The
Beckoning
Cat

Chris Lerpinière

Copyright

Jasami Acknowledgements

The Jasami team is integral to the production of all of our titles. They are talented, creative, and hardworking. Thank you!

Executive Editor

Calum Clarke

Editors

David Mackenzie

Lisa Daley

Formatting

Bethany Royle

Consultant Cover Designer

Ged Lerpinière

Acknowledgements

Firstly, thank you to my fantastic and supportive editing team from Jasami Publishing Calum, David and Lisa. They made editing for a newbie fun.

This book would never have been finished if it wasn't for the encouragement, bit of nagging, advice and support from Auntie Cannon (you know who you are!) Allan MacRaild, Johnathan Griffiths and Neil Healy.

Thanks also to Lyn Moir for my Newham retreat, such a special place to embrace creativity.

And finally thank you to all my friends and family who have witnessed my journey and never doubted I would eventually get here.

Dedication

Ged, Moni, and Anna
Couldn't love you more.

Table of Contents

Prologue	11
Chapter One	14
Chapter Two	19
Chapter Three	25
Chapter Four	38
Chapter Five	42
Chapter Six	47
Chapter Seven	51
Chapter Eight	62
Chapter Nine	71
Chapter Ten	78
Chapter Eleven	85
Chapter Twelve	91
Chapter Thirteen	108
Chapter Fourteen	115
Chapter Fifteen	119
Chapter Sixteen	122
Chapter Seventeen	128
Chapter Eighteen	136
Chapter Nineteen	140
Chapter Twenty	147
Chapter Twenty-One	156
Chapter Twenty-Two	160

Chapter Twenty-Three   171
Chapter Twenty-Four   176
Chapter Twenty-Five   182
Chapter Twenty-Six   189
Chapter Twenty-Seven   194
Chapter Twenty-Eight   197
Chapter Twenty-Nine   207
Chapter Thirty   210
Chapter Thirty-One   216
Chapter Thirty-Two   218
Chapter Thirty-Three   223
Chapter Thirty-Four   229
Chapter Thirty-Five   233
Chapter Thirty-Six   238
Chapter Thirty-Seven   241
Chapter Thirty-Eight   246
Chapter Thirty-Nine   250
Chapter Forty   255
Chapter Forty-One   258
Chapter Forty-Two   262
Chapter Forty-Three   269
Chapter Forty-Four   273
Chapter Forty-Five   287
Chapter Forty-Six   295
Chapter Forty-Seven   304
Chapter Forty-Eight   306
Chapter Forty-Nine   311
Chapter Fifty   315
Chapter Fifty-One   318
Chapter Fifty-Two   320

Chapter Fifty-Three   325
Chapter Fifty-Four   330
Chapter Fifty-Five   335
Chapter Fifty-Six   343
Chapter Fifty-Seven   351
Chapter Fifty-Eight   361
Chapter Fifty-Nine   365
Chapter Sixty   368
Chapter Sixty-One   372
Chapter Sixty-Two   377
Chapter Sixty-Three   383
Chapter Sixty-Four   390
Chapter Sixty-Five   395
Epilogue   405
About the Author   409

Chris Lerpinière

Prologue

He liked to watch, always had. He'd learnt that you could learn a lot from watching, just watching. He'd watched his mum when he was growing up, watched how she'd act, what was successful, what was not.

Now he was here, with his latest interest, watching, but this time was going to be so much more interesting, so much more worthwhile. Not like last time, that outcome had been disappointing; he hadn't prepared enough, hadn't covered every base. It wasn't like him. He hated to make mistakes.

'Don't be so hard on yourself,' his mum would say, lying on the couch, wrapped in some cheap nylon, imitation silk dressing gown, drawing heavily on her cigarette. 'Stop winding yourself up. Not worth it, babe.'

Nothing was ever worth it for Mum, which was why he had to try so hard. He had to succeed. He hadn't wanted to live like that, watching various men arrive at the house, for Mum to entertain them in her room. The sounds of her fake giggling and then fucking, so loud in his ears, the paper-thin walls of their flat only slightly muffling what was taking place less than a foot from his own bed. He was sometimes roped in, the first time being his first kiss. Everyone remembered their first kiss, didn't they?

He had been eight at the time, sitting in his room, colouring in - his favourite pastime. Making sure never to go over the black lines, making sure the colours didn't blend in with each other. His mother had a visitor, someone he had never seen before, but he was obviously fun because he could hear Mum laughing.

There was a knock at his door. He looked up and put an arm over his colouring. Mum was sometimes unpredictable, could be mean. She came in with cake. Chocolate cake, his favourite. Moist and rich.

'Look what I've got for you.'

He eyed her and the cake. Something didn't feel right.

A man came in behind her. Small, stocky, and dark.

'This him?' A question as if he was a disappointment, as if something better had been promised.

'This is him, he won't give you any bother, will you?' She looked at him, frowning, nervous, edgy. 'This is Les.' She nodded at the man. 'He brought us cake, I told him chocolate was your thing.'

'Thanks, Les.' Always mannerly, never rude.

'Les wants to spend some time with you, hun.' She turned and left, the worn heels of her dress-up shoes echoing on the linoleum.

He didn't remember much after that except the kiss. Bristles and heat, the soft slug of tongue pushing down his throat almost making him gag, the bitter taste of nicotine and the sweetness of beer. Les playing with himself as he held him down, forcing the very breath out of him. Then the groan, his colouring lying crumpled underneath them, the slimy wetness making the colours run.

There had been that jolt, though. A pleasurable thump in his groin as Les had exhaled in his ear, his warm breath setting off goosebumps. And a sense of power. He had done this, had made Les weak, the bigness of the man reduced to nothing by a simple action. Revolting as it was, there was excitement and there was power.

Later, at bath time, Mum was in such a good mood. His little green frog floated beside him, its arms behind its head, its boggling eyes watching, and its warty plastic face grinning inanely at him as he sank beneath the water. She let him stay in until the water turned cold and his skin was wrinkled. He noticed she had her nails done as she rinsed the shampoo out, digging the red hardness of them into his scalp as she sang an old favourite of hers, 'Going to wash that man right out of your hair, going to wash that man right out of your hair and send him home again.'

That was only his first kiss. There were many more chocolate cakes, manicures, and baths to follow. And so the die was cast, the dye was set, and the dying would follow.

Chapter One

T he smell of the locker rooms would change over a twenty-four hour period. At five in the morning, there was a staleness that matched the quiet. At six, the cleaner would come and transform it with disinfectant. At seven, the morning staff would arrive, bringing with them fresh air and fresh sweat from those who liked to exercise before work. The showers would run, emanating pine and cheap floral shower gel. Coffee would replace the shower's humidity as the last chance for a caffeine fix was taken. The room would quieten as work began, and then the smell would only alter if the locker room doors opening coincided with the work doors opening. That faint yet distinct whiff of fat charring as flesh was opened and blood vessels sealed, arresting any bleeding. The oily and foetid smell of gangrenous bowel which would rest in the nostrils and stay there long after work had finished. That odour, once smelt, was never forgotten.

Mirry loved the smell of the changing room, found it comforting. On this morning, at five, she breathed in the stale odour and the quiet of a night almost finished. Looking at herself in the mirror, she groaned, rubbed her eyes, and splashed water on her face. Just another hour and she would be tucked in bed, a mantra to keep her going. She dragged her fingers through her short blond hair, bringing it back to life. To shower or not to shower. The decision was not - bed was calling and she wanted to be home before the morning traffic. There would be no time for a morning romp with John; she would be lucky if she shared a cup of tea with him let alone anything else before he started his shift. She smiled inwardly, imagining him sleeping soundly on his back, his long limbs sprawled across their bed.

She looked around her as she quickly changed out of the theatre scrubs. Blood-spattered work clogs lay abandoned next to overflowing buggies holding the soiled linen from the night's work. Here lay the evidence of a busy but successful night. She had taken over from Debs at ten o'clock in the evening. Debs, as always, was running the retrieval of organs with military precision.

Debs with her shoulder length, curly, dark hair, almost black eyes, and olive skin, with a dimple above the solitary mole next to her full lips. Her appearance spoke of exotic promise, an original pear shape with slender waist ending in full hips and plump thighs. Outwardly, her look alluded to a cool, almost Aphrodite-esque being, but this could not have been further from the truth. Debs was a soft hearted soul with little or no awareness of the impact she could have.

The night's donor had been a twenty-two year old boy, just a lad really, full of promise. He'd fallen when climbing, doing the thing he loved most, out in the wilderness of the Cairngorms. His rescue had been well orchestrated, his arrival heralded by the helicopter's thrum, landing safely at the hospital. Everything was done to save his life, but the mountains had done their worst. His body had been battered, his spine broken in several places, and his head, his poor head, had struck the rocks with such force that no one could have survived it. They managed to keep him going for thirty-six hours. Enough time for his family to gather, shocked and disbelieving, trying to comprehend that he was dying - had died. Debs had taken them through the donation process, describing in quiet words what would happen to their son, brother, lover in the theatre as his healthy life-giving organs would be removed.

They had asked for a couple of hours to decide, to assimilate, to hold his unblemished hands and stroke his bruised face. It was his mother who led in the end. She could feel that her firstborn child had left his body, that what was lying in the bed was no longer her son but rather the vessel that he had inhabited. They were united in knowing that this was what their beautiful boy would have wanted, to help others in their time of need. He was a perfect donor for Debs, a strong, fit, and healthy young man with no past history of injury other than a broken wrist from falling off a rope swing while playing with his brother.

Mirry could tell this had been a hard case for Debs; they knew each other well enough. Debs had been her mentor when Mirry first started as a Donor Co-ordinator. An excellent role model and now a trusted friend. The handover had been concise, the retrieval already in full swing by the time Mirry had arrived to relieve Debs. She had been reluctant to leave, had wanted to see the case through to the end. Mirry's last words to Debs as she retreated out of the theatre were that she would take care of him and would text her when it was over. She knew that

Debs would have a fitful night, would not sleep, going over the day in her head. Mirry would have been the same.

Once the teams had left, Mirry and the remaining theatre nurse had covered the long retrieval incisions with stark white dressings. They had gently washed his bruised face and cleaned the remains of the mountain dirt from his ears. They labelled him, wrapped him, and then struggled a little to get the clean sheet underneath him. Both talking quietly to each other, where the organs were going, who would be waking up this morning to hear that their lives were about to be changed by the death of this boy. Mirry had stayed with him until the porters arrived with their distinctive metal box, stepping back as they pulled him onto the trolley and closed the lid. They joked with Mirry about the early hour of the morning - wasn't it her bedtime?

So here she was now, scrubs discarded and thrown in the overflowing linen buggy.

'What a sight.' She dragged her hands through her hair again to muss it up, making her look less like a tired toddler. She fiddled with her key to open her locker and pulled out yesterday's clothes. She pulled her jeans on, stuffing last night's pants into her rucksack. T-shirt sniffed before going over her head, remembering she'd only had it on for about two hours. Boots on, zipped and tied.

'Home time,' she breathed, pulling her battered leather jacket out of the locker and slinging it on, rucksack over her shoulder, quick check for mobile and keys.

Before leaving, she texted Debs. All good tonight, no probs, all organs and tissues accepted, sleep tight, catch you tomoz. She had one more look around the changing room and breathed in the quiet stale air before opening the door and heading out into the daylight and fresh morning sun. Home time.

Chapter Two

F ee and John knew immediately which house they'd been called to as soon as they pulled into the cul-de-sac. It was a pleasant estate, the gardens mature and well cared for, the houses in a sixties style, individualised with extensions, conversions, and log burning chimneys. A safe place to bring up a family. Good schools nearby, access to the bypass for a supposedly easy commute, within cycling distance of the shops, very idyllic Edinburgh. Or it was. The peace had been disturbed by the three police vans, an ambulance, and a flurry of activity in front of one of the houses. A uniformed officer unrolling blue and white tape around the garden railings, his tongue firmly clamped between his teeth in concentration. John manoeuvred in behind one of the vans. Confidently pulling on the handbrake and swiftly releasing his safety belt, he stared out at the scene. Cataloguing what he was seeing, senses alert.

'Ready?' he asked, turning to Fee.

'Sure am, Boss.' Fee was already releasing her safety belt, opening the car door, and jumping out onto the pavement.

John did the same, went round the car, and joined her in front of the ticker taped house.

'Before we head in, gonna do me a favour and get this fucking eyelash out my eye?'

Fee snorted, looking up at her boss. 'Now?' she said, raising her eyebrows in disbelief and shaking her head.

'Bend down, then, you lanky git!' she laughed. 'Right or left?''

John dropped to one knee, his eye squeezed shut.

'Right, right… hurry up, it's really nipping.'

'Good, serves you right,' she pulled his eyelid down, 'what is it with bloody men and their fabulous eyelashes? Yours are like a jersey cow.'

'Always been my best asset,' John laughed.

'Aye right, eyes of blue and curly coal black hair, proper throwback to your ancient Irish heritage… travelling in your nature, too?'

'Going to be a long day by the looks of things, let's not start the pish taking too early, Fee, eh?'

Fee fished the eyelash deftly out and put it on the back of her hand.

'Make a wish?' She gestured for him to blow. He puffed.

'Please, not an all-nighter,' he muttered under his breath as he stood up.

'Second that,' Fee said, rubbing her hands on the backs of her trousers as she followed John up the path, nodding to the constable standing at the front door when they reached the top, 'DCI Sneddon and DI Fee Smith.'

'Sitting room, first door on the right,' he said, nodding his head backwards, his serious face a little pale. 'Bit of a mess.'

John led the way through the glass door into a wide hall with immaculate wooden flooring. The walls were a deep red, the skirting bright white. It was warm and welcoming, a large mirror by the door making the space look bigger than it was. They could hear activity coming from the room on the right. John pushed the door open.

The room was a scene of devastation. Not like 9/11 or 7/7, but in the confines of a home, the impact of the scene took John's breath away. There were three bodies: two dogs and one adult. One dog lay disembowelled, the smell in the room putrid, the other its head misshapen with dried blood around its muzzle. There was a dark brown splatter sprayed high against the muted, patterned green wall behind the sofa. The pattern caused John to pause, shocked when he recognised the same familiar colour and design from home. There was evidence of a frantic struggle, a lamp on its side, a vase of flowers lying smashed on the wooden floor. Lilies, stark white, their strong funereal perfume mixing with that of the dogs. The clawing smell caught at the back of John's throat and turned his stomach with nausea.

The female adult lay at the door opposite from where John stood. She was crumpled in a heap as if kicked behind her knees, dropping where she stood. There was a dark red pool of blood, an animation balloon, leaking from her head. John pulled forensic gloves over his overalls as he walked over to her - it - and knelt down.

He tentatively moved dark hair away from the face: the eyes were closed, carefully applied eyeliner still visible. He took in the mascara smudges and perfect eyebrows. As a matter of habit, he felt at the neck, years of practice ingrained in his action. What he didn't expect was the responding thready, slow pulse he felt through the latex of his gloves.

'Fuck's sake,' he roared, 'she's got a pulse, get the paramedics in here now!'

He immediately rolled the woman onto her side, tilting her head as he did so to clear her airway. There was a commotion over by the door as the rest of the team yelled instructions into radios, summoning medical help and fast. John was quickly joined by Fee.

'Who checked this?' John asked as he tried to stop the blood leaking from the woman's head. 'Well?'

John looked over to an ashen faced officer standing with his head bowed. He knew that now was not the time to go ape shit, but the temptation to yell, scream, and let rip was immense.

'See me later, numb-nuts,' he growled under his breath. He looked up at Fee, shaking his head as he continued to press on the wound with his gloved hand.

'Check she's still breathing for me, Fee, will you?'

Fee knelt down on all fours and looked at the reassuring faint rise and fall of the woman's chest.

'Aye, it's faint but still there .'

The green figures of the paramedics arrived.

'What's the score then, John?' said the eldest of the two, laying a large kit bag down beside him. 'Been a while since I've seen you.'

'Great to see you, Jim- I've no fucking idea. We'd been called for a dead body, suspicious circumstances, but when I got here, I checked for a pulse and well…' John nodded down at the young woman now curled on her side.

The paramedic kneeled beside John and checked for breathing. 'What's her name?'

'Jenny, Jenny Anderson.' This from the ashen faced officer still standing by the door like he was rooted to the spot.

'Okay, John, go and shift yersel and let me in.' The paramedics took over assessing Jenny, talking all the while to her, trying to get a response. There was none coming.

'Think we'll scoop and shoot if that's okay with you, John, want to get her to ED ASAP.'

'On you go, I'll follow you in once I've got organised here.'

John stood aside and let them continue their work, like green flies around a red rose. The temptation to tell them not to disturb too much of the crime scene was immense, but John knew life had to come before evidence. What a bloody disaster.

'When's SOCO getting here, Fee?' John stared round at the room, trying to make sense of it, his brain continuing to catalogue the scene.

'Just arrived.' Fee nodded her head over to the open door where John could see the team assembling outside, pulling cases and overalls from the back of the discreet white van.

'Better go and bring them up to speed, then.' He looked over at Fee, she knew the drill. 'Okay if I leave you to it? Need to follow the boys in green.'

'I'm fine here, just keep me in the loop when you get up to the Royal.'

John nodded in agreement and headed out the door, following the paramedics, aware that they were now being watched by a number of neighbouring houses. Drama like this didn't happen very often in this part of Edinburgh, people would be talking about it for weeks. He jumped in the car and quickly pulled his safety belt on as the back door of the ambulance was slammed shut and Jim quickly made his way around to the driver's door. John turned the engine on in preparation to follow and quickly dialled Mirry's number. He knew that tonight's plans would need to go on hold as the likelihood of him being back before midnight was nil.

The call went straight to voicemail, Mirry was obviously still sleeping after her all-nighter.

'Hey Mirr, it's me, babe, really sorry, I know we were meant to be going out, but just to let you know, I'm not going to make tonight, shit's hit the fan here, maybe see if Pen can go with you instead? Love you, bye.'

John hit the hang up button as he reversed out of the cul-de-sac, following closely behind the ambulance whose blue light started flashing as its siren began. Mirry was going to be really pissed off with him. He hadn't been all that keen to go out tonight; ballet wasn't really his thing, but Mirry loved it, so he was trying his best. All this flashed through his head in a matter of seconds before his mind returned to the job in hand. It was going to be one of those days.

Chapter Three

Mirry sighed at John's message and put her phone back down on the bedside table, avoiding the half drunk water glass from the early hours when she had got in. She looked at the clock: 13:27, it told her, flicking to 13:28 as her brain tried to catch up and make sense of what time of day it was. She did the sums, probably had five hours' kip, got in at six, showered, had a cup of tea with John before he went to work, half an hour to unwind reading a chapter of her book. He'd been great knowing that she would be tired after being up all night. She loved John like she had never loved anyone else. Hearing his voice on his message took her right back to when they had first met.

It had been one of those nauseating emergency services football matches. An excuse for fun, frolics, and fucking between likeminded individuals whose jobs brought them into contact with the most challenging in society. Mirry had played a beezer of a game, loads of cheating and much laughter. She'd been first at the bar that night and had already downed a tequila shot before the losers had arrived. The night continued in raucous fun, dancing, and singing, but most of all drinking. He arrived late. Mirry had spotted him coming in - he looked fresh, clean, and something about his tall, confident attitude made him stand out. He made his way to the bar, being greeted by his colleagues with much back slapping, and joking. He bought a drink for himself and turned around to survey the room, his eyes sweeping over everyone as if casing the club, checking for exits. His gaze fell on Mirry and moved on in its sweep but almost instantly returned back to her. She smiled. He smiled back, then leaned in to talk in a friend's ear, still looking at her. His friend turned round, nodded at Mirry, and spoke back to John. The song ended, their interaction over as Mirry made her way back to her friends from the dance floor.

'Who the fuck is that?' she asked Pen, her eyes big and round as she nodded her head back in John's direction.

'New guy, apparently, just been moved from Perthshire, he's hot though.'

'Hot to bleeding trot, whoa boy, and bagsy the first to get a Lothian saddle on him!'

Pen snorted, 'Might come sooner than you think, babe, he's on his way over.'

Mirry stayed still until she sensed his presence, her heartbeat increasing. 'Get a bleeding grip!' she thought to herself.

'This seat taken?'

And so that was their first meeting, they got rip-roaring drunk together and stumbled out of the club at two in the morning. He came back to Mirry's, slept on the sofa, and had left by the time she got up late. Not even a kiss. But he'd left his number, a drawing of a bunch of flowers, and an apology for leaving without saying goodbye. Mirry was hooked.

She had left it a couple of days before calling. Pen's advice of course, don't be seen to be too keen, be cool. That was so not in her nature but there was something about John that had stayed with her. He didn't seem to be your run-of-the-mill bloke; they had talked long into the small hours of the morning and he hadn't even tried to make a pass at her.

Maybe she wasn't his type, she'd thought, maybe he had a girlfriend, maybe, maybe, maybe. She was never going to find out unless she called.

He'd answered on the third ring. 'Sneddon,' he said, officious and deep. She nearly put the phone down there and then. 'Hallo?' Questioning.

'Hi John, it's Mirry, we met a couple of days ago…' her voice trailing off. 'God, this was a bad idea.'

'Hey Mirry, good to hear from you.' Relief flowed through her, his voice now warm with that slight North East burr she remembered finding so attractive.

'Did you survive your shift?' she teased. 'Sorry I was in no fit state to be the hostess with the mostest and make you a cuppa. You must have left pretty early?'

'Yeah, went about seven, stuff to do before heading for work. Slept the sleep of the just Saturday night, though.'

'Would you like to get together?' Mirry said, finally out with it, hating the small talk of the phone, cutting to the chase.

'Sure, that would be great, what's good for you?'

They had eventually agreed on a lunch date, working around both their shifts. It had gone well, stretching further than lunch. Mirry had taken him to the Botanics, a favourite place for her, where they had laughed at the antics of the greedy squirrels terrorising children in buggies and marvelling together at the exotics in the glasshouse. Mirry showed him the donor garden, explaining a little about the creative thought that had gone into designing it and the significance of what it represented. They had kissed then, gently and deeply, Mirry's legs almost giving way with the flood of desire that had coursed through her.

He had walked her home at dusk, night shift for him and studying for her. It had been the best first date she had had with no uncomfortable silences, their conversation flowing naturally. John had made her laugh like no one before.

That had been three years ago now and Mirry had loved every minute of it. She smiled at the memory as she checked her phone for any work messages. Everything had been in order last night, she knew that, but double checked anyway before she could get on with her day.

There was just the picture of John at the top of Goatfell, his grinning face making her smile. Always did. That trip to Arran had been two months ago now, but it seemed like a lifetime. They'd had such a good time, the weather amazing in the west coast way, the cottage by the sea, remote, making it feel like they had the island all to themselves. They had made the decision there on Arran to start a family, had talked it over on the long hikes and evenings by the fire. Mirry had felt warm, relaxed, and so very much in love.

'Right', she thought, 'time to get on with the day.'

She knew that the ballet wasn't really Pen's thing, but she also knew that her best friend would always be up for a night out, with or without the added bonus of a spot of culture. Mirry quickly texted Pen, 'Been stood up for ballet tonight, fancy being my plus one?'

There was an almost immediate reply, 'Sure, as long as we have curry first and I can burp all the way through Swan Lake! Time and place?'

'Pear Tree, 5:30 then Mother India?' Mirry quickly texted her reply.

'Be there or be square,' was Pen's reply.

Her night now rearranged, she flung the covers back and padded through to the kitchen, avoiding the pile of tiles and new toilet bowl sitting in the hall. The sooner they got the renovations done to the flat, the better. Mirry was tired of living in what seemed like a permanent building site, water on water off - power on power off, cold showers, and sore feet from catching her toe on protruding nails. They never had enough time off together to get on with things, or to be in when the workmen came round.

She had demanded that the kitchen get done first. That was her safe haven. She loved the view from the big sash window looking out onto the garden below. This time of year, the lilac tree was in full bloom and she would inhale its perfume when she managed to get out to hang her washing. Turning on the kettle, she grabbed a mug, threw a tea bag in, and rammed some bread in the toaster.

Tea and marmite toast, her life saver, no matter what time of day. When it was ready, she took it through to the sitting room to sit at the bay window and looked down at the street, her own private scene. John laughed at her for this; she loved watching people going about their day, oblivious to her in her eagle's nest, making up tales about them and what they were up to.

Today was no different, the road was busy with lunchtime traffic, people out and about grabbing a bite to eat, heading for the nearby park for a bit of green space and beauty. Mirry was jealous; lunch break for her was usually stuck in front of her laptop, trying to catch up with patient notes, teaching sessions, and never-ending protocols. On the off chance that she managed to get out, it was for a brisk walk around the ever expanding hospital, up the hill looking down over the Forth, and over to Fife on a good day.

'So,' she thought to herself, 'looks like I've got the day to myself again, what to do, what to do?'

Getting up, she stretched, picked up the plate and mug and headed back to the kitchen, slaloming the bathroom DIY on her way.

'Alexa,' she shouted going into the kitchen, 'Debussy, L'apres-midi d'un faune.'

Mirry inwardly smiled at her attempt at a French accent, Madame Milne her old language teacher would have been delighted. Dishes in the sink and one more look out at the lilac tree before heading to the bedroom to dress. Run it was then, work up a sweat, and clear the sleep deprived cobwebs from her brain.

Her mobile rang out from the side of the bed. She picked it up, seeing Helen's name on the screen.

'Oh shit,' she thought, 'this will be trouble.'

'Hallo, hallo,' Mirry put a cheery voice on while pulling her joggers out of the washing pile.

'Afternoon Mirry, just up?' Helen's cool tones instantly put Mirry's nerves on edge.

'Pretty much, John had called to say he was going to be late, something big at work by the sounds of it.'

'Well, sorry to disturb you at home, but just wanted to know if you still wanted to go to that publicity training session over in Glasgow next month? Places are available and the funding's come through, but we need to be quick to get our names down.'

'Sure, sounds like a plan. Always fancied a bit of publicity training, I could be the new face of donation.' Mirry snorted to herself, the likelihood of that was a long shot with her bleached blonde crew cut and nose ring. She'd have to form an orderly queue behind Helen and the transplant surgeons, and she wasn't sure her ego quite stretched that far.

'Great, I'll put you down then. I'm going, of course, Cameron from the retrieval team is coming, and our new data guy Simon, don't think you've met him yet?' Helen said, Mirry imagining her boss visibly preening herself in anticipation of the attention.

'Sounds like an eclectic mix, Helen, surgeon, data analyst, and two old nurses. Anything else?' Mirry wanted this conversation over, wanted her own time and space back, didn't need to be reminded about work and the ongoing politics.

'Oh sure, sorry to have disturbed, you have a nice day and I'll catch you tomorrow.'

'No worries, laters.' Mirry hit the red telephone on her mobile and flung it onto the unmade bed.

She dressed quickly, plumped the pillows on the bed, and yanked the duvet up, instantly making the room look tidier.

Into the bathroom and brushing her teeth, she frowned at the pile of John's clothes half-heartedly thrown in the direction of the linen basket. Picking them up off the floor, she flung them in the wicker basket, pushed them down, and closed the lid with two hands. That would have to be dealt with later.

Trainers on, she strapped her phone to her arm, key in pocket, earphones in, and headed out, slamming the door behind her. The beat of her running music kicking in her adrenalin, she headed out onto the pavement, the spring afternoon bright as her eyes acclimatised. Off she went, head up, staring ahead, and running, running, clearing the sadness of last night's donor and starting a brand new day.

In the early evening, Mirry made her way across the Meadows, choosing to walk to meet up with Pen. The cherry blossom was in full bloom, the rich pinks almost hallucinogenic against the green of the grass. As always, there were joggers, dog walkers, office workers heading home, and groups of students congregating on blankets, laughing, chatting, snogging, and making the most of the warm spring air. She spotted Pen talking to a tall, well-built man outside the Pear Tree pub as she crossed the road from the university buildings. As always, Pen looked amazing with her blonde hair flowing free like some ridiculous Rapunzel, her black jeans tight on her endlessly long legs as she laughed at something the guy said to her. They had been friends since their student days in Dundee, and it was

Pen who had encouraged Mirry to move to Edinburgh, found her first flat share with Debs, and now the three were a tight team at work. She waved to Mirry when she saw her approaching, her broad, wicked smile welcoming her with its radiant brightness. Mirry caught the last few words of the conversation Pen was having, 'Yeah, you have a good evening too, nice speaking to you.'

'Hey gorgeous,' Pen said, throwing her arms around Mirry in a bear hug, engulfing her in her recognisable perfume, a mixture of bergamot, rose, and musk. Mirry loved the familiarity of it.

'Looking good, girl!' she said, stepping back. 'New top?'

'Looking pretty good yourself,' Mirry laughed, 'and yes it's new and no you can't have a loan of it!

'Anyway,' Mirry said, looking at the retreating shape of the man, 'who's the guy?'

'Oh, just some randomer, you know what it's like, someone sees a lone woman standing on the corner, makes up some excuse to chat.'

'Think that happens to you more often than anyone else, Pen.'

'Can't help being gorgeous,' she laughed, flicking her hair in an exaggerated fashion over her shoulder.

Mirry shook her head, smiling. She knew Pen had been brought up with four older brothers and she never took herself too seriously, especially where men were concerned.

'Anyway, time for that ruby,' Pen said, linking her arm through Mirry's, 'I'm bloody starving!'

The restaurant was busy when they arrived, the smell of onions, spices, and warm bread making Mirry's mouth water as she realised she hadn't eaten anything decent since lunch the previous day.

'How did last night go, what time did you get finished?' Pen said once they had ordered and had a couple of beers with a tray of poppadoms and chutney in front of them.

'All good, Debs had done most of the work, I was just finishing things off for her. Good result though.'

'Yeah, so I hear, Debs said the family were on board right from the start, makes it easier.'

'Mmm,' said Mirry, pushing an onion-laden poppadom in her mouth.

'John not make tonight, then?'

'Yeah, he called early doors, something big at work by the sounds of things, any excuse not to go to the ballet, not really his thing.'

Pen snorted, 'No, I wouldn't have thought so… How's things going with you two anyway, anything to tell your Auntie Pen?'

'Nothing exciting, and stop looking at me like that. You'll be the first to know should the stork come visiting.'

'Can't believe you two are actually going for it, never really saw you as the maternal type.'

'I know,' sighed Mirry, 'to be honest, not sure whether it's my clock ticking or maybe it really is the right time now that I've got together with John… I think he'll make a great dad.'

'Sounds like he's more into it than you?'

'Yeah, well he's a couple of years older than me and thinks that if we leave it any longer, he won't be able to play footie with his boy.'

Pen laughed. 'And if it's a girl?'

'Oh, the usual response to that one… as long as it's healthy! Anyway, we're having good fun practising and long may it continue.'

'Oh, TMI, girlfriend,' Pen said, screwing her face up in fake disgust, 'TMI.'

'Anyway, enough about me, what's happening with you? Anyone interesting?'

'Hmm, nobody special, there is the new data guy who's just started, but you know me, don't shit on your own doorstep.'

'Oh yeah, Helen was talking about him this morning,' Mirry said. 'What's he like?'

'I think he's come down from Dundee to sort out the ODR and our data, statistics, and all that stuff that is way above my head. Management decision you know what that's like.'

'Have you met him?' asked Mirry curiously.

'Yeah, Helen brought him in this morning like she had the prize bull at the Highland show… tall, blonde, good looking in that Slavic kind of a way, not really my cup of tea but good to have some new chat in the office. Helen was all over him like a rash mind, all smiles and fake bonhomie.'

'God, you're harsh sometimes, Pen!' Mirry laughed.

'Yeah, well, we all know where her interest lies at the moment, though, don't we?'

Mirry looked puzzled. 'No, what do you mean?'

'Oh, I'm saying nothing and I'll keep saying it, but just keep your peepers open around Helen and a certain surgeon.'

'You lot are just total gossips and I want nothing to do with it,' Mirry laughed, '… do you want that last bit of poppadom or can I have it?'

'It's all yours, Mother Teresa.' Pen pushed the plate towards her.

'Helen phoned this morning to ask if I wanted to do some publicity training through in Glasgow for some reason.'

'For a bit of colour, I would imagine,' said Pen. 'So far it's Helen and Cameron, say no more! Think you'll probably be asked to take your nose ring out, though.'

'Well, they can ask away,' said Mirry, touching the silver hoop in her nostril, 'that stays right where it belongs.'

Pen grinned. 'That's what I love about you, babe, total rebel.'

'Always,' Mirry grinned back, self-consciously spiking up her bleached blond hair. 'Rebel without a cause.'

'Well, let me know how it goes… Hurry up and eat that poppadom, I'm ready for my main course.'

By the time they made it to the Festival Theatre, they were late and had to make their apologies as they pushed their way along their row where everyone was already sitting. There were a few tuts as they went, with Pen swaying a little and bumping people's knees after a few too many beers.

'You are so embarrassing sometimes,' whispered Mirry, smiling broadly at Pen as they took their seats and the lights went down.

'Oh, shut it, you, just enjoy the dancing - I might have a nap!'

'Philistine,' whispered Mirry, settling down to enjoy the spectacle as the first of the ballerinas came on stage and the recognisable music began.

Pen didn't have a nap as it turned out, and Mirry was surprised at one point to glance at Pen and find her transfixed with her mouth ajar when the final act was being danced.

'Enjoy that?' asked Mirry when the lights came up and they made ready to leave.

'Aye, it was okay,' said Pen, 'beats the telly anyway!'

Mirry laughed as the two of them headed out with the rest of the audience. They said their goodbyes on the pavement and Mirry made her way back to the flat, the music and drama of the last act still ringing in her ears.

Chapter Four

John came home late. It was past midnight when he crept under the covers, trying not to wake Mirry.

'How you doing?' She mumbled sleepily, moving over to make more room for him.

'Totally shattered, babe, been a shit day.' John curled himself around Mirry, drawing her warm, slight body in towards him, smelling her, always the smell of her, like a warm balm.

'Wannae talk?' Mirry whispered into her pillow, fingers crossed the answer would be in the negative.

'Maybe in the morning, just need some kip for now,' John said, kissing the back of her neck.

He was asleep within seconds, his gentle, deep breath across Mirry's face bearing the traces of coffee, fried food, and stale air. Much as she tried to get back to sleep, it became impossible for her and she had to extricate herself from John's embrace without waking him. Gently, she rolled away with minimal movement.

'Damn,' she thought, 'never going to get my sleep pattern back at this rate.'

She was wide awake and knew it would be pointless going back to bed.

Mirry leaned over to the bedside cabinet and pulled her diary out of the drawer. She'd always kept an account of her life, sometimes just the mundane stuff, what she'd had for tea, who she'd met. Other times she wrote about her struggles and anxieties, things that kept her awake at night. It was cathartic, as if writing down the harsh realities of a day placed them somewhere else, not in her.

She'd been given her first diary by her favourite granny. She knew she wasn't meant to have a favourite, but in her child's mind, the one you see the most often, the one who plays with you and feeds you, the one who stands up for you when your mother is having a rant, is always going to win hands down on favouritism. Mirry loved the beginning of each year when she would get a fresh journal to start, the smell of the new unmarked virgin pages gave her such pleasure with the anticipation of starting off her year again. She had kept all her diaries and now as an adult, her journals. At uni, the nursing students were always being told to be reflective in their practice. To go over situations that were challenging and question what could have been done differently, what had gone well, and most importantly what could have gone better. Mirry had found this easy; it resonated with the way she lived her life. This week had been really tough, and Mirry wanted to write things down, to rid herself of some of her thoughts and worries.

She went through to the sitting room, taking her journal with her. She thought over what had happened in the last few days: it had been a tough week, full-on but satisfying, too. So many people's lives would be changed, some for the better, some for the worse. She switched the lamp on and curled up on the sofa with pen and paper. Within a few minutes, she was so engrossed that she didn't hear John coming into the room until a mug of tea was placed beside her.

'Jesus Christ!' Mirry jumped, almost upending the mug. 'Where the fuck did that come from?'

'I woke up and you weren't there, thought I would come keep you company. My head is buzzing too, not going to get back over now.'

'Tough day?' Mirry looked up at John, his dark eyes almost black in the low light of the lamp.

'Budge up, I'll keep your feet warm.'

Mirry moved over on the sofa, making room for John to sit down and stretch his legs out in front of him. His long, lean legs.

Mirry curled up beside him as he put his arm around her and she coorled in. 'Tell me,' Mirry said, 'I'm listening.'

John didn't need to be asked twice and, as he relayed the day's events to her, she was there with him, imagining the scene as he described what had happened. But he kept coming back to when he discovered that the woman, Jenny, had still been alive.

'I can't get her out of my head, she was lying there presumed dead and nobody knew. What if I'd got there earlier, would she have a better chance of recovery?'

'You can't blame yourself, John, you know that. You did what you could.'

'They worked on her for ages and she seemed stable when I left but you can tell things weren't looking good, you know what the medics can look like sometimes.'

'Yeah, I know that look,' Mirry said softly.

'She miscarried too, that was just too close to home.'

John shook his head and kissed the top of Mirry's head.

'Oh John, that's just too sad.'

'You know how you always say that some cases stay with you, Mirry. That you will always remember them. Like yesterday?'

'Mmm,' said Mirry in agreement, stroking the thick black hair on John's forearm.

'Well, this is going to stay with me for a long time. Still don't have a clue what happened to her either, going to be a tough case.'

She had never seen John quite so disturbed by his work before. They talked about it long into the dark of the night, but he couldn't get his head around the fact that he had thought Jenny to be dead.

Chapter Five

J ohn woke early the next morning and rolled quietly away from Mirry, who was sleeping soundly, her face beautiful in deep repose, almost angelic, if angels had piercings! He stifled a laugh and gently touched the silver ring in her small, perfect nose. A rush of love came over him as he looked down on her; she was the best thing that had ever happened to him, and he would do anything for her.

He left the bedroom and got ready for work, his mind very quickly reverting to the events of yesterday and the assault case. He wondered how Jenny was this morning. Thinking of her quickened his actions, and he was ready and out the door in minutes, coffee in a travel mug and toast crumbs still on his face.

He thought he would be the first in the office, but the lights were already on when he walked in and he found Fee ensconced in front of one of the PCs, an empty coffee cup beside her and her notebook already full of scribbles. John smiled, glad to see her. They both had the same work ethic and she was his best mate, even if she was female, which wasn't her fault, as he often teased her.

'Morning boss, you good?' Fee asked, her face serious.

'Yeah, didn't get much kip, but you were probably the same, eh? Shall we catch up before the team briefing?'

'Sure, I've been in touch with the Royal this morning and although she hasn't got any worse overnight, there's been no improvement either. Susie has been deployed as the FLO for the family, so that's good, she's loads of experience and knows the score.'

'Okay, I think we need to look at the surrounding CCTV, start door to door to see if anyone saw anything, and have our first interview, which'll be with her husband, think his name is Ray? He arrived in ED just as I was leaving and she was being taken up to ICU. Apparently, up in Dundee at some work thing? Does his alibi check out?'

John knew it would be the first thing Fee would have looked at.

'Yeah, I spoke to the hotel where his conference was being held. He had room service for breakfast yesterday morning and there had been a late meeting, so he was in Dundee the whole time.'

'Okay, he's the first one we should speak to, can you organise that? If needed, we can meet with him at the hospital.'

'I'll get on it, preliminary forensics should be coming through later today, so hopefully things will start coming together.'

'Yeah, I know,' John said, shaking his head. 'This is a weird one, though, looks like a random assault, maybe a burglary gone wrong, but something just doesn't sit right with me... we need more background.'

'Shall we say nine o'clock for team briefing and co-ordination?'

'Nine it is, boss, I'll get everyone organised.'

After the team briefing, John and Fee made their way to the Royal Infirmary and took the lift up to the ICU. The charge nurse opened one of the relatives' sleepover rooms for them to speak to Ray. He hadn't left Jenny's side since her admission yesterday afternoon when he had got back from Dundee. John and Fee sat on the individual plastic chairs as Ray was shown into the room and was invited to sit on the sofa in front of them.

He looked haggard and unkempt, his hair - or what was remaining of it - was cropped close to his head. The small relatives' room was dwarfed, as he was tall and well-built, wearing a white shirt which was crumpled with a small brown stain on the front where he had dribbled coffee.

John introduced himself and Fee to Ray and showed him their identity cards. Ray glanced at them but didn't really seem to register what he was looking at. The formalities over, John asked if Ray felt fit enough to answer their questions. His reply was instantly yes. Anything to help. He confirmed that he had been at a three day work conference in Dundee, that he was an IT specialist, and the company was getting ready to launch some new software. The conference had been full-on with meetings going on late at night, as international delegates dialled in due to the time differences.

Jenny and him spoke every night while Jenny was getting ready for bed. She always took the dogs out last thing, always headed for the nearby park, the dogs leading the way, their routine so engrained. This nighttime walk would take her about half an hour. There didn't seem to be anything bothering Jenny when they last spoke other than that the dogs had been very restless when they had got back. So much so that she had to lock them in the kitchen rather than having them in beside her, which she did when Ray was away overnight. He remembered joking with her that it was a full moon and maybe that was the problem. They had told each other they loved one another with their usual nonsense joke of who loved the other the most. At this, Ray's eyes filled with tears and he dropped his head to his chest, a sob, a deep breath, and then an apology as he looked back up at John and Fee. He accepted the box of tissues from Fee with a nod.

The one thing that drew Ray up short was when Fee said how sorry she was that Jenny had lost the baby. At this, he looked away and shook his head, mumbling something that neither John or Fee could hear. When John asked him to repeat what he said, he looked at them both and told them it couldn't be his, he'd had a vasectomy when he was married before. This news, of course, came as a bolt from the blue for John and Fee - did Ray have any idea who the father could be? He had shaken his head again, the tears coming quickly to his eyes as he stared at the wall above Fee's head. There was a silence then that nobody felt necessary to fill. After a few moments, John thanked Ray for his time and reiterated that they would be doing their utmost to find who had attacked Jenny. They all stood up together and Fee held the door open for Ray to return to Jenny's bedside. As he left the room, he looked at them both and said, 'She's my world, she's my absolute world.'

John and Fee left the ICU, nodding at the charge nurse as he pushed the button to open the exit doors; they didn't speak again until they had made their way out of the hospital and back to their car.

'Phew, that was tough,' said Fee, 'why is nothing ever simple?'

'Like I said this morning, Fee, I just don't think this feels right, there's something very odd about it all. Let's get back to the station and see what turns up from door to door and CCTV.'

'I'll see when we can speak with the friend, her name is Ali Swann, she found Jenny, think that's a priority.'

'Agreed,' said John grimly, 'maybe she can shed some light on the pregnancy.'

Chapter Six

The meeting with Ali had been organised for two in the afternoon at her house in a relatively new development. Fee remembered when there had been an orthopaedic hospital on these grounds of now impressive family homes and flats. She joked with John about visiting her granny who had been in for hip surgery. Fee and her brother had argued about sweets only to be put off when the patient in the next bed started using a bedpan and the whole family had quietly gagged.

The door to the house opened as they drew up to park. They were greeted by a beautiful, heavyset young woman wearing a dark green, all-in-one, designer jumpsuit. Ali's face was carefully made up, but it was obvious that she had been crying, no amount of foundation or powder could disguise her swollen eyes. She smiled grimly as they got out of the car, watching Fee and John as they crossed over the shale of the drive, their footsteps crunching loudly.

'Good afternoon… Mrs. Swann?' Fee asked as they reached the bottom of the entrance stairs. 'I think you were expecting us, DCI John Sneddon and DC Fee Smith.' Fee had her ID card on a lanyard and held it out for the woman to examine. She glanced at it half-heartedly.

'Yes, and please call me Ali, only my mother-in-law gets Mrs. Swann.' She looked at John's ID card more closely. 'Please come in.' She turned and led them into the house.

John was immediately struck by the beautiful decor and original artwork on the walls, the afternoon sun streaming in from the atrium above giving a sense of space and light.

'Beautiful house you have, Ali.'

'Thank you, the artwork is my husband's and the light in this part of the house shows it off beautifully… Can I offer you a tea or coffee?'

'No, thank you, I think we would like to get on to ask you a few questions about what happened yesterday if that's okay with you.'

Ali's eyes filled with tears. 'Of course. I spoke to Ray this morning to see how Jenny was, but he said there had been no change overnight, don't know if that's a good or a bad thing… This way, please.'

She showed them through to another brightly lit, impressive, and comfortable living room, decorated in muted greys and greens, and took a seat in the chair by the picture window. Fee and John sat down opposite her on a large sofa.

'Firstly,' Fee said, 'could you take us through what happened yesterday when you found Jenny?'

Ali sighed and very quickly recounted what had happened, how she had gone over to Jenny's as she did every other morning when they would both go out for a walk or run together. Ali was trying to lose weight - at this she looked down at her plump thighs and shrugged her shoulders. Jenny had been helping her improve her fitness, and they would exercise together with Jenny's dogs. When she rang the doorbell, nobody answered, and the dogs didn't bark, which was unusual. She had walked round to the back of the house in case Jenny was hanging her washing out. That was when she noticed that the back door was wide open, so she had gone into the house, calling Jenny's name.

Ali stopped at this point, took a breath, then carried on - that was when she found Jenny in the sitting room. She described the scene to Fee and John and, in retelling the events, they could see that the panic and shock she had experienced at the time was returning. She hadn't known what to do, with all the blood and mess she was sure Jenny was dead. She had called for the police straight away, and hadn't wanted to touch Jenny, she had been too scared. John asked her gently if she wanted to stop. Ali shook her head.

They asked her how long she had known Jenny, and Ali was quick to reply that they had been close since they had met at one of her husband's exhibitions four years ago where Jenny had bought one of his paintings. They had immediately hit it off and had become firm friends, seeing each other nearly every day. Fee and John looked at each other, their unspoken communication about the pregnancy and who was going to ask the first question. They needn't have worried, Ali sensed what their question was going to be and preempted them by saying the father of Jenny's baby was her husband, Matt. Fee and John tried to cover their astonishment at this revelation. Ali very quickly went on to explain that actually Jenny had agreed to be a surrogate for her, as she couldn't conceive, and they were desperate for children. Jenny had self-inseminated herself seven weeks ago and had only missed one period and wasn't ready to tell Ray yet. It was complicated, Ali said when she finished. There was nothing more to tell.

'Complicated?' Fee blurted out once they had left the house and were making their way back to the station. 'Complicated? Bloody hell, who inseminates themselves with their neighbour's spunk without telling their husband?'

'Each to their own,' said John quietly, 'each to their own. Let's head back and start putting things in order.'

They travelled back to the station in silence, both caught up in their own thoughts.

Chapter Seven

The office was stuffy and quiet when the call came through. Everyone was working quietly at their desks, the faint tapping of fingers on keys, some quicker than others, like jazz in staccato.

Mirry had been expecting it, the call. Chats had been had in the corridors, those in the know were subconsciously alerting one another, and, of course, there was John. So here it was, the call, a young woman, hypoxic brain injury, admitted in a flurry of activity through emergency, police in tow. Could she come now? Need for preparation before next conversation. Avenues to explore, discussions to be had. This was the time Mirry felt the knot tightening in her stomach. She brushed her hair, checked her teeth, blew her nose, and gathered the paperwork. Deep breath, radar on.

Arriving at the doors outside ICU, she was breathless, having taken the stairs two at a time. She breathed in deeply and exhaled out, then held her card up to the scanner. The thrill of being admitted unquestioningly still amazed her. She loved going through doors with 'No Entry' signs, 'Staff Only' notices, and those secret hospital areas that only those and such as those can gain access to. A silly feeling, but it made her smile. Always thought of as useless, but not now.

She knew this area well. The Medics' room gave good evidence of what kind of day it had been. Many empty coffee cups and discarded sandwich cartons; slow paperwork catch-up day. Empty of cups other than last night's pizza carry out boxes and mounds of paperwork; mental busy. The evidence showed it was mental busy, paperwork on three surfaces, bin overflowing with food wrappers, and a pair of blood-spattered clogs abandoned in the corner. Everyone was going to be stressed then.

Making her way down the corridor, she could hear the familiar electronic beeps of machines and quiet murmur of voices. Walking into the care area, a number of people turned to look… relatives visiting, their faces pale with worry, staff engaged in keeping track of life support, a cleaner scrubbing an empty bed space, a nurse already making up the bed for a new admission. The only people who didn't turn to look at her were the patients themselves - they couldn't, they were too sick. Lying in their individual spaces, hooked up to multiple machines, the brightness of the overhead lighting individually illuminating the seriousness of how ill these people were. It always reminded her of a car production line.

She knew immediately where her patient was, the one she had been called about. The side room with two police officers sitting outside, the lights low in the room. There were two people at the entrance to the door, deep in conversation. The taller of the two looked up when he sensed her there. Looked up and smiled. Mirry was relieved to see it was Craig. They had worked together over a number of years now, through which Mirry had had the pleasure of seeing him grow from a conscientious trainee anaesthetist to the strong and confident consultant he had become. Not friends as such but working colleagues with mutual respect.

'Hay,' he said, 'glad it's you, going to be a toughy…'

'Hay yourself,' Mirry said, smiling as she joined them. 'So what's new?'

In blue beside him was Sandie, her face serious. Mirry was relieved to see her too, they knew each other well. They had worked together as junior staff nurses, both starting in critical care at the same time. That would be twelve years ago now, and since then, their careers had taken different turns, with Sandie continuing with promotion within ICU and Mirry choosing the route of Donor Coordinator.

'Office?' Sandie said, her eyebrows raised.

The three of them headed back to the midden that was the Medics.

Craig spoke first.

'Not going to be simple. In fact, not sure at all whether this one will get past the PF.'

'She carried a card,' said Sandie, always the advocate.

'Okay, bring me up to speed,' Mirry said, looking at Craig.

Craig sighed.

'Already know some of it… John called it in; he's been working on this since.'

'Okay, that makes it easier,' said Craig. 'Her name is Jenny Anderson, she's a thirty-two year old female, found three days ago at home after a call from the neighbour who had gone in to take dogs for a walk. Every morning at 11 am, the two of them go for a 6 mile run/walk. Neighbour trying to lose weight, patient's a fitness trainer. Had been doing well, then, well, then you know what happened.' Craig's face grimaced.

'Dogs badly mutilated and dead. Patient initially thought to be dead, too, covered in blood with a blow to the head. Pulse was found, resuscitated at scene, brought in here through ED.'

'She was intubated, ventilated, scanned.' This simple sentence condensed the complex process of taking over a person's ability to remain conscious and breathe. Mirry could picture the scene in the ED, calm, almost robotic, everyone knowing their role. Instructions issued with confidence, teamwork personified.

'CT shows hypoxic brain injury…'

Mirry inclined her head, questioning.

'Evidence of strangulation, compression of the neck, not enough to kill her but enough to cause the oedema. Petechial haemorrhage obvious on CT, eyes, etc… Pupils fixed and dilated, obs all good now we've stabilised her, been off sedation for twenty-four hours, safe to say BSD is next step.'

'Family?'

'Husband, mother, and brother.'

'Dynamics?'

'Difficult to say, too shocked to take things in. Husband had been away for work, conference in Dundee, left the night before. They're up to speed with what's going on, well some of it. Police have done preliminary questioning and they have an FLO, which makes things easier all round for us as well as the family.

Mirry sensed something from Craig. 'Go on.'

'When she was being catheterised in the ED, the nurse noticed some vaginal bleeding. There was a thought that there had been sexual assault, but turns out it wasn't. She was pregnant, about six weeks. The foetal remains have been taken for evidence.'

Mirry looked away, the butterflies in her stomach lurching in a downward dive. This was close to home, personal. Craig saying it out loud made it so much more real.

'Does the family know?' Tentative question, so simple to ask.

'We told her husband when she was first admitted, but he hasn't taken it in - you can just tell. I don't know if he's let the rest of the family know either, but we'll have to revisit everything at some point today. Police finished questioning him yesterday. Apparently, his alibi stands up, so he's not a suspect.' Craig rubbed his eyes vigorously and shook his head.

'This isn't going to be easy either way, Mirry. We haven't spoken to the PF yet and depending who's on will depend on whether this goes ahead or not.'

'Well, as always we need to ask the question, don't we? No point going through a huge rigmarole if the family aren't on board.'

'But what about if the PF says no, Mirry? Then where does that leave the family?'

'There's always tissue donation, fiscal guys are usually cool with that.'

Sandie shivered, the vision of a busy fiscal post mortem room flashing through her head.

'Okay, ready, Mirry? Usual approach? Me, then over to you?'

'Girding my loins as we speak, Craig.'

'Gonna need it, girl, we're going to need it.'

Sandie and Craig headed back into the unit while Mirry went to sort the family room. Such a soulless place. No windows, just the overhead, artificial unforgivable lighting. Grey walls, the attempts to soften them with furnishings lost with the "no smoking" sign and the "violence to staff will not be tolerated" poster. Too many times in this room, the many instances of family grief and despair etched in its walls.

Mirry pulled two chairs in to form a group. She took the chair nearest the door. Always safe to have a clear exit. Memories of being trapped with an aggressive bereaved and unaccepting brother staying with her. That wouldn't happen again, reflective practice, it's called. Learning from experience, always learning from experience.

The door opened and Sandie led the way. Mother first, then a younger man, and the husband, so obviously the husband. His pallor grey, eyes red, the obvious lack of sleep emanating from him like a quiet, electrical humming.

Mirry stood. 'Please,' she said, indicating the sofa and armchair. Craig followed, the room starting to feel claustrophobic. Mirry sat down and everyone else did the same.

'Firstly, I would like to introduce you to my colleague Mirry, who is a specialist nurse who works closely with us.' Mirry nodded to them, maintaining eye contact.

'Ray, Jenny's husband, Kath, Jenny's Mum, and Kyle, Jenny's younger brother.' They all nodded at Mirry, Kath trying a smile, trying normal human niceties. Mirry hated this bit, the calm before the storm.

The rest of the conversation went as Mirry had expected. The explanation of treatment failure, severity of injury to brain, weaning off of the drugs used to keep Jenny asleep. The lack of response in any way, no coughing on the tube, no pupils constricting to bright light, no withdrawal to any painful stimulation either normal or abnormal. Said slowly and deliberately, as if each word had a cost, a price to pay, finishing with the inevitable, what questions do you have?

'Are you sure she was pregnant?' From Ray, his face still. Kath jerked as if a current had been passed through her.

'Pregnant? Pregnant? Where did that come from?'

'Kath, I'm sorry to say that when Jenny was admitted to the ED there was vaginal bleeding noticed - she was miscarrying at the time. The remains have been taken for analysis.'

Kath looked wide-eyed at Ray. She snorted when he didn't return her gaze.

Ray sighed, putting his head in his hands and rubbing his face.

'It couldn't have been mine, I've had the snip, you know, a jaffa.'

The silence was palpable. Ray continued to stare at the floor, his head bowed, his shoulders slumped.

'Who's was it then?' Kath again, her eyes flashing between Ray and Kyle. 'She wasn't seeing anyone, she would've told me, tells me everything my Jenny, always has.'

'Obviously not this time.' This from Ray, his head now up, his hollow eyes reflecting the pain that was so deeply being felt.

'Well, you wouldn't let her, would you? She had to bloody plead with you to get those dogs, you selfish bastard. All right for you, you've got your family already, your two boys. Good to them she's been, too. Never bloody appreciated that, though, did you? Hardly surprising she's gone off somewhere else looking for a bit of love.'

Mirry couldn't believe what was unfolding here. This was not how this conversation was meant to go. She looked over at Craig to take control of what was very quickly turning into a car wreck of a family approach. This one wasn't in the training manual.

'Mum, now is not the time.' This from Kyle, shaking his head. 'Can we just talk about what happens now to Jenny?' He looked over at Craig. 'Please doctor, what happens now, does she have to go to theatre or are there other drugs you can give to take the swelling away…?'

Craig exhaled. 'There is nothing more that can be done for Jenny. She is going to die, and I suspect that is what has already happened.'

'What do you mean, 'has already happened?' She looks okay to me - okay, she's a bit pale, and that bruising on her face isn't great, but…' Kyle's voice tailed off, his words falling into the silence, the reality too much to take in.

'The swelling in her brain has led to something we call 'coning'. With the swelling, there is nowhere for the brain to go other than down through to the area where the brain meets the spine. All the vital parts of the brain that keep us alive, the breathing, the heartbeat, are in that part of the brain called the brain stem. Once that area is irreparably damaged, there is no recovery. This is what has happened to Jenny. The ventilator is doing all the breathing for her, and we are keeping her blood pressure up with drugs. She will not breathe without it, and her heart will stop.'

The silence that followed Craig's words was almost palpable as their meaning became a reality for Jenny's family.

'Isn't there something more you can do? She's only been in for three days, and she's only thirty-two for god's sake.'

A desperate question, but finally back to safe territory for both Craig and Mirry. The stock phrases, nothing more to be done, the frequent use of the word brain death until the reality sank in and the final question was asked by Kyle.

'So what happens now?'

'We would like to confirm what we think has happened by carrying out some further tests.' Craig leaned forward to emphasise the seriousness of what he was saying. 'These tests will have to be done twice, once by myself and a second time by one of my colleagues so there is no doubt about the results. The test would confirm brain stem death, confirm that Jenny has died.'

'When will this happen? From Ray now, his head up. 'Can I be there to hold her whilst you do them? I've always been there for her. Please?' He looked at Sandie, at Mirry, at Craig. His eyes beseeching, a final question, quiet, 'Please?'

'We would like to do them this morning, and yes, you can be there, Ray, but I must stress the tests are very basic and may seem very crude. It may help, though, with coming to terms with what's happened to Jenny.'

Ray stood up. 'Right then, let's get on with it.'

'Please sit down, Ray, there is one more thing I need to discuss with you all at this stage.' Ray fell back down on the sofa, the thump of his weight making the old springs squeak in protest.

'At this time, it is our policy to always offer the opportunity for organ donation to families. Mirry is the specialist nurse for donation and we know that Jenny had signed up on the organ donor register to donate all her organs in the event of her death. Mirry?'

'She signed up when she joined the Bangholm GP surgery in 2010. She signed up to donate everything. Were you aware of her wishes, Ray, was it something you had ever discussed?'

'No, never, but that's so like her, she is always doing stuff for others, something to help; one of the things I love about her, she's so kind. Donating blood regularly, even had that pin they give you for the amount she'd given. Signed up for bone marrow transplantation, too, gave to that as well.'

'Well, not this time.' This from Kath. 'You're not touching my Jenny, she's been through enough, so no. Nice to meet you and all that, Mirry, but no.'

'Mum…' From Kyle, tentative and barely audible. 'It was what she wanted.'

And so it began, the to-ing and fro-ing discussion, the questions with answers given that nobody wanted to hear, the reality slowly taking its dark shape in the room.

Chapter Eight

Mirry went through the donor form slowly, double checking that every box was ticked and every question asked. The interview with the family had been harder than usual with more left unsaid than said. The conflict between Kath and Ray had been self-evident, but even in grief, they were holding on to politeness. Jenny had sounded like a beautiful, kind woman with a lust for life and a willingness to give everyone a chance. Mirry felt she knew her a little now, probably would have been friends had they met in another world.

This one would stay with her for a good while. She could see why John had been so upset; the fact that Jenny was pregnant made it seem all the more personal. The PF had given permission for kidney donation only after discussion with Paul, the forensic pathologist who would carry out the post-mortem examination post-retrieval. She had done a full body inspection and measurement. Well, Paul and her had. Going over the body with a fine-tooth comb, looking for evidence of bruising, grazing, and scratches for Paul - melanoma, drug abuse, tattoos, and piercings for Mirry. Nothing of note for Mirry, but for Paul, the distinct pattern of bruising around Jenny's throat was photographed and measured over and over again from every angle, her nails scraped clean, and for the final insult, her vagina swabbed, with Mirry and Sandie having to hold the flopping dead legs apart and still while evidence was gathered. There hadn't been much chat between the three of them; they knew each other well enough that small talk wasn't necessary. None of them were that good at it anyway, and on this occasion, there was no need. The reality of what they were doing kept them quiet within their own thoughts, allowing them to continue their work to the best of their ability for the dead woman in front of them.

The final straw for Mirry had been Jenny's beautiful bright red toenails, the colour speaking of fun, glamour, and confidence. The only time Mirry ever had the time or the patience to paint her toenails was the day before going on a summer holiday. They had never looked as good as these. Each cuticle perfectly shaped, the varnish unchipped and gleaming. Mirry had gently stroked Jenny's foot as she laid it back on the bed.

'That's me done, Mirry,' Paul had said, removing gloves and packing bags. 'She'll make a good donor for somebody.'

He looked over the bed at Mirry, no other words necessary, no trite phrases needed.

'Cheers, Paul, I'll finish up here and get her family back in. Will you advise PF for everything?'

'Think so, Mirry, we've enough evidence with the CT and bloods. There'll be a full pm tomorrow but it's not going to alter the cause of death at this stage. The bruising around her neck fits with the cerebral hypoxia. I'll be at the retrieval later anyway. You going to be there too?'

'Depends on timings, really. Hoping it's going ahead later today, but the retrieval team is out already, down in

Dumfries, so might not get done until early doors tomorrow.'

'Better get home for tea and a bit of shut-eye then.'

'Cheers, Paul, will you let Craig know for final PF decision then?'

'On it.'

With that, Paul had left the room, nodding at the two police officers outside, exchanging pleasantries and a wry joke.

Jenny's organ retrieval was to take place in the small hours of the morning, the returning transplant team responding with a quick turnaround.

Mirry shook herself, stretched her arms above her head, and exhaled loudly. Nothing more to be done here - home time, feet up on comfy sofa, bowl of pasta, and glass of wine. With any luck, John would be home by now, tea on the go. She had handed everything over to Pen earlier, who would see that Jenny's retrieval went to plan.

She shut down her PC and locked up the paperwork. Picking up her bag, she looked around the office one last time before turning off the light. First in and last out. Story of her life at times, inwardly groaning that it wouldn't be too long before she would be back here first thing tomorrow.

The other offices were in darkness as she pushed against the exit door. Heaving her rucksack onto her back, she made her way outside to the car park and found her car more by habit than recognition. Just before she started the engine, she looked up and saw a group of three figures huddled around the ticket machine. She knew instantly who they were and her stomach fell. They had talked about leaving later that day, saying their goodbyes, the realisation dawning finally on them that their Jenny was indeed dead. They would not have been encouraged to wait until Jenny was taken to theatre for retrieval. That would ultimately have been too painful.

Mirry started the engine and drove past them. She glanced into the ticket shelter, hoping that they wouldn't look out and see her, but also knowing that she would need to acknowledge them if they did. Nothing happened; they were too busy trying to find the right money for the ticket, too upset to be aware of anything else around them.

She decided to take a detour and drive home through the park, the evening May light bathing the Crags in a veil of warm yellow. As always, joggers and runners of all ages, shapes, and sizes were out and about. People walking their dogs, couples holding hands, tourists amazed that this area of hills and lochs could be in the middle of a city. The coconut smell of the yellow gorse akin more to a tropical island than the sweep of Edinburgh's countryside. She headed for town.

As always, it took her forever, or what seemed like forever. Every traffic light at red, caught behind buses and cyclists. By the time she found a parking space near the flat, she was frayed and hungry.

Mirry made her way up the flight of stone stairs. She was so tired; bone tired, her mum used to call it when she came in from a week of night shifts. Once more she questioned the decision they had made in buying a flat on the fourth floor. Yes, the views over Edinburgh were amazing, but sometimes lugging shopping, flat pack furniture, and a knackered body up these stairs was just not worth it. Her mind moved forward to a vision of carrying a baby buggy up too - she groaned inwardly at the very thought of it. Pushing that to the back of her mind, she put the key in the door, jiggled it to find the right angle, and walked in.

The first thing that struck her was the smell and humidity in the long, narrow hall. She could hear a rhythmical hissing and scraping coming from the sitting room. Dropping her bag on the wooden chest by the door, she slid out of her jacket and threw it onto the clothes hook.

'John, love, I'm home!' she called, pushing open the sitting room door. 'I'm heading straight for the shower…' Her words faded into silence as she surveyed the scene before her.

John was up a ladder, wallpaper stripper in hand, destroying the newly papered feature wall which had taken them hours of discussion and disagreement before settling on the patterned, muted green tones which had been the basis for the rest of the room. The last room they had finally finished in their first home together.

'What the fuck are you doing!' she screamed, covering her face with her hands, shutting out what she was seeing.

'Decided I don't like this green. Didn't think you would be home so soon, thought you were with Jenny's family?' John answered, out of breath as he reached up to the high cornice with the stripper, destroying all their previous hard work.

'Are you off your head?' She bent down and tore the plug of the steamer out of the wall. 'Really?' she yelled, kicking the box containing all of their DIY tools, the only box full of anything useful John brought when they first moved in together.

'Ach, Mirry, love, stop being such a drama queen. It'll take me no time to strip this, and then Fee and her brother are coming round to help finish off. I bought that paper you really liked the most, you know, the expensive one with the trees on it?' He climbed slowly down the ladder, not looking at her, running his hands through his hair, showing his agitation.

'What possessed you to do this now? This is the last room we had finished and now you've destroyed it because you've had another one of you harebrained fucking nonsense ideas!'

'As I said, Fee and Sam are coming round tonight to help me finish off. It's no big deal, it'll all be done by the morning. I thought you'd be pleased, you've got the paper you wanted.'

Mirry stood looking at him exasperated, shaking her head. Some battles were worth pursuing with John, but this one was going to take too much fight and she just didn't have the energy, certainly not after the day she'd had. Her head slumped to her chest.

'I'm going for a shower.'

'Can I get a kiss before you head off?' John asked, his head at that nauseating counselling angle he knew infuriated her.

'Get lost.' She turned and headed for the bathroom, unsuccessfully slamming the sitting room door behind her. Bloody dip and strip shite, door warped, her anger festering.

'Nightie-night!' He called after her.

'Pyjama, fucking pyjama,' Mirry muttered in response, closing the bathroom door on the madness in the sitting room, 'pyjama, fucking pyjama.'

Mirry undressed and ran the shower, closing her eyes as she stepped in under the hot spray, letting the force of the water hit her aching neck. She exhaled loudly and fumbled for the soap. She found it in the dish and breathed in the herby smell as she lathered quickly. The shower door opened, and before she knew what was happening, John was naked behind her, wrapping his arms around her waist and drawing him close to her.

'I'm sorry, Mirry,' he whispered in her ear, 'Really sorry.'

'I'm too tired for fighting, John,' she murmured, turning to face him, feeling his desire pressed against her belly.

The doorbell rang loudly.

'Ah shit, that'll be Fee,' John said, 'she's always bloody early.'

Mirry smiled and pushed him out of the shower. 'Off you go then, Mr. Fix-it, but lose the hard-on first, not sure Fee would be too pleased at that telegraph pole.'

John snorted with laughter as he wrapped a towel around his middle, pulling his dressing gown off the back of the bathroom door and shrugging it on as he headed off down the hall.

'Just coming,' he shouted.

'More than I'm doing,' Mirry thought as she rinsed off the lather and stepped out of the shower, reaching for the towel warming on the heated rail. She wrapped it round herself and put her robe on. Pulling the tie closed, she stepped out into the hall.

'Not disturbing anything, are we, love birds?' Fee was standing in the hall dressed in her usual off-duty clothes of ripped jeans, hoodie, and Doc Marten boots. Sam, her younger brother, stood awkwardly behind her, looking up at the ceiling, anywhere other than Mirry and John, the obviousness of their mutual showering making his toes curl in embarrassment.

'No, no, Fee,' said Mirry, 'a delight as always to see you, particularly now with the pig's ear he's made of my sitting room. Now, if you'll excuse me I'm off to get into my jammies.'

With that, Mirry turned and headed for their bedroom at the other end of the hall, closing the door on the madness behind her.

'Mirry have a hard shift?' Fee asked, raising her heavily pencilled eyebrows at John questioningly.

'Yeah, something like that, she got our case, who believe it or not is going on to donate. Been a nightmare for her from start to finish. You know what she's like with cases; they become her family, her donors.'

'Aw shit, that's a toughy. PF happy about giving permission?'

'Got there in the end, Paul helped out by the sound of it. It's hard to say no to Mirry and the team when healthy organs are at stake. Something positive had to come out of that shit show. Thanks for coming, I couldn't live with it the way it was. You'll see…'

John led Fee and Sam through to the sitting room. Fee took one look at the remains of the patterned muted green wallpaper, a flashback to a similar wall, but splattered with dog's blood, excrement, and fur. She shook her head and pulled her hoodie off.

'Right, I get it, let's get this over and done with or you'll never hear the end of it.'

Chapter Nine

The following week, Mirry was stuck in the office, watching the interminable blue circle go round and round on her PC screen. She blew exasperatedly out the side of her mouth. This was doing her nut in, trying to get on with her reports and write a teaching session for a school talk, but no matter what she tried or how she tried it, nothing was working. She could feel the confines of the windowless office starting to close in around her. Debs was talking quietly into her mobile in the corner, her face partially obscured by the ridiculously green potted plant that she insisted on having on her desk in a vain attempt to bring some oxygen into the room. On Pen's desk; a multitude of piled up files, her PC screen covered in different coloured post-it notes, their order and relevance known only to her.

The last person they shared an office with was Cath. She was the longest-running member of the team, her quiet knowledge, gentle manner, and grace always making Mirry feel slightly in awe of her. Cath was happily married, and it was no secret that she was trying for a family too. There had been great sadness over the last few months as she had had two miscarriages. Despite this, she had remained positive, never changing, returning to work not long after each heartbreaking disappointment. Mirry knew that

Cath's deep faith was what brought her comfort, that and the love of her close, supportive family. Cath's desk, as always, was ordered, with nothing personal on it, just a PC and a keyboard.

Mirry dropped her head into her hands for the umpteenth time that morning and groaned with frustration, rubbing her short blonde hair in furious circles, causing it to stick up at odd angles.

'Aaaach, I bloody hate this, makes my life a misery! Why doesn't the bloody thing do what it's supposed to do?' Mirry said out loud.

Debs smiled, knowing Mirry's impatience with all things electronic. 'Give Colin a shout,' she said. 'You know how much he loves you!'

Mirry's frustration escalated as she realised just how much she still had to do, not just the school talk but database entries, patient record updates, letters to families, and she was on call that night, so no glass of something chilled for her. If she had had a baseball bat, the life of this particular desktop would now be in the balance. Taking a deep breath, she phoned Colin, the team's IT guru, for help.

'It's your friendly neighbourhood Luddite again,' she said when Colin answered the phone on the second ring. 'Can't get anywhere with the database this morning, can't get any results for my clinic this afternoon - in fact, can't get eff all, and unless you come down here with a solution or some diazepam, there will be no machine left to torture me, as it will be in small pieces and I'll have my P45!'

Colin chuckled. 'Don't let the bastard get you down,' he said. 'Got a couple of things to take care of here, then I'll be down in a minute. Go and grab a coffee and some fresh air and stay away from the bridge, you know that's not good for you.'

'You know me too well.' Mirry's nicotine habit was common knowledge, as were her frequent attempts to give it up. However, this time, it was different since she had started taking folic acid and made John a promise that she would stop. The Zippo had been ditched and nearly all temptation removed. So far she had been doing okay.

'You're a lifesaver, Colin,' she said.

'No, that's you, Mirry,' murmured Colin.

'Ah, get out of here, you big sap! Debs is in the office, so I'll catch you later, alligator.'

'Got our new guy with me today - okay if I bring him over to meet the team, if you've time?'

'Yeah, great, although there's just me and Debs here at the moment... Oh, cancel that,' she said, watching Debs getting up and signalling that she was heading out in a poor charade of leaving, gesticulating wildly and reaching for her jacket. 'Looks like she's skiving off somewhere.'

'So just you then, Mirry. Be down in ten,' said Colin.

'Where you off to, Debs?' asked Mirry, putting down the phone. 'You had a call?'

'Came through when you were shouting at your PC,' Debs smiled. 'Off to 118, sub arach that came in last week not looking good, time for a chat with the family.'

'Oh, well, good luck. Colin's bringing down the new guy, you met him yet?'

'Eh, not yet, but I hear he's from Dundee, bit of a looker by all accounts. Think he knows it though, according to Pen.'

'God, you lot are so judgemental. Give the guy a chance, he's only just started.'

'Ha, listen to you! Fill me in with all the details when I get back. Probably be handing this one over to you anyway. You're on tonight aren't you?'

'Yeah, for my sins.' Mirry groaned inwardly, the vision of her night cosied on the sofa with John dissipating into the ether.

'Family might say no; she wasn't on the register and she's been in a week, could be a non-starter.'

'Go and do your thanng,' said Mirry. 'I'll let you know how I get on with Crocodile Dundee.'

'Oh, I see what you did there, very funny!' Debs picked her briefcase up and headed out the office, sorting the collar on her jacket and running her hand through her hair.

Mirry turned back to her PC, the blue circle continuing to torment her. She pushed her seat back, stretched her arms up, and exhaled loudly. Standing up, she shook her shoulders and bent down, letting her arms drop, moving them in a circle first clockwise then back again, loosening the tension, breathing slowly in and out.

The door behind her opened.

'Woah, Mirry, nice view!' This from Colin, walking in laughing as Mirry quickly stood upright, experiencing a sudden head rush as she became vertical again.

'Ever heard of knocking?' Mirry smiled, pleased to see Colin, comfortable with the banter after their years of working together.

'Hey Mirry, this is Simon… Simon, Mirry.'

Mirry looked at the man who had followed Colin in. She saw immediately what the fuss was about. Tall, blonde, with such piercing blue eyes they almost looked unreal. He had a relaxed look about him, the words of a Bowie song coming into Mirry's head for some inexplicable reason, 'Lets him loose, hard to swallow', long and lean, tall, blonde, and hugely fuckable. This last thought took Mirry a little by surprise - where the hell had that come from?

Mirry gave a winning smile, holding her hand out.

'Hay Simon, nice to meet you, welcome to the team. I hear you've come down from Dundee?'

'Yeah, thanks, Mirry, nice to meet you too, just starting to find my feet.'

He looked down on Mirry, his height exaggerated by Colin's short stature. His handshake was strong, Mirry's hand felt small in his grip. His hand was warm, and as she released her grip first, almost reluctantly, she noticed a dressing on his wrist. He seemed to be appraising her too, almost slightly amused by the effect he was having on her.

'Careless Stanley knife accident opening packing boxes,' Simon said, seeing Mirry looking at his wrist as he pulled his sleeve down. 'First aid has never been my strongpoint!'

'Hope you gave it a good clean, wouldn't want it to get infected. I could have a look if you like?'

'Aw thanks, Mirry, that's really kind,' Simon smiled. 'It's okay for now, but I'll keep your offer in mind.'

They continued to look at each other until Colin spoke up.

'Simon is pulling together the databases from NHS and UK Transplant so that they speak to each other,' he said, breaking the silence, slightly amused at what he was witnessing. Mirry was staring at Simon, and Colin watched her as she scanned, radar on, reading, assessing. He was used to Mirry's ways. Sometimes it could be disconcerting to be caught in her gaze, there was nowhere to hide. If she had been born in an earlier time, she probably would have been burnt as a witch. Insightful to a tee. Colin knew she could read a room like a fortune teller would read leaves in a cup. The only difference being Mirry would read it right nine times out of ten. It was what made her so good at her job.

'Well, good luck with that one, Simon, been needed for a long time, will make our job so much easier,' Mirry said, returning quickly to business. 'Anyway, thanks for coming down, Colin, can I leave this with you? Just not connecting to anything. Going to grab a bite to eat and get some daylight.'

'Sure, Mirry, no worries, we've got this.'

She walked over to where her jacket was on the coat stand, reached up on her tiptoes to take it down, aware that she was being scrutinised from behind by those piercing blue eyes. She felt a thrill go up her spine as she stretched, felt eyes removing her shirt, sliding her trousers down... 'Get a grip, Mirry,' she thought, turning round to find Simon's eyes quickly leaving right where she knew she had felt them.

He smiled broadly, unabashed at having been caught out. 'Enjoy your lunch, think it's nice out there.'

'Cheers, Simon,' said Mirry, her usual confidence off-kilter slightly as she shrugged on her jacket. She patted her trouser pocket for money and phone, a gesture more out of habit rather than a conscious act, aware again that she was under the blue eyed scrutiny. Shaking herself back to normality, she said: 'Maybe have a welcome coffee with the rest of the team when you've got your bearings.'

'Great,' said Simon, 'I'll look forward to it.'

Colin glanced at Mirry, aware that the atmosphere in the room, which had become charged very quickly, was now returning to normal. Looking at Mirry, he was puzzled by the unfamiliar blush she had.

'Nowt as queer as folk,' he thought, sitting down at her PC, adjusting the chair, and pulling the keyboard towards him.

'Dinnae be disturbing my perfect ergonomics!' Mirry laughed as she headed out the glass door of the office. 'Thanks again, Colin, catch you later, guys.'

Mirry strode down the brightly lit corridor, smiling to herself. 'Now he's something else,' she thought ruefully. 'Once upon a time.'

Chapter Ten

John was reading through the reports of the door to door interviews his team had done with Jenny's neighbours. His concentration was broken with the sudden shrill ringing of his desk phone.

'Sneddon,' he said, not taking his eyes off the paperwork in front of him as he continued highlighting areas for further discussion.

'Hey John, it's me, got some interesting preliminary results back from your assault case last week.' John instantly recognised the Aberdonian accent of Mark, the senior forensic scientist.

'Oh thanks, Mark, did you hear she didn't survive? It's now a murder investigation.'

'Yeah, Fee let me know what happened and that she went on to donate. Mirry involved?'

'Yeah, she was, keeping it in the family so to speak,' John said wryly. 'Can you email what you've found?'

'Actually, it would be better if we got together, there's a few things I want to run past you. I might be overthinking this, but there's a couple of odd things you need to be aware of.'

'Do you want me to come to you then?'

'Good idea, and you could bring some coffee with you too, you know how shite our stuff is!'

John laughed out loud. 'On it, might even squeeze in a bun.'

'I shouldn't really, but a muffin would be very welcome, you know my favourite!'

'See you about eleven thirty then?'

'Great, I'll let front desk know you're coming.'

John put the phone down, his curiosity already starting to go into overdrive. Mark was always very measured with his analysis and reporting; it was unlike him to want to discuss his findings so early.

John could see Fee sitting in deep concentration in front of her PC going over the CCTV recordings that were available from around where Jenny had lived. It had picked up Jenny taking her dogs for a walk at ten twenty-two on her way to the park and thirty minutes later when she returned. Fee was literally going through frame by frame looking for anything unusual. Knocking on his office window, he waved for her to come in.

'What's up?' she said, leaning in from the door.

'Been on the phone with Mark at Howdenhall, says he wants us to go down for a chat. You free?

'Yeah, sure, let me grab my jumper and keys, and I'll meet you out front.'

John closed his laptop, grabbed his mobile, and pulled his jacket off the back of his chair, shrugging it on as he headed out.

'Just heading down to Forensics,' he announced to the remainder of the team as he was leaving. 'Reconvene at end of play today.'

Fee was waiting in the car at the entrance to their office as John signed out and pushed the exit button to open the glass doors. As soon as he had fixed his seatbelt, Fee pulled away.

The drive through town was slow, making them both tense. It was late May and Edinburgh was full of tourists and would only get busier as the summer progressed, culminating in the end with the madness of the Edinburgh Festival. Fee stopped at a pedestrian crossing as a hoard of teenage schoolchildren were being herded across by two very stressed teachers. John wondered where they came from. He could hear an excited babble of what he thought was Spanish through the car's open window. He smiled when he made eye contact with one of the teachers and swept his brow in a mime of wiping off sweat. The teacher grinned at him, nodded, and waved before quickly returning to her shepherding duties.

'God, that looks so stressful, doesn't it?' John said as they pulled away.

'Bloody madness, give me an assault case to investigate any day!' answered Fee, laughing.

They stopped off for a tray of coffees and a bag of muffins before pulling into the car park at Howdenhall. Going into the building, the receptionist buzzed them straight through to the corridor where Mark's office was. John knocked on the door and walked in without waiting for a response.

Mark was sitting with his back to them in front of three screens. He was a heavy-set man whose tight shirt wrinkled around the very obvious spare tyre he was carrying round his middle. On hearing John and Fee come in, he swivelled round on his chair, his face breaking into a huge grin with squint teeth when he saw the tray of coffees and the brown paper bag.

'That was quick, mate!' he said, standing up. 'Come in, come in, good to see you both.' He gestured to two seats opposite his desk.

'Hey Mark, brilliant to see you, how's the kids?' Mark and John had worked together on a couple of cases and had immediately got on well, each recognising a kindred spirit with their no bullshit outlook on life.

'Growing like weeds and eating me out of house and home. Carol's got me on yet another diet,' he said, slapping his expansive midriff, 'so today's goodies are a lifesaver… you know what she's like, lettuce and water!'

John and Fee both laughed as they opened the muffin bag and handed out the coffees.

'She just wants to have you a wee bit longer, that's all Mark, just taking good care of you,' John said, handing Mark a lemony coloured sponge confection and smiling, seeing Mark's eyes light up in delight.

The coffees and muffins handed out, they sat down as Mark went through what forensic results they had so far. It turned out that the house had revealed very little and Jenny's swabs had not come up with anything unusual. However, there had been tissue taken from the biggest dog's mouth, and Mark explained that he thought the dog had probably bitten the assailant quite badly.

'So there may be some DNA available then?' asked John as he finished off the last dregs of his coffee.

'Looks like it, the way the dog was killed it looked like it was done in anger - to be disembowelled that way. Whoever did it knew what they were doing and killed the dog with real force. The other animal had been bludgeoned to death.'

'Nasty,' said John, but he could tell that Mark was holding something back. 'But that's not the reason you've got us down, is it, what's going on?'

'Hmm, well, this is where it gets interesting. When I was looking over the SOCO photos, I noticed that the Ramsay ladder to the attic was down. The team went up to check the roof space, and this is what they came back with.'

Mark clicked the mouse to bring up a photograph of the loft area in Jenny and Ray's house. There was the usual paraphernalia of suitcases, boxes, and what looked like an artificial Christmas tree. Mark pointed with his pen to an area to the side of the tree.

'What's that?' John asked.

'Well, to me, it looks like someone has been sitting there. The dust has been disturbed and whoever it was had leant against the wall because, believe it or not, we've managed to find a couple of hairs that were pulled out by that small nail jutting out of the beam.'

'Wow, that's impressive work, Mark, but what does it mean?'

'Okay, go with me on this… I think whoever assaulted Jenny had been in the loft for some reason and took her by surprise when they came down the Ramsay ladder.'

Fee shivered. 'You think someone was hiding up there whilst she was in the house?'

'It looks like it, why else would the dust be disturbed like that?'

John was staring at the screen, looking at the picture of the loft whilst his brain went into overdrive.

'Remember Jenny had said to Ray the night before that the dogs had been really unsettled when they got back from their walk?' John said, looking at Fee for confirmation.

'You don't think someone got in whilst Jenny was out walking the dogs?'

'Could be a possibility, but that means that he must have known that she always walked the dogs at that time and that there was a Ramsay ladder to the attic.'

'Well, we'll run DNA on the hair samples too and see if there's a match. Should have those results by the end of the week.'

'This is great, Mark, really helpful, there are so many things to work with here. Think we need to get back to the station and see where we go from here.'

'A pleasure as always,' Mark said, standing up and showing them to the door. 'Just keep me in the loop, will you?'

'For sure,' said John, shaking Mark's hand, 'great to have something to work with.'

It wasn't until they were both back in the confines of the car that they were able to discuss what Mark had just told them.

'God, that gives me the creeps to think that whoever did this was hiding in the loft,' Fee said, pulling on her safety belt and starting the engine.

'It does mean though that whoever did this planned it rather than it being some random attack, don't you think?'

'Is that meant to make me feel less creeped out then?' Fee said, her imagination working through what must have happened when Jenny had realised there was someone in her home.

'I think it means that we have to go through Jenny's life with a fine-tooth comb and revisit all of the CCTV from around her house in the last few weeks.'

'Agreed,' replied Fee quickly. 'Let's get back and set the team to work, something has to come up, surely.'

Chapter Eleven

Mirry swore to herself as she mounted the stairs two at a time. 'Bloody hell, bloody hell, bloody hell!'

From outside the glass doors, she could see that the main office was already empty, meaning everyone would be in the meeting room and she was late. She hated being late, thought it rude and inconsiderate, engrained from years of turning up on time for shift changeover.

She burst into the meeting room with full force, exclaiming her apologies before even taking in who was in the room.

It was another soulless place in the hospital, used by different teams. There had obviously been some medical teaching going on, a picture of a liver crudely drawn in blue pen still evident on the whiteboard.

The office coffee flasks were out on the table like silver sentries guarding the tray of cups and, more importantly, the plate of biscuits.

Mirry looked around the gathered team, taking in who was there as she pulled out a seat nearest to the door.

'Morning Mirry,' said Helen, sitting at the top of the table, 'not like you to be late, so we thought we would give you five minutes before beginning.' Helen shuffled the pile of papers in front of her. 'I think we can just get going now, looks like everyone is here.'

Mirry scrabbled in her bag for something to write with as Pen pushed the printed agenda over to her, winking as she did so.

'Mirry, if you could take the minutes, that would be much appreciated.' This from Helen, her passive aggressive tone self-evident, more left unsaid than said.

Mirry looked around the table to jot down who was present, inwardly groaning at the thought of having to take the minutes. This was a job she absolutely hated; it meant she had to remain focused throughout the meeting and, by the looks of the agenda, it was going to be a long one. There was Helen, superior and enigmatic, Pen grinning knowingly at her, Debs sympathetic, Cath distracted by something on her phone, and Colin scribbling on a piece of paper in front of him.

And there he was, Simon, the new guy looking around the table, taking everyone in.

'Firstly, I'd like to introduce and formally welcome Simon Grey to our ever expanding team.' Helen nodded over in Simon's direction.

Simon smiled and said, 'Looking forward to working with you all.'

His gaze stopped at Mirry, smiling, looking straight at her, almost through her, causing an unexplainable lurch in her stomach.

'Is Grey with an "a" or an "e"?' Asked Mirry, smiling straight back at him.

'An "e" thanks, Mirry, as in Earl Grey rather than "a" as in the unit.'

'Mmm, bergamot,' said Mirry out loud as she continued to scribble. There was a quiet guffaw from Pen.

The meeting continued to follow the agenda and, after an hour, Mirry's mind was beginning to wander. 'Hopefully stop for coffee soon,' she thought, staring wistfully at the two flasks on the table, 'not long now.'

As if she had heard her thoughts, Helen said, 'Before we break for coffee, there is one last thing I want to cover which might lead to a bit of a discussion over said coffee.' She looked around the table, her face serious.

'As you know I have been studying for my MBA. There are a number of ideas I have been introduced to that I think we can implement into donation services from industry to improve performance.'

Mirry sighed, looking at Helen, her boss's self-importance coming out of every pore.

'Firstly, I'd like to introduce a donation leaderboard to the office where we can see on a month by month basis how we are all progressing with our numbers and indeed who is the most successful at taking donation through to transplantation. We can then reflect on the practice of our most successful co-ordinator, take apart their practice, but most importantly learn, learn, learn from each other.'

There were a number of furrowed brows around the table at this announcement.

Pen, as always, was first to speak.

'So, are you putting us in competition with each other then, Helen?' she asked. 'I think we all work pretty damned hard and collegiate at the moment, not sure team competition is required.'

'The very opposite, in fact, Pen. This is not meant to be seen as a threat, merely as an incentive. For example, how many of you know who has been the most successful co-ordinator this year?' Helen looked around the table, her eyebrows raised in expectation.

'By successful, Helen, do you mean who has had the most retrievals or the most referrals?' Mirry said. 'Surely that depends on how many on-calls you've done?'

'No, not really, it's fairly simple using an equation that I have worked out. From our number of referrals to successful donations tallied with the number of on-calls, there is a clear leader at present. That happens to be you, Mirry.'

'I think that's luck, to be honest, Helen, right time, right place, right family.' Mirry frowned. 'Right?'

'Actually, luck has very little to do with it,' Simon said from the top of the table as everyone turned to look at him. Undeterred he continued, 'Statistically, if it was luck, then Debs would be out in front as she has had more referrals, but actually, Mirry, you have more success in turning your referrals round into actual donors, proving that your practice is obviously commendable.'

Mirry looked around the table. 'I don't see how…' she started.

'Oh don't be so bashful, Mirry,' Helen said, 'I think everyone around the table would agree that you do an amazing job. Your practice can be a little alternative for some people's taste, but your results speak for themselves. It is also for that reason that I've invited Mirry to be part of the upcoming publicity training that we are doing.' Helen's patronising tone was beginning to grate.

'Who's we?' asked Pen.

'Well, mainly Cameron, as the lead transplant surgeon and me, of course, are giving the major contribution. Simon is going to oversee the statistical analysis, data management, and PR feedback whilst our very own Mirry will be the face of the team.' There was silence from everyone as the details were absorbed.

'Anyway, we'll keep you all posted as to how it goes and will be looking for positive feedback once some of the promotional material is ready for editing.'

'Can't wait,' mumbled Pen under her breath.

'Right, shall we break for coffee now, everyone? Get back together at what,' Helen looked at her watch, 'eleven o'clock sharp? Still got a lot to cover.'

Helen shuffled her papers in front of her, stood up, and pushed her chair back, bringing the meeting to a conclusion.

After the meeting, Debs, Pen, and Mirry headed back to the office together. Mirry was uncomfortable about what had been discussed and the way Simon had commented on Debs' practice.

'I'm sure what the figures say isn't true, Debs,' Mirry said uncomfortably..

'What do you mean, Mirry?' said Debs as they all stepped aside to let a porter and nurse push a patient on a bed down the long bright corridor.

'About me having better numbers.'

'To be honest, Mirry, I don't really care about the numbers and who is ahead, we already share all our experiences and practice, don't we?'

'Yeah, I suppose so…'

'Well, we do, look at that really tricky case you had the other week with the assault victim. I know you didn't manage to get the heart and lungs, but if you and Paul hadn't managed to persuade the PF to give permission, two people would still be on dialysis, one of them being that young lad from Glasgow.'

'I know, but that is a case in point, that was a team effort.'

'Ah, stop getting your knickers in a twist about Helen and her ideas,' said Pen. 'We all know what we're doing, just enjoy your day out in Glasgow. Rather you than me, to be honest, a whole day of publicity training… I'd rather stick a red hot needle in my eye!'

With Pen's acidic conclusion, the subject was closed and they headed back to the office, each distracted by their own thoughts.

Chapter Twelve

Mirry arrived at Waverley half an hour before their train to Glasgow was due. Even at this early hour of the morning, there was a buzz of energy. Commuters walked about looking at train times, mobiles, and watches, unaware of their fellow travellers around them, each concentrating on their own day, their own destination. The morning sun was bright through the high metal work of the train station roof, the odd pigeon already out and about flapping raggedy wings, little beady eyes searching for a morsel left by some unthinking traveller. Mirry didn't mind the city's pigeons; they were everywhere, and during the festival, they were in fierce competition with the seagulls for any abandoned food. Sometimes not even abandoned, the seagulls being braver than the pigeons, carrying out a swoop and grab on an unsuspecting tourist not paying close enough attention to their sandwich.

The coffee bars were open and trading, but as yet the queues had not built up. Mirry made her way over to her favourite bagel bar. She looked up at the menu wondering why she was bothering as she always had the same thing.

'Morning love, what can I get you?' This from the young man behind the counter, his smile warm and welcoming.

'Great customer service, the boy deserves a medal,' thought Mirry.

'Wholemeal marmite bagel and cappuccino with an extra shot, please.' Her order rolled off her tongue so easily. She just loved the simplicity of it; it ticked all her early morning boxes.

'God, you never change.'

Mirry turned around and there was Helen. She was dressed in a formal navy trouser suit, her auburn hair sleek and shining, full makeup already in place, slightly overdone in the harsh morning light. She smiled down at Mirry, her perfect white teeth marred by a dark smear of red lipstick.

'Can't beat perfection,' laughed Mirry, winking at the young lad as he handed over her breakfast.

'Same order for you?' He grinned at Helen.

'You must be joking,' snorted Helen. 'Salmon and cream cheese and a double espresso for me. Kickstart the day, brain food and a heart-starter.'

As Helen waited for her order, Mirry wandered over to look at the timetable board to see what platform they were on.

'Ours is the seven-fifty, platform thirteen,' Helen said, walking purposely by her, carrying her breakfast in one hand, their tickets in the other. Mirry followed, as always wondering at Helen's ability to stride so quickly in high heels, her presence being noticed by a number of men who were sizing her up as she strutted past them. Mirry could never wear heels comfortably, they made her feel like an unbalanced prawn, like a child in her mum's dress up shoes. Femininity, or whatever high heels were, was not for her. Pen always laughed at the practicality of Mirry's shoes, where Pen had a vast selection of heels and boots, some that she referred to as her 'house' shoes. Shoes for play only, a different kind of dress up, their spiky heels giving off an aura of danger and risk. Pen to a tee.

They made their way through the ticket barrier, Helen taking charge, handing over Mirry's tickets as well as her own. Mirry smiled at the guard but he was too intent at looking after Helen, watching her hips sway exaggeratedly from side to side, sinewy and snakelike. The train was busy, filling up with suit-wearing men and women, some already deep in conversation on their mobiles, oblivious to their fellow travellers around them. Helen found their reserved seats and indicated for Mirry to squeeze in beside the window.

'Looks like we may have this to ourselves then,' said Mirry, opening up her still-warm breakfast, slightly salivating in anticipation of the salty, buttery bagel.

'That ain't going to happen. This stops at Haymarket, so we'll probably have company all the way.'

Mirry didn't say anything, becoming irritated at Helen - sometimes, she could be such a condescending pain in the arse. Mirry checked herself, 'going to be a long day, girl, just go with the flow.' She took a big bite out of her bagel, the melted butter running down her chin as she grabbed the paper napkin to stop it from going on her skirt. Helen glanced over as she delicately tore a piece from her own bagel and popped it in her mouth, avoiding smudging her lipstick.

'So, Mirry, you looking forward to today?'

'Don't really know what to expect,' said Mirry, 'just going with the flow, you know me.'

'Hmm, yes, well, it really is a fantastic opportunity for us both, these places are as rare as hens' teeth. I had said I needed publicity training, what with the way donation is going in the future. It's all about engaging with the public, promoting the benefits of donation, how many lives can be saved by transplant, that kind of thing.'

'There are times though, Helen, do you not think, they should maybe concentrate a wee bit more on the experience of the donor families? Let them have more of a voice?'

Helen looked over at her, smiling as she wiped non-existent crumbs from the side of her mouth.

'Oh, that's so typical of you, Mirry, you are sweet at times. Always on the side of the donor family. The reality of it is that death just isn't sexy, whilst life-saving surgery is. That's what makes all the difference to people's perception of donation, it's all about the life-saving.'

'Not sure too many donor families would agree with you there.' Mirry could feel her blood beginning to boil as it always did when she had these conversations with Helen.

'Well, I know what your feelings are about all this, Mirry, which is why I recommended that you come today, might give you a different perspective when you really know what goes on with publicity and marketing.'

'Donation is not about publicity and marketing,' snorted Mirry, angrily pushing her empty coffee cup away from her.

'Oh, I think that is where you're a little naïve. On the course I'm doing - you do remember I'm doing an MBA, don't you - marketing can be applied to any scenario in the workplace. Take my new initiative of the leaderboard for example - you must admit that it has concentrated the team to try and perform better. Introduced a bit of competition?'

'Have you forgotten what it was like to be an ODC, Helen?' Mirry asked, exasperated. 'Donation is about doing what is right for the donor and the families irrespective of the success or not. It's the families that have to live with it.'

'I'm well aware of that, Mirry, and no, I haven't forgotten what it was like to be an ODC. I'm just a little more realistic about what our goals are than you. Organs save lives, Mirry, and that, after all, is what we are employed to do.'

'I give up!' Mirry sighed, shaking her head in exasperation. 'You and I are never going to agree on this, so let's just agree to disagree.'

'Fine by me,' answered Helen, sitting back in the seat and pulling a file from her bag. 'Now, if you don't mind, I've some work to catch up with.'

They travelled the rest of the journey in silence with Helen concentrating on her work and Mirry looking out the window as the bland scenery of central Scotland whizzed past. By the time they arrived in Queen Street Station, the silence between them had changed to amicable companionship and the two women stepped down from the train and into the bustle of the crowd. 'Taxi rank is at the front,' Helen said, striding off purposefully as Mirry avoided a group of students blocking her way. She caught up with Helen just as she opened the door to the first black cab in the rank.

'Morning hen,' said the driver, 'where you two lovely ladies off to?'

Helen gave the address as Mirry followed in behind her and sat down, pulling the safety belt over and clipping it in.

'Work, is it then?' asked the cabbie, talking to them in the reflection of the mirror, which Mirry noticed had red rosary beads dangling down from it. 'So very Glasgow,' she thought, smiling to herself.

'Yes, that's right, doing a bit of publicity training today,' said Helen, straightening out her jacket under the safety belt.

'Publicity, you say? What's it you two do then, let me guess, radio, politics, television?'

Helen scoffed. 'Nah, nothing so glamorous. We're Organ Donor Co-ordinators.'

'Woah,' laughed the cabby, 'didn't see that coming!' And so their conversation took off as they discussed the merits of presumed consent and the donor register. As always, both Helen and Mirry advocated for the benefits of donation with family agreement. By the time they pulled up outside the building where the training was to take place, they had convinced the driver to not only sign up to the donor register but to tell his family what his wishes were.

'Good job done there,' Helen said, laughing as they made their way inside the glass fronted building.

'Two pronged attack always works,' laughed Mirry, holding her hand up for a high five, the atmosphere between them now well and truly cleared.

'Let's get on with our day then!' said Helen, high fiving Mirry back and giving her a hug.

Going through the glass doors of the office building, Mirry was struck by the difference between this workplace and her own. There were tall green plants, chrome fittings, big windows, and a general feeling of success and productivity. They made their way to the reception desk and were met with a broad smile from the handsome dark-skinned young man sitting at a computer.

'Good morning ladies,' he said, 'how can I be of help this morning?'

Helen quickly explained who they were there to see, and just as the receptionist was about to give them directions, Mirry heard the swish of the revolving doors behind her. Turning around, she saw Cameron and Simon come in from outside, laughing as they entered the hall. Mirry's stomach flipped upon seeing Simon and realising that they would be spending the whole day together.

'Ah,' Cameron said, 'looks like the ladies have beaten us to it, Simon.' Cameron strode confidently over, shaking off his expensive coat and tucking it over his arm.

'Looking great today, Helen, if I may say so,' said Cameron, 'and Mirry, good to see you too, my two favourite nurses. Going to be a good day.'

'Hi Cameron,' Mirry said, her confidence a little off-kilter in this new environment. She had only ever spent time with Cameron in a retrieval theatre, usually in the small hours of the morning, or a clinic, explaining transplantation to sick and desperate patients. He was a handsome man, a great surgeon, but he carried that Edinburgh air of superiority that Mirry disliked.

'Cameron, how lovely to see you,' Helen said, reaching forward and taking his arm. 'Simon.' She acknowledged him by nodding her head.

'Hi Helen, hi Mirry, good to see you both. Looking forward to today,' Simon said. 'Think we're in for a bit of a grilling, I saw the day's agenda last night.'

Just at that, they were joined by a tall, willowy woman made even more ethereal by her taupe trousers and gossamer cream blouse, her elegance making Mirry feel like a dowdy middle aged spinster.

'Edinburgh Donation team, I believe?' Willow Woman said, her welcoming smile making her seem less like something from a fairytale. 'My name is Anna, please follow me and I'll take you to our training room. We have a busy day ahead of us.'

The training was intense and challenging but enjoyable. There had been a lot of laughter as they all relaxed in each other's company with lively discussions and debate. After her photo session at the end of the training, Mirry made her way to the breakout room. A name that always made her smile - what was about to breakout, a riot? Or was it a throwback to the 80s song from Swing Out Sister that her friends at school used to blare out, dancing in her bedroom. She grabbed a cup of lukewarm coffee from the machine and flopped onto the mocha coloured sofa which engulfed her like an insipid chocolate mousse. Everything in the room was cream and beige. 'Dull, dull, dull,' thought Mirry to herself. 'Very corporate'

She could hear Helen laughing in the corridor outside the breakout room, or rather giggling. The door opened and she came in curling a long strand of hair behind her ear, her face flushed and her eyes bright. Cameron followed behind her, also grinning. 'And so I said, "absolutely not," and you can imagine how much she hates somebody saying no to her.'

Helen giggled again. 'Cameron, you're terrible sometimes,' she said, laying her hand on his arm as she walked through the door.

Mirry was watching their interaction as if it was being played out in slow motion before her. How could she have been so naïve and not spotted this before? Cameron and Helen were having an affair, or at least shagging! She suddenly felt quite prudish - as if she was anyone to judge - but Mirry knew Cameron was married. His wife Kate and two young children were dragged to every work social event or publicity funding. The great lifesaving transplant surgeon and his loyal supportive family. The children often bored, Kate smiling and shaking hands, agreeing with everyone when she was told how marvellous her husband was.

'What a load of lies,' Mirry thought. It made her wince inside. The obvious deceit and cover-up sitting uncomfortably with her.

'Oh, hi Mirry, you still here?' Helen said, making her way over to the coffee machine.

'Think I had the last of the pictures taken just now.'

'Well, you may as well make your way back to Edinburgh then if you're done,' said Helen. Mirry felt like she was six again, being given permission to leave the classroom. 'Cameron and I are staying on to have a look at the proofs and discuss our next publicity event.'

'Sure you are,' said Mirry, her tone dripping with such sarcasm that it drew Helen up sharply, looking over at Mirry as she passed Cameron his coffee. Mirry noticed

Helen had added sugar to it without even asking him what he took. How had she not picked up on this before?

'Can I have my tickets then, Mum?' Mirry smiled, feeling more and more like a recalcitrant teenager. Why oh why was she behaving this way?

Just at that, the door opened and they were joined by Simon. Mirry couldn't help but admire his presence. He had on the whitest shirt and his blonde hair had been cropped short, enhancing the strong Slavic contours of his face.

'Hey Mirry, you still here too? Jeez that was uncomfortable. "Look natural," he says whilst you're sitting underneath a white umbrella being cooked alive by enormous spotlights!'

'No, I'm done,' Mirry said, getting to her feet and pulling on her jacket. 'Once Helen gives me my tickets, I'm heading for the station, might even get back before the rush hour.'

'Great, I'll chum you then.'

Helen was already in her bag, rummaging for her purse. Locating the tickets, she handed them to Mirry.

'Good day's work, Mirry, safe journey home, and I'll let you see the final product before it gets released.'

'Great, Helen, thanks, it's been a really interesting day, in more ways than one.' She took the proffered tickets. 'Nice to see you again, Cameron, albeit so briefly but in proper clothes.'

Cameron grinned. 'I know, don't we scrub up well?'

Mirry pocketed the tickets and looked over at Simon.

'Coming, Simon?'

'Lead on, McDuff,' said Simon, bowing his head and gesturing to the door with an outstretched arm.

Outside, it was a relief to be in natural light again, the warm early evening glow softening the harsh outlines of the high buildings around them.

Mirry took a deep breath of the fresh air and exhaled loudly. 'Taxi or shanks' pony?'

'Oh, taxi, I think, Mirry, after the day we've had, all expenses paid and all that!'

Simon looked down the busy street and put out his arm, signalling to a black cab on the other side of the road.

The cabbie deftly did a U-turn in the street as buses and cars made way for his manoeuvre, accompanied by brief toots of horns.

They jumped in the back and Mirry recognised the red rosary beads hanging from the rearview mirror.

'Ah, it's you again, darling,' laughed the cabbie into his mirror. 'Twice in one day.'

'What are the chances of that?' Mirry laughed, pulling on her safety belt as Simon joined her in the back seat.

'And I see you got lucky today too!' grinned the cabbie, looking at Simon as he settled himself, pulling on his belt.

Mirry laughed and glanced over at a puzzled Simon. 'Must be doing something right!' She laughed again as she watched Simon try to put the pieces together. 'Same cabbie Helen and I got this morning,' she grinned, finally helping him.

'Back to Queen Street then, darling, or are you headed up the west end for a bit of scran?'

'Nah, unfortunately home for us, work is done for the day.'

The cab pulled back out into the traffic, the cabbie waving at the tooting cars and narrowly missing a pedestrian who jumped back onto the pavement, sputtering in shocked anger.

'Woah, that was close!' said Mirry, her heart in her mouth.

'Could've been one for you,' joked Simon, smiling out the rear window at the still-gesticulating pedestrian, fading as the rear view was replaced by buses and cars.

'What you up to this weekend, Mirry? Not on call, are you.' A statement rather than a question.

'Nah, free this weekend. What about you?'

'Nothing planned, bits and bobs, you know how it is.'

'No,' thought Mirry, 'I don't know how it is, don't know anything about you.' She studied his profile as he looked out the window, wondering what was going on in his head. He was an enigma to her and was starting to get well under her skin, in more ways than one. They had exchanged pleasantries at work, nothing more. But Mirry recognised the almost tangible attraction between them, the shared smiles, the stopping to chat in corridors, the butterflies whenever he was around.

'John's off too, so we'll probably get on with fixing up the flat some more. Like to have it finished by Christmas - not much left to do, just the bathroom and spare room to finish off.'

'Sounds like domestic bliss,' said Simon, barely keeping the boredom out of his voice.

'Yeah, well, we would have been much further on if John hadn't decided to change the wallpaper in the sitting room. I'd just got it the way I wanted it too.'

'Oh yeah, what happened?'

Mirry went on to relate the episode with the wallpaper change. The frustration of coming home from work to the smell of steam and the mess he had created. Simon was smiling at her obvious irritation and nodding encouragingly as she recounted and embellished the story. By the time she got to them both standing in their dressing gowns in the hall when Fee arrived, Mirry was starting to laugh, as was Simon.

'Did you ever find out why he wanted it changed?' said Simon, grinning. 'John doesn't sound like a Llewelyn-Bowen kind of a guy to me.'

'No bloody idea. It was a beautiful calming green with faint leaves, but he said he had gone right off it. Fee knew something was up though, something to do with work, I think. Anyway, it's done now, and actually, he probably has a point for all of my moaning. I ended up getting the design I had wanted in the first place.'

'So all's well that ends well in Papergate at Mirry's,' Simon laughed as the cab pulled into Queen Street. 'Think that's why I live alone!'

'Yeah, well, you might have the right idea there!'

Simon paid the cabbie and they bade their farewells, laughing at his banter about going back to the dark side of the east.

They ran to catch the train that was looking ready to leave, managing to get on just as the whistle was blown and it began to move.

The journey back to Edinburgh was spent catching up about work, discussing the obvious affair between Helen and Cameron, with Simon laughing at Mirry's shocked realisation that this had been going on under her nose and she hadn't spotted it. Mirry found herself laughing out loud for the first time in what seemed an age, loving the gentle teasing from Simon as he played up to her prudishness.

Mirry felt disappointment rise in her as the train finally slowed as it drew into Waverley. She glanced out of the window at the end-of-the-week commuters busy on their individual journeys. She wasn't ready to go home yet, knew that the flat would be empty. John would be at work, his breakfast dishes probably still piled up beside the sink, waiting for her to come and tidy up. He'd been so caught up in Jenny's case she had hardly seen him over the past few weeks.

Simon seemed to sense her change in mood.

'Fancy a drink before heading home?' he asked as he pulled his rucksack and coat from overhead.

'Easy for him,' Mirry thought to herself, subconsciously wondering just how tall Simon actually was, her mind starting to stray to places it shouldn't.

'Ah, go on,' said Mirry. 'Decision made,' she thought to herself, her spirits lifting, dirty dish resentment abating, and empty flat blues banished for another time.

'There's a fab wee wine bar I like just up from the station if you fancy…' Simon suggested.

'Ecco Vino, one of my favourites. Hope we can get a seat.'

They left the train, Simon letting Mirry out the door first, his presence seeming to clear the way for her instead of having to fight her way through the crowds.

They went out the back entrance of the station in companionable silence and made their way up the steep, steep steps of Fleshmarket Close, inhaling the familiar smell of damp, stale piss and the remnants of a thousand weary tourists.

Neither of them were out of breath at the top, Mirry noticed, and they both grinned at each other in silent, mutual congratulations.

They walked down to the wine bar in sync, chatting about nothing and everything.

By the time Simon ordered another bottle of wine to accompany the remains of the cheese they had devoured, Mirry's guard was gone and she found herself flirting outrageously, enjoying Simon's attention and very obvious attraction to her. He was funny, recounting stories of when he had arrived in Dundee from down south, wondering if the locals were actually speaking English, the dialect and accent being so strong to his untuned ear. Mirry, too, had found herself a stranger in Dundee when she had started her nurse training there, and had her own new-kid-in-town stories to tell.

His chat had her in stitches, but was soon brought up short when Simon said how much he liked her smile, said in such a way that there was no doubt what was meant, his words creating an almost tangible space between them, the air now charged.

Mirry lowered her gaze and mumbled something inaudible about being from a good gene pool. She didn't know how to get out of this one, the sudden realisation that here was a work colleague and, like Pen, she had an unwritten rule never to engage in a relationship at work, her phrase, 'don't shit on your own doorstep' resounding in her ears. And, of course, there was John.

The palpable silence was finally broken by Simon patting her on the knee and saying, 'Home time, the weekend excitement awaits.'

By the time they had paid and found themselves out on the street again, the atmosphere had lifted.

'I'm going to get a cab if I can,' said Mirry, looking up the street in anticipation.

'No worries, I'll wait with you until you get it.'

'It's okay, Simon, you don't have to.'

'I know that, Mirry,' he said, moving closer, close enough for her heart to start up a notch. He bent his head down and kissed her gently on the mouth, not moving his hands out of the pockets of his coat, his mouth causing sparks to fly throughout her.

'I can't,' she said, looking up at him.

'John?' Simon asked, remaining close, the warmth from his breath stroking her cheek.

'Yeah, John,' she said almost regretfully, but the mention of his name brought her right back to reality, clearing the magic from between them. 'Friends?'

'Don't think that's going to be possible, Mirry,' Simon said, pulling back from her, a slow smile on his face.

'Okay, any reason why?'

'Sure, it's pretty simple - I'd find it difficult to be friends with someone I want to fuck as much as I do you.'

Mirry snorted out loud, her laughter breaking the tension between them.

'Well, that's honesty for you,' she said as he grinned down at her.

'I've always found that the best way, Mirry, and let's just say the offer is always open should you wish to be more than that.'

'I'll keep that in mind, you gorgeous man. Now get me a cab.'

Within minutes, Mirry found herself alone in the back of a cab heading for home, smiling to herself about the day, a little regretful but knowing she had made the right decision. Temptation had been right there and she had resisted. She felt proud of herself; this would definitely be one for the diary!

Chapter Thirteen

I t was a week after the publicity training that Simon was moved into Helen's office beside the team. An office within an office, the glass windows looking out on all their desks. Helen was moving up a floor to be on the main corridor with the medical staff, next to the transplant unit.

'Funny that,' Pen had joked sarcastically, 'apparently Helen needs to be nearer to Cameron... I wonder why... oops, there goes my zip down my back!'

Mirry still couldn't quite understand what was going on in that relationship. To Mirry, they both had so much to lose: Helen had her reputation which was so important to her, and Cameron his wife and family. It made Mirry a little nauseous; she didn't know why but suspected it was a reflection of what had happened to her as a child. Mirry's family was dysfunctional, and although relations had improved over time, there remained much unspoken bitterness.

Mirry was eight when her parents divorced after her father had the obligatory affair with his secretary at work. Mirry remembered it coming as a complete shock to her and her younger sister when they came home from school to find two suitcases in the hall and raised voices coming from the sitting room. He left that evening, and they didn't see him again until after Christmas. The festive season was always a difficult time for her.

Her mother had cried for weeks with a revolving number of her friends coming round to commiserate and give support, wine, and advice, their words dripping with vitriol which their mother soaked up like a bitter sponge. Her father's name became taboo in the house, but there was no getting away from the fact that Mirry missed her dad hugely. They were always close and she was his undeclared favourite. Not having him in her life had been heart-wrenching, and at such a young age, she didn't fully understand why. Why her mother couldn't forgive him and why she and her sister were no longer able to see him every day.

It was many months after that her dad picked her up from school and took her to his 'bachelor pad' as he called it. This image jarred in Mirry's young mind. All she could think about were the connotations of tomato soup and why he was so proud of his pokey one-bedroom flat. It turned out that the affair had petered out once the excitement of the clandestine nature of their relationship had been normalised. The woman had gone abroad to work, apparently 'needing the distance' to help her heal, leaving behind a broken family and an even more broken man. The divorce had been tough on her dad financially; he never did forgive himself for destroying the family home on a middle-aged man moment of madness. Mirry's mum had been given the house as part of the settlement but had had to return to work for a few years. She had met Andrew, an unassuming greying divorcee with a penchant for vintage

Airfix soldiers. He moved in with them just as Mirry started puberty. It did not make for a happy home. Mirry was full of teenage angst and wanted to kick out at everything, including this usurper of her father's rightful place. As soon as she could, she left home and moved into a flat. Seeing Cameron, a supposedly happily married man, having such a brazen affair stuck in Mirry's craw and she was struggling to come to terms with it.

It didn't take Helen long to pack up what few belongings and files she had in the office, with Colin helping to disentangle and move her PC and printer.

Mirry, Pen, and Debs were all in the office the afternoon Simon took up residence. His PC - Mirry could tell - was high spec, with two screens, a printer, and a very obviously expensive ergonomic chair.

'Like bloody NASA,' Pen grumbled out the side of her mouth as she watched Simon unpack his belongings through the glass office wall. The only thing that Helen had left behind was the new whiteboard with the donor referrals and retrievals numbers next to each DC.

Mirry watched Simon as he organised his new space. She smiled to herself when he brought out an oriental, ornamental cat, popular in Chinese restaurants and placed it next to his phone. Its left paw began bobbing slowly up and down, rhythmical and hypnotic.

'Anyone want anything from downstairs?' Mirry said, standing up, having finished catching up with her notes. 'I'm going to grab a coffee and maybe some buns to welcome our new housemate.' She nodded her head over towards Simon, his back to their office as he placed black file after black file onto the shelves above his desk.

'Yeah, grab me an Americano please,' said Pen, looking up from her screen, 'and defo a bun of some sort from M&S - do you want any money, Mirr?'

'Nah, you're all right, my treat. Debs, you want anything?'

'Just a tea for me, please,' said Debs, not raising her dark head from her screen, still deep in concentration.

Mirry grabbed her bag from under her desk and walked over to Simon's office, knocking gently on the door before leaning in. Simon turned, saw it was Mirry, and broke into a broad smile.

'Just popping down for coffee and buns, Simon, and wondered if you um… fancied anything?' Mirry knew she was flirting but just couldn't help herself.

'That would be great, Mirry, thanks,' said Simon, still smiling broadly, his blue eyes once again sending sparks through Mirry. 'Black Americano with an extra shot if I'm to make it through to the end of the day. Do you want any cash?'

'No, my treat to welcome you to the office. Loving your ornament by the way,' Mirry said, looking at the rocking cat sitting on his desk. 'It's meant to bring good luck, isn't it?'

Simon stroked the top of the cat's head gently with the top of his index finger, not taking his eyes off Mirry.

'Yes, she goes everywhere with me, meant to bring luck and prosperity. She was a present from an old friend.'

'I love it, we could all do with a bit of that,' laughed Mirry. 'Hope she brings us a bit.'

'Need to wait and see, won't we?' Simon grinned, still stroking the cat's head.

'I'll go and get those coffees, see you in a bit.'

Mirry left the office, smiling to herself about the lucky cat. Maybe Simon was right, maybe it would bring luck and prosperity to the office. She wondered if there was a similar cat for fertility; she would need to look that one up.

When she brought the coffees and cake back, they gathered around Debs' desk for their routine afternoon break and catch-up. Pen invited Simon to join them. Mirry noticed that the waving cat from Simon's desk had now been moved to the shelf above the donation whiteboard in the main office. She smiled to herself about the powers of superstition.

'See she's got a new home then?' Mirry said, nodding up at the slowly waving cat.

'Yeah, thought she could bring the whole team luck and prosperity rather than just me,' smiled Simon, accepting the coffee Mirry was handing him.

'How kind,' said Pen, taking in Mirry's reaction to Simon disapprovingly.

'I think she looks great there,' said Debs, 'the rhythm of the waving is quite therapeutic, don't you think?'

'Every little helps, Debs, doesn't it?' Simon said.

'Ching, ching,' said Pen patting her backside. 'Sorry, team, got to get back to it, no time for chit chat. Thanks for the coffee, Mirry.'

Pen nodded to Mirry, her face serious as she made her way back to her Post-it littered desk. The ambience of the group was broken and everyone returned to work.

At the end of the day, Mirry and Pen were making their way back to the staff car park together.

'What's going on with you and the Ice Man then?' Pen blurted out after an unusual silence between the two of them.

'What do you mean?' asked Mirry, knowing full well what Pen was implying.

'Oh, don't play cute with me, Mirry, you forget how well I know you!'

'Och, I don't know, just something about him, he's got under my skin,' admitted Mirry, looking up at Pen.

'Well, stop right there,' said Pen, her face serious, her mouth fixed.

'Nothing's going to happen, Pen, what's your problem?' Mirry was surprised at Pen's vehemence and a little dismayed.

'I don't like him,' said Pen, 'I don't trust him coming in here taking over the office - who does he think he is? Helen's our boss.'

'All he's done is put that daft cat on the shelf!' retorted Mirry defensively.

'That's not all, did you know that he's taken over our rostering from Helen? The whiteboard turns out to be his idea and now he's ensconced in Helen's old office where he can keep us under that cold, blue-eyed surveillance. I don't like it.'

'Nobody likes change,' said Mirry, trying to placate her friend.

'Just watch yourself, Mirry, don't trust him. Think he's all about Simon and you've too much to lose.'

'Listen to you, as always being John's biggest fan,' laughed Mirry.

'Well, you've a good one there and you don't want to fuck it up with some selfish egomaniac who would just dally and drop.'

'Not going to happen,' replied Mirry, linking her arm in with Pen's. 'Not going to happen.'

'Good!' said Pen, squeezing Mirry's arm affectionately.

The sun was shining when they left the hospital, the brightness temporarily blinding them both after the artificial atmosphere of the office and its lack of natural light. They both rummaged in their bags for their sunglasses, Pen with her huge designer Ray-Bans and Mirry with her clear plastic bargain buy.

They hugged at the crossroads of the car park with Pen going in one direction and Mirry the other.

'Just remember what I said,' Pen said in Mirry's ear as they hugged goodbye, 'that man is no great shakes and he's not to be trusted.'

Mirry returned her embrace with feeling. 'Not going to happen, Pen, don't worry.'

Their conversation stayed with Mirry for her journey home. John was pleasantly surprised when he came home after work to a beautiful meal and Mirry wearing very little but his favourite perfume. There was nothing better to take both their minds off work.

Chapter Fourteen

John awoke later than usual the following morning. His mouth was dry, and he recognised the thick feeling of too much wine and not enough sleep. He kissed Mirry lightly, but she just mumbled and turned over, pulling the duvet with her, leaving him no option but to get up and get going.

He had wanted to go for a run before work, but that wasn't going to happen now, he neither had the desire nor inclination. 'Cold shower, black coffee, and toast is what I need,' he thought, stretching his arms up to the ceiling and sighing out loud. Just before leaving, he made Mirry a cup of tea and left it by her bedside, then kissed her briefly and made his way quietly out the flat.

The traffic wasn't bad as it was still early on a Saturday morning and not many people were up and about. As he drew the car up at the station, his mind was already planning what the day had in store. Hopefully, Fee would be in too, and they could assess all the work that had been done on Jenny's case so far. His feeling being that they needed to reconvene and start from scratch - they were so obviously missing something.

The team came together at nine o'clock and discussion ensued about what Mike and his team at Forensics had turned up. Nothing much had been gleaned from the door to door investigation. The neighbours were all still very much in shock and devastated at Jenny's death. Nobody had a bad word to say about the couple and there seemed to be true support for the grieving Ray. Fee did however want to share something she had discovered on CCTV analysis with the team.

John nodded his assent and Fee pulled up a series of CCTV images on the screen. The images were grainy and in black and white and at first not easy to decipher.

'As you can see, these are the images taken at night the week before Jenny was attacked,' Fee said. 'If you look at this area here, it shows the trees that are at the back of Jenny's estate. If you look closely here, you can just make out a bike leaning against the fence. It's there every night for five nights between the hours of nine to eleven, the time that Jenny always took the dogs out for their final evening walk… and if you look here,' Fee ran the video forward, 'you can see the person leaving and picking up the bike. Notice anything unusual about him? Assuming it's a him.'

'Other than it's a weird time to be out on your bike, and why is he all in black?' John said.

'My thoughts exactly,' Fee said earnestly. 'What exactly is he doing, and why is he there?'

'Can we get a good look at his face?'

'No, he keeps his head down all the time and his helmet obscures any clear shots. However, we can see the make of the bike, and let me tell you this, it ain't something from Halfords!'

'What about CCTV from a wider area when he's left?' asked John, concentrating hard on the frozen image of the man on the screen.

'I think that's probably where we should be looking now to see if we can pick him up elsewhere. Also start looking at bike suppliers and where someone could buy a bike like that.'

'Agreed,' John said, getting up and coming to the front of the meeting room to give out instructions for his team going forward. After discussion and agreements, the team set to work on the next stage of the enquiry.

John returned to his office, his head buzzing with this new information. Fee followed him in.

'Great work, Fee,' he said, sitting down at his desk and booting his PC up.

'Well, it gives us something to work on,' Fee said. 'Also, just to say the team are planning to head out to the pub after work, fancy letting our hair down a bit. Big game on TV in the Three Sisters if you fancy joining us?'

John was still feeling the effects of last night's wine and lack of sleep, but the thought of having a laugh with the team after the week he had had was sorely tempting.

'Yeah, why not, I'll join you just for a couple though before I head home. Mirry is off today too and we were going to try and do something together. We haven't had much time recently.'

'No worries, we'll give you a shout when we're heading out. Mirry could join us if you like? Be good to see her.'

'Nah, I'd better just pop in for one with you guys then head home. We had a bit of a skinful last night, not sure I'm up for a sesh!'

'Right, catch you later.' Fee left his office, closing the door behind her. He watched her making her way across the office, joking with the rest of the team before resuming her desk, her face disappearing behind the screen of her PC.

John returned to looking at his own PC, his head still full of what they had found to date.

The day passed quickly and at four o'clock, Fee popped her head round his door again.

'You coming?' she said, pulling on her jacket and struggling to hold the door open at the same time.

'Yeah, why not,' John said resignedly, 'not getting anywhere here. Just one, mind.' He laughed.

'I ain't your keeper, boss,' laughed Fee. 'Meet you downstairs.'

John had a final look through his emails before closing down for the day. Unsurprisingly, there was one from Charlie, his boss, requesting an update on the case for Monday morning. John's heart sank a little at this. They had made very little progress with Jenny's case. It meant that he would have to come into work tomorrow on his day off to have another run through everything. There was something they weren't finding, there had to be.

He logged off and stood up to stretch before picking up his jacket from the back of his chair and heading out with his team. 'One drink would do it,' he thought, 'just the one.'

Chapter Fifteen

Mirry woke late. The bedroom was bright with the morning sun filtering through the long cream curtains accompanied by the faint chat of the birds in the lilac tree outside. She stretched starfish style, luxuriating in the width of being alone in bed.

She looked over to the bedside clock: 10.20, the red lights blinked back at her. There was a mug of cold tea next to the clock and a faint memory of John waking her this morning with a kiss before leaving for work. 'He must be bloody knackered,' she thought, smiling at the memory of the night before. They'd drank too much wine and had ended up having clumsy sex in the early hours. Mirry realised that they had both been desperate to reconnect, to find each other again after the prolonged distance that had grown between them because of work. She had even managed to turn herself around after. 'Assuming the position', John called it, pillow under her hips, her legs raised and resting on the headboard. 'Maybe this time it would work,' she thought to herself. She'd stayed that way long after John had fallen asleep, his deep breathing calming her. Maybe this time.

'Oh, I need some tea,' she thought to herself, swinging her legs over the side of the bed, her feet landing on the cool wooden floor. She reached down for her abandoned robe and felt the slow release of fluid from between her legs. 'Whoa, that was some orgasm last night,' she thought, but quickly realised it wasn't last night's semen when she looked down and saw the red trickle flowing quickly down the inside of her thighs, reaching the top of her ankle almost before her brain registered what was happening.

'Oh fuck,' she swore out loud, now trapped in the indecision of how to make it out of the bedroom without getting blood everywhere. Pulling her robe between her legs, she waddled duck-like around the island of the rug and made her way to the bathroom.

Sitting down on the seat there was another loss of blood, leaving her in a warm rush. Mirry's resigned disappointment was registering as she did the sums of how many months it now was that they had been 'trying'. She knew John would be disappointed too, but as yet, he hadn't seemed too concerned - in fact, it was him who would shrug and say, 'Maybe next month, babe.'

'Maybe it's my fault,' she thought, 'maybe subconsciously I'm making my body hostile to this.' She knew this wasn't how it worked, but realistically, the thought of having a baby terrified her. They were good together, her and John, they understood each other's work demands and she wasn't sure they needed anything else. It had taken her a long time to get to this stage in her career and she knew having a baby would change things professionally for one of them. And it would be her. She had witnessed it so many times before in her female colleagues, flying high, great prospects, then bam, off on maternity leave where people very quickly forgot your capabilities. Staff move on, and coming back part-time never has the same kudos as before.

She shook herself. Okay, so not this month then, just need to keep practising. Mirry stirred herself from the toilet, reaching behind her to the wooden box that sat atop the cistern. She scrabbled to find a large tampon, unwrapped it quickly, and inserted it without thinking. With a perfunctory wipe of toilet paper, she made her way to the shower to wash away the evidence of yet another failure of her and John's coupling.

Chapter Sixteen

Mirry was lying cradling a hot water bottle when John came crashing through the front door, falling over the table with the key bowl, swearing heavily. Mirry could hear him attempting to hang his jacket up accompanied by more loud expletives and not much success.

'Hi honey, I'm home,' he shouted. 'You in?'

He stumbled clumsily into the sitting room and instantly took in what the blanket and Mirry's demeanour meant.

'Oh shit, Mirry, not again?' He lurched in and flopped down beside her, clumsily patting her on the knee.

'Where have you been, thought we were going to do something together?' Mirry asked, trying not to sound peevish.

'Oh, forgot to tell you - we went for a few pints after work and the footie was on so…'

'Hmm,' said Mirry, quietly rearranging the blanket and hot water bottle to make room for him.

'It's just not happening for you, is it?'

'For me, John?' Mirry asked, raising her eyebrows at him.

'Oh, you know what I mean, Mir, sorry it just came out wrong.'

'Hmm,' said Mirry non-committedly. 'Good night with the boys then?'

John snorted. 'Yeah, it was a good laugh, Fee was there, I should've phoned, sorry, we won too!'

'We? Were you playing then?' Her tone dripped with sarcasm.

'Ha!' John replied, staring at her blearily with one eye shut.

'How's you?' he asked, seemingly oblivious.

'Sometimes you are such an arse!'

Mirry threw back the blanket and got up from the sofa, still clutching the hot water bottle protectively.

'I'm off to bed'.

Mirry could barely keep the tears from falling. Her disappointment again at not being pregnant was growing with each unsuccessful month. What had initially been exciting and freeing when they first started to try now felt more of a chore, the spontaneity not having the same erotic pull that it once had. John didn't seem that bothered, was enjoying the freedom of unprotected sex with none of the accompanying worry. His attitude was starting to irk; was this the right time for them to bring a baby into this world? Mirry wasn't so sure, it always seemed to be down to her to organise the flat, down to her to look after herself, to not party, to take the folic acid, to always be a willing participant in their coupling.

Mirry went through to the kitchen and filled the kettle to refill her cooling bottle. She looked out into the back garden, the heavily flowered lilac tree standing tall and comforting, silhouetted from the glow of their neighbours' sitting room lights. She refilled the bottle and held it close to her aching belly as she made two cups of tea, an automatic response now, one for her, one for John. She took it through to the sitting room and couldn't help but smile at the sight of him now slumped lopsidedly on the sofa, his long legs stretched out in front, his mouth slightly ajar, accompanied by soft rhythmical snoring. Perhaps she was being too hard on him; they had both been so caught up with work it was hard to find the middle ground sometimes. She placed the mug of tea on the coffee table in front of him and pulled the blanket over him.

'Sleep well, my prince,' Mirry whispered, kissing him on the top of his head, 'sleep well.' She turned and headed to their bedroom to get ready for bed and sleep.

John woke early on Sunday morning and groaned. He knew immediately that the dryness in his mouth and his thick head meant a hangover. Coupled with this, he remembered his conversation with Mirry when he came in and the immediate drinker's guilt set in. He looked over to see her small outline in the bed beside him. This was a good sign then, they had slept in the same bed. He had a vague memory of waking in the darkness of the sitting room and fumbling his way under the covers. Time to make amends, he knew that.

He rose quietly, looking at the clock and seeing that indeed it was still early, not yet seven. Coming to the kitchen, he saw that Mirry had left out a meal for him last night, a plate of now congealed pasta lay forlorn under the microwave cover. He quickly scraped it into the bin and put the empty plate in the dishwasher. Filling the kettle, he looked out of the window down onto the garden. A white cat was patrolling the garden, looking up at a blackbird sitting in the lilac tree. Whilst waiting for the kettle to boil, he swallowed a couple of paracetamol with a long drink of water, almost gagging in protest as the cold water hit his stomach. He made tea for them both and carried the mugs through to the bedroom, quietly placing one down on Mirry's side.

'Cheers,' Mirry mumbled out the side of her mouth. 'You okay?'

'Yeah,' John said, plumping the pillows up beside her and sitting back down on the bed, leaning on the headboard.

'Sorry about last night, Mirry, I'm an arse.' He took a sip of tea and looked over at her, knowing this could go one of two ways.

'That you are, John Sneddon,' Mirry said, rolling over on her side and staring up at him, her face creased with sleep on one side. 'However, you're my arse and I wouldn't want you any other way. Don't be beating yourself up about it, you're allowed a blow out every now and then.'

'I know, but...' he faltered, a memory of himself coming into the flat last night and Mirry sitting with a hot water bottle flashed across his vision. 'Shit, Mirr, I'm sorry about, you know, your period and that.'

'I know, it's crap and I'm disappointed too, but we just need to keep trying.' Mirry pulled herself up until she was level with him and stroked his face. 'Not going to be parents this month.'

'Just as well, really,' John said, looking down at her and taking another sip from his mug, 'I've got to go into work today for a few hours, sorry.'

'Oh fuck, John, not again.' Mirry shook her head and reached over to lift her mug from the side. 'What time will you be back?'

'Well, the sooner I go, the sooner I'll be back.' John put his mug down on the side table and got up out of bed, stretching his arms above his head.

Mirry watched him. She was always amazed at his uninhibited nature when naked. He pulled out clean underwear and socks from the chest of drawers and chucked them on the chair before heading off to the bathroom. She couldn't help but admire his physique and smiled to herself as her gaze stayed on his buttocks.

After towelling himself and coming back into the bedroom, he quickly got dressed and blasted his hair with her dryer, instantly returning the dark curls that she loved.

He leant over to kiss her as he was strapping on his watch, the smell of toothpaste and heady aroma of freshness enveloping her.

'See you later, love, I'll text and let you know when I'm finishing. Maybe go out for tea tonight?'

Mirry kissed him back and gave his neck a quick hug. 'Yeah, just let me know. I'm going to pop over to see Debs this morning, she might fancy a walk down by the canal. Just keep me in the loop. Love you.'

'Love you too, Mirry, and really sorry again for being an arse.'

When he arrived in the office later that morning, John relished the quiet; there was no one else in. It would give him time to catch up with no interruptions.

He quickly finished the coffee he had picked up. 'Right,' he thought to himself, switching on his PC and pulling up his chair, 'time to get on with the day.'

Chapter Seventeen

Mirry languished in bed until she felt her stomach cramping and a warm wetness coming from her, reminding her she needed to get up and change. After a quick shower, she stripped the bed and put on a wash. She listened to the news as she tidied the bedroom, finished changing the linen, plumped up the pillows, and neatened the patterned throw at the bottom of the bed.

After drinking her breakfast coffee whilst watching next door's black cat chasing imaginary mice, it's antics making her smile, she phoned Debs, knowing she would be up, being an early riser. Debs answered on the third ring.

'Hey Mirry, how's you on this gorgeous day?'

'Hi Debs, thought you would be up, not disturbing you, am I?'

'Nah, just sitting here with Marcus, reading… Can you hear him purring?'

Mirry could hear Debs putting her phone next to Marcus, her spoiled rescue ginger tom who got away with wrecking Debs' plant collection on a regular basis due to his hard beginnings. For all his feline flaws, he was devoted to Debs and would position himself like a sentry looking out the window when she was out, awaiting her return. Debs had even fashioned a bed for him there so he would be comfortable. He was not, however, as receptive to visitors. If approached, he would hiss menacingly before retreating at a fast pace under the safety of the large blue sofa in Debs' sitting room, his green eyes peering out from underneath. He tolerated Mirry now, accepting the occasional stroke when she was tasked with feeding him. Marcus' saving grace as far as Mirry was concerned was his loud and comforting purr which would vibrate through his whole body if he honoured you by sitting on your lap. On this occasion, Mirry likened it to rolling thunder, rhythmical and comforting.

'He's on form this morning, Debs, sounds like a happy boy.'

'Oh, he's loving the attention for once. Anyway what you up to, you're off as well today, aren't you? Not seeing John?'

'Nah, he's had to go in for work, says he'll be home for tea, but I'm not holding my breath. Fancy getting together, maybe do something in town? Bit of brunch, looks like it's going to be dry - we could head up Arthur's Seat?'

'Ooh, I haven't been up there for ages. Last time, I think, was with that weirdo I dated for a few weeks - remember him, the one who turned out to be married?'

'Oh God, yeah, I remember him. Jason or something, wasn't it? Promised you all kinds of things early on.'

'I know and, as always, I swallowed it hook, line, and sinker. When will I ever learn, Mirry? Think I'm off men for now, just me and Marcus.'

'Oh, never say never,' Mirry laughed, 'there are plenty more frogs needing a snog from you before you find your prince.'

'Not sure I can be bothered anymore. To be honest Mirry, I've stopped looking; it can come and find me!'

'Right then, let's have a girls day out - brunch, then a hike. Come round for me about eleven, eleven thirty.'

'Fab, make it eleven thirty, got a few things to catch up with, you know me, got to leave the place sparkling!'

Mirry went through to the kitchen to get the washing out of the machine in preparation for taking it outside to hang up to dry. All the while, she was thinking about Debs, looking forward to catching up with her. She had loved staying with Debs for the few months they had lived together when she first came to Edinburgh, but sometimes Debs' obsession with keeping her house like a sterile theatre suite had been hard to live with. A glass couldn't be put down without it being whisked away, washed, and in the cupboard. Hell mend you if anything was left on the draining board! Mirry smiled to herself at the memory. There had been good times all the same; it had allowed Mirry to settle into life in Edinburgh which could sometimes be a cold city to get established in. Coming from Glasgow, it had taken Mirry many months before she thought of it as home. Now living with John, the plans they had together had changed that. Maybe she could have a word with him to see if he knew of any suitable men at work they could introduce to Debs. And then there were always Pen's brothers, surely they might have a mate. Mirry smiled to herself, making a mental note to chat to Pen about it. There had to be someone out there.

Going out into the garden with her full washing basket, Mirry noticed that their downstairs neighbours had planted up a multitude of pots containing herbs and flowers, giving the garden an almost Mediterranean feel. The lilac tree whispered gently in the morning breeze and Mirry could hear the scissors of a blackbird snipping away in the background. No one else had their washing out, so she commandeered both lines with the sheets and pillowcases, grabbing the clothes pole that was leaning up against the wall and pushing the line high in the air. 'With any luck it will be dry before Debs comes round,' Mirry thought. She headed back upstairs to the flat and could hear her mobile ringing as she pushed open the door.

'Feck!' Mirry swore, running through to the bedroom, remembering too late that she had left the phone in the kitchen. By the time she got to it, she could see that John had left her a message. She hit reply and listened to his voice.

'Hi Mirr,' his message started, 'missing you! Just wanting a bit of a chat about something that's come up at work. Can you give me a call when you get this?'

Mirry hit the redial number and waited to be connected. John picked up almost immediately.

'Hey babe, that was quick, where were you?'

'Hanging the washing out, good day for it. Anyway, you rang, my lord?' Mirry giggled.

'Yeah, just wanted to run something by you about the case.' John knew he didn't have to explain what he was talking about; Mirry knew immediately.

'Go for it,' Mirry said, wandering over to look out the kitchen window, absentmindedly picking a cup off the draining board and returning it to the cupboard.

'What do people donate bone marrow for?'

'Hmm, usually for patients who need a stem cell transplant for leukaemia, I think.'

'Why would someone do that?'

'What do you mean, why would someone do that? The same reason people donate blood, to help, it's called being part of the human race!'

'Have you registered for it then?' John asked.

'Yeah, because I'm a blood donor too, but it's unlikely I'll get called. It doesn't tend to be white Caucasian women that they need the most. What's this got to do with Jenny?'

'She was registered as a donor for organs, blood, and stem cells. Does that strike you as odd?'

'Not in the slightest. Remember, she was even going to be a surrogate for her pal, that's what kind of person she was.'

'So how do you end up getting called to donate then?' John asked.

'All your details are on a database, tissue typing and clinical info. When they are looking for a donor, they run the system to see if there's a match anywhere. A bit like what we do when we have an organ donor, see what the best match will be. Basically so the organ stands the best chance of not being rejected.'

'Right, I get you.'

'Any help?' Mirry asked.

'Yeah, thanks for explaining, just pulling together everything I can about her. Not sure if it's relevant, but you never know. Anyway, love, what you up to?'

'Heading out with Debs for brunch and a walk up Arthur's Seat, we'll think about you!'

'Cheers, sorry about this, but you know what it's like. Hopefully be back about six, love you.'

'No worries, love you too. Hope you get somewhere today, see you when you get in.'

Mirry rang off. John's call took her back to the bed space in Intensive Care, checking over Jenny's body with Paul, the perfect red toenails and the grief of her family.

'Please, God or whoever is out there, let John find out who killed Jenny, for everyone's sake.' Her mood had darkened now, the lightness she had felt this morning dissipating with the weight of the memory.

By the time Debs arrived, Mirry had finished tidying up, the washing had been taken in and was airing on the pulley in the kitchen, and she had had time to put on a little make-up.

'Hallo my lovely,' Mirry said, opening the door with a flourish, bowing extravagantly, 'welcome to our humble abode.'

'Why, thank you, dear maiden,' Debs laughed. 'Good day for a walk, and I brought a picnic for us. I couldn't walk past the deli without thinking of you.' Debs handed Mirry a laden carrier bag. 'Need to make up some rolls, but I got your favourites!'

'Oh, Debs, you're an absolute star!' Mirry grabbed the bag from Debs and peered inside as she made her way to the kitchen.

Debs followed Mirry, laughing at her enthusiasm. It didn't take them long to make up the rolls, which they packed with crisps and a couple of bottles of beer into a haversack.

'Anything healthy?' Debs asked. 'Especially with you know what?'

'Not this month unfortunately,' Mirry said, remembering that she would need to change before setting off.

'Oh, I'm sorry, Mirr, didn't mean to put my foot in it.'

'Och, don't worry, it's not a problem, we've only been trying for a few months, not getting too worried, if it's meant to be.'

'Hmm, I know, but it's still a bit tough, especially now with Cath's news.'

'What news?' Mirry asked, but she could sense the answer.

'Yeah, Cath's three months gone, longest she's gone yet, had her first scan yesterday and all looking good.'

'Oh, that's just brilliant news, she'll be delighted! Please let everything be okay for her this time. How's she feeling?'

'All good so far,' Debs said as she wiped down the chopping board and tidied up the remains of their roll making, 'taking it very easy, I think.'

'We'll need to take extra special care of her,' Mirry said thoughtfully, imagining what Cath must be feeling now she had actually managed to get to her three month scan. It would be too hard if she was to lose her baby now.

'Right, is that us then? Rolls, check, crisps, check, beer, check, stop off for some sweets on the way?'

'Got that covered too,' laughed Debs, pulling out two bars of chocolate from her handbag and dropping them in the haversack. 'We'll no go hungry the day!'

'Come on then, my Sherpa friend, if you take the bag, I'll meet you downstairs. I just need to nip to the loo.' Mirry's mood had lifted now that Debs was here. She had company for the day ahead, and it looked like it was going to be fun.

Chapter Eighteen

John put his mobile back on charge after catching up with Mirry and went into the staff kitchen to make himself a tea. He needed to clear his head, sit back, and try to make sense of all the evidence the team had gathered about Jenny. Going into the fridge for milk, he found a packet of cheese sandwiches from the staff canteen that were still in date, and he realised from the empty feeling in his stomach that he hadn't had any breakfast.

'Result,' John thought to himself, tearing open the cellophane and grabbing the first sandwich. He ate half of it before he had finished making his tea and took the spare one through to his desk with his mug. Sitting down at his PC, he pulled out some paper and started writing down what was going through his mind. He always meant to use his PC for note taking, but years of using a notebook from when he was a constable in the community was a hard habit to break.

Looking at the evidence, it seemed that whoever had attacked Jenny had been watching the house. They would have known that Ray was away and what time Jenny took the dogs out at night. The team had also discovered that the couple had applied for planning permission to put a room upstairs in their attic. The plans of the house were on the public council website. The notice that changes were being planned for the house were tied to a lamppost directly outside their house. Anyone could have had access to the plans and seen the layout of their house. This made John nauseous, how exposed Jenny had been without even realising.

John came back to the grainy images on the CCTV and cursed that they weren't clearer or that there wasn't better cover. There was no more footage of the suspect on CCTV in the surrounding area of the estate. It was as if he had disappeared into thin air. The bike had been identified as a Ridley Fenix and, although top of the range, would, in all probability, be impossible to trace.

Mark had got back with the forensics of the hair found in the attic and the skin samples taken from the dog's mouth. At least there was a link there. Whoever had been hiding in the attic was the same person who had been bitten by the dog, and the samples matched a blood spatter on Jenny's T-shirt. Mark had also confirmed that the DNA from the foetal tissue collected when Jenny miscarried matched that of Ali's husband.

John had met up with Paul whose preliminary pathology report had confirmed that the cause of death was cerebral hypoxia caused by forced decompression on the hyoid cartilage. There had been bruising around Jenny's throat that Paul suspected had been caused by a ligature of some kind. John made a note to check all the evidence that had been taken at the scene. It appeared that Jenny had been completely subdued. Clumps of her hair were found at the kitchen door; it looked like she had been grabbed from behind and thrown to the floor. Paul had said that Jenny would have lost consciousness very quickly and would not have been aware of what was happening. Even so, John could almost feel her terror when she realised she was being attacked. Two of her fingernails had been broken as she scrabbled on the floor. There was bruising on her upper arms where the attacker had pinned her down with his knees, watching her terror as he leaned over her and strangled her. 'But why?' John thought, 'It was so carefully planned.' The deep laceration to her scalp had probably been caused by striking the edge of the coffee table, causing profuse exsanguination but no underlying skull fracture. There were no other injuries, no sexual assault, just what seemed a cold, calculated attack. The report ended with a note that the kidneys had been surgically removed for transplantation and the uterus had evidence of a recent miscarriage. This final fact made John wince, too close to home. He knew how much this case had impacted Mirry.

He brought up the file that had all of Jenny's personal information. There were transcribed interviews with her friends, her neighbours, and, of course, Ray. In every single interview, the shock was evident. Jenny had no enemies. She worked hard as a personal trainer, having been a PE teacher for five years. All her clients were women. Her relationship with Ali and her husband had been very close. Ali had recounted how Jenny had inseminated herself with a turkey baster seven weeks prior to the attack. They had drawn up a contract that they had both signed, but Jenny had insisted on waiting until they were successful before telling Ray their plans. The FLO had written a concise account of what she had witnessed of the family dynamics.

It was obvious that Jenny's mum didn't like Ray and had never approved of their relationship. Her thinking being that Jenny could have done better than an older divorcee with two children. Ray's relationship with his ex-wife was amicable. They had both fallen out of love apparently. The couple had met when Jenny was a PE teacher to his boys in primary school. His sons loved her because she knew everything about football and they all supported Hibs. She would happily take them to the matches at Easter Road and yell, sing, and shout along with the crowds. There was nothing remarkable showing up in the interviews, nothing that raised alarm bells. The surrogacy agreement being the only oddity in her life. She gave blood regularly and had signed up as a bone marrow donor after one of her pupils at her old school had developed leukaemia.

John sighed and stretched. His tea was now half drunk and cold, so he got up to make a fresh cup. The frustration that there was nothing obvious was beginning to irk. He knew that they wouldn't have the considerable manpower that they had at the moment for the case. Very soon, it would be wound down if something didn't turn up. He asked himself yet again, what was it they were missing?

Chapter Nineteen

John felt prepared for the meeting on Monday; he couldn't have spent anymore time gathering everything together for the report. The team knew that they had collated as much as they could. They also knew that some of them would be getting moved on soon as no progress had been made.

'Good luck,' Fee said to him as he left the office.

'Is what it is, Fee,' he said, 'we've gone over this so many times now. Can't make evidence up.'

John slowly made his way up to the suite of offices on the top floor, deep in thought. The summer sun was bright in the stairwell and had warmed it almost to the point of unpleasantness. The air was close and he could feel sweat starting to bleed onto the back of his shirt as he opened the door to the top floor. This was where all the major decisions were made. So far removed from the reality of what happened in the offices below. He nodded at the blonde PA sitting like a sentry at the desk next to his boss Charlie's door. He always got on well with Charlie, she was no nonsense, knew the score and how hard everyone worked. She respected the way John ran his team and he respected her for her direct approach. Management, however, was not for him and handling budgets and answering to the public and councils came with just too much heartache.

He knocked on Charlie's door and, on her gruff 'Enter,' pushed open the door.

'Morning John,' Charlie said, standing up and coming round her desk. 'You good?'

'Doing okay, thanks, boss, how about you?'

'Yeah, same old, same old… Want to bring me up to speed on this case then? There's been a bit of breathing down my neck going on so I'm just passing the love on.' Charlie grinned wryly. 'Let's sit down and see where we're at.'

John acknowledged that Charlie had said 'where we're at' - made it feel less like them and us.

They both sat at the round glass table in Charlie's office, usually used for meetings. John spread out the evidence across it and went through what they had found systematically. Charlie listened intently, only interrupting when she wanted something clarified. John made notes as they went along.

'Looks like you've covered most things, John, where do you want to go from here?'

John sighed and rubbed his eyes. He knew this question would come up, and if he was being honest, he had been at a loss. When he had discussed it with Fee, she had mentioned maybe making the case more public. A crime reconstruction and putting it on TV. John knew that it was very rarely done and took a lot of time and effort.

'We were thinking about a televised crime reconstruction?' he said. 'Somebody must have seen something, we just need to jog the right somebody's memory.'

'Yeah, I get it, John, but you know as well as I do how much work that is to set up.'

'Think it would be worth it. This is such a random attack and whoever did it is still out there.'

'Okay, let's give it another week, chase forensics. Whilst you're doing that, I'll have a word with finance and see what the plan should be to take that forward.'

'Brilliant,' John said, standing up and letting out a sigh of relief, 'gives us a wee bit of breathing space. Something has to come up, like I said, this case is just too weird.'

John gathered up all the paperwork and filed it back into the folder. Charlie and him exchanged pleasantries, neither wanting to linger now that the work had been addressed. John took his leave and headed back down the stairs, squinting in the bright sunlight as he went over the evidence in his head one more time.

When he got back to the office, he instantly sensed that the atmosphere from this morning had changed. Fee was standing by her desk, holding her phone close to her ear with her shoulder whilst scribbling on the pad in front of her. She was frowning in concentration as she wrote. He stood listening for her conversation to finish, only picking up a few words that were being said but instantly recognising that something bad was going on. He didn't need to wait long before Fee ended her call and looked at him.

'A body has been found by a dog walker up Calton Hill. Looks like a sex game gone wrong; forensics are there now.'

'Woah, okay, let's head over, you can fill me in on the way.'

'Why is it always a dog walker?' Fee asked rhetorically as she shrugged on her jacket and ran to catch up with John who was already strides in front of her.

By the time John pulled up at the top of the hill, access to the public had been closed. Not easy to do in the late summer months; Edinburgh was still teeming with tourists. The telltale blue and white tape was out under some bushes and the surrounding area near the National Monument. The white of the forensic tent stark against the vibrant green of the trees and grass. There was a group of uniformed officers standing chatting, waiting for further instructions but enjoying the views of Edinburgh that the hill provided.

'I love this place,' Fee said. 'Well, during the day anyway.'

'Yeah, me too,' John said, looking around as he pulled his jacket from the back of the car and slipped his ID lanyard over his head. 'Different place at night though.'

'Telling me,' Fee said laughing. 'My mate works for the council and you should see how many condoms are picked up here after a weekend!'

'Right, let's go and have a gander, looks like SOCO have got the place secure.'

They walked over to the tent, nodding to the uniformed officers and flashing their ID.

The zip of the tent opened and a white figure emerged. John immediately recognised Paul and felt relief knowing that they were in good hands.

'Hey John, thought this would be for you,' Paul said, unzipping his suit once he was outside the cordoned off area, rolling it down before pulling it off.

'What we got?' John asked, his face serious, having caught a glimpse of pale skin and blonde hair when the tent was unzipped.

'Nineteen-year-old lad, name of Ryan Blackwell, a known frequenter up here - been brought in a couple of times for possession and cruising. Appears to me like a gasping game might have gone wrong. There's a blue rope still around his neck, behind which were multiple bruises and some severe chafing. Looks like there was one too many times.'

'Any witnesses that we know of, Paul?'

'Nah, you know this place, John, it would be difficult to get anyone to admit to being up here after midnight. He probably died between the hours of four and six this morning. Core temp still recordable.'

Fee shivered at these words, knowing what that meant.

'I'll be able to do the post-mortem later this afternoon,' Paul continued. 'Think Colin is free too, so we should have preliminary results for you by the morning. I'll leave you to it.' Paul placed his suit in a plastic bag and put it into one of the many trunks in the back of the SOCO van.

'Cheers, Paul,' said John, 'think Fee and I will have a look. You know what I'm like, want to get a feel of the place.'

'All yours,' Paul said, handing them both pre-wrapped forensic suits. 'Poor lad, he's had a hard life for one so young.'

John and Fee quickly pulled on the white suits and donned the blue overshoes offered to them by another officer before they bent and entered the tent.

The enclosed space felt claustrophobic after the open skies outside. Two white clad figures were preparing a body bag to wrap the figure lying prostrate on the ground before them. Paul had been right; he was just a young lad, his face pallid, his lips tinged blue. Looking down, John could make out the emaciated body underneath the dark baggy jeans and grey hoodie. He had dirty blond hair that, on further inspection, was obviously dyed, the dark roots showing through. There was a flash from the SOCO camera which illuminated the scene in much more graphic detail, creating an unreal image, like a scene from a play, before it returned to normal. If there was such a thing.

'We've finished here, John, ready to go, are you needing a bit more time?'

John's concentration was broken, so he shook his head. 'No, I think we're done. I'll catch up with Paul later on, thanks, mate.'

They made their way out of the tent and stripped off again in the warm sunlight, the obscurity of the beautiful Edinburgh view contrasting starkly with what they had just witnessed.

'Right then,' John said, sighing as he ran his fingers through his hair, 'family first, I think, and then we'll take it from there.'

'I got next of kin details when the call came through,' Fee said. 'Somebody is going to need to ID him. I'll get uniform onto it.'

'Thanks, Fee, let's head back and start a case file, let the team know and we'll see what Paul has got for us later.'

John looked around him, breathing in the fresh air, knowing that it was going to be another long day.

Chapter Twenty

Mirry had been called to Fife. For a child, for a boy, a little nine-year-old boy who had fallen from a motorway bridge. He'd been larking with his friends, bunking off school, which had led to this, his end. Mirry hated summer for these events. They always started in May with the lighter nights, when people are more active, out and about, freed from the confines of the coldness of April. Accidents always increased. She drove across the Queensferry Crossing, forever marvelling at the clean white sweep of perfect metal strats, the almost impossible engineering keeping the road, and all that traversed the Forth, in the air. She looked over at the old bridge with a swell in her heart as she remembered her Mum calling it Grandpa's bridge. He had worked on it during the early construction in the sixties. Had many a tale to tell. And then the older iconic shape of the railway bridge, the matt rust girders solid and timeless. Traffic wasn't bad as she pulled off the junction for Kirkcaldy, with her satnav instructing her, the automated voice taking her the way she already knew.

Parking up, she reached down to the passenger footwell to grab her case. Her case of goodies, John called it, paperwork for the dead.

Arriving at the paediatric ICU, she buzzed the entry door. No ease of entry here, not her patch. A voice spoke out of the intercom, 'Hallo, can I help you?'

'Hi, yeah, it's Mirry Colville. Got a call from Dr. Rae?'

Questioning, never sure what to say to the intercom. How to introduce herself to a faceless voice unaware of who else might be listening in the unit. Not wanting to be identified yet by family or others.

'Oh, right, been expecting you.'

The intercom buzzed and Mirry pushed her way through the doors. Bright lights in the corridor illuminated the incongruous cartoon figures on the wall, their garish colours shouting and stark. There were two nurses standing at the desk when she walked into the care area. The dark haired one looked her up and down, appraising Mirry, taking in her neat tailored navy suit, a double take at the silver nose ring.

'You here from the transplant team?'

'Donor,' Mirry said. 'Donor team.'

'Donor team, right,' came the reply, sarcasm and detachment self-evident. 'Dr. Rae, Ross, is in the medics room, know where that is?'

'Just down the corridor?' Mirry said questioningly, giving her best smile, not too sweet, not too sickly.

'Sure,' Nurse of the Year replied, turning her back on Mirry and looking over at her colleague. They carried on their conversation, looking at something of great interest on her mobile phone.

'Thank you' Mirry said, feeling an overwhelming urge to say something but knowing it was pointless. She had a job to do, there was no point making a fuss - for now. That particular nurse's card was marked though, Mirry wouldn't forget her in a hurry. Heading down the corridor towards the medics' room, she thought back to the last time she had been here. That had been for a much younger child, an accident at home with a curtain cord, Mirry shivered as she remembered. Ross as always had been the consummate, caring professional he was but she knew that he had found that case particularly difficult. He had a son at home the same age, had gone home and cut all the curtain chords in his own house despite his wife's initial, confused protestations. Fallout from work they called it, whoever 'they' were.

'Hi Ross,' said Mirry, walking into the medics' room.

Ross looked up from the desk. His face broke into a wide, welcoming smile, as he got up and held out his hand. 'Hi Mirry, long time no see. So good to see you, it's been a while.'

'Good news for some,' Mirry joked, giving his hand a firm shake, 'you must be doing something right. What's the story?'

Ross pulled out a chair for her beside his at the desk and sat down. 'It's like I said on the phone: wee lad, Darren, out playing chicken with his pals on the motorway bridge yesterday tea time. Lost his footing, fell on to the hard shoulder - fortunately, not the main drag or there wouldn't be much left of him. Looks like he fell on his head, fracture at C3 and carotid dissection, pupils were fixed and dilated on admission. We did the first set of tests this morning, not worth prolonging this one for anyone.'

'Where are we with family?'

'Looks like there's just Mum,' sighed Ross, 'and she's twitching; social work's been involved, other kids have been taken into care. Darren had been left with her because they thought he was old enough. Old enough at nine.'

'Okay. Police, PF? What's the story there?'

'Police all good, report in the process of being finalised before going to PF. Initial discussion with Rob looks promising. He advises approach first and see where we go from there. If you like, I'll just get Sam in, she's looking after Darren today, spent the most time with Mum, give me a sec.'

With that, Ross left the room. Mirry shrugged off her jacket and hung it over one of the office chairs. She took out her mobile and turned it to silent mode. Opened her case and took out fresh donor paperwork. Breathing slowly, in and out, keeping her heart rate down, movements slow and calm.

Ross came back in.

'This is Sam, Darren's nurse today.'

Sam smiled nervously at Mirry.

'Hi, this is my first kiddie donor so...' Sam left that statement hanging, didn't need to add anymore, her anxiety self-evident.

'No worries, Sam, I'll take you through everything if we progress. Children are the hardest and it never gets any easier for any of us, believe me.' Mirry smiled warmly. 'Can you bring me up to speed with what Darren's obs are like and how Mum is?'

'Sam was good, Sam was professional; it made it easier for everyone,' Mirry thought. When faced with the horrendous reality of what had happened to this wee lad, not just his accident but his whole life, it was a saving grace to keep professional, keep feelings away, far from the harsh reality of what was being faced, of what was ahead.

Despite his impoverished and undernourished background, Darren was holding his own. Mirry knew though that it wouldn't last. Children could go as quickly as the blink of an eye. The speed at which they could deteriorate never ceased to take her breath away.

Once Mirry had caught up with all the clinical history, it was time to meet Mum. Sam took her through to the relatives' room. The blind was down and the room was dim; it smelt stale, it smelt of sadness and hopelessness. 'If hopelessness had a smell,' thought Mirry as she followed Sam in.

And there she was, curled up on the bed in a foetal position. On hearing Sam and Mirry come in, she pushed herself up and swung her thin denim-clad legs over the side of the bed. Mirry took in all of it in an instance - Mum was withdrawing. Mirry recognised the signs, a feral haunted look in her eyes, the shivering and trembling spreading through her like electric shocks. Mirry knew that this was not going to be easy. Could Mum even give consent for donation in this state?

'Trish, this is Mirry - the specialist nurse I was telling you about earlier,' Sam said quietly as she sat down slowly next to Trish.

Trish looked up at Mirry, her dark eyes puffy and red.

'Yeah?' Trish said questioningly. 'What is it yer after? I'm needing to get out of here, I've other kids to look after.' The lie falling from her lips so easily that Mirry was almost impressed, the power and authority of addictive drugs could get a person to do anything, say anything, in the desperate attempt to return to oblivion.

Mirrry began her well-honed introduction, watching Trish's reactions which were difficult to interpret through the jolts and shivers. Her introduction finished with a question: was donation something that Trish would consider?

It turned out it was. This came as a surprise to Sam who had found it hard to see the human being under the condemned exterior of this young woman. She shared her thoughts with Mirry at the nursing station as Mirry began to make the initial arrangements for donation.

'I know what you mean,' Mirry said, 'but one of the things that this job has taught me is never make assumptions, things are not always what they seem.'

However, there was no denying the speed that Trish wanted to leave the unit once the second set of tests had been done and the paperwork completed. A scraggy scarecrow of a man came to pick her up, stood numbly beside her when she stroked her son's hair and said her goodbyes. He had shuffled from foot to foot and looked at anything other than the reality of a little nine-year-old boy lying connected to a ventilator, his mouth pulled to the side by a tube, his bed surrounded by machines. The soft rhythmical hissing could be heard above the quiet words that Trish was saying to her son as tears fell from her eyes.

Finally, she turned away from the bedside and Sam led her quietly out of the room, the scarecrow following behind, his head bent down.

Later in the early evening, Pen arrived to take over from Mirry. The donor team had arrived and were preparing theatre. Pen was quiet and subdued for once, and hugged Mirry when she arrived in the empty doctor's room.

'Tough day, babe?' she whispered in Mirry's ear.

Mirry nodded silently as she turned and gathered up the completed paperwork before handing Darren's case over. She wanted to stay, felt responsible for the little body now being moved over to the operating table. Her eyes filled.

'Time to go, Mirr,' Pen whispered, gently pushing her towards the door, 'I've got this.'

Mirry left then, her own tears falling as she made her way out of the hospital to the car park. 'This job was too hard sometimes,' she thought.

Her drive back to Edinburgh was done on autopilot. So many thoughts were going through her head about what she had just been part of. Life was so very precious and could be taken away by one simple stupid mistake. Mirry knew that others would benefit from Darren's death, but at the moment, this did not take away the despair she was feeling.

It was after seven by the time she got back home. For once, there was a space just outside the flat which she was grateful for. She pulled her bag out of the footwell, checked her mobile for messages and sighed before getting out of the car. She took the stairs up to the flat slowly, deep in thought.

Opening the door, she called out but very quickly realised that John wasn't home yet. There was a stale smell in the hall and the evening sun was shining through the sitting room door, illuminating the dust motes. She hung her jacket up, kicked her shoes off, and threw her keys into the bowl. Going into the sitting room, she went over to the bay window and opened the large middle window as far as it would go, letting the evening air in along with the faint noises from the street below.

She stuck her head into the bedroom and inwardly sighed at the rumpled unmade bed, the curtains pulled halfway open and lopsidedly askew. There was the stale smell in here too, but stronger, more pronounced. Walking over to the long picture window, she grabbed the curtains and roughly pulled them completely open, quickly shaking them into alignment before throwing open the window and feeling the evening breeze on her arms.

Mirry went through to the kitchen, opened the window wide and pulled at the fridge door, already knowing what was in it but hoping for some inspiration. As expected there was milk with a debatable expiry date, some dried out cheese, beers, and a vast assortment of condiments. She pulled out one of the beers, found a bottle opener in the drawer, and had downed half the bottle before she made it to the kitchen window.

When John came in from work much later in the evening, he found Mirry curled up on the sofa fast asleep. There was a pile of empty beer bottles and a pizza box with its remains cold and unpalatable spoiling on the coffee table.

'Mirr,' he said, gently shaking her. 'Mirr, wake up, babe, think you need to go to bed.'

Mirry stirred and opened her eyes, trying to focus on his face. She squeezed her eyes shut and opened them again, grunting, 'What time is it?'

'Just coming up to midnight. Think you need to go to bed, babe.'

'Where you been?' Mirry slurred, sitting up, rubbing her hands through her hair and wiping her mouth.

'Work, where else?' John answered. 'Been one of those days.'

'Hmm,' Mirry murmured, 'tell me about it. I ordered pizza but ate all the good bits.'

'So I see,' John said. 'Away to bed, love, I'll tidy up here.'

'You had any tea?' Mirry asked, sitting up.

'Kind of, just going to make some tea and toast before bed. You want any?'

'Nah, I'm heading for my scratcher.' Mirry got up unsteadily from the sofa, stroked his head, kissed his cheek, and headed out the door.

Alone, John looked around the sitting room, taking in the wall that he had repapered at what seemed an eon ago. Leaning down, he crammed the remains of the pizza into the box, picked up the empty beer bottles, and made his way through to the kitchen, cursing the open window where the now cold night air was blowing through.

Chapter Twenty-One

J ohn was so very tired. It had been ten days since the body of young Ryan had been found, and so much evidence had been gathered that he was struggling to make sense of it all. Coupled with that, they had finally got permission to organise a crime reconstruction for Jenny's last known movements. The final preparations of finding dogs similar to Jenny's were in place so the drama could be filmed tonight. Sarah the FLO had been liaising with Ray to make sure he and the rest of her family were on board. They were all to contribute to give a picture to the public of the person Jenny was.

John felt like one of those vaudeville performers spinning plates, trying to keep on top of everything and keep his team grounded. They were all working above and beyond. Ryan's identity had been confirmed by his mother. She had wailed so loudly in the City Mortuary at the Cowgate John was sure it must have been heard all the way up to the Royal Mile. Ryan had many friends who had come forward voluntarily to speak to the police which was unusual in a case like this. The feeling being that a lot of them were thinking, 'there but for the grace of God.'

Apart from work, he had had such little time with Mirry. She had been on call and had been out with a donor on the last full night off he had had. Sitting eating a pizza on his own at home had been no fun - they would have to do something special to make up for it. He looked at her picture sitting on his desk and inwardly smiled. He loved that photograph of her messing about on the walk down from Goatfell. They had played Pooh sticks on the bridge where she had cheated outrageously, but he had conceded her victory whilst doubled up laughing. His reminiscing was interrupted by his desk phone ringing. He sighed and picked up.

'Sneddon,' he said, looking out through the glass wall separating him from the rest of the team.

'Hi John, it's me.' The unmistakable Aberdonian accent of Mark from Forensics.

'Hey Mark, how you doing?'

'I'm okay, but not sure you're going to like what I've got to tell you.'

'Hmm,' said John non-commitedly.

'I've some good news and some bad news. What do you want first?'

'Oh, go for the good news first, why don't you, then you can knock me down!'

'Okay, you ready for this? The good news is we've managed to obtain some DNA from that young lad off Calton Hill; there were a couple of pubic hairs lodged in some chewing gum that was found at the back of his mouth.'

'Nice,' John said, an image of the boy's last few hours on earth springing to mind that he quickly quashed, 'and the bad news?'

'We ran it through the database and it's come up with a positive match with a case down in Newcastle.'

John immediately sat up straight. 'You're kidding me?'

'No, I'm not, and this is where the bad news comes in… when I was putting in the data I realised that there was no entry from that assault/murder case you had earlier in the summer, you know the one, the young woman that…'

'Yup, I know who you mean,' John interrupted, realising that his heart rate had increased.

'Well, it looks like there was a bit of a balls-up there. Her data wasn't entered until now.' Mark paused and John could hear him clicking and unclicking a ballpoint pen. 'Her case is related to the Calton Hill case and the one in Newcastle. Same DNA taken from all three cases.'

It took John a few seconds to absorb what Mark was saying and a cold chill ran down his neck as the realisation hit him.

'Are you saying what I think you're saying, Mark?' John said.

'Yes, I'm afraid so. Same perpetrator for all three - looks like you've a serial killer on the loose.'

'Ah, fuck,' John swore, 'fuck, fuck, fuck, fuck.'

'I feel your pain, mate,' Mark said. 'Do you want me to come to you? Go through everything with you?'

John's head had gone into a tailspin and all the plates came crashing down around him. The seriousness of this revelation knocked him for six. He looked out the glass partition at his small team of four gathered around Fee's desk, laughing at something she was sharing with them on her PC screen.

'Right,' John breathed out heavily, realising he had been holding his breath. 'Can you come up at two this afternoon? I want to get the team organised and I'll need to let Charlie know. We were planning a reconstruction to go public, but this puts a whole new slant on things.'

'Yeah, I'll come to you at two,' Mark said. 'Really sorry about the balls-up on our part. There will, of course, be an investigation, but that's not much good to you at the moment.'

'Thanks, Mark,' John said, 'see you at two.'

John put the phone back on its cradle and sat looking at it. He breathed in and out slowly as his thoughts started to come together. First things first, he would need to let Charlie know. 'Better to do that in person,' he thought, getting up and pulling on his jacket. This was a major development, and not a good one.

Fee had seen movement in his office and was watching him getting ready to leave. He beckoned to her to come in.

'Boss?' Fee said, concern in her voice, seeing the seriousness on John's face.

'Shit's hit the fan, Fee, going to need to go and tell Charlie. Chum me up the stairs, will you, and I'll fill you in.'

By the time they were standing outside Charlie's office, the colour had returned to Fee's face. When Charlie opened the door to them, she was met with a force of determination from two of her most senior officers.

Chapter Twenty-Two

Over the following days, Mirry couldn't get Darren out of her head. His little white body leapt into her mind at random times, flicking through like the old projector slides her grandad used to show the family holidays on. Click, whirr, little skinny body, click whirr, grimy dirt ingrained neck and heels, click whirr, short dark hair shaved tight to head, click whirr, smell of old cooking fat mixed with that sweet foetid aroma of depravation, poverty, and hopelessness. It was messing with her. She had been for a run, pounding the pavements down along the canal, avoiding cyclists and buggies, hoping her mind would clear with the beauty of the trees and the dappled light on the water. It wasn't working, not this time.

The flat was a no go area, John was asleep after getting in from work in the early hours. She had to be quiet for him to have a dreamless sleep from which she knew he would not wake up refreshed. Some sleep was better than none at all. She crept into the bedroom and grabbed her book off the bedside table, looking down at John sleeping in the semi-darkness of the room. She loved the outline of him, his dark head on the white of the pillow, the temptation to get in beside him made her smile... maybe later.

She was going to head to her favourite beach to watch the waves crash and the relentless tides, their rhythm constant and never changing. Happier, younger, carefree summers spent laughing, getting wasted, and getting laid. A reminder of what it was to be and stay alive. Grabbing her car keys from the wooden bowl in the hall, she headed out, down the tenement stairs two at a time, swinging on the worn wooden bannister at the bottom landing with two feet together. Out to the car, jammed tightly between a white van and a Merc. Fuck's sake, how was she going to get out of here? Selfish bastards. The reversal warning beeping immediately, she changed gears - forward, back, forward, back - all the time, her irritation and anger growing - selfish, selfish bastards.

Finally free and down to Ferry Road, window down in the summer sun, starting stopping all the way through Leith to Seafield road with its spectacular view down the coast. This was making the itch in her to be free of the city and by the water even stronger. Then finally hitting the bypass, gaining speed at last. She flipped her music on, found Iggy, found Lust for Life, foot to the floor, she was off flying. The road was quiet, empty as she drove harder, yelling at the top of her voice, 'I've got a lust for life, lust for life…' staring hard at the road in front, all thought of Darren gone, screaming, 'Lust for life, lust for life, I'm just a modern girl'. Suddenly there in front of her, a tractor appeared, trailer bouncing behind it, a load of muck littering in its wake. She braked and braked hard, managing to slow inches from the back of it, so close she could see the sharp silver of the plough's edges and the dirt ingrained in the smooth curves of the blades. Her heart was in her throat, hammering so hard she thought it would burst. Shakily, she exhaled, realising she had been holding her breath for the whole of the slow motion action. Just in time to take the turn off down to her favourite place. Tantallon Castle standing russet and resilient as always, its towers strong against the blue of the wide East Lothian cloudless sky. Down the hill, the countryside spread out before her in patchwork fields of ripe yellow and verdant green.

Silent prayer as she turned onto the farm road, hoping it would be quiet, too early for day trippers. She slotted her money in the ticket machine and the barrier lifted. Driving through the forest, she marvelled at the trees, the birds singing, her heart slowing. The car park was empty. She pulled in, turned the engine off, and sat with the window open, listening to the bird song and the quiet sound of the waves on the beach. She reached over to the glove compartment, opened it, and took out the joint Pen had given her, nestled in the box of tissues. She smiled to herself, guilty secrets, just for her. She fished her lighter out of her bag and sparked up, inhaling deeply, the smoke catching the back of her throat. She exhaled loudly, feeling the rush of green to her bloodstream. Mirry looked about; no one here, just her. She drew on the joint again and closed her eyes, feeling the high settle into a wave and with it a sense of calm.

Grabbing her water bottle, she slipped her mobile into her back pocket and stepped out the car, slamming the door behind her and flicking the key at it over her shoulder, hearing the click of the lock. Pulling another drag from the joint, she headed carefully down the rocky path to the empty beach. The tide was out, the sand stretching far out in front of her. She headed off towards the cliffs to find the secret tiny harbour where she loved to sit.

She took her hoodie off, threw it on the ground and sat down, her back to the cliffs, just staring out at the sea. The Bass Rock looked different from this angle, iced in white from the nesting gannets, the lonely lighthouse standing solid and sentry-like. Fresh sea air increased the burning of her joint as she inhaled again finally, finally coming down from her wound up, brain-tight state. Lying down, Mirry looked up at the true blue sky with the sound of the waves and gulls in her ears and lay still, listening to her breathing, smelling the fresh sea air, feeling the gentle morning breeze causing small goose bumps on her uncovered arms. 'At last,' she thought, finishing the joint, 'some fucking peace.'

Mirry stayed at the beach until she was no longer stoned. She had walked from one end to the other slowly, paddling through the clear water at the shoreline and watching the seabirds swoop and dive. It wasn't long before she was joined by a couple with their dog, but the beach was so vast she couldn't even make out their faces. The dog, a collie, was chasing the ball being thrown hard and fast, returning it with lightning speed, its pink tongue laughing, hanging out the side of its mouth. Mirry could feel herself beginning to unwind, the tension in her shoulders lessening and the tightness in her brow softening. By the time she got back to the car, the munchies had set in and the desire for a bacon roll and hot coffee had replaced her previous angst.

She drove slowly out of the car park, avoiding the potholes and bidding the beach farewell. Coming back to the main road, she headed for North Berwick, hoping to find a coffee shop open. She wasn't disappointed and settled down on a bench at the harbour to savour her roll, the grease and sauce dripping out onto the napkin as she sipped her strong hot coffee. Once she had finished, she walked down onto the sand and found a space in amongst the tough beach grass where she settled with her book. She was very soon engrossed, the background noises of the town fading.

It was the laughter of a group of women of different sizes jumping the incoming waves that brought her back to the present. She watched them for a while as they shouted to each other, with some swimming parallel to the beach and the others treading water and chatting. Mirry thought about her own camaraderie with her team, how much she valued Debs and Pen's friendship, how happy she was for Cath. It made her realise that it had been ages since they had been out all together and it was time to rectify that. So easy to get caught up in the busyness of life, sometimes taking a bit of time out together was badly needed. She got up, stretched, and packed her book into her bag. The women were coming out of the water now and she caught snippets of their conversations, the joy and exhilaration from being in the sea together was so very obvious. Maybe Pen and Debs would give it a go. She laughed out loud at the thought of it, knowing instantly what Pen's response would be.

Over the next few hours she wandered aimlessly around the High Street, avoiding other pedestrians on the narrow pavements and browsing the shops. She bought a couple of postcards and, by the time she returned to the car, she felt like she had been on holiday. Her thoughts went to John who would be stirring from sleep after his late night. She went into the butcher's and bought two fillet steaks. She smiled to herself, thinking about how pleased he would be. Life was good.

By the time she got back home, the traffic was starting to build up for the after-school run, and she realised she had spent a whole day without speaking to another human being, other than in the shops and cafe. She jogged up the stairs to the flat with the shopping banging against her thigh. Opening the flat door, she could hear that John was already up and in the shower.

'Hay Gorgeous,' she said, pushing her head around the bathroom door. John had his back to her and she could see him lathering shampoo on his hair, the suds dribbling down the curve of his spine. She didn't need to think twice and quickly stripped off, joining him in the warmth of the spray before he realised she was there. He jumped in surprise when he felt her arms circle him and turned with a huge grin on his face.

'Where have you been, ya minx? I've missed you,' he said, pulling her against him and kissing her on the mouth.

'Spent the day down East Lothian way, just chilling, did me the world of good.'

'So I see,' said John. 'We've the rest of the night together, what do you fancy?'

'Well, being the best girlfriend in the world, I got us a couple of steaks. Thought we could pig out, watch the telly, and maybe get some baby practice in.' Mirry smiled up at John as she cupped him gently in her hand.

'Sounds perfect, practice now or later?'

'Now would seem appropriate, don't you think?' Mirry wiped the last of the lather from John's face, and taking his hand, led him out of the shower, grabbing a towel off the rail, and led him through to the bedroom.

John laughed as she placed the towel on the bed, lay down, and reached up for him. He bent over her, smiling as he pushed himself gently into her and Mirry gasped at the initial resistance and drew her legs around him pulling him in further.

'God, I love you,' John whispered in her ear as he moved slowly.

'And I you, you beautiful man.'

They both lay quietly together once they had finished. Mirry threaded the dark hairs on John's chest through her fingers, stroking and gently pulling, an odd habit she realised she had developed that helped her to relax.

'How was work last night?' Mirry asked, finally breaking the silence between them.

'It's totally crap to be honest,' John replied, kissing Mirry's forehead. 'I'm going to have to go down to Newcastle for a couple of days.'

'Newcastle?' Mirry looked up at him. 'Didn't think that England was in your remit.'

'Yeah, well, there has been some developments that have blown everything out the water.'

'What's going on, John, anything to do with Jenny's case?

'I can't say, Mirr, other than I'm going to be pretty caught up until things are sorted.'

'Bloody work, maybe we should just jack it in and go for something less stressful? You could do something in security and I could maybe try out-patients.'

'Aye, right, like that would suit either of us.' John chuckled, pulling Mirry closer.

'How's Jenny's family?' Mirry asked, remembering the sadness of her husband Ray the day Mirry took consent for donation. She had been able to give Ray the news that both of Jenny's kidneys had been successfully transplanted, hoping that may have brought him a little solace.

'Claire has kept them up to date - well, as much as she can with what we have. I think knowing that Jenny had wanted to be a surrogate was a double-edged sword for Ray. On the positive, he knew she hadn't been unfaithful, but he was still hurt that she hadn't told him. You wouldn't do that to me, Mirr, would you?' John looked down at her, his dark eyes intense.

'Of course not, my love, you'd be the very first to know; it's just taking a bit of time is all. I'm enjoying the practising though,' Mirry giggled, snuggling her head into the warmth of his chest.

'Me too, babe, me too.' John looked up at the ceiling as his mind strayed back to work, and that ever present question, what had they missed?

They both fell into a doze, comfortable and warm until the banging of the neighbours door and their shouting in the close woke them both up.

'Bloody students,' mumbled John as he stretched his legs fully and Mirry sat up, raising her arms high above her head.

'I'm hungry now, how about you?'

'Bloody starving, didn't you promise me steak?'

'Indeed I did. I'll get started. Could you pop down to the car? I bought a couple of bottles of red in North Berwick and fancy having one tonight.'

'You're spoiling me, Mirry.' John rolled off the bed and headed off to the bathroom. She followed him and had showered before he left.

'Where's your car?' he asked, picking up the keys from the wooden bowl.

'I had to park at the bottom of the street. You know what it's like, bad timing coming in at 5.'

'See you in a wee while then, can we have chips too tonight? Spoil ourselves!'

'On it.' Mirry kissed him briefly on the cheek as she headed down the hall to the kitchen, smiling to herself and looking forward to their night in together, the darkness that she had woken up with completely erased.

'Life is good,' she thought for the second time that day as she started on the evening meal, pulling lettuce out of the fridge and switching the oven on, 'life is good.'

She had everything pretty much prepared when she heard the front door open and slam and lifted her head as John stormed into the kitchen.

'I thought you'd given up?' John blurted out, his face dark with anger.

'Given up what?' Mirry said, knowing immediately what John was talking about.

'Your car is stinking of the stuff, Mirry, for fuck's sake! What if I needed to give one of the team a lift? How good would it look, eh? Boss' ride stinking of green?'

'Oh, give it a rest John will you? I just needed a bit of downtime, head has been frazzled last few weeks, it was only one jay.'

'And where did you get it from, I wonder? Pen, I suppose, or one of her bloody brothers.'

'Like I'm going to tell you!' retorted Mirry, anger at her ruined vibe starting to rise.

'You said you'd given up!' snapped John.

'I said I would try.'

'Oh, don't fucking nitpick!'

'Oh, John, Jesus, don't do this, I thought we were going to have a good night. I'm sorry, I just needed to get out my head for a while.'

'You know I can't condone it, Mirry. I'm asking you for the last time, please, give it up, especially now when we're trying for a child.' He stood at the door, staring unflinchingly at her and Mirry knew that this was a make or break moment.

'Okay, I promise I'll give it up.'

'Promise?' John said, his face serious.

'Promise,' Mirry answered, feeling what she realised was a sense of loss, yet another part of her having to compromise, but she knew how important this was for him.

'I promise, John. Can we drop it now and get on with the rest of our night please? Those steaks cost a small fortune and I'm hungry?'

'Yeah, okay, sorry for being a bear. You know how much I hate it.'

'I know John,' Mirry mumbled as he pulled her into his arms. They stood holding each other for a few moments as the bitterness of their exchange dissipated.

Chapter Twenty-Three

A few days later, Mirry was on her own in the office, the rest of the team were away taking clinics, teaching, or on catch-up from being on call.

Simon's office was in darkness, with only the faint glow from the standby lights of his printer and PC visible like two disconnected red eyes.

She liked these occasions when the quiet would allow her time alone, undisturbed, to reflect on events and be a little at peace. She breathed in deeply and exhaled, looking around the office and smiling to herself at the place she was in - great team, good mates, and a challenging job.

Her eye was caught by Simon's beckoning cat see-sawing slowly from its new resting place on the shelf above Debs' desk. She smiled to herself, thinking about what might have been with a man like Simon. Their flirtation had continued but no longer stirred the fiery sparks it had once lit. Even so, there was still something about him that continued to get under her skin.

She knew that Pen remained adamant that he was not to be trusted, and his warm relationship with Helen had definitely cooled in the last few weeks. Mirry couldn't help but admire his work ethic though and his apparent commitment to donation. He could often be found at his desk when everyone else had gone home, the angle-poise lamp   illuminating his strong features, the outline of his physicality stirring something in Mirry still. She knew very little about him and his life outside work, even now that he had been with the team for a few months. He kept himself to himself, and Mirry was aware that he deflected personal questions with skill, giving little away. This, Mirry thought, was one of the reasons that Pen disliked him. They knew he cycled to work and that seemed to be his main hobby, spending his weekends with a local cycle group. Mirry wondered for a moment what he looked like in his Lycra but very quickly dismissed that thought, chuckling to herself. That would be one to share with Pen.

An email dropped into her inbox, and she inwardly groaned when she realised it was from Helen with an ominous red exclamation mark next to the heading, 'Learning opportunities'. Mirry clicked on the message and read through the latest from Helen. She was organising a study session with the national donor coordinators so that they could all log hours for their professional development, share practice, and discuss taking the service forward. Would Mirry give a talk on the difficulties experienced when asking for permission for donation from the PF, using Jenny's case as an example of the collaborative nature of the professions?

Mirry shook her head in disbelief; she knew how much extra work this would be. Everything would have to be run past Helen, torn apart, and redrafted multiple times before it would be passed fit for public consumption. Then there was the emotional rollercoaster Mirry still felt about Jenny's death and subsequent donation. She was uncomfortable about making Jenny's case public in this manner, reducing her death to nothing more than a teaching session.

She emailed Helen back, outlining her concerns about this being a good example - surely there was something more suitable and not so hard-hitting?

An email was sent back almost immediately which took Mirry by surprise - Helen would barely have had time to read her reply before responding.

Helen insisted that the case was a perfect example and could be used to encourage other PFs to not be so 'timid' about granting permission for donation in difficult cases, the word immediately grating on Mirry.

Mirry's eyes filled as she read Helen's response and her use of the word 'difficult'. A flashback of checking Jenny's body, of her red toenails, and the devastated and lost look of Ray. She pushed herself back from the desk and stood up to stretch and wipe her eyes.

As she sat back down again, the office door opened and Simon came in, holding two cups of coffee on a cardboard tray.

'Hey Mirry, you good? Thought I'd bring you a coffee. Knew you were on your tod today.'

He smiled down at her as he placed the tray on her desk.

'You okay? You look a bit…' He didn't finish the sentence, left it hanging as he eyed her with his brow furrowed.

'Not really, Simon,' she said, and before she knew it, she had recounted what Helen had suggested and how it had made her feel.

'Jenny's case still really difficult for you then?' Simon said as he leant his hip against her desk, sipping on his coffee.

'Not just me, Simon,' Mirry said, shaking her head, 'not just me.'

'John too?' he asked. It came as a surprise to Mirry that he remembered John's involvement with the case.

'For everyone.' Mirry wanted to shut this down; she could feel the tears starting to well again as she thought of all the people who had been affected by Jenny's horrendous death.

'It was actually me that suggested it to Helen, if I'm honest, Mirry. I think it's a great example of what can be achieved when the PF is on your side and may also help with you coming to terms with her death.'

Simon's calm admission drew Mirry up short.

'You did?' Mirry asked.

'Yeah, Helen and I were catching up after the publicity training, you know, brainstorming what opportunities were out there for promotion and the like.'

'And you thought this case was an opportunity for promotion?' Mirry asked, shaking her head in disbelief.

'Well, not so much an opportunity, more a great example of excellent collegiate practice which others may not have experienced.' Simon leant in. 'You're one of the best, Mirry, people need to see that.' He smiled down at her. 'Have a think about it,' he said, straightening up from her desk. 'Enjoy your coffee.'

With that, he headed to his darkened office, gently pushing the Chinese cat's paw as he passed, causing it to rock frenetically for a few seconds before resuming its gentle hypnotic rhythm. The automatic lights of his office came on as he went in and Mirry was left staring numbly at his back. She sat for a few moments holding her coffee and sipped the hot bitter fluid slowly, thinking over what had just happened.

'Bugger it,' she thought, pulling her keyboard towards her. She would tell Helen she would give the talk just as long as she could deliver it in her own words. Helen's response came in much later in the afternoon: she was delighted Mirry had had a change of heart and looked forward to seeing how Mirry planned to do the presentation. A date was set for the next national co-ordinators meeting in four weeks time. Mirry breathed a sigh of relief. That would give her enough time to prepare.

Chapter Twenty-Four

The tension in John's shoulders and neck was not helping his temper. The weekend bag that was stored at the very back of the cupboard and the frustration of trying to get to it was taking its toll. He had finally managed to grab it by his fingertips when he accidentally dropped a box of lightbulbs, three of which smashed. It was a finicky job tidying the fine, fragile filaments of glass and was accompanied by much swearing. Throwing the case on the bed, he grabbed clean underwear from the pile on top of the chest of drawers that Mirry had put there the night before. He often wondered why she never put his clothes away; it would be so much tidier.

His running gear was sitting on the chair, taunting him. He hadn't managed out for a few days and could do with the head space. He grabbed it and optimistically chucked it in the case too. After adding his wash bag, a clean shirt, and jeans, he closed up the case just as his mobile vibrated in his pocket. It was a text from Fee; she was on her way in a taxi to pick him up so they could get to Waverley together. Grabbing his jacket off the back of the chair and picking up his keys from the bowl in the hall, he headed out the door and ran down the stairs, two at a time.

It was a clear summer's morning. The school run had been and gone, leaving the street in a hiatus, awaiting the next event. He heard the recognisable diesel engine of the black cab before he saw it. It had barely stopped before John jumped in the back beside Fee, pulling his case in after him.

'Morning Boss,' Fee said, her face serious.

'Hi,' John answered tersely, 'you alright?'

'Yeah, good thanks, you?'

'Could do without this,' John said, sorting his seat belt and looking out the window as the taxi drove on.

'I've got all the forensic info with me on a stick. Mark sent it over last night.'

'Hmm,' John said, glancing at the driver and giving a shake of his head, just enough that Fee knew to change the subject.

'Booked us into the nearest Travelodge for a couple of nights - don't think we'll need any more time than that, do you?'

'No, hope not. Spoke to the lead down there, he's got things organised for us, meeting the team this afternoon. Chloe alright with you being away for a few days?'

Fee snorted. 'Considering I've not been in much the last week or so, she says it's nothing new. Think I'll need some major brownie points to make up for it though. What about Mirry?'

'Same, we're a bit like ships that pass in the night at the moment with her on call and what's going on with the case. Don't think there's going to be any change there for a while either.'

It didn't take long for the taxi to arrive at the back of Waverley, and they made the train to Newcastle with time to grab a coffee to take on board. The train was busy with a mixture of shoppers, families, and what looked like hen and stag parties. There was a lot of banter, making John and Fee grin at each other, listening to the nonsense. It was a relief for them both knowing that, for at least this two hour journey time, they could put the case aside.

Arriving in Newcastle, they were met by a heavyset dark haired man with a broad and welcoming smile. He introduced himself as Grant Melrose, DI for the case. John and him shook hands, both men genuinely pleased to be seeing each other face to face after the numerous phone calls they'd had on the lead up to the visit. He led them through the barriers and out to a waiting car parked on double yellow lines, the warning lights flashing.

Fee had never been to Newcastle before, which took Grant by surprise.

'Need to get down here, pet, when all this is done, do a bit of shopping and sightseeing. Not all pubs and football, ya knaw.'

The conversation continued in the car until they reached the station. Grant's team were waiting for them in the meeting room and they were welcomed with a coffee and sandwich.

The discussion centred around the DNA from their case matching the two cases in Edinburgh.

'What can you tell us about the victim then, Grant? Trying to find a common theme is proving impossible.'

'I'll let Jason talk you through what we have - he's the family's FLO and is up to speed with everything.'

Jason stood up and briefly outlined what they had gathered. The victim was a female twenty-seven year old second-generation Chinese data analyst. She was still living with her parents and three younger siblings, all of whom worked in the family-run restaurant and carry-out. She was employed by the National Blood Transfusion Service and her remit covered keeping track of blood donors in the North East of the country. When not at work, she would often help out in the restaurant. Being good with numbers, her parents would leave her to cash up at the end of the evening and lock up. Three years ago, her father had opened up the restaurant in the morning to find Susie's body. The kitchen door leading out to the back had been open and there were no CCTV or any witnesses to anyone leaving the premises.

Susie had been strangled with a long piece of blue nylon rope which had been left around her neck. The rope had left burn marks that looked like pressure had been applied again and again. There was bruising on her upper shoulders where her attacker had held her down with his knees, sitting astride her. There was no sign of a robbery, no sexual assault, and no obvious signs of a break-in. Indeed it looked like Susie had known her attacker, as there was a pot of jasmine tea and two cups in the sink. Forensics had gleaned very little from the scene, but the pathologist had obtained three hairs entangled in Susie's earring and the same hair was found on Susie's coat.

Her family were understandably distraught. The language barrier had been difficult as English was not her parents' first language. Susie's younger sister Kay had been the main point of contact. The team had drawn nothing but blanks. Susie was a quiet, studious young woman who didn't have many friends. There was no boyfriend that they knew of, but Kay had said that she thought there may have been someone. Susie had become quite secretive before her death, showing up late to the restaurant on a couple of occasions and refusing to let on where she'd been. There was nothing on her phone. There had been extensive interviewing of the few friends she had and some of her work colleagues, but still nothing had been found. Susie cycled everywhere, a habit that had been passed down from her grandfather. All in all, there was nothing remarkable to find about her and no apparent motive for her murder.

Fee and John listened intently to Jason, interrupting him every now and then with questions. When Jason had finished, they stopped for a break and some more coffee.

Reconvening after about half an hour, it was John's turn to present. Fee had done an amazing job of getting all the pertinent facts and information onto the USB. It was a simple matter for John to go through what they had. He realised he almost didn't need the slides he knew the case so well. When he finished, there was a collective sigh around the room.

'Might be a good idea for you to meet Susie's family whilst you're here,' Grant said. 'Jason could take you to see them tomorrow; he's got to know them well and has built up a good relationship with them.'

'That would be great, Jason,' said John. 'Could we do that in the afternoon? I'd like to have a look at all your forensic material in more detail in the morning if possible.'

'Absolutely,' Grant said. 'I'll give Forensics a shout and tell them you're coming in. In the meantime, I'll show you what else we have.'

The rest of the day was spent going through the interviews that had been had with Susie's friends and family. There was absolutely nothing showing up - the only similarities in the cases were the apparent randomness of the attacks and the DNA samples. The team had even had a trichologist examine the hair in an attempt to gather more information. Surprisingly, the samples had shown that they were from someone who was losing their hair. The follicle was weak, which is probably why it had come out so easily when attached to Susie's earring.

John's head was buzzing when they finished up at six that night. Grant asked them to join the team for a curry, a bit of Geordie hospitality, he had said, and neither John nor Fee could refuse. Both were desperate for a drink and an opportunity to think about something other than the case.

Going back to the hotel to change and freshen up, John and Fee went to their separate rooms with an agreement to meet in reception at seven. The curry house was within walking distance of the hotel and John was looking forward to stretching his legs. When he got back to the room, he flopped spread-eagle on the bed and called Mirry. He sighed when she didn't answer; he'd really wanted to hear her voice.

'Love you, Mirr,' he said to her answerphone. 'Missing you.'

Chapter Twenty-Five

It was unusual for Pen, Debs, Cath, and Mirry to find themselves all in the office together at the end of the day. There were no donor cases pending and there was a feeling of lightness in the air.

'Shall we all go out for tea tonight?' Pen asked. 'We've not had a proper time to celebrate Cath's predicament and it would be great to catch up.'

'I've nothing on, John's away for a couple of nights,' Mirry said with enthusiasm. 'What about you two?' Mirry smiled over at Debs and Cath.

'Well…' Cath started, 'I'm…'

Her words never left her mouth before Pen jumped in, 'Right, that's it, girls, laptops off, jackets on, let's head down to Mother India, quick curry, and then you'll be home before you know it.'

'Oh, okay,' Cath said, 'but nothing too spicy, my indigestion is doing my nut.'

'Brilliant,' said Pen. 'Bring your Gaviscon, I've seen you glugging from the bottle when you think nobody's looking!'

There were guffaws all round the four of them. The banter culminated in everyone piling into Cath's car. It was decided that she was now going to be their designated driver, as not only could she not eat spicy food, she could no longer drink.

'S'pose being pregnant is good for your mates,' laughed Pen, squeezing her long legs into the back seat beside Mirry.

By the time they got a table at Mother India's, the smell of the herbs, spices, and warm naan were working their magic. They all ordered, agreeing to share.

Throughout the evening, there were many laughs, but things got a little serious when Mirry confessed to what John and her had argued about.

'Oh, he can't stop you having a spliff now and again, Mirry,' Pen said, taking a deep slug of her red wine, the rim of the glass leaving a half moon of dark purple on either side of her mouth.

'Och, I know, it's just obviously with his work and us trying for a baby, it's probably not the most sensible thing to be doing.'

'Who needs sensible?' asked Pen, looking around the table. 'Honestly, you lot need to liven up a bit, as we all know you're a long time dead!'

'Enough, Pen,' Debs said, 'Mirry has a point, sometimes you have to compromise when you're in a relationship.'

'Aye, that will be chocolate,' snorted Pen, 'I ain't compromising for anyone!'

'And how's that working out for you then?' asked Cath quietly.

'It's absolutely fine by me,' said Pen. 'I don't have to answer to anyone but myself, and I have to say I've never been short of gentlemen callers!'

The four women burst out laughing, lightening the atmosphere.

'What about you, Debs,' Pen asked, 'anyone taking your fancy?'

'Nah,' Debs said, looking away just a little too quickly.

'Oh my God, there is someone, come on, spill the beans.'

'There is nobody,' Debs said firmly, 'just stop digging right there, Pen.'

At the end of the meal, Cath gave Pen a lift home to Leith, and Mirry and Debs headed off in the opposite direction together, walking off the excesses of what they had eaten.

'God, I'm stuffed,' Mirry said, laughing as a spicy burp escaped. 'Sorry about that, Debs.'

'Not the only one,' said Debs, rubbing her stomach. 'How come we always eat too much when we go there?'

'Cos it's bloody delicious and we deserve it. That was just so nice tonight catching up. Cath looks great, doesn't she?'

'Yeah, so very happy too, shame about the indigestion though. What you thinking, Mirry?'

'Och, you know, John and I have been trying for a while now, and I know I shouldn't worry, but I thought it would just happen much quicker than it has.'

'Don't overthink it,' Debs said, taking Mirry's arm and giving her a squeeze, 'it'll happen in its own time.'

'I know that too, deep down, but, what with his work and my on-call, we never seem to get any quality time together. When we do, we seem to be at odds with each other.'

'I think that was more about you smoking a spliff in the car, do you not?' asked Debs, smiling at Mirry. 'Man's got a point there.'

'Oh, don't you be taking his side too,' laughed Mirry, shoving Debs. 'I need some back-up. Anyway, enough about me, who've you got your eye on? You went really pink when Pen asked you.'

'None of your business - I'll let you know when there is something to tell.'

'Ooh, that's too mysterious, come on, spill the beans!'

'Nothing to spill for now, but don't worry - you lot will be the first to know if things change!'

The late summer sun was beginning to set by the time they got to Debs' flat and they laughed as they watched Marcus mewing at the window and rubbing himself against the glass when he saw Debs in the street looking up.

'Who needs anyone when you get a welcome like that?' Debs said, giving Mirry a quick hug as she rummaged in her bag for her keys. 'Want to come up for a cuppa?'

'No thanks, just going to head home. Don't think John will be back yet, so I'm going to have a long bath, jammies on, and settle down with a good book.'

'Might do the same,' Debs said, unlocking the door. 'See you tomorrow.'

'Yeah, see you.'

Mirry was deep in thought as she made her way back to the flat. There was part of her that was in awe of Cath who seemed so at peace with herself and her pregnancy. She knew that Cath had been through the mill to get to where she was now, but Mirry was almost jealous of Cath's serenity at becoming a mother. For Mirry, there were still doubts. She wasn't sure that having a child was really what she wanted and felt that she couldn't talk to John about her misgivings. He wouldn't understand. The thought of losing her own independence and identity was troubling her and she wasn't sure she was unselfish enough to truly love a child. Her own parents' breakup stayed with her. Life would never be the same, and once the child was born there would be no going back.

She stopped at the canal path entrance to let four cyclists join the main road. They were chatting and slightly out of breath, the first two nodded their thanks at Mirry. What she didn't expect was for one of them to speak to her.

'Hey Mirry, what you doing here?' It was Simon, smiling down at her as he removed his helmet. 'Nah, on you go, lads,' he said to the men he was with, 'I'll catch you later.'

'Hey Simon, just been out with the girls catching up.' Mirry suddenly felt a little flustered; seeing Simon out of context was a little weird but not unpleasant.

'You live round here then?' Simon asked as he ran his fingers through his hair, which was damp with sweat.

'Yeah, just walked Debs back and now heading home for a bath and an early night.'

'Hmm, lucky John,' Simon said, grinning.

'Ah, stop it, Simon, he's not there to appreciate it, work has got him in its clutches.'

'Working late again, Mirry?' Simon asked sympathetically. 'Tell you what, I'm meant to be meeting the boys for a pint down at Winstons before heading home, you want to join us?'

'Nah, you're all right, wouldn't want to gatecrash,' Mirry said, trying to remain focused on Simon's eyes and not let her eye travel down his Lycra-clad body. She could smell him, like freshly cut grass, feel the warmth emanating from his body.

'You sure? Don't like the thought of you going back to an empty flat, boys wouldn't mind at all.'

Mirry could feel the temptation to go with him pulling her like a physical force, especially after the thoughts she had just been having.

'No, honestly, Simon, thanks, but I'm going to head home.'

'No worries, Mirry, see you tomorrow then.' Simon reached over and cupped her face in his hand, his blue eyes holding her still. 'It's lovely to see you.'

'Yeah,' Mirry said, stepping back from him uncertainly, 'see you tomorrow, and don't be having too many pints if you're cycling home.'

'Just the one, purely for rehydration purposes.' Simon laughed, breaking the tension between them as he put his helmet back on. 'Bye Mirry.'

'Bye,' Mirry said as she watched him cycle away. She couldn't help but feel a little disappointed that she hadn't gone with him, especially when she got back to the empty flat and just a short answerphone message from John.

Alone again, she ran a deep bath and sunk under the warm water with Simon still very much on her mind. Later that night, she pulled her journal out from her bedside drawer and wrote of her doubts, her disappointment, and her conflicting emotions. When she reread what she had written, she felt better, the cathartic nature of writing helping her once more to put things into perspective. She closed the journal, put it back in the drawer, turned off the light, and snuggled down to sleep.

Chapter Twenty-Six

The meeting with Susie's family had been organised for eleven the following morning. Jason came by the hotel to pick them up, then they drove through the city centre to a more residential area.

'This is Jesmond,' Jason told them. 'Bonny part of Newcastle.'

The car pulled up in a street of red-bricked townhouses, the sun reflecting off the bay windows that could be seen from the road. They all had neatly maintained front gardens, and it was obvious that this was an affluent neighbourhood.

'It's number seven,' Jason said, reversing into the only parking space in the street, 'just down here a bit.'

The three walked down the road as Jason explained that it would be Susie's parents and her sister that they would be meeting.

'Kay has been amazing with all the help she's given us,' he said. 'She and her parents are anxious to meet you both. I let them know why you're here.'

Jason stopped in front of a black wrought iron gate, clicked it open, and then walked up the short path to the front door. There was a white jasmine in full bloom climbing up the wall, and the perfume from its flowers was exquisite. They waited on the bottom step after Jason had rung the bell.

The door was answered by a petite young woman dressed in jeans and a yellow long sleeved shirt that was the perfect backdrop for her thick black bobbed hair. The resemblance to the pictures they had seen of Susie was uncanny - it was obvious this was Kay, her sister.

'Jason,' she said, smiling, 'welcome.' She bowed to Fee and John as she opened the door further and ushered them in.

Jason introduced John and Fee, both of who smiled uncertainly, both feeling a little off kilter.

'So kind of you to come,' she said graciously.

'No, not at all, Kay,' John said, 'thank you for agreeing to see us. We realise how hard this must be for you all.'

'Come through to the conservatory please, my parents are waiting.'

She led the way through to the back of the house where the conservatory had been added on to the kitchen.

Susie's parents were already standing when they came into the room and introductions were made. Kay went to make tea as Jason made stilted conversation with the couple. Susie's mum had the worn look of deep grief etched on her face. John could sense that time had not been much of a healer for her. The couple sat close together on a bamboo sofa. Directly opposite, there was a display cabinet that had many framed photographs, the most prominent being of Susie. It was the same one the police had used when her death had hit the papers three years ago. John's eye was caught by something moving on the ledge that bordered the conservatory. It was a large ornamental golden cat, its paw waving rhythmically in the sunshine, its inane smile a little disturbing. The irony of what seemed to be a good luck charm did not pass John.

They stayed for over an hour whilst Jason explained what had happened in Edinburgh and why John and Fee were down in Newcastle. Through Kay, they were able to ask about Susie, apologising if the questions were repetitive or appeared intrusive. Kay took them upstairs to Susie's bedroom which had been left exactly the way it was on the day she died. There was nothing remarkable about the room. It was comfortable with fitted wardrobes, a desk, and a dressing table. Beautiful silk embroidered pictures of birds of paradise were above the bed and there were a number of books on the bedside table, all in English. Her linen basket had been emptied by SOCO and there was some evidence of fingerprint dusting around the mirror. The window to the bedroom was open and the recognisable smell of the jasmine from the front door was wafting in on the summer breeze. The essence of Susie was very much still in the room and John and Fee could understand why nothing had been disturbed.

The only time during their visit that there seemed to be a problem was when they asked if Susie had a boyfriend or was seeing anyone. Her mother swore in her own language, at which point there was a heated conversation with Kay.

'I think Susie was seeing someone,' Kay said, 'but she would have kept it hidden from my parents as they wouldn't have approved of her seeing someone who wasn't from our community.'

'What makes you think she was seeing someone, Kay, did she tell you?' Fee asked gently.

'Not as such. Susie began to take more care with her clothes and make-up. There were a couple of times that she was late coming back from work and the restaurant at night and she was secretive about where she had been.' Kay's eyes filled with tears as she spoke and her mother seemed to admonish her.

'Susie had never had a boyfriend or not anyone serious anyway,' she continued, steeling herself a little. 'Even at university, she didn't socialise much, She was a very private person.'

For John and Fee, meeting Susie's family made them even more resolved to find the killer. It was obvious that Susie was very much missed by her family who were still existing in a kind of limbo, not knowing who was responsible for her death. Going back to the station with Jason, they discussed what had been said and their options. There were no theories, just dead end followed by dead end.

Returning to Edinburgh later that evening, John and Fee were deep in thought. All the files that the Newcastle team had on Susie's case had been downloaded onto both their laptops. They passed the journey in companionable silence as they worked their way through the evidence. Fee concentrated on the interviews with Susie's work colleagues whilst John looked at the forensics and the scene of the crime. He was careful to ensure that other travellers couldn't see the SOCO photographs of Susie's body. She had been found in a booth, lying on one of the banquette seats, her body partially hidden by a table. The background was unremarkable, with red wallpaper, decorative lanterns hanging from the ceiling, and dark wood latticework separating the booths. The booth was directly opposite the bar area in the restaurant and, as John studied the photograph, he could make out the figure of an ornamental, golden cat by the till, the flash of the SOCO camera reflecting on its body drawing his attention.

'Those cats seem to be everywhere,' he thought, moving to the next picture.

Chapter Twenty-Seven

It was late when Mirry woke to hear the flat door close. She looked over at the clock and inwardly sighed when she saw it was past midnight. She could hear John in the kitchen putting the kettle on and the chink of a spoon in a cup. Slowly, she swung her legs over the side of the bed and slipped her feet into her slippers. Walking into the kitchen, she could smell toast being made and her mouth watered in a Pavlovian response.

'Want to put a bit on for me?' she said to John's back.

John jumped. 'Oh, hay Mirr, sorry, love, I didn't want to wake you.'

'That's okay,' Mirry said, adding another piece of bread to the toaster, 'you know what I'm like, sleep really lightly when you're not here. How was Newcastle?'

John sighed, rubbing his face hard. Mirry realised how very tired he looked. He had a grey, haunted look she had never seen before, his usual strong demeanour diminished somehow.

'Really sad, to be honest. This case is just growing - looks like we have the same guy for three murders now.'

'Three?' Mirry exclaimed. 'Connected to Jenny's case?'

'Looks like it. Suffice to say I'm going to be full-on for the next few weeks. We might get the reconstruction we wanted though, which is good - anything to help because we have bugger all other than the bastard's DNA.'

Mirry began buttering the toast as John finished making two mugs of tea.

'Does that mean more late nights?' Mirry asked, her heart sinking. She had been looking forward to spending some time together.

'For sure, Charlie has said we can have some more manpower to help out which is great, but once we have the reconstruction, we'll be swamped with calls - always are.' John kissed the top of Mirry's head. 'Fancy taking these to bed?' he said, picking up the two mugs of tea.

'Yeah, I'll bring the toast, but no crumbs allowed.' Mirry laughed, following him through to the bedroom.

'I'm going to nip for a quick shower, don't eat my bit.'

'Be quick then,' Mirry said, getting back under the covers, her place in the bed still warm.

By the time John came back to bed, Mirry had finished her toast and drunk half her tea, her eyes beginning to feel sleepy.

'How's you anyway, my love?' John asked, getting in beside her. 'Missed you.'

'I'm good, was out with the girls last night catching up. Did I tell you Cath was pregnant?'

'No, that's great news, they've been trying for a while now, haven't they?'

'Yeah, hopefully this time she'll go to term. She seems to be keeping well, bit knackered, but aren't we all?'

'Sure am,' John said, finishing the last of the toast and slugging the dregs from his mug. 'Too tired for a bit of practice, Mirr?' He asked, reaching over and pulling Mirry towards him.

'It's one o'clock in the morning, John,' Mirry laughed, snuggling into his arms. 'But I have missed you.'

Their love making was quick, both achieving orgasm together and falling asleep almost immediately afterwards… once the toast crumbs had been brushed out from underneath them.

Chapter Twenty-Eight

T he study day came around much quicker than Mirry had anticipated and, as always, she was left frantically scrabbling to finish her PowerPoint presentation in time. Helen had finally approved what she had done and she was pleased with what she had pulled together. She hoped it would promote a good question and answer session and perhaps a sharing of experiences.

Pen, Debs, and Mirry made their way over to the main lecture theatre in the Chancellor's Building in the university's medical school facility. It was a sparkling bright morning and the sun was pouring through the glass doors of the entrance hall, illuminating the modern wood and chrome design of the foyer. Helen was already there and had set up a welcome desk at the door, programmes printed out and ready for distribution, some donor memorabilia, pens and lanyards in a box ready for delegates to purloin.

'Ah, the Spice Girls have arrived,' she said, smiling over at them. 'Looking forward to today? Think we've got a good turnout.'

'Yeah, I am actually,' said Mirry, 'and just you remember you're still a Spice Girl yourself. You may have been promoted, but you will always be Ginger Spice to us!'

Helen laughed, the atmosphere between the whole team relaxed for a change, the positive effects of the sunshine and light lifting everyone's spirits.

'Pen, can you and Debs do the register as delegates arrive please?' Helen said. 'Mirry and I need to set up and make sure the running order and presentations are all downloaded and ready to go. Got some good speakers today and lunch should be a treat as I managed to wangle some money for a decent buffet for a change.'

'Huzzah,' said Pen, 'looking forward to that already!'

Pen slid behind the desk, followed by Debs, as they sorted the delegate list and started to make welcome packs out of the programme and freebies.

Mirry followed Helen through to the auditorium just as the first delegates started to arrive. She could hear exclamations of recognition as the co-ordinators from Glasgow were loudly welcomed by Pen. The anticipation of the day started to build and, walking into the lecture theatre, Mirry felt the butterflies start to take flight in her stomach. She breathed in and out slowly as she followed Helen's confident stride down to the front of the auditorium.

'Can you do a screen check for me, Mirry, whilst I get this set up?' asked Helen, pushing various buttons on the desk in front of her, her brow furrowed in concentration. 'I always hate this bit. We've no IT help this morning from the uni, their guy is off sick.'

'Uh oh,' Mirry thought to herself, hating everything IT related, her nerves beginning to jangle. 'Screen is blue so far, Helen,' she said.

Helen continued to push various buttons. But the screen stubbornly refused to change.

'Bloody hell, what time is it?' Helen snapped, her irritation becoming palpable as she pulled her mobile out of her pocket.

'It's quarter to… we've fifteen minutes before we start… people will probably start coming in soon.'

'Don't you think I'm aware of that? Fuck, I'll just need to call Simon and see if he can come down and help.'

She punched numbers into her mobile and held it to her ear.

'Simon? It's Helen, listen, we've got our big day on today and there is no IT cover from the uni. Could you pop down? I can't get anything I've downloaded up on the screen. '

Helen paused as she listened to the response; Mirry could tell her irritation was climbing.

'Do you not think I've tried all that already? Delegates are going to be coming in fifteen minutes, you need to come and sort this, you're meant to be the expert after all.'

Helen closed down her phone and put it back in her pocket.

'He's on his way, luckily he's just downstairs, but he's none too happy.' Helen went back to looking at the console in front of her. 'Could you let people know we're running a wee bit late and get them to wait in the coffee room?'

'Sure,' answered Mirry, heading back up the stairs of the auditorium. As she came out into the corridor, she ran straight into Simon.

'Woah,' he said, catching her by the arm as she stumbled, 'really sorry, should look where I'm going. Helen sounds a little uptight and rude as always.' Simon smiled down at her.

'Yeah, she's a bit stressy - important day and I'll be your biggest fan if you get it working. Without my slides, I'll be lost!'

'For you then, Mirry, shouldn't be a problem.' He carried on into the auditorium as Mirry went to tell the delegates about the delay.

It wasn't long before Helen texted Mirry in the coffee room to say people could now come in. Pen and Debs showed people where to go and Mirry made her way back to the front of the auditorium where Helen and Simon were in deep discussion.

'Okay, thanks, Simon,' Helen was saying. 'Mirry, if you sit at the front, it will be easier for you when you have to get up to speak before lunch… ah, there's Cameron, he's doing our opening address.' Helen's attention was immediately taken over when she saw Cameron walking down the auditorium steps, her face lighting up and a broad smile forming for the first time that morning.

Mirry went to take a seat in the front row and was joined by Simon after he had greeted Cameron, shaking him by the hand, both men grinning broadly at each other, sharing a joke.

'Better stay for the morning to make sure there's no more glitches.' Simon stretched his legs out in front of him as he made himself comfortable. 'Looking forward to your talk the most though, Mirry, be good to see you up there doing your stuff.'

'I'm bloody bricking it,' Mirry laughed, 'hate this side of work!'

'You'll be fab, got your biggest fan sitting in the front row cheering you on, what more could you need?' Simon leaned over and straightened Mirry's jacket collar, looking her straight in the eyes as he did it. Mirry found her heart doing a couple of somersaults as once more she looked into those blue eyes, a thrill going up her spine.

'It's all your fault I'm here in the first place!' Mirry said, smiling at him. 'I would have told Helen where to go otherwise.'

'I think everyone would like to tell Helen where to go sometimes,' Simon said. 'Oh, look there she goes again, simpering up to Cameron.' Simon nodded his head at the front of the auditorium where Helen was fixing a microphone to the lapel of Cameron's jacket, the intimacy of the gesture not lost on Mirry.

'I wish they wouldn't make it so bloody obvious,' said Mirry shaking her head, 'half the country's donor co-ordinators are here and people love to gossip.'

'Doesn't look like they're that much bothered,' Simon said. 'Anyway, back to you, when you on?'

'Just before lunch, could be the kiss of death.'

'Nah, I think you'll find what you have to say will spark lots of interest. PF giving permission for donation after what turned out to be a murder is pretty impelling stuff, not many will have achieved that before, Mirry.'

'Thanks for your vote of confidence, Simon, it means a lot.'

'As I say, Mirry, always your biggest fan, in more ways than one as you well know!'

'Simon, stop that right now, I'll never be able to concentrate!'

'It's good to have an admirer though, Mirry, is it not?'

Mirry felt a blush coming up and was annoyed at herself at how easily Simon could make her feel like this. She had to get this into perspective and knew that her desire for him would probably pass. But at the moment, there seemed to be no evidence of that.

Helen's voice broke the spell between the two of them as she began the day with her introduction of Cameron as the morning's first speaker.

As it turned out, Mirry needn't have worried about how her presentation would go down; Helen had to eventually call time on her slot as there were so many questions and much discussion that they had run over into the lunch break.

The buffet table had been set up in the back of the canteen with an impressive collection of sandwiches, sausage rolls, chicken satays, falafels, dips, bread, cakes, and fruit. The noise level was loud as conversations were had, the morning's sessions having stimulated much debate.

Mirry was helping herself to some fruit when there was a tap on her shoulder and a throaty laugh. She turned around and came face to face with a tall, skinny man grinning all over his face with his arms wide open.

'Anthony, my God, how the devil are you?' Mirry put her plate down and jumped into his embrace, the pair of them shrieking so much with laughter it drew the attention of those gathered around them.

'How long has it been?' Mirry asked.

'Well, now let me see… I left Edinburgh ITU ten years ago to go to Newcastle at the same time you were heading off for donation. My God, Mirry, you haven't changed a bit, bloody gorgeous and still not grown!'

'And you are still a cheeky git. What you doing in Edinburgh?'

'Saw the light, babe, bit like you, and joined the donor team in Freeman's, on the recipient side though, doll. Loved your talk this morning, check you, all confident and professional.'

'Oh, thanks, not really relevant for England though, is it?'

'Well, I think there were a couple of similar cases that came across our desk last year that didn't proceed though. Coroner stymied them in the end.'

There was another yelp from beside them and they were joined by a red headed, freckled woman who was the same height as Mirry but double her width.

'Fran, my God, today just keeps getting better!' she said. 'You down from Aberdeen? Saw your name on the register and was hoping we'd catch up.'

'Loved your talk this morning, Mirry,' Fran said. 'We've had a couple of cases like that up our way in the last year, and the PF refused donation there too.'

'What, cerebral hypoxia cases after assault?'

'No, they were apparent failed suicides but PF just wouldn't contemplate donation. One reason being he thought it too hard for the families.'

'Well, I think what I spoke about this morning is why the PF did give permission; he knew how hard it was for the family but donation was important, there were two excellent matches for the recipients. It's important to have the forensic pathologist on side too and we're so lucky to have Paul. He goes out of his way for us despite how busy he is.'

'That was such a weird case though, wasn't it? And is it true that they still haven't found anybody for it?'

'Yeah, I shouldn't really be telling you this, but confidentially it's John's case and they are no further forward with any suspects, though there's other stuff about to hit the news. But it was so random, a real case of stranger danger. Makes you paranoid.'

'Hmm, interesting, speaking of confidentiality, is that Simon Grey working with you?' Anthony asked, leaning in and lowering his voice.

'Yes, it is… do you know him?' asked Mirry, her curiosity instantly sparked.

'Yeah, he was with us for a while until he moved up to Dundee I think… about three years ago. He here now?'

'Yeah, he's overseeing all the donor stats, publicity, and stuff all a bit over my head!'

'Last time I saw him was at clinic in the summer, he was with his mum.'

'His mum?' Mirry asked.

'Hmm, she had a kidney transplant. Not my case, came in whilst I was on holiday.'

'Really?' Mirry said. 'He's never said anything, but that's maybe why he's so committed to donation. Makes sense.'

'Probably shouldn't have said anything, Mirry, keep that to yourself, eh?'

'No worries,' Mirry said. 'He's great, actually, Anthony, helped me out a few times.'

Anthony snorted. 'I bet he has, Mirry!'

'Not like that.' Mirry shoved Anthony on the shoulder and could feel herself starting to blush.

'I think you protesteth too much. He is bloody gorgeous though - you know of course he bats for both sides?'

'Bloody hell, Anthony, you haven't changed a bit,' laughed Mirry.

'Well, you both looked very cosy sitting beside each other this morning, I saw you! Just thought I'd give you the heads up!'

'Mirry Coville, you are kidding me, I'll take your John off your hands any day if you've finished with him,' snorted Fran.

'Bloody hell, will you two bugger off and give me a break!' Mirry laughed. 'Still happy with John, thank you very much, there will be no taking him off my hands, Fran. And as for you, Anthony, wind your neck and imagination in! He's a colleague… doesn't hurt that he also happens to be extremely good looking though!'

'That's my girl!' Anthony said. 'What was it you and Pen always used to say back in the bad old days… You can look but you can't touch!'

'Ha! And don't you forget it!' Mirry wagged her finger exaggeratedly. 'Anyway, lovely as it is chatting to you both, I can see Helen giving me the evil eye so I had better get on and circulate. Fancy meeting up for a drink later?'

'Yeah, brilliant, I'm staying over tonight, catch you at the end of the day when Helen is off your back.'

'Great, catch you later.' Mirry gave them both a quick hug and made her way over to where Helen was waiting for her. Mirry could see her tapping her foot in impatience.

Chapter Twenty-Nine

The week after the conference, Mirry decided to run to work in the mornings, making the most of the light before the clocks changed and the darkness of winter descended. She wasn't on call for a few days and relished the sense of freedom it gave her not being tied to her mobile. They had a new member on the team in preparation for Cath going on maternity leave and she was undergoing her training. That, Mirry knew from bitter experience, could be brutal as she would have to be available twenty-four seven to gain experience whenever there was a referral. Liz, the new girl, seemed to be okay with it though; she was used to on-calls, having spent four years working in theatres. They already knew her fairly well as she had been part of the donor retrieval team. 'Their loss, our gain,' Mirry thought as she headed into the changing rooms for a shower before work.

The last few weeks had been tough. John was always late home from work, if he got home at all, and the strain was beginning to show in him. Mirry was trying to be supportive, leaving meals out for him, doing the washing, tidying, and cleaning, but she was missing spending time with him. Maybe he'd get a couple of days off now the reconstruction had gone out on TV last night, she thought. But John had warned her that the work would probably double, every call would need to be logged, investigated, and followed up.

'Morning Mirry,' Pen said the minute she came into the office, 'didn't John do an amazing job last night and so very handsome too - what's it like being with the Police's answer to George Clooney?'

'Oh Pen, piss off, will you!' Mirry said, dropping off her bag and hanging her coat up. 'If you knew the half of this case, you wouldn't be making jokes. He's bloody knackered and never home.'

'Oh, sorry, Mirry, it looks really serious. Wee bit close to home too with one of them being our case from the summer.'

'I know,' Mirry said, 'not sure what the recipients would think if they knew. Have they been told, do you know?'

'One of them has written to Ray via Helen saying how grateful they are, but Ray doesn't want to respond... understandably. Think he's just glad they're doing so well.'

'Doesn't make up for not finding who's responsible though, does it?'

'Nah, but anyway, we've got enough on our hands. Debs is off to ICU out at St. John's this morning with Liz - think it's a subarach that came in last night. Horrendous by the looks of the CT, and they're not planning on transferring to DCN.'

'Good practice for Liz though. Sooner she's up and running, the better.'

'Yeah, she's great. She's got good experience and looks like she might be a bit of fun!'

'New Spice girl to the team then; the only name left is Baby, which is probably appropriate, seeing as she's the youngest.'

'Not sure she'd appreciate that nickname yet, maybe wait until she knows us a wee bit better, eh?'

Mirry sat down at her desk and switched her PC on just as Simon came into the office.

'Morning ladies,' he said, 'everyone alright this morning? Saw John on TV last night, Mirry, doing that reconstruction. Did a good job, looks like a tough case.'

'I was just saying exactly the same thing Simon,' Pen said, 'and isn't he a handsome dude?'

'Very,' said Simon, looking directly at Mirry. 'You won't be getting to see much of him just now, Mirry, I bet.'

'Ships that pass in the night,' Mirry answered. 'It'll be worse now that it's gone out on TV. Hopefully generate some new leads though.'

'Bit stuck then, are they?' asked Simon. 'That's usually why they have to do a reconstruction.'

'Think so,' Mirry said, 'he can't really discuss it with me.'

'Really?' Simon said. 'Not even a bit of pillow talk? He must have to offload to someone, Mirry, surely?'

'No, like I say, we hardly see each other as it is. I think the last thing he wants to talk about is work when he's at home.'

'Hmm, I get that,' Simon said, unlocking the door to his office. 'Still, he has to unload at some point I would have thought.'

Chapter Thirty

John decided to follow Mirry's lead and ran to work too on the morning after the reconstruction. He knew it would be busy when he got in and so there would be no other time when he would have the chance to exercise. As he rounded the corner, he spotted two of his team with the same idea trotting in front of him. He caught up with them, going through the back door to the changing rooms, and had a bit of good-natured banter about who was the fittest.

After his shower, he took the stairs two at a time up to the office. He could see that everyone was already gathered. Fee was writing on the huge whiteboard that had been put up at the front of the open plan office within clear sight of everyone.

'Morning,' John said, addressing the whole room. 'Planning a catch-up at eleven, see where we are with everything. Fee… could you come to my office? Need to look at staffing for the next few days.'

Fee nodded, grabbed her coffee and files off her desk, and followed John.

'You want one?' she asked, lifting her mug. 'Fresh pot just made, I'd get in whilst it's fresh.'

'Would you mind, Fee?' John asked, pulling his chair out from behind his desk and sitting down.

'Ha, just because you've been on the telly doesn't mean you get special treatment, boss.'

'Ah, go on, milk no sugar.'

'Like I didn't already know that,' Fee laughed, heading out the door. 'Give us two ticks.'

When she came back, not only did she have coffee but a couple of bacon rolls as well, which one of the team had purloined having done a swoop of the work's canteen.

'Oh, result,' John said, unwrapping the greasy package and taking an enormous bite. 'Right, let's get down to it… who's in today, who's got holidays booked, might need to be cancelled once we have a look at the response to last night. What's it been like, you had a chance to get a feel yet?'

'Phones have been ringing non-stop apparently, both here and down in Newcastle; it's going to be tough sifting through everything. Think we are going to have to cancel leave, unfortunately.'

'Oh, that'll go down well, maybe see if we can offer overtime to sweeten the blow. Christmas is not that far away, they might appreciate the extra cash.'

'Will do,' Fee said, throwing her empty paper bag into the bin and wiping her mouth with the back of her sleeve. 'In the meantime, do you want to see what we've got so far to feed back to the team? Need to prioritise jobs to be done, mainly chasing up leads with potential witnesses.'

'Brilliant work, Fee, let's have a look then, let's get this bastard before something else happens.'

The morning passed so quickly John had no time to look at the clock. As predicted, the response to the reconstruction had been overwhelming and John and Fee sectioned off the team into pairs so that each couple had a separate responsibility. It was late in the afternoon before he had a minute to text Mirry to let her know he wouldn't be in until after seven. He asked her if she wanted him to bring a carry-out home, and that he fancied a Chinese for a change. She was quick to reply, yes, she'd have a carry-out and just surprise her. 'Surprise her,' he thought to himself ruefully. The surprise would be if he actually got home for seven at all.

It was indeed after seven before John got to their local Chinese to pick up the carry-out. As he stood at the till waiting to pay, his eye was caught by a small ornamental golden cat waving its paw on the shelf. 'Seems to be following me around,' he thought with a shiver, remembering the crime scene photographs and Susie's home. 'Why is it grinning like that ?' He shook his head as if trying to remove a physical object from his brain. Once the food was handed over, he quickly paid and smiled to himself, spying the prawn crackers at the top of the bag. The disturbing images soon crumbled and disappeared as he crunched crackers on the way to the car.

'Hi Mirry, been out hunter-gathering!' John shouted, coming into the flat.

'In here,' he heard her shout from the kitchen.

'Wait 'til you see how much food I've…'

His voice trailed off as he came into the kitchen and saw that Mirry was not on her own. There was a tall, blonde man sitting opposite her at their kitchen table, a couple of bottles of beer opened and half-drunk and Mirry looking a bit flustered.

'Hi,' said John uncertainly.

'John, this is Simon,' Mirry said. 'We work together; he just popped round to drop off some work stuff.'

'Pleased to meet you, Simon. Sorry, I would have got more if I'd known we had company.'

'Oh no, no, not a problem, John, I was just on my way,' Simon said. 'I've been keen to meet you, especially as Mirry talks about you all the time.' He stood up from the table, smiling with his hand outstretched.

'I do not!' Mirry laughed. 'Might have mentioned how much a pain in the backside you are if anything.'

'Good to meet you too, Simon,' John said. 'It's data stuff you do, isn't it? Mirry mentioned you were doing a great job getting things in order.' He took Simon's hand and gave it a firm shake.

'Yeah, pretty dry compared to what you're working on, John. We were just saying in the office what a great TV personality you'd make.'

John snorted. 'Yeah, for all the good that did,' he said resignedly, 'it's tough at the moment, long hours with very little to go on. Obviously I can't say too much, but at the moment it's like herding cats trying to find a needle in a haystack.'

'Ha, love the mixing of metaphors there,' Simon laughed. 'Still can't be easy on you both, what with Mirry's on-call commitment and your long hours.'

'Nah, it's not,' John said, 'hence the carry-out on a weekday!' John went over to put the food on the side whilst he got out cutlery and plates. 'Sure you don't want to stay? I always order too much, there'll be loads.'

Mirry was looking at him with raised eyebrows, and he knew instantly he had said the wrong thing.

'Well, if you're sure I'm not intruding…' Simon said, looking at Mirry. 'I've no plans and that bag does look pretty full.'

'Settled then,' John said, putting the plates and cutlery on the table. 'Let me grab a beer and catch up with you two.'

Despite Mirry's discomfort, John and Simon seemed to hit it off, helped by a few beers and the sharing of food. As it turned out, there was more than enough to go around and conversation flowed as if Simon and John were old friends.

John told them about seeing the ornamental cat at the Chinese restaurant, telling them how creepy he found it, with its inane grin.

Mirry burst out laughing. 'Yeah, we have our very own one at work, don't we? Simon brought one with him when he moved into the office; it now sits in pride of place, waving away incessantly, keeping an eye on us all from above Debs' desk. Where did you get it from again, Simon?' Mirry asked, tidying up the empty containers.

'Apparently, it's beckoning not waving, Mirry,' Simon said, correcting her. 'I was given it by somebody special when I lived in Newcastle.' Simon looked down at the table. 'She said it would bring me luck and prosperity, but that's not happened yet! I thought it would be good in the office though, a kind of talisman for organ donation.'

'Oh,' Mirry said with interest, this being the first time Simon had mentioned anyone before, 'somebody special, you say?'

'Yeah, she was my first actually - things didn't really go as planned, which is one of the reasons I moved up to Dundee.'

'Oh, sorry to hear that, mate,' John said sympathetically, 'time's a good healer though, eh?'

'Yeah,' Simon said wistfully, 'it certainly helps. Anyway, enough about me, thanks so much for your hospitality but I don't want to intrude any more on your evening. I know how busy you are, John.'

'Nah, it was nice to meet you, Simon, maybe go for a beer one night? Show you some of the sights in Edinburgh.'

'That would be great,' Simon said, standing up.

'I'll see you to the door,' Mirry said, pushing back her chair.

'Bye then,' said John, collecting up the dirty dishes and putting them in the sink.

When Mirry came back into the kitchen, John was filling up the bin with the empty carry-out containers.

'Nice bloke, Mirr,' he said, busy with his task.

'Yeah,' Mirry said, feeling a little guilty, 'really nice bloke.'

Chapter Thirty-One

Mirry couldn't believe what had just happened. The last person she had expected to have in her flat had been Simon; she hadn't realised he even knew where she lived. She'd got a text from him when she had got in from work that evening to say that he had some really good feedback from the study session which he wanted to share with her. There was talk about putting together an annual national training event and would she be interested? When she had replied that of course she would, he had texted that he was going on annual leave and asked if he could drop off the USB with all the details on it on his way home from work. So, there he was, at her front door.

When she let him in, for some reason, she had begun to feel a little uncomfortable. Having Simon in her own space had felt a little awkward; she wasn't sure how to behave with him here. The flirtations in the office were one thing, but to have him standing in her home was a different matter altogether. Simon had seemed to pick up on her discomfort, played up to it by asking where John was, seemed to enjoy seeing her squirm. She had taken him into the sitting room where he'd commented on the feature wall, remembering what she had said when they were together for the publicity training. He was mildly amused by the whole situation and had looked around almost disdainfully, as if what John and her had worked hard for was nothing.

She'd invited him into the kitchen and offered him a drink, meaning a tea or a coffee, but instead he had asked if she had any beer. Mirry hadn't felt she could say no, in that ridiculous way of not wanting to appear rude. Actually, the beers helped to relax the tense atmosphere between them, but she still hadn't enjoyed having him there in her space and she couldn't quite work out why.

It was a relief when John came home with the carry-out. She'd thought that Simon would do the polite thing and leave, but John had invited him to stay despite her trying to signal otherwise. Now it looked like Simon and John were going to be best pals and this all felt a little weird to her. Weird and very uncomfortable.

Getting ready for bed later that night, John was in a good mood, having company seemed to have helped him to relax. By the time Mirry had finished tidying up the kitchen and turned the lights off in the sitting room, John was already in bed, his bedside light off and quietly snoring. 'There'll be no baby-making tonight then,' she thought ruefully. 'Cheers, Simon.'

Chapter Thirty-Two

It wasn't until John was changing the picture on the calendar in his office that he realised that a whole month had passed without him noticing. Staring at November's scene of the Machrie Moor Stone Circle on Arran took him immediately back there and his time with Mirry. Such a magical place to visit, and the day they were there in March, it had been so very peaceful, with not another person in sight. 'Oh, to go back there and away from this madness,' he thought, returning the calendar to the spot above the filing cabinet. He had a team briefing to prepare for and then a meeting with Charlie for a catch-up. His heart sank at the thought of it; he knew they were no further forward and had no suspects. He looked out at the whiteboard at the front of the office which was now covered in photographs of the victims, arrows, boxes, and maps, the composition of it all only making sense to those on the team. The pressure was on.

His mobile vibrated in his pocket and he pulled it out, not recognising the number. It was a message from Simon, asking if he wanted to go out for that pint sometime. John inwardly sighed, regretting that he had offered to show Simon some of Edinburgh. 'Poor bloke,' John thought, 'he's probably a bit isolated.' He texted back that yeah, why didn't they meet up tonight at the Devil's Advocate?

Simon's response was almost immediate with a thumbs up and 7.30pm question mark. See you there, John replied and then quickly texted Mirry to let her know he wouldn't be in for tea.

The meeting with Charlie in the afternoon turned out to be a total grilling from her and her superior, leaving his head busted. The outcome was that the team had to go back to the beginning and go over all the evidence, interviews and CCTV for all three victims again. Charlie was convinced there was something that must link all the cases. John didn't feel he could be sarcastic and say yeah, same guy killed them all. There had been an idea floated that they should look at other strangulations that had occurred just to see if there were any other similar cases. John knew that this would be a huge amount of work for him and Newcastle. He also knew that his team's motivation was beginning to lag.

When he got back to the office everyone was away home for the day. He sat down in front of his PC to see if any more emails had come in and ended up spending another hour catching up with those, making a list of all the things that would need attending to in the morning. By the time he'd closed down his PC, he was seriously looking forward to that pint.

He headed out, crossing over the Pleasance and making his way to the Bridges. It was a cold night, the air was clear and bright. It was busy around Surgeons' Hall, and John could make out groups of people heading to the Festival Theatre, its lights leading them like moths to a flame. He carried on down until he reached the Royal Mile, then headed up the High Street. Despite it being November, there were still tourists about which made him smile. He could understand though, Edinburgh was such a beautiful city. He had grown to love his time living here and now even more so, setting up home with Mirry. He walked past St. Giles and avoided the heart in the road that usually had a revolting amount of gob on it, the only place where it was accepted that you could spit outdoors. Crossing the road, he ducked down Advocate's Close, the dark, archaic walls closing in around him. He could see the welcoming lights of the pub and pushed the door open to be met by a gust of warm air and the loud babble of voices.

Looking around, he immediately spotted Simon already sitting at one of the tables with what looked like a half drunk lager in front of him. He waved and made his way over.

'Hi mate,' he said, shaking Simon's proffered hand. 'Sorry I'm a bit late. What you having whilst I'm at the bar, looks like you could do with a refill?'

'I'll get the next ones then,' Simon said, sitting down and taking a large swig of his drink. 'Make mine an IPA, goes down so easily. Shall we get some food?'

'Yeah, I'll grab the menu and bring it over.'

By the time their food came, it was time for another refill and the bar staff brought their pints over to them. Their burgers didn't take long to disappear and it would have been obvious to anyone watching that both men were ravenous.

'God, I needed that,' John said, pushing his empty plate away from him and taking a long drink from his pint.

'Me too,' said Simon laughing. 'Couple of Neanderthals, the two of us, you would think we hadn't been fed in days!'

John could feel himself starting to unwind with the help of the beer and food. Simon was easy to talk to and they seemed to have a bit in common, both liking sport and the outdoors. They empathised with each other about having office jobs, and John lamented for the days when he was a bobby on the beat and spent much of his working day outside.

'How's work going anyway, John?' Simon asked. 'Last time we met, you were up to your eyes in it and had just been on TV. You any further forward?'

'Nah, still really full on, hoping something will come up soon.'

'Yeah, Mirry had said you were working hard. I think it means a lot to her, particularly as one of the cases was her donor.'

'I know,' John said, wiping off the condensation on his beer glass with his finger, 'she's not the only one that it means a lot to.'

'Must be tough though, after all that work, what with the reconstruction and things. Nothing showing up at all?'

'Them's the breaks. Something will materialise soon enough, I'm sure. Anyway, enough about work, what you up to at the weekend?'

Their conversation flowed easily until the bell was called for last orders. John's heart sank when he saw that Simon had come back from the bar with a half pint and a whiskey chaser. However, it didn't stop him demolishing them both. By the time the two of them were ready to make their way home, they were laughing uncontrollably and unsteady on their feet.

'God, I'll get it in the ear when I get in,' John said, clumsily helping Simon with his jacket, closing one eye.

'Man's allowed to let off steam now n' again,' Simon slurred, pushing his arm into the proffered sleeve from John. 'Cheers, mate.'

'Och, I know, Mirry's all right, just this case is taking up so much of my time, can't think of anything else.'

'Yeah, she's okay is Mirry,' Simon said, opening the door of the pub for John as they made their way out to the dark close outside.

'Need to get this bastard soon though,' John said, more to himself than Simon.

'Good luck with that one, sounds like he's got you beat so far.'

'We'll get him,' John said more firmly.

'Sure you will,' Simon said. 'I'm heading down to Princes Street for a bus, good to see you.' Simon offered an outstretched hand to John who took it and pulled Simon into a rough embrace.

'Need to do this again one night. Cheers, Simon, see you soon.'

Both men separated in the dark, amber lights, going in opposite directions, John swaying slightly as he made his way unsteadily up the stairs to the High Street. By the time he got home, it was past midnight and there was a definite cold shoulder waiting for him in bed. Cheers Simon.

Chapter Thirty-Three

John and Mirry became even more distant over the following days. Work just seemed to be overtaking both of their lives in time and thought. Each time Mirry had been on call, she had had a referral. Two cases had been successful, with the donors going on to fully donate. It had been tough though, and Mirry was beginning to think it might be time to look for a different job, one without the on-call commitment. This latest referral had been the hardest yet.

It had been a difficult case for everyone concerned but, when it came down to it, the family had made the decision that was right for them. Mirry couldn't help feeling disappointed though; sure, the patient was young - only seventeen - but even so, he had put his name down on the ODR to donate everything but his eyes. He had even talked about it with his mum and dad, but they still couldn't bring themselves to give permission for donation in the end.

To add insult to injury, Mirry had to ask them to sign the authorisation withdrawal form. This was an added blow. They felt they were going against his wishes, which of course they were - perhaps taking final parental control when all else was lost. His case was so very sad; he had hung himself, but not completely. He'd been found out in the garden when his parents returned from their weekly immersive French class to find their only son garrotted by a blue rope hanging on the garden fence. Mirry could tell their shock was numbing, the full devastation of his death yet to hit. They couldn't comprehend how their happy, healthy young son had come to do this to himself. Just the day before, they had been joking about getting him a hamster for his Christmas to keep him company when he was studying. His family had asked Mirry to stay with them when his life support was withdrawn. She had witnessed this process before, but it never got any easier watching the colour drain and the heart rate slow when the ventilator was withdrawn. His mother helped wash and prepare him for the mortuary and his sister brought in his favourite woolly hat and socks so he wouldn't be cold.

By the time Mirry was making her way back to the office, the light outside had disappeared and she realised she hadn't seen the sun the whole day. She sighed inwardly, knowing that this change in light meant that winter was well on its way, accompanied by the darkness of the days stretching through until February.

Mirry half-heartedly pushed through the door that led from the corridor to the office. There was a low light coming from within. 'Somebody must be working late tonight,' she thought with a little relief. It would be good to go over what had just happened.

Looking through the glass door, she could see that it was Simon, sitting in front of his PC, the rest of his office in darkness, just the glow from his screen illuminating his features. He looked up when she came in, a slow smile came across his face; he looked genuinely pleased to see her.

She walked over and leant against the open door. 'Hi, you working late too?'

'Yeah, you know how it is, sometimes easier to work when there's nobody here, can concentrate better. You been up to 118 for a donor?' he said as he swivelled back to face his screen again.

'Mmm,' said Mirry, 'very sad, family said no.'

Simon sat bolt upright and swung round in the chair to face her. 'What do you mean the family said no? I thought he was on the donor register.' A statement rather than a question.

'Family still have to agree, Simon, and they just couldn't bring themselves to say yes in the end.'

'Fuck's sake, that's total nonsense! They shouldn't be able to do that! All that bloody work for nothing! He would have been a perfect donor!' Simon spat out the words with such venom, Mirry was a little taken aback at his vitriol. 'Could you not have persuaded them, Mirry? I thought that was what you were good at?'

'It's not that simple, Simon,' Mirry said, straightening up. 'It has to be right for the family; they're the ones who have to live with the decision they make, not us.'

'Does it not make you angry though, Mirry? You're always the one banging on about the donor's rights. You've just lost us a perfect donor, someone whose wishes were to donate and because his family feel guilty about his suicide, they withdraw authorisation.'

'How do you know he committed suicide, Simon?' Mirry asked. She didn't remember him being in the office when the call had come in earlier.

'Oh, I was just having a look on Trak to see what the ICU cases were like…' Simon addressed his computer screen with a shrug of his shoulders and then looked over at her, his mouth now set in a firm line.

'Hmm, didn't know you had access to what was going on in the wards like that.'

'Yeah, well, I need access for data collection about potential cases and occupancy figures, that kind of thing.'

Mirry stared hard at Simon who had returned to looking at his computer screen again. She was aware from his manner, that had been warm when she first came into the office, had become decidedly cold, his attitude changing to an almost non-verbal dismissal of her.

'Well, I'll just log today's case and then I'm heading home. You staying on a bit longer?'

'Yeah, few more things still outstanding. See you tomorrow.' Simon didn't look up at her but went back to concentrating on his screen.

'Yeah, see you tomorrow.' Mirry returned to her own desk, fired up her PC, entered the case into the database, reliving the conversation she had had with the family as she ticked the 'No' box for 'did donation proceed?'

Simon's words were still ringing in her ears as she made her way out to the car park. Perhaps she should have tried harder with today's family. Would they regret their decision later when the trauma and guilt of their son's death had become less acute? She would never know; she could only do what she thought was right at the time. After all, she was there, Simon wasn't.

Climbing the stairs when she got home, the tiredness engulfed her with each heavy step. Coming into the flat, she was met with the acrid smell of burnt toast mixed with stale air. She shrugged off her coat and hung it up, kicking off her shoes and putting them on the rack next to John's enormous brogues. There was the sound of some game show coming from the sitting room, she poked her head round the door to say hi. John was lying sprawled on the sofa, fast asleep. He was in his running gear, the television blaring, its psychedelic colour illuminating the dirty dishes and empty mug lying on the coffee table. Mirry shook her head and made her way into the kitchen. The bitter smell was more pronounced, and the black scrapings of the cremated bread were all over the sink. The torn remains of the loaf were on the counter, the bread knife lying haphazardly beside the empty butter dish. For some reason, Mirry's eyes filled with tears. She tidied up, rinsing the blackness away and wiping down the surfaces. Opening the fridge, she sighed at the contents. 'Scrambled egg again then,' Mirry thought, taking out two eggs in preparation. By the time she had made her meal and poured herself a glass of milk, her sadness was being replaced with a corroding annoyance.

'Just for once could he not have made some food for me too?' she thought self-pityingly. 'Selfish git.'

She ate quickly, still standing at the worktop, staring out at the blackness in the garden, not tasting anything. Once she had finished, she opened the kitchen window slightly to let the fresh night air in to dilute the bitterness. Switching off the light, she went through to the sitting room where

John had not moved, the programme now changed to the desert plain of some far off land where a deer was being stalked.

'We all know where that's going,' Mirry thought, picking up the remote and closing down the scene with one push of the button.

The change from noise to silence woke John, who opened his eyes to find Mirry staring down at him with an expression that he knew was trouble.

'Hey Mirr, when did you get in?' John said, pulling himself upright and rubbing his eyes, 'God, I'm knackered.'

'You're knackered?' Mirry said accusingly. 'Not that knackered that you could manage a run, leave the kitchen in a tip stinking of burnt toast, eat all the bread, and lounge about waiting for the maid to come in!'

'Bloody hell, Mirry, where did that come from?'

'Just have a fucking thought sometimes, would you?' Mirry spat at him, shaking her head as she headed out the door.

'Mirry, wait,' John said, rubbing his eyes before getting up and instantly regretting not stretching when he got in, his legs tight and sore. He stared at the closed door and decided to just leave her, huffy cow. He flopped back down on the sofa and grabbed the remote, switching the television back on just as a deer was being suffocated by a lioness.

'How very appropriate,' John said to himself, settling down again. He didn't hear Mirry weeping in the bedroom.

Chapter Thirty-Four

They were both up early the following morning. John made Mirry a cup of tea and left it on the kitchen table whilst he went for his shower. It was still there growing cold when he heard the bang of the front door as Mirry left. He got ready for work, quickly made the bed, and threw last night's discarded running gear into the laundry basket.

His mood didn't improve on the drive to work. Hitting potholes and avoiding idiot cyclists dressed in black had darkened it further, in line with the early morning winter gloom. There was nobody in the office when he arrived, which came as a relief; he wasn't in the mood to speak to anyone just yet. In the kitchen, he put on the coffee to percolate and warmed some milk in the microwave.

'Morning Boss,' Fee said, coming into the kitchen, bringing the smell of the outside with her.

'Mind yourself,' she said, trying to reach behind him to put what looked like her lunch into the fridge.

'Fuck's sake, Fee,' John said, getting out of her way but spilling some of his hot coffee over his hand.

'Oops sorry! Like a bull in a china shop, me, sometimes,' she said, grinning at him guiltily. 'You alright this morning?'

'Och, yeah, sorry for being a grumpy git. Had a bit of a spat with Mirry last night,' John said, wiping down the spilt coffee on the counter. 'Think we could both do with a holiday.'

'Tell me about it,' Fee said. 'Chloe was having a go at me last night as well for always being at work. It's okay for her, at least teachers have got regular hours and great holidays.'

'Yeah, but let's be honest, Fee, would you want her job? Adolescent kids and all those hormones? She must have the patience of a saint!'

'You're right, she is pretty cool, puts up with me most of the time, and that isn't easy. What's up with Mirr?'

'Just think I've been a bit of a slob recently. This case is just doing my head in.'

'Think the whole team is feeling the same way. Might need a bit of pep talk this morning, bit of brainstorming.'

'Charlie had said yesterday that maybe we should have a look at other cases of strangulation in the past couple of years both here and in Newcastle.'

'Yeah, that sounds like a good idea. I think the profiler's report is through too. Saw an email heading with that this morning but haven't read it yet.'

'That'll be my first job today. It'll be interesting to see what she makes of what we have. Catch up at nine-thirty? Get the team together?'

'Sure thing,' Fee answered, filling her own mug with coffee and heading out of the kitchen.

John sat down at his desk and opened up his PC. He immediately went to his emails and found the report that Fee had mentioned.

The report was concise with no surprises. For John, it reaffirmed what the evidence had provided, but to see it written down in black and white from another professional was reassuring. At least his head was in the right place. They knew the murders were all committed by the same person, but the difference between the victims was interesting. The profiler had separated each case. The first murder may not have been planned, but the evidence of multiple bruising around Susie's neck raised questions. Was there a sexual element to this case or was it just about power? Susie seemed to have known her attacker, as there was no sign of a break-in. The second case that they were aware of, Jenny Anderson, looked much more planned. The house had been watched and her movements monitored. The killer had hidden in the attic overnight. The attack was much more measured, but the anger against the dogs spoke of a volatile personality. The third case seemed totally random; definite sexual element again where fellatio had obviously taken place. Was he homosexual?

Impression: male, fairly well built, strong and fit - obvious from the CCTV of the suspect on the bike - personality disorder of sorts but probably a high functioning narcissist who enjoys what he's doing. Concern that there may be other victims that have not been identified. Obviously losing his hair, blonde.

John pushed his chair back from his desk and looked out into the main office whilst he absorbed what the profiler had written. The randomness of the cases when written down in black and white was stark. Perhaps this was a clue in itself. The more he thought about it, the more John was convinced that they should explore if there were any other cases that were similar but had flown under the radar.

Chapter Thirty-Five

Mirry jumped on hearing the front door slam when John came in from his morning run. They had barely spoken the last few days, and Mirry was still smarting from their exchange a couple of nights before. She knew that they were both off today and, normally, they would have planned to do something together, but John hadn't bothered to ask. She closed up the book she was reading, folding down the page for later. Going through to the kitchen, she could hear the shower running and for a split second thought about joining him, but quickly shook that idea away.

The faint morning light was glowing through the big sash window, and Mirry looked down into the garden, noticing the bird feeders their neighbour had hung on the lower branches of the lilac tree. There was much activity of pecking and fluttering, each bird seeming to take its own turn before flying off with full beaks.

Opening the fridge, she took out the sausages, bacon, eggs, and mushrooms she had bought last night on her way home from work. It wasn't long before she had everything cooking, the coffee made, and toast keeping warm at the side of the hob, the routine of the tasks easing the rusting resentment within her. Her mood began to soften. She set the table, even putting out napkins that were joined by the milk jug, butter, and sauces, brown and red. Mirry smiled to herself, remembering John's preferences of brown with sausages, red with bacon. She whisked the eggs together, added seasoning, melted butter in a pan, and then plopped the eggs in over a low heat. The final stages.

'John,' she called through the kitchen door, 'breakfast is ready.'

She heard him come in behind her as she slowly stirred the eggs.

'This looks great, Mirry, thanks.' John pulled his chair back and sat down, pouring himself a coffee out of the pot.

'Thought it would be good to start the day off well,' Mirry said, plating up the food and putting it down in front of him.

'Wow, Mirry, you've outdone yourself this morning, this is fabulous, just what I needed.' John hammered sauce onto his plate, picked up his cutlery, and attacked his plate with gusto.

Mirry brought her smaller portion to the table and sat down, mirroring his sauce additions and spreading butter on her toast.

'So, how's the case going?' Mirry asked through a mouthful of toast.

'Nowhere,' John said. 'Do you mind if we don't talk about it? Would like to forget about it today.'

'Sure,' Mirry said, 'been a tricky time for me too.'

'Hmm, sure it has,' John said non-committedly, taking out his mobile and looking at his messages.

'Yeah, we had a really difficult case a few days ago, just a young lad, committed suicide.' Mirry stared off out the kitchen window, the image of pulling Jack's woolly hat on before wrapping him in a shroud flashing across her vision.

'Hmm, tough,' John said, swiping through his phone.

'John, you listening to me?' Mirry asked, her irritation noticeable in her voice.

'Yeah, babe, sorry.' John put down his phone and looked across the table. 'What were you saying?'

'Och, just it's been a tough few weeks, what with one thing and another. My last referral was really hard for everyone, and I don't know if I handled it properly.'

'You will have done, Mirry, don't be doubting yourself. At least yours had some resolution.' John wiped the dregs of bacon fat and sauce up with his last bit of toast. 'Not like us, totally consuming and not getting anywhere.'

'Yeah, I know, John, but we weren't talking about your case. You said you didn't want to, whereas I would like to talk about mine with you, just to get another perspective on it.' Mirry pushed her half eaten breakfast away from her, her appetite disappearing, the feeling being replaced by a different type of gnawing.

'Mind if we don't, Mirr?' John asked, oblivious to Mirry's growing resentment. 'Just want to catch up with you and leave work out of it.'

'Fine,' Mirry said, 'what you fancy doing? Head up the Pentlands for a hike? Bit of fresh air, get out the town?'

'Em, no, actually, I've already promised Fee I'd give her and Chloe a bit of a hand with their garden. Chloe wants a veg patch, and I said I'd go over and help clear some of the bushes and stuff for them. I said you would come give us a hand too.'

'John, we've hardly seen each other, can we not just have the day to ourselves?'

'It'll be fun, you like Fee and Chloe. Bit of hard graft, might take your mind off things.'

'I don't need fucking hard graft to take my mind off things,' Mirry said between clenched teeth, 'what I need is to spend time with the person who is meant to care about me.'

'Well, not if you're going to be a miserable cow, I'm not,' John said, pushing his chair back and collecting their dirty dishes together.

Mirry swallowed hard, staring at him as he cleared the table, putting the dishes in the sink. She could feel tears starting to come.

'So you don't think a seventeen-year-old lad hanging himself in the family back garden isn't something to be upset about?' Mirry shouted at him. 'When did you get so bloody cold?'

John turned around from the kitchen sink. 'Did you say hanged himself, Mirr?'

'Yes,' Mirry said, wiping the tears from under her eyes with both hands, 'his mum and dad found him just in time, or so they thought. But the damage had already been done.'

John felt the blood drain from him - could there be a connection? His mind was trying to make sense as his thoughts pinballed.

'John?' Mirry's voice brought him quickly back. 'What is it, you look like you've seen a ghost.'

'Not sure, Mirry, sorry… just that there's a familiarity about your case that is making me really uncomfortable. Was there any suspicious circumstances?'

'John, you don't think…' Mirry stared at him, the meaning of what he was saying starting to dawn on her too.

'We were thinking about looking to see if there had been any other suspicious hangings that we might have missed. Nothing has been turning up, Mirry, I'm at my wits end.'

'Well, maybe you should have a look at his case then,' Mirry said, her anger dissolving. 'You'd better hurry though, his funeral is next week.'

'Hmm, maybe clutching at straws,' John said more to himself than Mirry. 'Need to chat to Fee about it this afternoon; you'll need to come now, Mirry, definitely.'

'Okay,' Mirry said, realising the seriousness of what John was suggesting, 'let's finish these dishes and get out to Fee's.'

Chapter Thirty-Six

Fee and Chloe lived out past Haddington in an old farm cottage that they had bought the year before. They had spent all their free time doing it up themselves, bit by bit. The end result resembled something that would not have looked out of place in an interior design magazine. The kitchen was warm and welcoming with a wood burning stove and a large picture window that looked out onto the garden. At this time of year, the garden was dormant, the lacy brown heads of the three hydrangea bushes lending a nodding structure to the flower bed. The small lawn stretched down to the wooden gate in the fence, which in turn led out onto the adjoining fields.

Fee was already at the door when they pulled up in the drive, her arms crossed and her face serious. John had called her from the car to say that something had come up that he wanted to talk about.

'Hi Boss,' Fee said. 'Hi Mirry, good to see you. In you come.'

They followed her through the front door, the warmth of the tiled entrance hall mixing with the fresh winter's air outside.

'Chloe's gone out for a run when I told her you would need to talk about work. Think she's planning a 10k, so will be gone about an hour. Come through to the kitchen, the fire's on, and I've made some coffee.'

They made small talk whilst Fee busied getting the coffee and putting a plate of biscuits on the table. Mirry shook her head when Fee offered her one; she was still full from breakfast.

'So what's going on?' asked Fee once they were settled with steaming mugs in front of them.

'I'm not sure, and I might be clutching at straws, but Mirry had an odd case at work.' He paused when he said it. 'Go and explain to Fee, would you?'

Mirry quickly outlined Jack's case, when he had been put forward for donation, and what had happened.

'There will be a police report about that for sure; it must have gone to the PF by now, John. Nobody will look at it until Monday,' Fee said once Mirry had finished. 'Definitely think it's worth going through though.'

'You don't think I'm jumping the gun?' John said, looking for reassurance. 'This case has been so all-consuming sometimes, I feel I can't see the wood for the trees.'

'The way things are at the moment, I don't think we can ignore anything - think we should head in this afternoon, to be honest. You and I can do a bit of digging, and if we don't find anything, at least we tried.'

Mirry cleared her throat. 'I'm a little worried about confidentiality here,' she said tentatively. 'Neither of you should know about this case, I shouldn't have said anything.'

'Don't worry,' Fee said reassuringly, 'Charlie told us a few days ago that we had carte blanche to look at all hangings and suspicious deaths that come in through the PF. This is definitely in that criteria.'

'Right, let's head in then,' John said, standing up, 'the sooner we get in the office, the better. Fee, can you drive me in and Mirry can take my car home?'

'Sure,' Fee said, clearing the mugs from the table, 'let me leave a note for Chloe.'

Fee left the kitchen and they could hear her running up the stairs, leaving Mirry and John standing waiting for her.

'Oh, this could be something big, Mirry,' John said, rubbing his hands through his hair.

'Yeah,' Mirry said, 'bang goes our weekend again.'

'Ah shit, I know, Mirry, but what can I do? We need to get this bastard before anyone else gets hurt.'

'Och, I know, John, don't worry, I'll maybe go and start a bit of Christmas shopping or something. Think I'll just head now then, leave you two to get on.'

'Great,' John said, 'I'll text you later, let you know what's happening. And thanks, Mirry, this could be really important.'

When Fee came back down to the kitchen, they made their way outside to the cars, Fee locking the door behind her and putting the key under the boot scraper sitting at the back door. Mirry's feelings of resentment started to dissipate as she realised that Chloe was in the same position as her, yet another weekend ruined by work.

Chapter Thirty-Seven

Going into the empty office later that day, John and Fee were on a mission. As the overhead lights flickered on and illuminated the whiteboard with all the victims' photographs, arrows, and evidence scrawled in different coloured pens, it made them both more determined. Fee went straight to her PC to find the police report for young Jack Lewis, the boy's name that Mirry had reluctantly given them only after they had reassured her that it was okay. It didn't take her long to find it and print it off before taking it to John's office. On the face of it, the case looked like a suicide. Jack had been found by his parents hanging from the bough of an apple tree, his feet just inches off the ground. They had cut him down quickly and his mum had found a slow pulse whilst his dad had called for the emergency services. It was the paramedics who had alerted the police, requesting an escort to get them through the Edinburgh traffic. Fee made a note to get in touch with the community constable whose name was on the report.

The clinical team had contacted the on-call PF when Jack had died to discuss whether or not they would be able to issue his death certificate to the family. As there seemed to be no suspicious circumstances, the PF had agreed to prevent further distress to Jack's family. John's heart sank on reading this; he knew what they were about to do would cause major problems and upset.

'Nothing for it, Fee. First things first, going to have to discuss this with the PF.' John rubbed his eyes and face, taking a deep breath and exhaling loudly.

'At least have the conversation,' Fee said. 'One way or the other we need an answer.'

John quickly made notes of the case, scribbling down the important details and, in doing so, bringing his pinball thoughts into alignment. He found the PF on-call number and called, his heart in his mouth.

The conversation had gone as well as he could have expected. Fortunately, it was the same PF who had been on call when Jack had died and he remembered the case well. Unfortunately, he wasn't happy about his decision being questioned, so John had to keep an even tone to his voice in an attempt to not aggravate the situation. He gave John permission to contact the family to retrieve Jack's belongings and to ask preliminary questions. He was under strict instructions to not mention the possibility of a post-mortem or investigation at any point until the case had been discussed with Charlie and Paul, the forensic pathologist.

'Decision is out of our hands for now,' John said, relating the details to Fee over a coffee in the kitchen. 'Let's make the call to the family and see what we get from them.'

The journey to Jack's home was made in mutual silence as both John and Fee realised the enormity of what they were about to embark on. Jack's father had been surprised to hear from them. He was confused about the necessity of their visit. The family home was full of people who had come to offer support. Could they not come next week, he'd asked, after the funeral?

They parked on the street parallel to Jack's house and walked to the front gate. Jack's dad was at the door before they had a chance to ring the bell, having been spotted by a young girl sitting on a chair positioned in the bay window.

He led them inside and up to Jack's room, the only room in the house that didn't have anyone in it. He then went to fetch his wife, leaving them uncomfortably leaning against the window in the room, not wanting to sit down on Jack's bed. It was a typical teenager's bedroom: various film posters on the walls, a jumble of clothes at the bottom of the bed, a desk with an open laptop and a pin board above full of postcards, what looked like old tickets, and other memorabilia.

When Jack's parents came back to the bedroom, they brought with them the emptiness of grief and the sharpness of shock. His mum looked at them both in suspicion before sitting down beside her husband on Jack's bed.

John outlined why they were there, repeating the word 'routine' like a mantra to stave off any dissent.

'There's nothing routine about this for us,' Jack's mum said dispassionately, 'nothing at all. Our only son is dead, officer, so please do us the courtesy of not using that word.'

'My apologies,' John said, looking down at the ground, 'it was not my intention to cause you any more pain. I'm sorry.'

'I'll go and get the hospital bag for you, we haven't been able to open it since we got home,' Jack's dad said after an uncomfortable silence, 'though why you would want that is beyond me.'

'We need to make sure that the report that goes into the PF is as complete as possible,' Fee said.

'I thought the PF had had all the information from the doctors in ITU when Jack died,' his mum said.

'Unfortunately, due to the nature of Jack's death, we need to ensure that everything has been looked at; collecting his belongings is the last thing that needs to be done. The officers with Jack when he was first admitted should have taken them then, but unfortunately they were pretty new and didn't know the process.' John could feel the beginnings of a white lie starting to form and his discomfort was obvious.

'Will they be returned?' his mum asked, tightlipped, holding back tears that were beginning to well.

'Yes,' Fee said, 'I will ensure that happens personally.'

Jack's dad came back into the room, holding a large white bag with 'patient belongings' in red writing on the side. He gave it to John without looking at him and sat down next to his wife again.

'As I said, we haven't opened the bag since we got it back - we couldn't.'

When John and Fee left the house, they could feel that they were once more being watched by the little girl sitting at the bay window, like a solitary, infantile sentry set apart from the adults.

'Christ, that was hard,' John said, exhaling loudly in the car.

'Had to be done though,' Fee said. 'Better get these off to Mark and his team now. I'd given him a call before we headed and he should be in the lab by now.'

'Okay, let's do this,' John said, starting the engine and pulling out onto the road. 'Hopefully it will have been worth it.'

Chapter Thirty-Eight

Mirry was early getting into work on Monday morning. John as always had brought her a cup of tea at six when he had left. She hadn't lingered in bed once it was finished. They had both had an early night the evening before, with Mirry feeling worn out from her early Christmas shopping, battling through the crowds, early revellers, and excited children on Princes Street. She could never work out what the point of all this fuss was for just one day but, at the same time, she hoped her request for time off at Christmas would be granted. It was her turn, after all, she had been on call the last three Christmases.

John had got in last night just after eight o'clock, had a shower, eaten his roast chicken dinner, and shared the remains of the bottle of wine Mirry had started. He hadn't said much about how the case was progressing. She knew that the PF, Charlie, and Paul had all agreed that a post-mortem should be done to exclude any foul play. As the most senior officer, it had been Charlie who was left to make the call to Jack's parents to let them know of the developments and the necessity for further investigation. To say that they had been upset would be an understatement. John had come in for particular criticism from Jack's mum and that had stung. Paul was able to reassure the parents that there would be no change to funeral arrangements as he was doing the examination first thing on Monday morning. He would speak to them personally straight afterwards to give them his findings. Everything possible was being put in place to try and alleviate any more suffering and contain the fallout. Mirry knew that this would be particularly hard for Jack's parents as the reason they had denied donation was because they didn't want their son's body disturbed. Sadly, they had no choice in that decision now.

Coming into the office, she was surprised to see that the decorations had gone up and then remembered Debs' love of all things Christamassy. There was tinsel hanging in swathes from the ceiling, holly adorning the whiteboard, and an artificial tree complete with baubles and lights in between the desks. Mirry smiled at the words 'Merry Christmas' sprayed in fake snow on the glass door of Simon's office.

'That's going to be a bugger to get off in the New Year,' Mirry thought as she pulled out her chair and made herself comfortable at her desk. Switching on her PC, she pulled out her diary and had a look at what she had on for the rest of the week - only one on-call, thank goodness, and a school talk. This would give her time to get her notes ready for clinics and have a look at some of the latest research that had come in about the new immunosuppressant treatments for recipients. She put her headphones on, found her work playlist on her phone, and started reading. Pen and Debs came in together, with Pen raising her eyebrows at Mirry over the festive decorations. Mirry just smiled and nodded, knowing Pen's dislike of all the tat cluttering the office. Cath and Liz came in later, but left soon after when a donor call came through from Fife.

Simon arrived at ten and had brought coffee and much applauded bacon rolls. Their previous sour exchange from the week before seemed to have been forgotten, much to Mirry's relief. Indeed, Simon was delighted with the Christmas decorations and jokingly chastised Pen for being a Scrooge about Debs' efforts. There had been the usual chat about the weekend, with Simon commiserating with Mirry about John having to work. The conversation moved on to the Christmas work night out. As she did every year, Debs had once more made all the arrangements and was chasing everyone for their final payments.

'You coming to the night out, Simon?' Mirry asked later in the morning as she filled up her water bottle from the dispenser outside his office.

'Yeah, I thought I might,' Simon said, pushing himself away from his desk and stretching his arms wide above his head. 'Not usually one for work dos, but it would be nice to have a night out with the team and see everyone let their hair down.'

Mirry couldn't help but feel a little rush of pleasure at the thought that Simon might be coming.

'Have you let Debs know?' Mirry asked.

'Yeah, although I think I'm too late for the meal choice, just have to take what's offered. Looks like a decent venue though, booked a room for myself,' Simon said, pulling his jumper down and stretching his legs out in front of him.

'Not going to be sharing with anyone. What about you, Mirry?'

'Pen and me always share, cheaper that way and seems to keep us out of mischief.'

'Oh, that's a shame,' Simon said, smiling at her, 'everyone loves a bit of mischief, don't they?'

'Hm,' Mirry said non-committedly, chastising herself for the blush she could feel spreading tellingly up her neck. 'I think my mischief days are over.'

'I doubt that very much,' Simon said with a grin, 'and if they are, that's too bad.'

'There was a time, Simon, believe me,' Mirry said, laughing as she screwed the top on her water bottle.

'Never say never,' Simon said to her retreating back as she giggled, making her way back to her desk.

Mirry's giggle was soon suppressed when she looked over at Pen who was staring stoney faced at her across the office, mouthing, 'Stop it.' Mirry stuck her tongue out in response, causing Pen to just smile and shake her head as she looked back at her PC screen.

'Night out might be fun,' Mirry thought to herself as she looked back into Simon's office to catch him staring straight at her, smiling, with his hands behind his head. A shiver went up her spine and a small voice chastised her from inside.

Chapter Thirty-Nine

Jack's post-mortem was booked in for first thing
Monday morning. John and Fee had arrived at the
City Mortuary in plenty of time. They exchanged
pleasantries with the mortuary staff over a coffee in
the staff room before heading into the respective changing
rooms to get into scrubs. Paul arrived just as John was
folding his clothes and pushing them into a locker.

'Morning John,' Paul said, 'you joining us this morning?'

'Yeah, Fee's here too. Just want to see this case through,
you know how it is.'

'I've asked Cat to join us,' Paul said, pulling on a pair of
white wellingtons over his scrubs. 'PF wants it to be a two
person job given the circumstances.'

'Yeah, totally understand,' John said, slipping a pair of
blue overshoes over his brogues. 'Might not be anything,
but Mark got back this morning to say that they had found
blue rope in his belongings; I think they had just cut the
rope down without taking it off him when he was found.'

'No doubt he'll be examining that and adding it to his
report. Anyway, shall we?' Paul said, holding open the door
to the entrance of the PM room. John nodded and walked
through, holding the second door open for Paul. He hated
this part of the job. 'At least there would be no other cases
going on this morning,' he thought. At times, he found his

senses overwhelmed in the PM room when multiple dissections could be going on simultaneously. The graphic sights and oppressive smells were made more unreal with the tinny music playing from the radio that sat on one of the shelves.

Fee and Cat were already changed and standing by the large metal dissection bench, looking over the report together. Fee was bringing Cat up to speed with the case. The two mortuary technicians were busying themselves laying out sampling kits and preparing the dissection trolley with its array of scalpels, knives, and high powered drill. The air in the room was charged, like the wait for a performance to begin, only the main attraction hadn't arrived yet.

Once everything was prepared, tubes labelled, and the microphone ready for recording above the PM table, Paul nodded for Jack to be brought in. John and Fee stepped back to observe from the side. The body of the boy was pulled onto the table, identification checked once more by both Cat and Paul who had stepped forward to begin. The stark lights above the table emphasised the pale skin and blue hue of the naked Jack. He was hairless apart from the dark bush cradling his limp, inert penis curled on his lower abdomen. His body was rolled, photographed, and checked by both Paul and Cat, issuing quiet instructions to the two mortuary technicians assisting. They paid particular attention to the area around Jack's head and neck, pointing out the odd abrasions and bruising at the back underneath Jack's hairline. They combed through his hair meticulously and scraped the samples into one of the universal containers. John looked away when the first incision was made; he could never get used to that, it always made him feel lightheaded. He looked at Fee standing beside him, intently studying something on the ceiling, and realised that she was feeling the same. She glanced over at him and smiled at the shared moment of apprehension, shaking her head and squeezing her eyes shut.

Cat and Paul worked methodically over Jack's body, removing organs, weighing and sampling as they went. John and Fee looked ceiling-wards once more at the end when Jack's scalp was pulled back over his skull once his brain had been examined. Paul nodded to the technicians and stepped away from the table with Cat as they removed their gloves and threw them in the orange disposal bin. The technicians then busied themselves sewing Jack together again, the Humpty Dumpty nursery rhyme coming inexplicably into John's head. Paul motioned for John to join him in the changing room while Fee followed Cat.

'I'll get the initial report finished by close of play today, John,' Paul said, stripping off to his underwear and pulling a towel out of his locker. 'My initial thoughts though are that he was subdued before being hung from that rope. There are areas of bruising that don't match the rope abrasions, but I'll know more when I examine the photos in detail later. In the meantime, I think it's safe to say that this was not suicide - someone else was involved in this lad's death. Whether it's the person you're after, who knows.'

'Thanks, Paul,' John said, 'at least we know it wasn't all for nothing and gives us something to work on.' John couldn't help but think of Jack's parents who would be receiving this news later from Paul. His heart sank at the thought of their distress.

John waited in the foyer of the mortuary for Fee to join him when she came out of the changing rooms. She shook her head when he asked if she wanted to stop off to pick up some lunch. He was relieved, as he didn't feel like anything either. They didn't speak until they had cleared the barrier letting them exit the car park and drove on to the Cowgate, the buildings, as always, dark and oppressive around them.

'Cat say anything to you?' John asked as he indicated to drive through the Grassmarket.

'Not much,' Fee said. 'You know what she's like, plays things close to her chest, doesn't want anyone making assumptions before they have all the facts.' Fee looked out the window, taking in the Christmas street decorations and the festive lunchtime trade in the pubs and restaurants.

'Does it not make you feel a bit weird seeing all this after what we've just been doing?' she said to the passenger window rather than directly to John.

'Yeah, know what you mean,' John said, braking to allow a gaggle of giggling women stumble across the road in front of them, the last one at the back bowing and blowing him a kiss before tripping onto the pavement.

'If only they knew,' Fee said, staring out the window.

'Just as well they don't,' John said, accelerating slowly away and heading up Victoria Street, 'they wouldn't sleep at night.'

'Paul say anything more to you?' Fee asked, bringing their thoughts back to work.

'No, he'll have the preliminary report to us by the end of today but he says it wasn't suicide so that gives us reason to investigate further. Let's go back to the beginning with Jack: friends, hobbies, that kind of thing, there has to be something they had in common.'

'Other than they were all on the Organ Donor Register?' Fee said absentmindedly. 'That's the only thing I can see.'

'Them and half the population of Scotland, Fee, not exactly narrowing things down there.'

'Got to start somewhere, Boss, got to start somewhere.'

By the time they got back to the office, their melancholy had lifted slightly, enough to stop off at the work canteen and grab the last couple of bowls of soup and a sandwich. It was going to be a long day.

Chapter Forty

The run up to Christmas was frenetic as always. Mirry was quietly delighted when she was given the time off that she had requested. Helen wanted to acknowledge the extra work she had put in with the publicity launch which had turned out to be a raging success. The tune 'Funky Town' with its catchy chorus of 'Talk about it' was on all their TV ads and radio jingles that Helen and the PR company had put together. So much so that the song had been re-released and was heading for the number one slot for Christmas. Mirry knew Helen was getting major credit for this as it had been her idea that had got the ball rolling in the first place. The number of people signing up to the Organ Donor register had increased by thirty percent in the last month, something that had never happened before. Helen was on a high and obviously feeling generous.

When Mirry told John she had the week off, he was delighted. Christmas was falling at the weekend, and for once, John was insistent that he and his team would have the time off. They had all been working extra shifts but as yet were still no further forward. The tension in the office was taut, tempers frayed, so when he announced that they were to have Christmas off this year, there had been a round of applause and much hilarity.

Mirry and John talked over what they would do, neither wanting to spend it with either families, the dynamics just too pressurised for them both.

'Why don't we just lie low and have Christmas at home for once, just you and me?' John suggested.

'You mean just totally ignore the outside world?' Mirry said.

'You know what, why don't we see if that cottage is free on Arran, the one we had in March?'

'Not bloody likely to be free at Christmas.' Mirry laughed at John's enthusiasm.

'Right, I'm going to call them now.' John leapt from the sofa and grabbed his mobile off the top of the bookcase where it was charging.

'Now let me see,' he said, his brow furrowed in concentration as he scanned through his emails. Mirry smiled at his enthusiasm and could feel the excitement generating off him like something from a breakfast cereal ad.

'Got it,' Mirry heard him say, his voice muffled through the wall as he made his way out of the sitting room, heading for the kitchen. After what seemed a lifetime, he came back in with a broad grin on his face. 'They just had a cancellation this morning, so it's ours, my love, for four days over Christmas, can you believe it?'

Mirry whooped in delight and jumped off the sofa, flinging herself at John. 'You are amazing and I love you! Oh, we're going to have a great time… What we gonna say to the family though?'

'How about a bit of honesty with them?' John said, holding Mirry at arm's length and looking her straight in the eyes. 'How about we've both had a really tough few months and just want some peace and quiet together to chill and reconnect?'

'And what's going to be the trade off for that, do you think?'

'Well, maybe if they leave us in peace, there might be a new addition next Christmas.'

Mirry laughed at that but, in her heart, felt a dull ache; it was seeming less and less likely and the worry was starting to gnaw.

Chapter Forty-One

It was a few days after their trip to the City Mortuary that John received an excited call from Mark. The forensic results from Jack's post-mortem had come back and once more the samples combed from Jack's head matched the other cases. John was surprised at his own response of dejected acceptance at what Mark had found. He had known deep down that the case was going to be another murder and he felt resigned rather than elated.

When he met with Charlie, they had agreed not to release this new information to the press for fear of creating a public panic. The frustration that nothing was connecting was beginning to chafe, and chafing badly. John's every waking hour was spent thinking about the case and he could tell his stress levels were at breaking point. The rest of the team were picking up on this too. They knew that they were really no further forward; the evidence was great but, without a suspect, it was worthless.

He called yet another team briefing. He reported back the results from Mark which confirmed it was the same individual who had been involved with the deaths of Sarah, Jenny, Ryan, and now Jack. An FLO had been assigned to Jack's parents. Fee had spoken at length with them when she went to tell them why they couldn't return Jack's belongings as promised. That had been a tough conversation and the team had supported Fee as much as possible when she came back to the office.

The meeting ended with John trying to portray a positivity that he didn't feel. It was back to square one, it had to be. Returning to witnesses that had come forward after the reconstruction, contacting bike shops, searching CCTV from all areas covered, not just necessarily where the victims were found. This was Fee's idea; they knew vaguely what the perpetrator looked like, so maybe he would be caught on camera somewhere else in the surrounding area at the time of Jack's assault.

Leaving the office later that day, John's mood was low. At least he had Christmas away with Mirry to look forward to, he thought, as he made his way out to his car. He realised that he probably hadn't been very easy to be about the last few weeks, but he knew Mirry understood the demands of his job. It was bizarre how their work had collided in such a major way. Mirry was still very quiet about Jack's death. When he told her that the forensic results had confirmed he had been strangled, she had burst into tears. Not being able to discuss it with any of her confidantes he knew was also hard for her, but he had had to stress that this information was not to be disclosed. Trust was such a major part of their relationship, he realised, and it brought him comfort knowing that Mirry had his back.

Pulling up in front of the flat, he decided to nip up to Bruntsfield to get her a present. Hopefully the shops would still be open. He knew her work Christmas night out was at the weekend and she had said she had nothing to wear. They had seen a red dress in one of the boutique windows the last time they had been out and about. John knew that Mirry had coveted it. However, she said she didn't want to splash out so much on something that would probably only be worn a couple of times. Seeing the dress in the window confirmed to him that it was perfect for Mirry. She would look amazing in it. The sales assistant wrapped it carefully in tissue paper and removed the price tag at John's request. Walking back down towards the flat, the spring in John's step had returned and he couldn't wait to see Mirry's face.

Coming into the flat, he was delighted to hear the sound of the shower running and Mirry's running gear abandoned on the hall floor. He went through to the bedroom and unwrapped the dress, hanging it up on the wardrobe door so it would be the first thing she saw when she came out of the bathroom. Going into the kitchen, he pulled open the fridge door to see what to make for tea. The simple actions of normality starting to dissipate his previous low mood.

'Going to be a pasta night,' he thought, taking out the garlic, onions, red peppers, and bacon from the fridge. His mouth watered at the thought of it. Hearing Mirry's squeal from the bedroom made him smile. She came running into the kitchen wrapped in just a small wet towel and threw herself at him, wrapping her arms and legs around him in a full bear hug, giggling the whole time.

'How did you know, you gorgeous man?' she said breathlessly in his ear.

'Thought you deserved something nice, my love, I know I've been a total pain in the arse recently.' He gently unwrapped her from around him and placed her back on the ground.

'Oh, John, it's just perfect! I'll wear it this weekend for my night out.'

'That's what I bought it for, Mirr, just disappointed I won't get to see you in it.'

'Well, that can soon be sorted,' Mirry laughed. 'I can model it for you now if you want, I'll need to make sure it fits anyway.'

'Go for it,' John said, 'I'll get on with tea.'

As it turned out, tea was abandoned until much later. The dress fitted Mirry so exquisitely that it didn't stay on for very long. John had taken even more delight removing it than he had when he bought it.

Chapter Forty-Two

Pen took another glug from her glass of fizz and reached for crisps with prehensile fingers, black varnish still drying on her nails. 'Who doesn't love a Christmas night out?'

'I hate them.' Mirry was straightening her hair, not happy with the forever kink at the front. 'Everyone off their face with booze, too much rich food, and fake bonhomie, it sucks.'

'God, you're a party pooper, I remember the day when you would have been first at the bar, margaritas all round, dancing on the tables, and that was before the turkey!'

'That was a long time ago,' Mirry smiled. 'Saw the light.'

'Saw John Sneddon's cock more like!' Pen snorted, inspecting her talons.

'You are an awful woman,' Mirry laughed, softly spiking her hair with her fingers.

'Your words not mine, babe. Always remember the day after he'd stayed the night, you positively cooing over how fabulous his body was… "Ooo he must work out three times a day"… barely able to ride your bike to work, I seem to remember!'

'You're like a bloody elephant, you, never forget anything.'

'Not sure the size of John's cock could be forgotten, gotten pretty legendary in the office,' Pen giggled, ducking when Mirry threw her rolled up towel at her.

Mirry laughed and made her way to the brightness of the bathroom to make her face up, smiling at the memory of that night that changed her life. Their relationship had had its ups and downs the last few months, but they were still able to reconnect. It was just that, with each month passing with no result, it was beginning to trouble her more. Would she ever conceive?

'Oh, fuck it,' she thought, tonight was not the night to think about it, time for fun and nonsense with her friends. She grabbed the beautiful dress John had bought her off the back of the door and shimmied into it, no zip or buttons - just a knitted tube of bright red.

'Ha!' said Pen when she returned to the room. 'Check you, girlfriend, sassy!'

Together they linked arms and headed for the lift in the hotel to take them down to the party hall, fixing their make-up in the lift mirror, anticipation of the night ahead rising.

The doors opened in the glossy main reception area, the atmosphere buzzing. Partygoers in small groups laughing, holding the obligatory free glass of bubbles. Waiting staff doing the rounds with trays of drinks, carefully weaving through those obviously well on their way with the celebrations. A corny Christmas carol being crooned in the background by some ancient long-dead singer.

'See our lot?' This from Pen as she grabbed two glasses of fizz from a passing tray. 'Get that down you.'

Mirry smiled at Pen. It reminded her of old times when the pair of them went out on the lash together - time to man up and let her hair down.

'Down in one, Pen, let's get this party started!'

'That's my girl!' They clinked glasses and threw back the fizzing, lukewarm liquid together, snorting as the bubbles hit the back of their throats.

Pen let out a loud belch. 'Man, that stuff is rank. Let's get a decent glass, halfies on a bottle of Blush?'

The two of them headed for the bar and found the rest of the team huddled around it.

'Don't we all scrub up well?' said Mirry, smiling broadly at her friends. Debs looking amazing in figure-hugging emerald green, her dark hair curled in a complicated arrangement adorned with sparkling pins. Liz less dramatic in black, safe and chic. Helen in a long purple velvet gown, looking like a medieval queen. Colin grinning all over his face like a freshly laundered cherub, dress trousers replacing his usual work jeans. Simon tall and quiet to the side of the group, crisp white tailored shirt, close fitting over dark trousers. Mirry smiled over at him, there was something about a man in a white shirt. He nodded back. 'Looking good tonight, Mirry, true Lady in Red.'

'Cheers, Simon, that was the plan.'

She took the glass of wine offered to her from Pen, feeling a slight blush spreading up from her neck. Why did this always happen whenever she was around Simon? Not for the first time, she told herself to get a grip.

'Who's on call tonight?' Mirry asked.

'Cath volunteered to take it,' Helen said, pouring tonic into her gin, with cucumber of course, never lemon.

'Ah, good on her, not really her thing anyway seeing as she's six months gone,' said Liz, comfortable now with the team.

Pen glanced over at Mirry to check her reaction. Mirry smiled back and shrugged; she wasn't dwelling on that tonight.

'Think the Glasgow and Dundee team are here tonight.'

'Going to be some night then, let's look at where we're sitting.'

The group made their way through to the large reception hall past the enormous tree festooned with baubles and lights. There were multiple large round tables set with white tablecloths, cutlery, and gold crackers.

'We're over here,' Debs waved, heading for a table across the dance floor, wobbling slightly on her heels, the height of them exaggerating the sway of her backside. The group followed, carrying bottles and glasses, giggling and talking as other partygoers came into the hall, the noise level growing, the anticipation of the night heightening.

Simon sat down beside Mirry, putting his glass next to hers.

'Not drinking tonight, Simon?' She looked him straight on, taking in the contours of his face up close, the pale stubble on his face just within stroking distance.

'Not tonight, Mirry.'

'Not tonight, Mirry, what?' Mirry replied playfully.

'Drinking.'

She wasn't sure how to reply to that. Impressed at his cool, self-assured manner, in control of himself, as always, total control.

'Wish I had your resolve,' Mirry replied, picking up her glass of rosé and taking a sip. 'Always been rubbish at saying no.'

'It's not been difficult for me, I can take it or leave it.' Simon took his glass and turned it so the lemon was facing them. 'Alcohol was never something I saw as a good thing, causes too much damage. My dad was an alcoholic; Mum left him in the end but, by that time, the damage to her had been done.'

'Oh, I'm sorry, Simon, sometimes I can be a bit insensitive.'

'No need to apologise, Mirry, it was a long time ago and, as they say, don't repeat the sins of the father. Some old minister told me that once. Mum's good now, getting better every day.'

'Even so, Simon, it can't have been easy.'

'Everyone has stuff in their past, some more than others. It's how we deal with it that counts, don't you think? Take control and deal with it.'

'Too true,' Mirry smiled, thinking of the way John sometimes behaved, didn't show his emotions very well, had been taught never to cry. Wasn't what real men did - an often said quote from his father, tough working man, never took a day off work, point of pride for him, being a man.

'Anyway, are we here to party or what?' Simon leant over Mirry, picked up the bottle of rosé and filled her and Pen's glasses. 'Here's to a good night, ladies.' He winked and briefly touched Mirry's shoulder, giving it a gentle squeeze.

'Cheers to that.' Pen raised her glass, looking straight at Mirry with raised eyebrows - she'd noticed the body language between them. Never missed a trick did Pen, thought Mirry, raising her glass back and shaking her head slightly, communicating, 'nothing to see here, Pen, move on.'

The starters arrived, and Debs with her list in front of her was organising who was to have what. Mirry couldn't remember what she had ordered - who would when the dinner choices were made in August?

'Mirry, you and Pen chose prawn cocktails, everyone else went for smoked salmon. Simon, that okay with you? Think you were away when we made our choices. You're not veggie are you?' Debs asked.

'No, Debs, I'm not veggie, but I don't like smoked salmon or prawns, to be honest, bit slimy for me,' Simon replied. 'Don't worry, there's plenty bread and butter.'

'Oh no, no Simon I should've asked, I'm so sorry…' Debs got up flustered, gesturing to the nearest waiting staff. 'What's the veggie option?' she said. 'Please could we have one for the gentleman over there?' She gestured to Simon.

'Surely, madam,' from the waiter, 'mistakes happen all the time.'

'I didn't make a mistake,' said Debs to the waiter's retreating back.

'Honest, Debs, it's no big deal.' Simon was up now standing beside her, his hand on her arm, looking down at her. 'You weren't to know. You've done an amazing job so far getting everyone organised, it's a bit like herding cats, I imagine.' He smiled warmly at her.

'Oh, you've no idea, next time some other bugger can organise this.'

'Oh no, Debs,' came the cries from around the table, 'please no, if we leave it up to someone else, we'll all be queuing up in the hospital canteen for dry turkey and mushy sprouts!'

Debs shrugged her shoulders. 'Just as long as you lot appreciate the bloody effort this takes.' She shimmied back to her seat as the waiter returned with what looked like a plate of mozzarella and tomato.

'Ah,' sighed Simon, 'the good old veggie standby, always a favourite.' He sat back down again and winked at Pen.

'Somebody saying grace?'

'Grace!' the table shouted, the traditional cry bringing everyone back together again as they picked up their cutlery and began to eat.

Chapter Forty-Three

Mirry groaned as she leaned forward on the toilet, surrounded by the noise of drunk women, cackling, laughing, swearing, and snorting.

'Women, worst drunks ever,' thought Mirry, her head spinning as she sat up. 'Bloody hell, water for me for the rest of the night.'

'Anyone got any bog roll?' came a voice from the cubicle next door. 'Dinae want to drip dry on my good frock.'

'Nothing worse,' said Mirry, pulling a line of paper from her own dispenser and passing it under the cubicle wall. 'Can you reach without dripping?'

'Oh, cheers, love, that's brilliant!' The line of paper was swiped and disappeared.

Mirry took her own clump, wiped, stood up, pulled up her tights, and smoothed out any wrinkles before pulling the red tube of her dress down. Turning round, she flushed and walked out to the sinks which were commandeered by women in various states of inebriation, some applying more make-up, fixing their hair, a couple in the corner comforting some blonde haired creature whose eyes were puffy with crying, the blackness of her mascara smudged under her eyes making her look like an albino panda, if there was such a thing, thought Mirry.

She squeezed her way between the preening women to the basin, running the water, wetting her hands, and applying soap before lathering, subconsciously counting.

'Ha!' said the woman joining her from the previous cubicle. 'You a nurse, babe? Can always tell, good hand-washing technique!'

'Aye,' said Mirry, 'some habits never change.'

'You one of the Edinburgh lot?'

'Yep, that's right, like to get away for our Christmas night out, means we can let our hair down without bumping into anyone. What goes on tour stays on tour and all that.'

'Sure thing, I'm Alice, data processor with the Dundee team.'

'Hay, nice to meet you.'

'Yeah, thanks for the bog roll by the way.'

Mirry laughed, 'always helping a lady in distress!'

'See you've got Simon working with your team now?'

'Yeah, just started in the summer, knows his stuff.'

'Yeah, he's good, actually, he's pretty brilliant,' said Alice as she fixed her lipstick, carefully framing with red pencil before filling in with gloss. 'Just as well, really…' she said, tapering off.

'What do you mean?' Mirry's curiosity sparked.

'Oh nothing, just saw him tonight with your mate in the green dress out by the bar; she looks pretty hammered. Might be worth keeping an eye on her, Simon can be a bit weird at times.'

'Weird in what way?' Mirry said, trying not to sound over-interested, carefully reapplying her own red gloss, rubbing her lips together before pouting in the mirror.

'Think he's into some kinky stuff. Each to their own as far as I'm concerned, but things got a bit out of hand up our way, which I think is one of the reasons he left Dundee. Nothing bad really, just rumours. You know what gossip is like.'

'Don't I just. People like nothing more than a bit of dirt on you, been there, bought the teacup!'

'Ha! Good expression!'

'Well he seems to have settled in. The team like him, even if he's a bit controlling at times, but yeah, I'll keep an eye on Debs. She's never been that great with booze… or men for that matter.'

'Enjoy the rest of your night, maybe see you at breakfast.'

'You too, good to meet you.'

Alice did a final take in the mirror, pouted at her reflection, grinned at Mirry, and then headed out the door.

Mirry ran her fingers through her hair and pushed it off her face, checked her teeth for lipstick, then followed Alice back out to the party.

As she headed to the ballroom, she glanced into the bar area. There were men in various stages of dishevelment propped up at the bar, with raucous laughter coming from a group she didn't recognise. Precariously perched on a corner stool, Mirry recognised the back of Debs leaning on Simon. Her beautiful emerald green dress now ruched up under one thigh, exposing a small but very obvious ladder in her black tights, the pale cream stripe of flesh showing through like a scar. Simon was supporting her with both hands round her waist leaning down, his face close to her ear. Debs threw her head back in laughter. She then leant forward, putting her forehead heavily on his chest. Simon looked over Debs' dark head straight at Mirry, cool and intense. She nodded and smiled, cursing herself as she realised Simon was making a play for Debs. The green fingers of jealousy slowly coiled around her throat, her disappointment taking her by surprise. What was it about that man, she thought, like some kind of itch you just can't scratch. Not for you, girl, forget it; he's frying other fish tonight.

She continued on to the ballroom and pushed open the swing doors just as she heard the first bars of 'Sisters' and Pen yelling, 'Get your toosh over here and dance with me, Mirry!'

Party time - take two.

Chapter Forty-Four

It was the sound of Pen's alarm that woke her in the morning. The beeping was accompanied by swearing from Pen as she fumbled for her phone, cursing as her mobile fell to the floor still beeping.

'Fucking thing, bloody noisy fucking thing, shut the fuck up.' Finally finding the off button, Pen fell back on to her pillows, exhaling loudly.

'Oh God, I feel like shite,' Pen moaned. 'Who put aniseed in my mouth?'

'Think that was your brilliant idea just before bedtime,' said Mirry, 'flaming bleeding sambucas, your party piece.'

'Oh, listen to you, Mrs. Bleeding High and Mighty, no, I'll just have a cleansing ale.' Pen did a fabulous imitation of Mirry, taking the piss mercilessly.

'At least I managed to keep mine down,' laughed Mirry, 'and a thank you would be nice, I just love holding your hair back whilst you spew.'

'God, I'm too old for this nonsense. Make us a cup of tea, babe, will you?'

Mirry threw the duvet back, the starch in the covers barely changed because she had slept so soundly. She padded over to the tray and took the kettle into the bathroom to fill up.

'Good night though, Pen, you must admit, that lot from Dundee are a real hoot.'

'Yeah, so they were. Did Simon not use to work with them? He didn't seem to chat to them much.'

'Think he was too interested in getting his hands on our Debs, do you not? Did you see them snogging at the bar? They weren't there when we went to bed, hope Debs is okay.'

'Do I detect a wee bit of the green monster there, babe?' Pen as always astute even with a hangover.

'Ah, shut it, you, it's okay to look…'

'Just don't touch,' laughed Pen in answer.

'Just don't touch!' they choroused together.

'Hurry up with that tea, won't you, something has definitely died in my mouth and it needs flushed out.'

Mirry quickly made tea for them both, pressing as much flavour out of the cheap hotel tea bags that she could. She handed Pen a cup followed by a glass of water and two paracetamol.

'Did I ever tell you I love you?' Pen said, pushing herself up in bed before taking the glass and tablets, which she quickly swallowed.

'Cupboard love I think that is,' laughed Mirry. 'Get that down you whilst I go for a shower, then we can raid the breakfast buffet - I need to eat something!'

Once they had both showered and dressed, they made their way down to the restaurant, following the smell of bacon and toast, greeting people along the way. Colin and Liz were seated by the window, sharing a joke. Mirry looked around for Debs, but couldn't see her anywhere, couldn't see Simon either.

She pulled a chair up beside Colin who was busy buttering toast in anticipation of attacking the mound of fried food on his plate.

'You always love a full Scottish, don't you, Colin?' Mirry laughed as she watched him empty sauce onto his plate.

'Only reason I come to these dos, Mirry, you know that. Not a social animal, me.'

'Not like Simon,' grinned Liz, 'I don't think Debs made it back to her room last night, and I don't see them down for breakfast yet.'

'Did you guys not share then, Colin?' asked Pen.

'Nah, too old for bunking up now,' said Colin. 'Prefer a room to myself - that way I can snore to my heart's content.'

'Oh, I love a new romance,' said Liz. 'Last I saw was Simon propping Debs up in the lift at midnight.'

'Enough of that, Liz, remember, what goes on tour, stays on tour!'

Mirry poured coffee into her cup, remembering the times when it would have been her that people would be gossiping about after a night out. Times had so changed, she thought. Now she had John to think about, a more settled life.

'Penny for them?' said Simon, sliding into the empty chair beside her.

Mirry jumped, startled by his arrival and conscious of his fresh smell amongst the breakfast odours.

'Oh, morning Simon, how you doing? Looking better than the rest of us that's for sure.'

'Mind that wouldn't take much,' giggled Pen, returning to her seat with a full plate of fried food, balancing a mug of coffee and orange juice.

'Oh, Pen, you are a monster,' said Mirry, her stomach churning with the post-party nausea. 'How can you?'

'How many times do I have to tell you, Mirry, after all these years? Gotta get some carbs into you, sort the hangover no problem. Just glad you're driving is all I can say.'

'Yeah, well, that ain't going to happen 'til after eleven at the earliest.'

Mirry got up and walked over to the heavily laden breakfast table. She really couldn't face anything, but she knew she'd feel better if she got some food down her. She picked up a warm plate and joined the queue of last night's revellers. She listened to their banter, the relentless teasing of one young lad who was turning an unusual green colour. They were merciless, and Mirry began to feel a little sorry for him, the rites of passage to adulthood.

She could sense someone behind her and turned round to be caught by Simon's intense, blue gaze.

'You don't look that bad, Mirry.' He smiled, reaching behind her, his arm brushing against her lower back. 'What time did you and Pen get to bed?'

'Oh God, that woman is going to be the death of me one of these days. She had us doing sambuca shots at two am with your old team from Dundee, then I spent the next hour holding her hair back as she puked.'

'Nice,' said Simon with a note of condescension that irked Mirry a little.

'Debs okay this morning?' Mirry asked, regretting it immediately as she dropped her eyes from the intensity of his and reached for the spoon to ladle scrambled eggs on her plate.

'Far as I know,' he said, shaking his head when she offered to spoon some eggs on his plate. 'She was a bit wasted so I dropped her off in her room. Probably still sleeping.'

'Hmm,' said Mirry, 'never seen Debs that bad before. She usually stops when she gets squiffy.' Mirry smiled to herself, remembering a few nights out with Debs when she first joined the team. Debs' posh public school accent. 'No more for me, darling, I'm nice and squiffy!'

'Known Debs long then,' said Simon, 'you're quite close, aren't you?' Casual conversation but Mirry could sense something from his question.

'Yeah, she's a good girl - doing the job we do, you get to know somebody pretty well. She gets pelters for being the posh one of the team, but she always has your back. I've total trust in our Posh Spice.'

'Which one are you then Mirry… let me guess, I'd have you down as Sporty having seen the state of your trainers.'

'You got it and Pen,' Mirry nodded over to their breakfast table where there was loud raucous laughter coming from them all, watching Pen pulling a face of disparagement which she suspected was meant to be an imitation of Mirry last night chastising her for being so drunk, 'our Pen is total Scary Spice.'

'Yeah, that wouldn't be hard to work out,' said Simon, smiling.

'I might just pop up to Debs' room and check she's okay,' said Mirry, adding a couple of bits of toast to her plate. 'Would you take that to the table for me, Simon? I'll be quick!'

'Wouldn't hear of it. You have your breakfast, Mirry, I'll nip up and check, I know which room she's in. Could you just grab me a yogurt and a bowl of that stewed fruit stuff, don't really fancy the full fry up.'

'Always the gentleman then, Simon,' Mirry said teasingly. 'Revisiting the scene of the crime?'

Simon's smile fell quickly from his eyes but remained on his mouth, fleetingly but noticeable enough for Mirry.

'Can't think what you mean, Mirry,' he whispered conspiratorially as he handed her a bowl. 'Not too heavy on the prunes, I'm pretty regular already.'

Simon smiled again and winked as he turned and headed out the restaurant, waving a greeting at Helen as they passed at the entrance. Helen joined Mirry in the queue as Mirry was slopping yogurt on a bowl of fruit.

'Not like you to have fruit, Mirry... you watching your weight?'

'No,' Mirry replied, slightly irritated at Helen's comment and assumption, 'they're for Simon.'

'Oh, so he's got you running after him as well as everyone else,' said Helen, flicking her hair over her shoulder as she reached for a plate and began helping herself to eggs and toast.

'What's that supposed to mean?' said Mirry, her irritation obvious.

'Oh forget it, Mirry, just something about that man, he has all you young women swooning after him like he's bloody Prince Charming. He's not fooling me though, it's an act, a bloody good one, I'll give him that, but if what you have is of no benefit or use to Simon, the chivalry and charm very quickly disappears.'

Mirry wondered where this vitriol had come from; Helen might be a pain in the ass at times, but she was very seldom bitchy. She knew that there had been a few management meetings that Helen had come back from in a temper but Mirry didn't know why.

'Yeah, well, I said I'd get him something whilst he was away checking on Debs,' Mirry said.

'Debs not down yet then?' Helen raised an eyebrow in interest. 'Not like her.'

'Girl's allowed a long lie, Helen, she was partying hard last night.'

'Well, good luck to her if she was partying hard with Simon, she'll need a blow torch to warm him up.'

'Not like you to be so negative about one of the team, Helen.' Mirry couldn't help herself, her curiosity sparked by Helen's out of character behaviour.

'He ain't no team player, Mirry, have no doubts about that.' Helen looked over at the rest of the group sitting at the breakfast table. 'Just be warned, Mirry, he is not all that he seems.' She picked up some butter and jam and made her way over to the team, greeting them warmly and squeezing in beside Pen who was noisily insisting that everyone move round for 'the boss'.

Mirry shook her head, thinking how glad she was not to be in management. She really did hope that Debs had got it on with Simon now just to piss Helen off. She weaved her way back to the table, balancing Simon's bowl of fruit and yogurt with her eggs and toast.

Sitting back down, she put the bowl in the empty space beside her and began her breakfast. Now that she was a bit more awake, she was ravenous. The conversation bubbled around her as she concentrated on buttering her toast and stirring sugar into her coffee.

Taking a sip, she grimaced.

'What's up, babe?' asked Pen.

'Tastes like old wood chipping,' Mirry said, adding more milk to her cup.

'Oh hotel breakfast coffee, cannae beat it. Get it down you, it's wet and got caffeine in it, what more can you ask for after last night?'

Mirry snorted and fell back into the teasing and chat of the night before.

Mirry quickly finished her breakfast as everyone chatted around her. She looked at Simon's empty place and uneaten yogurt.

'Hey, I'd better go and take this up to Debs' room for Simon, otherwise it'll get thrown out.'

'Not sure that's such a great idea,' whispered Pen, looking at Mirry from under her raised eyebrows.

'Why not?' Mirry said but instantly regretted it, realising why Simon had not come back to the table.

'Might be best to let sleeping dogs lie,' Pen said, conspiratorially grinning all over her face. 'Looks like Debs has got the man of the match, shall we say?'

Helen's words stuck with Mirry when Simon finally returned to the table, accepting his fruit and yogurt with a wink and a smile.

'Debs okay?' asked Mirry, innocently concentrating on buttering another piece of toast, not looking at Simon.

'Bit rough, she says she's going to miss breakfast and will catch us on Monday. Anyway, what's everyone else got planned for the weekend? Deep joy for me, I've to take my mum Christmas shopping.'

'Oh, good luck with that, Simon, the shops are mental,' Liz said, having already told everyone she had finished hers in October.

After breakfast the team dispersed from the restaurant with various shouts of 'see you Monday,' and 'enjoy what's left of the weekend.'

Mirry and Pen got in the lift together, Pen's incessant chatter about last night starting to get on her nerves.

'Can you remember what room Debs is in, Pen?' Mirry said. 'I just want to pop in to see if she wants anything or a lift back home.'

'She's second floor, 206, I think. I'll pack up our stuff then whilst you do that, you got the key?'

Mirry hit the two buttons in the lift before rummaging in her handbag and handing over the key. The doors closed, and Mirry caught sight of herself in the mirror. 'Okay,' she thought to herself, 'I've looked a lot worse.' Christmas was coming, perhaps next year she would look very different, maybe have a bump and a baby glow. She smiled at the thought of it and was surprised by the feeling of warmth she felt.

The lift stopped at floor two, and Mirry stepped out into the bustle of the hotel corridor. The housekeeping staff were already hard at work cleaning rooms, a linen buggy and a huge cart partly blocking the ease of access to the rooms.

She made her way down the corridor, taking in the uniformity and blandness of the hotel. Finding room 206, she knocked tentatively at the door.

'Debs?' she said. 'It's just Mirry.'

There was silence, so she knocked harder. 'Debs,' she said, raising her voice, 'you all right, lovey?'

'Think she's gone, love.' This from one of the housekeeping staff as she came out of the opposite room. 'She left about 5 minutes ago with some tall bloke. She didn't look that clever, to be honest, but he seemed to have a good hold of her.'

'Oh, cheers,' said Mirry, turning and heading back to the lift. It wasn't like Debs not to have let them know she'd left. Force of habit from the team to let someone know your whereabouts. Mirry took out her mobile and texted her.

'Sorry to have missed you this morning babe, hope all good xxx'

Mirry got back to her room and knocked for Pen to let her in.

'How's she doing then?' said Pen, making Mirry internally squirm as she watched Pen stuff her red dress into a bag, pushing it down.

'She's gone,' said Mirry absently, 'looks like she left with Simon.'

'Oooh well, then she'll have a tale to tell on Monday, looking forward to that one.' Pen laughed. 'Posh takes one for the team!'

'That's not even funny, Pen, and stop stuffing everything in my bag like that, you dozy mare, that dress cost an arm and a leg!'

'I just want to get out of here,' said Pen, grabbing her jacket out of the wardrobe. 'I've things to do and people to meet today and can't hang around here babysitting Debs. Just glad she's let her hair down for once.'

'Yeah, you're right, let's get going, I've loads to do this weekend too. Let's get on with the day. Should be safe to drive by now.'

Pen snorted. 'Yeah, I think so, babe. You forgetting you were sick too, or had that just slipped your mind when you were slagging me off?'

Mirry laughed and gently pushed Pen towards the door. 'What goes on tour remember?'

'Not another word,' joked Pen, placing her finger on her lips, 'these babies are sealed.'

They both did a final sweep of the room before going out the door and closing it behind them. No more thought given to Debs.

By the time Mirry had driven back to Edinburgh, cursing the December weekend shopping traffic and dropping Pen off on the other side of town, her hangover was well and truly established. Her head was thick and thumping. Added to that, the periodic waves of intense nausea were making her groan. She managed to park near the flat and slowly made her way up the stairs, one step at a time, head down, bag heavy on her back. Mirry noticed that the air in the close was cold, the bannister icy under her hand, and her breath coming in clouds of mist. It reminded her of when she was a child, desperate to be an adult, and would pretend with her sister that they were smoking, sitting in the garden sharing a straw between them. The memory made her smile and instantly reminded her that she hadn't talked to Celia in an age. Both so caught up in their own busy lives.

Opening the door to the flat, the warmth of the hall gusted out to welcome her and she quickly came in, closing the door behind her. Hanging up her coat, she became aware of the smell of spices, warm and comforting as the aroma lingered and tantalisingly led her down the hall. Coming into the kitchen, the scene that met her filled her with pleasure. John was busy at the hob frying up onions into a thick unctuous paste which she immediately recognised as the beginnings of her favourite curry. He had his back to her and she could see him swaying from side to side to an unknown rhythm that was coming from the headphones clamped tightly to either side of his head.

'John,' she called, delighted at the scene of domesticity, the kitchen clear for once, with just the peelings of onions, garlic, and ginger piled neatly next to the chopping board.

'John,' she called again, waving her hands to attract his attention. Even this didn't work and it wasn't until she stood beside him with an inane grin on her face that his concentration was broken.

'Jesus, Mirry, I didn't hear you coming in,' he smiled down at her, removing his headphones and turning the heat down under the pan. 'How you doing?'

'Feel like total crap! You know what Christmas nights out are like, too much rich food and drink.' She took the wooden spoon that he had been using out of his hand and stirred the onions around, breathing in their strong aroma and realising her belly had rumbled, a good sign.

'Yeah, well, I am the best boyfriend in the world because I knew you would feel like shite so I'm making you your favourite rogan josh with dahl and naan, few beers in the fridge, clean sheets on the bed, and the sitting room is all ready for you to crash. And I've taken the rest of the weekend off so…' He pulled her into his chest, squeezing her so tight she squealed in delight.

'Oh my God, John you are the bestest boyfriend ever and I love you with all my heart… What time's tea?' Mirry grinned up at him, stroking the side of his face and kissing his cheek.

'Shall we say about six-thirty? Once I get this on, I've a few emails to send then the night is all ours. Go and get into your jammies and chill out.'

Mirry didn't need to be told twice. She left John to his cooking and headed into their bedroom, picking up her overnight bag and digging out her mobile before collapsing on the bed.

She scrolled through her messages, laughing at Pen who had sent nothing but a screenful of green faced emojis and the words 'when will we ever learn?' The last text was from Debs: it was short, saying, 'I'm okay, feeling foolish, don't know what happened last night but head is swimming still. Simon got me home, he's still here btw, so all good xxx'. Mirry felt a twang of something which she realised was disappointment. So Simon had made his move good and proper then, he'd set his sights on Debs. It dawned on Mirry that she had missed all the signs of Debs's attraction to him. Looking back, she realised that there had been a couple of occasions where Debs had been in his office, her dark head and his light head close together as they had discussed something on the computer screens in front of them.

What an idiot, she thought to herself, smiling ruefully - that puts an end to that dalliance. She realised there and then that this was actually what she had needed to rid herself of her obsession with Simon. He was obviously no longer interested in her, and all Mirry could think was fair play to them both. She put the phone down beside her and stretched luxuriously on the newly made bed. What did she need him for anyway? Time to concentrate fully on the bestest man in the world making her her favourite curry. She knew with delight that it wasn't just going to be curry on the menu tonight.

Chapter Forty-Five

The rest of the weekend was uneventful. Sunday was spent with them both lazing in bed, luxuriating in their rare time off together. For once they felt part of the human race. They walked down to Stockbridge, had a leisurely brunch, and headed to the Botanics, taking in the palm house and breathing in the peace and tranquillity of the gardens. Even in December it was a beautiful place. It was cold and crisp, the low winter light casting an almost magical glow over the Edinburgh skyline. They were both quiet but comfortable in their joint silence. By the time they got back to the flat, the light was changing once again and the winter darkness had replaced the weak brightness of the afternoon. John closed the curtains in the bay window of their sitting room, put on the lamps, and lit the candles. Mirry made a pot of soup and they sat together sharing cheese, bread, and a bottle of wine. 'Life is good,' Mirry thought.

Her hangover was completely gone by the time she was back in the office on Monday. So much so that she had decided to run to work, leaving the flat early whilst it was still dark. John had teased her that she didn't have to feel guilty for being such a slob over the weekend. By the time she was running beside the Meadows, she was in her stride, her breath coming easier, allowing her mind to wander with the rhythm of her steps. She wondered what kind of weekend Cath had had. Mirry hoped there was nothing for her to pick up, as she was on call for the rest of the day and night.

The traffic up to Little France was a mixture of buses, taxis, cars, and bicycles. It was always busy this time of day, so many people going to work at the same time, the hospital disgorging its tired night duty workers to be replaced by the day shifts. The car park attendants trying to maintain some semblance of order in the nightmare that is hospital parking. Mirry slowed her pace as she ran past the university buildings and the Anne Rowling Clinic. By the time she got into the hospital itself, she was cooling down and starting to sweat. She headed over to the changing rooms for a quick shower before grabbing a coffee and heading up to the office.

Mirry could see the lights were already on as she made her way along the corridor. The Co-ordinators room was empty but Helen and Simon were sitting in his office in front of his PC. There was obviously something interesting being discussed as they both looked very serious. Helen was pointing at the screen and glaring at Simon. Mirry knocked before putting her head round the door.

'Morning Team,' she said in the bright voice which Pen often said was the most annoying thing about her.

'Oh, you're here, Mirry,' Helen said, 'just as well, looks like the proverbial is about to hit the fan. Cath got taken in to Simpson's last night, she might be losing the baby, she's had some heavy bleeding and Debs is off sick… I wonder why?' She looked pointedly at Simon.

'Oh no,' Mirry said, 'did you have to take over last night then, Helen?'

'Yeah, of course. It was all quiet, thankfully. You're on today and tomorrow by the looks of things, but Simon and I are trying to work out a roster. I, of course, could step in again, but as you can imagine…' Helen left it hanging. They both knew what that meant - their roster was tight at the best of times with very little leeway for sickness. It was almost impossible to get cover from the nurse bank as no one else had the skills and knowledge that the coordinators had. To have two off sick was going to push the donor programme to the limits and it was possible they may have to turn potential donors down.

'I think Liz is ready to go solo, Helen, she's been out about four times now, and all her objectives have been signed. She just needs you to finalise.'

'I'm well aware of that, thank you, Mirry,' Helen said, not lifting her eyes from the computer screen. 'Not much help at the moment though, as she's on holiday for the next two weeks.'

'Have you let the retrieval team know yet?'

'Not yet,' sighed Helen, 'I'm not going to say anything until I've worked out a solution. We may have to ask Glasgow and Dundee to help out. Once Simon and I have seen where our gaps are, I'll give them a call. There isn't anything to hand over from the weekend, fortunately, so if you don't mind, Mirry…?' Helen gestured with her eyebrows and Mirry felt herself being dismissed.

She went back to her desk with a multitude of thoughts going through her head. Her immediate one was for Cath;

she knew how much this baby meant and Cath had been visibly relaxing as the weeks of her pregnancy had passed without upset. Now the threat of losing her baby at six months would be terrifying. It was also very unlike Debs to be off sick. She never took time off, it must be something serious.

The sound of the office door being flung open brought Mirry quickly back from her thoughts. Pen came in backwards, her arms full of case notes, her brow creased in concentration.

'Morning Mirr,' she said, 's'pose you've heard the shit has hit the fan then?' Pen nodded her head to Simon's office. 'Poor Cath.'

'Oh, Pen, it's such a worry,' said Mirry, 'you know how much that baby is wanted.'

'It's crap, I know,' Pen shook her head, putting the case notes down on Cath's empty desk. 'Think we should go and see her at lunchtime, Helen says she's probably going to be in for a few days.'

'Yeah, good idea, maybe take her something?'

'Like what? A get well card ain't going to do it, is it, and flowers are out, not allowed anymore.'

'I think she would just be pleased to see us.'

'Yeah, you're right,' answered Pen, 'and what's up with Debs? She's never off… must have been some weekend.' Pen had her back to Simon's office but her expression said it all as she indicated with her eyebrows.

'Yeah, I'll give her a call once Helen has gone. In the meantime, let's just get our heads down.'

The morning passed in a flurry of activity with various emails flying backwards and forwards as Helen tried to cover the service. By lunchtime, it looked like the rota was set for the next week and there was an almost tangible sigh of relief in the final email that had the new rota attached. Dundee were happy to cover Cath and Debs' on-call, and it also meant that Helen didn't have to join the rota again.

At lunchtime, Pen and Mirry made their way over to Simpson's to visit Cath, picking up some sandwiches and fruit on their way past the ever-busy Marks & Spencer's outlet. The hospital foyer was bustling with a vast assortment of people, from theatre staff in their white coats over their scrubs, to patients in pyjamas, some being wheeled outside for a cigarette with their drips on poles beside them despite the large no smoking signs littering the entrance. There was an elderly couple looking lost and confused in the melee of the human traffic. Mirry couldn't help but ask them if she could help. It was the usual problem of trying to find the right outpatient department in the confusing layout of the ground floor corridor and the anxiety of being late for their appointment. Mirry gave them directions and reassured them not to worry about being late, saying that clinics were notoriously behind in appointment times.

'You're such an angel,' Pen joked as they set off at a brisk pace down the main foyer.

'Have you spoken to Debs yet?' asked Mirry, taking one of the bags that Pen was carrying.

'No, but I did speak with the Iceman,' Pen said, looking down at Mirry with a grin.

'You never did, you cheeky mare!'

'Well, if anyone would know what was wrong with Debs, he would, don't you think? Especially after the weekend they must have had!'

'Sometimes, Pen, you astound me,' Mirry laughed. 'So, what did he say?'

'Something about her having a sore throat,' Pen giggled, making ridiculous hand gestures indicating fellatio. 'Hope she hasn't forgotten how to do it. We know it's been a while for our Debs!'

'Pen, stop it, someone will see,' Mirry retorted. 'It's just not like Debs to be off, I'll give her a call later. She'll want to know how Cath is anyway, I'm sure.'

'Yeah, I know, and get the goss on you know who.'

'Not interested in that side of things, Pen,' Mirry said as they both side-stepped a herd of medical students coming out of a lecture, their own self-importance making them immune to everyone else in the corridor.

'God, they are so rude!' snorted Pen, glaring at the passing students, none of whom were paying a blind bit of notice to the tall, elegant blond and her small companion.

'You sure you don't want to find out?' Pen asked again. 'I know full well you and Simon have been dancing round each other for a few months. If it wasn't for John, you would have shagged him by now, Mirry!'

'Pen, enough, will you?' Mirry laughed, shoving her hard with her shoulder. 'He got under my skin for a while. I suppose I could have taken it further, but like you said, John and me are solid now, wouldn't risk that for something that

I think would just be a couple of fuck dates. Simon doesn't strike me as being the romantic relationship kind of guy.'

'Yeah, you're right there, just as long as he's good to Debs. Who knows? She might show him the way,' Pen said. They continued walking until they got to the maternity part of the hospital. Here the atmosphere was very different to the main concourse. It was still busy, but there was an atmosphere of hopeful expectation. They stopped outside the entrance to the ward that Cath was in. 'You ready for this?'

'Yeah,' said Mirry, the seriousness of what they were about to witness bringing them back to reality, all joking ceased as they made their way in.

They didn't stay long with Cath. There wasn't much they could say and, though she looked relieved to see them, she was still so very pale. She had had some serious bleeding and cramping, but so far, the baby's heartbeat was strong, and the bleeding had stopped. It was a relief when Cath's mum arrived and they could make their excuses to leave. They both gave Cath a hug with reassurances not to worry about work and that they would pop in later.

Coming back through the foyer, they were quiet, caught up in their own thoughts. Seeing Cath and the other pregnant women in the antenatal ward had once again made Mirry wonder if she and John were ever going to succeed in getting pregnant. They hadn't been using contraception for months now, and yet still nothing, no success. The sound and vibration of the pager on her waistband brought Mirry back to reality. She recognised the number immediately as being St. John's ICU, and her stomach did its usual flip.

'Better get this,' Mirry said, and they both quickened their pace back to the office.

Chapter Forty-Six

John was late going into the office on Monday morning. He'd decided to walk so that he could have some headspace to think about the best way forward, hoping for inspiration along the way. Walking past the local primary school, he smiled at the children playing frenetic games in the playground whilst harassed parents made late drop-offs. The school day hadn't started yet, but John could see through the illuminated windows the handmade Christmas decorations and angel mobiles floating down from the ceilings. He could imagine the excitement of the children in their anticipation of what the winter holidays would bring. Thinking of his own family, he felt a little pang of guilt for the decision they had made about going away for Christmas. They would see them in the New Year, and nobody seemed that bothered when he'd called his parents. His brother and his children would be with them on the day itself, and he knew it was their grandchildren that brought his mum and dad the most pleasure. Maybe next year. His thoughts strayed back to work and a sadness came over him as he realised how many families would not be celebrating Christmas this year because of one man.

Arriving in the office, his body was warm from the walk, and he was relieved to take his coat off. Hanging it up, he looked out at the whiteboards and his team. Fee was on the phone and concentrating on something on her PC screen. There were a few paltry decorations hanging with a desultory nod to the festive season. Considering what was on the whiteboard, that was hardly surprising. It seemed inappropriate somehow, especially now Jack's picture had joined the others, his broad smile shining out, his youth so apparent dressed in his school uniform.

John made a mental note to remember to get in touch with Jack's FLO to see how they were bearing up. Fee glanced into his office when she came off the phone, and he beckoned her to join him.

'Morning boss,' she said, coming straight in, 'how's you?'

'Okay,' John answered, 'decided to walk to work this morning to get some headspace. Anything new over the weekend?'

'Absolutely zilch.' Fee looked out at the whiteboard. 'What oh what are we missing?'

'When were we last in touch with Newcastle? Anything from them?'

'Not so far, but might be worth a call to Jason?'

'Yeah, I'll get on to that this morning.' John rubbed his face in frustration. 'What about you?'

'I've been doing my favourite CCTV watch, but there's not much cover where Jack lived.'

'Team meeting at two then for a catch up?'

'Yeah, I'll let everyone know,' Fee said, standing up. 'I'll leave you to it.'

'Cheers, Fee,' John said, switching on his PC, his screen immediately illuminating, asking for his password. His day was about to start.

At eleven, John went through to the staff kitchen to grab himself a coffee. Coming back into the main office, he had a bit of banter over taking the last dregs when the main door opened and Charlie came in. John felt a thud of discomfort in his belly. Charlie's face was serious; she didn't greet the team, just said 'Office' tersely to John as she made her way to his room. He had very little choice other than to follow. And that was when the shit hit the fan. He was being taken off the case - not enough progress was being made, the news of Jack's death was about to hit the press, and the powers that be wanted things a bit more under their control. Not that he was doing a bad job, Charlie reassured him, it was just semantics, really. That and the fact that Jack's family were raging. They had plans to go public with what had happened to them, including the 'lying' detective who had come to visit and withheld the truth about their son's death.

John left the office devastated. Charlie had advised him to take some annual leave and hook it on to Christmas so all in all he would be out of the office for about three weeks. In normal times, he would have been delighted to have so much time off, but this was not through choice. He felt frustrated and angry that he was being sidelined but, above all else, he felt bereft. The case had taken over his life in recent weeks. There was a part of him that knew Charlie was right. The decision had been taken to run another reconstruction to include Jack's parents who had insisted that more publicity was needed. It had to be somebody more senior than him who would be seen to be in charge. She had reassured him that, when he came back from leave, the case would be shared. That didn't help.

He regretted having walked to work now, he just wanted to get home. Coming out of the office, the cold afternoon air hit him as he wrapped his scarf around his neck and quickened his pace. He avoided some drunk students who were singing 'Flower of Scotland' at the top of their voices. John would have thought a Christmas song more appropriate given the time of year. He smiled to himself, what was he now? The carol police?

'Bugger it,' he thought, 'no point rolling in self pity, that isn't going to help anyone.' He pulled his mobile out of his pocket and hit Mirry's number, she would help lift his mood. The ringing was answered by her recorded message, and he couldn't help but feel disappointed. Quickening his pace, he decided to head down to Princes Street and the Christmas market to take his mind off things. A bit of glühwein and a ridiculously priced hot dog would do his mood the power of good.

The market was bright with multicoloured lights and heady with the smell of cinnamon, roasted meat, and candy floss. The yells from the chairoplane swirling above added to the festival atmosphere. John lost himself in the crowds, meandering round the stalls, dumbfounded at the price of some of the absolute tat that was for sale. He stopped at one of the glühwein vendors and ordered a large glass, which he took over to an upstanding barrel being used as a table. Taking a large gulp of the warm, heady drink, he shut his eyes and breathed deeply. Opening them, he looked out across the crowds, his mood lightening a little. His gaze was caught by a tall recognisable form sitting on the benches outside the burger stall. It was Simon. John picked up his drink and wandered over.

'Hey Simon, fancy seeing you here.'

Upon hearing his name Simon looked up and seeing it was John, instantly got to his feet.

'Hey John, nice to see you, didn't think this would be your kind of thing,' Simon said, 'and drinking on duty, I see.' Simon grinned, nodding at the steaming cup in John's hand.

'Yeah, well, not on duty today,' John sighed. 'In fact, not on for a few weeks. What you doing here anyway?'

'Just here with my mum, she's up visiting for a few days and she fancied the market. I've told her everything is a rip off, but she's not having it,' Simon said. 'Oh, here she comes now.'

John turned to follow Simon's gaze and saw an older-looking woman wrapped in a thick burgundy coat coming towards them, the bag at her side bulging awkwardly as it banged against her legs.

'Simon, go and grab that,' the woman said, passing the bag to him, 'and who is this good looking gentleman, pray tell?'

'This is John,' Simon said, taking the bag from his mother's outstretched hand and tucking it under the table. 'He's the partner of one of the co-ordinators I work with. John, this is my mum, Karen.'

'Nice to meet you, Karen,' John said, stretching out his hand, 'looks like you've been busy.'

'Nice to meet you too, John. I know I've probably been ripped off, but I can't resist a Christmas market, isn't that right, Simon?'

'That's right, Mum.' Simon sighed and rolled his eyes.

'Why don't you join us, John, finish your drink?' Karen said. 'Simon, go and get me one of those glühwein things, get me in the spirit.'

'Not sure that's such a good idea, Mum,' Simon said quietly, 'not great with your medication.'

'Oh, one won't hurt, don't be such a party pooper,' Karen said. 'He's such a worrier, my boy.' Though she'd stroked Simon's face as she spoke, her tone had been firm. 'Go and get me that drink now whilst I keep John company.'

Simon reluctantly made his way to the bar whilst Karen sat down on the wooden bench at the table and patted the seat beside her.

'Do anything for me, my boy,' Karen said, watching Simon, 'absolutely anything. Now then, John, which co-ordinator is yours? Simon has told me all about his team.'

'Mirry is my better half,' John said, joining Karen, squeezing his legs uncomfortably under the table.

'Ah, yes, Mirry, I think she's one of his favourites. They do an amazing job, don't they?' Karen said, taking her gloves off and rubbing her hands together. John noticed the burgundy polish on her nails matched the colour of her coat.

'Yeah, Mirry works really hard. More of a mission for her rather than a job at times.'

'And what do you do then?' Karen asked slightly flirtatiously. 'Let me guess, with your build I bet you're probably a PE teacher or personal trainer.'

'Ha!' John guffawed. 'No, I'm in the police for my sins.'

'Really?' Karen said, raising her heavily pencilled eyebrows. 'Would never have had you down as that. What department?'

'I'm with the Serious Crime Unit,' John said, 'or I was until recently.'

Simon returned to the table with three steaming mugs of glühwein and a couple of brandies. He gave Karen one of the mugs and passed the brandy to John whilst he picked up the other.

'Cheers,' Simon said, knocking back the glass.

John thought for a moment and then followed Simon's lead. The harsh burning at the back of his throat turned warm and comforting.

'John was just telling me he works for the Serious Crime Unit, Simon, did you know that?'

'Yeah, I did, think he's been working on that case that was in the news recently, Mum.'

'Oh, that one,' Karen said, 'how very interesting. Doesn't sound like you're getting anywhere though.'

'No, tricky case,' John said, reluctant to speak about it. 'I've been taken off it for a few weeks anyway.'

Simon's interest was immediately piqued. 'Really, mate, that's a shame, last time we spoke you had hoped the TV reconstruction would throw something up.'

'Hmm, can't really say much about it, I'm afraid,' John said. 'Anyway, what are you two up to for the rest of the day?' John was keen to change the subject, didn't want to talk about work.

'Finish my Christmas shopping and then Simon and I are heading out on the town tonight. What about you, quiet night in with Mirry?'

'Think she's on call tonight, isn't she, John?' Simon said. 'In fact, I think she may be out for a donor, one came through just at lunchtime there.'

'Seems you know Mirry's movements better than me, Simon,' John said, laughing, 'I've been trying to get a hold of her, but it keeps going to voicemail. Makes sense if she's with a family.'

'Why don't you come out with us then?' Karen asked, patting John on the arm. 'No point you being all on your own.'

'That's very kind, thank you, Karen, but I need to get home, it's been a tricky day and I just want a quiet night in.' John picked up his now cooled glühwein and swallowed half the mug quickly. Simon lifted his own mug, raised it to John and joined him in downing half too.

'I can't finish that, I'm afraid, Simon,' John laughed, 'one is always enough for me.' He extricated himself awkwardly from under the table. 'Nice to meet you, Karen.' He extended his hand. 'Good luck with your shopping.'

'A pleasure to meet you too, John,' Karen said, taking John's hand in both of hers, 'and good luck with your case, sounds like you may need it.'

John withdrew his hand from Karen's. 'Thanks, Karen.' He looked over at Simon. 'Maybe go for a catch-up pint before Christmas, Simon?'

'Sounds a plan,' Simon grinned, 'I'll give you a call. Regards to Mirry when you see her.'

John made his way slowly through the crowds, the effect of the glühwein and brandy making him feel a little merry, and headed up the steps to Princes Street before turning back to wave to Simon and Karen. They were both watching him, their heads close together, smiling his way. Simon raised his hand and John waved back before he was swallowed in the melee of Christmas shoppers.

Chapter Forty-Seven

Mirry got home in the early hours of the morning. The case had gone very smoothly with no glitches. A full retrieval had gone ahead. The team from Newcastle came for the heart and lungs before Edinburgh retrieved the liver, kidneys, and pancreas. So many lives were going to be changed through the evening's work. Mirry was exhausted but content; she knew she had done a good job and that the donor's family would be relieved that everything had gone so well. She had a quick shower before getting into her pyjamas and carefully climbing in beside John, the heat and familiar smell of him warming and comforting. He stirred when she put her arm around him but didn't wake up. For once, Mirry was asleep within seconds.

John's alarm going off woke them both at seven o'clock.

'Put that bloody thing off,' Mirry mumbled from under the covers. John silenced the alarm and fell back on the bed. After a few minutes, Mirry opened one eye to see John wide awake and staring at the ceiling.

'You okay, babe?' Mirry asked, cuddling up to him.

'Kind of,' John said. 'Bit shit, actually.'

Mirry opened her eyes and looked up at him. 'What's to do?'

'I've been taken off the case,' John said, saying the words outright, making the reality of his situation real.

'Fuck, John,' Mirry said, sitting up, 'what happened?'

'Too much heat being put on Charlie by the looks of things. We're not getting anywhere and now going public about Jack. Maybe just as well, think I made a mess of things with his family.'

'So what happens now,' Mirry said, 'with you, I mean?'

'Apparently I've leave to take, so that's me until the New Year. By that time, hopefully things will have moved on, but I ain't holding my breath.'

'Christ,' Mirry said, taking in what John was saying. 'On a positive note, does that mean we've longer off together at Christmas?'

'Sure does, Mirry, but I'm going to keep in touch with Fee on the QT, I still need to know what's going on for when I get back.'

'Well, in that case you can get me a cup of tea, I don't have to be in at work until after eleven.'

'Fancy taking my mind off things first?' John asked, rolling over and pulling Mirry into his arms.

'Nah, tea first, you horny devil, then we'll see!'

John laughed before kissing the top of her head and climbing out of bed.

'Your wish, as always, is my command, my lady!'

'Sucker,' Mirry said, stretching herself out on the bed starfish-like, 'and pop in some toast whilst you're at it,' she said to his retreating back. Everything has a silver lining - just got to look for it.

Chapter Forty-Eight

Mirry arrived at the hospital just before eleven and, as always, had trouble finding a parking space. It was a cold and damp December morning. She was glad she had her gloves and scarf for the ten minute walk to the main foyer. She nodded acknowledgement to the reception staff who were frantically busy at the front desk. Not a job she envied, having seen them being harangued on many occasions by irate visitors. She grabbed a sandwich and water from the shop and made her way up to the office. Pen was sitting at her desk with her headphones on, and she could see Simon through the snowflake graffiti on his office window.

'Morning Pen,' Mirry said, cheerily coming in. 'Fecking cold out there today!'

'Morning Gorgeous,' Pen said, looking up and taking off her headphones, 'good result yesterday, eh?'

'Yeah, textbook stuff,' Mirry said.

'Good news,' Pen said, 'Cath got out today. She popped in just before heading home - looks great and really relieved. Baby is all good, and the bleeding has stopped.'

'Oh, that's great,' Mirry said, 'what a relief.'

'Yeah, she's coming back next week, can't afford any more sick time apparently.' Pen rolled her eyes at this.

'Means the rota will be okay for Christmas. Have you spoken to Debs yet?'

'Nah,' Mirry said, shrugging off her coat and hanging it up, 'haven't had time, but I'll text her, maybe pop in and see her on my way home tonight.'

'Good plan,' Pen said, 'I'm on tonight, but doubt anything will come through.'

Simon's door opened and he came in with a whiteboard duster in his hand.

'Morning Mirry, nice to see you,' he said, grinning, 'I believe another successful case for you last night? I'll just make amends to the leaderboard, keep things up to date.' He leaned over Debs' desk and changed the numbers next to Mirry's name. 'Top again, Mirry, good job.'

'Thanks, Simon,' Mirry said uncomfortably. 'As I always say, team effort.'

'Hmm,' Simon said, 'speaking of team efforts, did John tell you he met me yesterday at the Christmas market? He was saying he's been taken off his case for a few weeks.'

'Really, Mirr?' Pen asked.

'Yeah, he's gutted, think they're planning some more publicity and there was a bit of disagreement with one of the families,' Mirry answered. 'John said he'd met you with your mum?'

'She's up for a bit of Christmas shopping and a catch-up. I'm not spending Christmas with her this year, so we thought we'd celebrate a bit earlier.'

'How's she keeping?' Mirry asked.

'She's good, thanks, Mirry,' Simon said, 'why you asking?' His tone had changed slightly and his face had become serious.

'Oh, nothing really, just one of the Newcastle co-ordinators had said that they recognised you from their recipient clinic.'

'So much for patient confidentiality,' Simon said, 'nothing is bloody private in this place, is it?'

'Sorry, Simon,' Mirry said, 'I was just asking.'

'Yeah, well, she's doing great. The Newcastle team have looked after her really well, given her her life back. Anyway, stuff to do, catch you later, ladies.'

Simon turned and went back into his office, closing the door behind him. Mirry looked over at Pen.

'Think you and I need to go for a bit of lunch and a chat later, do you not?' Pen said. 'Bit of catching up to do methinks!'

'Oh, Pen, just leave it, nothing more to say about it!'

'Whatever,' Pen said, pulling on her headphones, 'you and your morals, Mirry!'

Mirry grinned and stuck her tongue out before sitting down at her desk and getting the paperwork out from the day before - so much to follow up on and it was only Tuesday.

Later that day, Helen came in to catch up with Mirry and Pen. The stress of covering the rota resolved and a successful donor had made her ebullient. Helen said that, now Cath was coming back, there would be no changes to the Christmas rota and Mirry could still take her annual leave. The thought that her time off might have been cancelled had never entered Mirry's head. As always, Helen was making her feel truculent - who was she to bestow her favours like some over inflated fairy godmother? She wasn't doing her any favours, Mirry was due her holidays.

'Any word from Debs?' Mirry asked. 'I was going to pop in and see her on my way home from work.'

'Yeah, she phoned this morning to check in,' Helen said. 'She thinks she'll be back on Thursday.'

'Is she okay?' Pen asked. 'Not like Debs to be off.'

'Says she's got some bug or other,' Helen said dismissively, 'suppose it's that time of year. Right, better get on, catch you both tomorrow.'

Helen nodded to Simon before looking up at the leaderboard and giving him a thumbs up. She headed out the door, flicking her hair over her shoulder with a final 'have a good day.'

'Why does she always get under my skin?' Mirry said out loud. But Pen hadn't heard her, her earphones were back in and she was concentrating on something on her screen.

Mirry took out her mobile, found Debs' number, and sent her a message saying she would pop by on her way home from work. Her reply took Mirry a little by surprise.

'Be great to see you but Simon's coming round tonight, catch up tomoz.' So things had progressed, Mirry thought to herself. Good on Debs.

'No worries, see you on Thursday, hopefully,' Mirry answered whilst looking through the glass into Simon's office. He was staring at something on one of his screens and the light was illuminating his strong profile. She could see Debs and him together, and it made her smile.

Debs answered with a heart and a thumbs up.

Chapter Forty-Nine

J ohn was at a total loss once Mirry had left for work. He'd been for a run, changed the bed, showered, and now was left staring at the wallpaper opposite the sofa. It would forever remind him of Jenny's sitting room. Maybe Mirry was right, when the baby comes they should move. The flat was pretty much completed now, the bathroom all finished thanks to Pen's brothers, just the spare room needing attention. He should get on with that now he was off, but his motivation for decorating was zero. Instead, he phoned Fee. His call went straight to her voicemail and he stumbled through a message asking her to call him when she was free.

He decided he couldn't sit about doing nothing but think about the case. He fired up his laptop and made himself comfortable on the sofa. Opening up the files that they had been given down in Newcastle was like visiting a familiar friend. It felt like such a long time ago, so much had happened. He wondered how Susie's family were doing now the winter had set in. They were no further forward than they were when Susie was murdered three years ago. Looking at the case again felt like he was seeing it with fresh eyes and his heart lifted a little.

The file with the scene of the crime was the first he opened. Susie's body had been at such an odd angle, stuck under the table, lying on the banquet, it had been difficult for SOCO to get clear photographs. There was a computer-generated image of the layout which made it easier to understand where the table was in relation to the rest of the restaurant, including the kitchen.

Susie must have known her killer, as jasmine tea had been found in her stomach and a teapot with two small china cups had been found washed up in the kitchen. Washed so thoroughly that there were no fingerprints found - unusual, to say the least. The hairs that identified her attacker were found tangled in her earring and on her coat. John thought about this, running through a scenario in his mind. He realised that one of the ways the hairs may have got caught in her earring and on her coat was if the two were in an embrace. If that was so, then Susie must have been having a relationship with someone, as her sister Kay suspected.

He went back to the interviews with Susie's family, friends, and colleagues meticulously. He realised that the question of whether Susie had a boyfriend had only been directed at the family and, of course, her parents were adamant that she hadn't been seeing anyone. Okay, he thought, something to revisit and maybe go back to her friends and colleagues to ask. If Susie was keeping it a secret, he doubted they would know, but it was worth asking if anyone had any suspicions.

After a few hours, John realised that the time had run away from him and the sitting room was now dark with the end of the short winter day. He got up to close the curtains and put the lamps on. He stretched and groaned. His phone rang loudly from the table. Picking it up, he could see it was Fee and immediately answered.

'Hey Fee,' John said, 'how's it going?'

'Hi Boss, just returning your call,' Fee said. 'More importantly, how are you doing?'

'Och, just a bit pissed off,' John answered, flopping on the sofa. 'Anything new today?'

'Nah, just the usual. Charlie has got the team going through everything again, and the plan is to go public at the end of the week.'

'Just in time for Christmas then,' John said.

'Yeah, Charlie and I are heading down to Newcastle tomorrow to catch up with Jason face to face and do a bit of brainstorming.'

'That's what I would do if I was Charlie. Whilst you're there, see if you can get them to reinterview Susie's friends and colleagues again and ask the specific question about whether she was seeing anyone.'

'Okay,' said Fee, 'any particular reason?'

'Just been going through her files this afternoon and forensics showed that she had his hair caught in her earring and on her coat. It just reminded me of when I hug Mirry, sometimes my hair gets caught in her earring and she always yelps. Long shot but maybe she was intimate with her attacker, meaning she obviously knew him well. There was a hair found on her coat that was hanging in the kitchen as well, so she must have been with him at another time.' John exhaled. 'Am I making too much of this, clutching at straws?'

'Definitely not,' Fee said, 'I'll discuss it with Charlie on the way down, but I'm not sure I can say anything about you, can I?'

'Nah, best not,' John said, 'I am totally persona non grata! Best to say this comes from you.'

'I know, this is total shit, we miss you. When will you get back in?'

'Charlie thinks it won't be at least until after Christmas. Once the publicity has quietened down, hopefully with all the festivities that will mean sooner than later.'

'Well, whatever happens, I've got your back,' Fee said. 'I'll keep you in the loop, wish me luck.'

'Thanks, Fee, catch up when you get back.'

'Will do, take care, don't be going up the wall.'

'You know me too well,' John laughed. 'Bye for now.'

'Bye John,' Fee said warmly before ringing off.

John put the phone down on the table, realising that this was probably one of the rare times that Fee had called him by his name. For some reason, he was genuinely touched.

Chapter Fifty

When Debs came back to work, there was very little said about her absence. She looked pale, with shadows under her eyes, but was embarrassed about being off, especially when Pen teased her about the Christmas night out. Later in the day, they stopped for lunch and a walk at the back of the hospital. It had taken Mirry a lot to encourage Debs to keep her company, but Mirry had persevered, complaining that she needed some daylight otherwise she would wither.

Their conversation was casual as they made their way out of the hospital to the back path that led up the hill to the trees. It was cold, so they quickened their pace. As always, they had to stop a couple of times to pass the time of day with other colleagues out and about grabbing lunch or heading for the canteen. Their chat had been pretty mundane and, once they had caught up with work, there was an uncomfortable silence. Mirry couldn't help herself, she asked the question, fully addressing the invisible elephant that had come between them.

'So how's things going with Simon then?' Mirry asked, smiling, hoping she hadn't overstepped her mark. Debs went a little red and shook her head.

'You and Pen been chatting?'

'No,' Mirry said, 'you know me. After the chat we had in the summer, I wasn't sure where you were with potential suitors.'

'Listen to you,' Debs laughed, 'potential suitors! What year do you think this is, Mirry, 1899?'

'Och, you know what I mean!' Mirry shoved Debs hard.

'Well too early to say yet, I think. Simon wants to keep things low key, you know what it's like trying to date someone at work. Can get very awkward.'

'Yeah, that's a tricky one,' Mirry said, staring down the hill, watching a couple stop in front of a burned-out motorbike in the grass.

'Also think he had his heart broken when he worked down south. So we're just going to take it slow, not go public.'

'Sounds wise, Debs, just as long as you're good that's all I care about.'

'And you okay about me seeing him?' Debs asked.

'What do you mean?'

'Well, Simon did say that there had been a bit of a thing between the two of you.'

'Did he?' Mirry asked, genuinely surprised. 'Have to say I did fancy him for a while, but I've John to think about, and I wouldn't want anything to mess that up.'

'That's what I thought, Mirry, but I wanted to ask anyway, just to be sure.'

They both stopped in companionable silence and looked down on their workplace.

'Wow, things have changed so much in the last couple of years,' Debs said.

'Haven't they just,' Mirry said thoughtfully, 'and not just up here.'

They made their way back down the hill, past the abandoned motorbike, the rough grassland, and the back of the mortuary, before returning to the warmth and the buzz of the hospital.

Chapter Fifty-One

The rest of the week was uneventful for Mirry as she readied herself for going on holiday. She had a gentle fizzing in her stomach as she thought about the time off with John. Although he wasn't in a great place, her enthusiasm was beginning to wear him down. He had gone out and done the food shop for taking away with them. Their fridge was now groaning, filled with treats for Christmas Day and beyond.

They watched the reconstruction together when it was aired at the end of the week. Charlie came across really well, emanating an air of confidence and determination. Fee even featured, being filmed as one of the officers working diligently at her desk. There were interviews with Ray and Jack's parents. The latter being the hardest to watch as they spoke about how lovely their only son had been. Watching them, Mirry's eyes filled with tears as she remembered washing his body with his mum in preparation for the mortuary.

John was quiet after the programme. Mirry left him to his thoughts as she went to make them both a cup of tea. Coming back into the sitting room, she placed the two mugs on the table and sat down beside him, curling her legs up underneath and pulling his face round to look at her.

'For the next week, my love, there is nothing you can do about this, and we are going to our safe place.' She stroked his face, running her finger across his lips.

'I know, Mirry, it's just really tough to walk away, I feel such a sense of responsibility and failure.'

'You're not walking away. You know what Charlie said - once the publicity had calmed down, you would be back.'

'I just want him caught before anyone else gets hurt. Who knows what he's thinking or who his next victim might be.'

'Well, if anyone can do that, John, I know that you, Fee, and your team are the best ones for the job.' She bent forward and picked up the two mugs, handing one to John. 'Now drink your tea and tell me what food you got for us, the fridge looks stuffed.'

The rest of their evening was spent planning what they would do when they were away, looking at walks they had yet to discover and a good beach for a Christmas Day dip.

Packing up the car in the morning and getting organised, Mirry could feel John beginning to relax a bit more. By the time they got to the ferry port at Ardrossan, their moods had lifted and the holiday daft banter had begun. The water was calm and the sun was shining brightly despite the cold. The top of Goat Fell had a smattering of snow and the Christmas lights of Brodick twinkled on the shore. They stood outside on the deck together, wrapped in each other's arms in quiet contemplation as the ship made its way into harbour. Mirry knew they were going to have an amazing time, and her heart was filled with love for the man standing beside her.

Chapter Fifty-Two

Pen was taking down the Christmas decorations in the office the week after Mirry came back from her holiday. She was balanced precariously on one of the office chairs which she had jammed up against Debs' desk.

'Bloody hell, Pen, what you doing, trying to kill yourself?'

'Oh, just hold the bloody chair, will you, I've nearly got it,' Pen said. 'Debs always makes such a fuss about getting the deccies up, it's time they were down. Think she's coming back today, be good to get the place back to normal. Hate all this cheap nasty tinsel anyway.'

With that, Pen unceremoniously ripped the last bit off the wall, causing Mirry to grab the chair as it rolled away backwards. Jumping down, Pen crumpled up the silver fronds and bunged them in the bin.

'You not want to keep that for next year?' Mirry asked, already knowing the answer and grinning as Pen brushed herself down.

'Aye right!' Pen said, making her way over to her desk and sitting down. 'Think we can afford something a wee bit more classy next year, eh? Hate the office looking like a primary school classroom at Christmas time, all we need is the baby Jesus in a little cardboard crib on some ancient cotton wool. Does nobody know it doesn't snow in Bethlehem?'

'Wee bit pedantic there, Pen,' Mirry laughed, 'where's your festive cheer?'

'Went out the same way as that fecking tinsel. Enough already, let's get on with the New Year.'

'Where is everyone?' Mirry asked, pulling out her own chair from under her desk and sitting down.

'Liz had a donor last night. She needed a bit of hand-holding to start off but did really well.'

'And Cath?' Mirry asked.

'Think she's got an antenatal appointment and then she's heading out to St John's to have a chat with the team in A&E, think she's hoping to up the corneal referrals.'

'What about Debs?'

'Well, she's due back today, I think. She was on holiday last week, remember?'

'Oh yeah, forgot about that.'

'You alright, Mirr?' Pen asked. 'You look a bit peaky.'

'Och, I'm fine, just a bit knackered, John and I decorated the spare room over the weekend and I feel like I've done a marathon.'

'Helen has asked for a meeting this afternoon with the four of us, probably to discuss Cath's maternity leave, so be prepared for extra on-calls.'

Mirry looked up and saw Simon pushing the door open, coming in backwards carrying a cardboard tray full of coffees with a paper bag balancing on the top.

'Morning ladies,' he said, turning round, 'thought we could have a caffeine hit to get the day going, celebrate the New Year with a wee bit of pastry to clog the vessels.'

'Oh, sell it to us, why don't you, Simon?' Pen said, getting up and taking the paper bag off the top of the tray.

'Hi Mirry, good to see you,' Simon said, smiling down at her. 'Good weekend? John okay?'

'Hey Simon, and yeah, it was great, thanks.' Looking up at him, Mirry realised that her feelings for him had gone; there was no longer that unstoppable rush that his presence usually brought. Mirry couldn't help but feel relieved. 'How's you?' she continued. 'Haven't seen you since Christmas, did you head home to see your mum?'

'Nah, just stayed in Edinburgh, bit of work to catch up on and a few things to sort out in my flat, you know how it is, single man on his own.'

'You still single then, Simon?' Pen asked, her eyes innocently wide, looking up at him from behind her desk as she reached for her coffee.

'Yup, still single,' said Simon, 'for my sins! Anyway, catch you ladies later.'

Simon put the tray of coffees down and took a cup for himself, shaking his head at Mirry when she offered him a croissant.

Once his office door was closed, Pen looked over at Mirry with her eyebrows raised.

'What a gentleman, eh?'

'Yeah, Debs had said that neither of them wanted it to go public yet, you know what work relationships can be like.'

It wasn't until the late morning that they realised Debs hadn't come in and there had been no phone call. Pen called Helen to check, but she hadn't heard anything either. Simon had left the office at eleven and said that he wouldn't be back until tomorrow so there was no point asking him where Debs was. Mirry texted her, but there was no reply forthcoming.

In the afternoon, it was just Pen and Mirry who were at the meeting with Helen. As Pen had suspected, it was about Cath's maternity leave and there followed quite a heated debate about their on-call cover. Both Mirry and Pen were reluctant to increase their sessions, but it looked like there was going to be no choice. Mirry inwardly groaned at the thought of more weekend work.

'On a positive note though, it does mean some extra money,' Helen said cheerily as she brought the discussion to an end.

'Yeah, which the tax man has a fair portion of,' Pen grumbled, picking up the pager from the table and fixing it to the waistband of her trousers.

'Will you catch up with Debs for me, Mirry?' Helen asked. 'Think she must have thought she'd taken annual leave for today. You popping round to see her?''

'Yeah, probably, I'll keep trying her number though, see what she's up to.'

'Great,' said Helen, 'in that case, meeting adjourned.'

Pen and Mirry made their way back to the office quietly fuming. Not for the first time, Pen echoed Mirry's thoughts when she brought up the subject of changing jobs. Mirry knew that Pen's interest lay in teaching and the lure of a nine to five with weekends off was very attractive.

'Don't be going yet, Pen,' Mirry pleaded, giving her arm a squeeze.

'Nah, I'll wait until you're off on maternity leave and then go. Shit would really hit the fan then!' Pen laughed. 'So hurry up before I say something to Helen which will get me my P45.'

Giggling at the thought of it, the two made their way back to the office to finish up for the day.

Chapter Fifty-Three

Mirry called Debs again and, for the fourth time, got her cheery answering message. Listening to it, Mirry remembered the laugh they had had in the office making the recording. Debs hated hearing her own voice and her first few attempts had Mirry in stitches - she had sounded like a funeral director, very clear and solemn. Eventually Debs had been persuaded to shut her eyes and speak naturally, with Mirry holding the phone for her. That had been last summer when life had been bright and hopeful, to match the warm light and sunshine.

Mirry didn't leave a message this time, couldn't think of any new way of saying she was worried about her, to call her back. She decided she would pop round to Debs' after work. She still had her spare key, having been given the responsibility of feeding precious Marcus before when Debs was on holiday. Mirry stopped off to collect some flowers and a bar of Debs' favourite chocolate as she made her way round to her flat.

It was damp, dark, and dismal by the time Mirry got home from work. The January afternoon cold permeated Mirry's red raincoat, making her wish she had put on something warmer. She increased her pace, walking across the metal bridge, looking down at the brown mirror of the canal water reflecting the amber glow of the street lights back up to her. By the time she reached Debs' block a couple of minutes later, her heart rate had increased slightly and her breath was forming fine misty clouds. Out of habit, she looked up at Debs' sitting room window, expecting to see the curtains drawn and a light on. Instead, the big bay window stared down at her in darkness, Marcus' empty bed just visible above the window frame.

Mirry unlocked the entrance door and made her way up the common stairwell, admiring Debs' community plant collection at the stair window. Mirry knew Debs' neighbours loved her. It was a settled block mostly comprised of young professional couples. The elderly couple next to Debs adored her.

Mirry rang the bell and waited, her ear slightly tilted, expecting to hear Debs coming to the door. There was nothing, just silence, a silence that began to worm a thread of anxiety into Mirry. She rang the bell again, this time for a little longer, more insistent, bordering on rude. Still nothing. Mirry pushed open the letter box and called through.

'Debs, it's just me, your friendly neighbourhood psycho armed with flowers and chocolate.'

The only answering sound was a faint, plaintive mewing. Mirry instantly recognised Marcus' call and she shouted out his name. His mewing got louder as he ran towards the sound of her voice. Mirry's unease was growing, the thread of anxiety now feeling like something solid. Without a further thought, Mirry put the key in the door and walked in.

She called out again as she closed the door behind her, but the only sound was coming from Marcus, now weaving himself in and out of Mirry's legs, purring loudly.

'Hallo lovely boy,' Mirry said, bending down to scratch him behind his ears, 'where is she then?'

'Debs?' called Mirry as she popped her head around the sitting room door. Everything looked in order, the coffee table clear with just a small bowl of oranges and the remote sitting silently in front of the blue sofa. The plants in this room were Debs' pride and joy, but even Mirry recognised they had not been watered. Their foliage was drooping, giving them an unfamiliar neglected look. Marcus was now mewing insistently beside Mirry, looking up at her, his green eyes staring.

Mirry turned and went back into the long hall. There was a faint whiff of ammonia that Mirry realised was coming from Marcus' litter tray. Mirry walked into the pure white of Debs' kitchen and noticed a glass upside down on the otherwise empty draining board. Mirry knew now something wasn't right. Debs never left anything on the draining board. Marcus' feeding bowls were both empty and his figure of eight around her legs was getting more insistent.

'Okay, tiger,' Mirry said, reaching under the sink for his food pouches. She quickly emptied one into his bowl, which he immediately started eating. This wasn't like him. Debs thought that he had an eating disorder and would only eat when nobody was watching.

Mirry made her way back out to the hall and it was here that she noticed another faint smell, slightly sweet mixed with mothballs. She called out again as she made her way down to Debs' room. Pushing open the door, the overripe smell was stronger now. The room was in darkness. Mirry fumbled for the light switch beside the door and the room was suddenly illuminated. And there she was. Debs, her best friend, hanging by a long scarf wrapped around her neck and attached to the coat hook at the side of the wardrobe. The hook that had hung Debs' uniforms when she worked in the transplant unit, had hung her dresses before a night out, had hung her coat when it got wet in the rain, and now… and now it hung Debs. Mirry blinked twice at the shock, trying to take in what she was seeing, like seeing a jet before you hear it, visual reality catching up with her thoughts.

Mirry could tell that Debs was dead. Her beautiful curly dark hair had fallen across her face, her body slumped and skewed, like a macabre rag-doll, her face a pallid blue. She was dressed in underwear that Mirry had never seen Debs wear before. Black corset, fishnet stockings, black, spiked heeled boots which were crumpled underneath her. Mirry backed out of the room, her hand over her mouth, her eyes filling with tears, her breath coming in quick pants. She fumbled in her pocket for her mobile, her hands shaking so much she could barely make sense of John's face smiling out from her screensaver. She hit John's number and heard it ringing. Please answer, please answer, Mirry inwardly prayed.

'Bet you've decided to stay for a glass, tea's nearly ready so make it just the one,' John answered, his voice smiling.

'John, you need to come to Debs', John please come now. Oh, John, come now, my God, John…'

'Mirry, what the fuck?'

'Just come, John.'

Mirry hit the red telephone button and leant against the hall wall before her knees finally gave way. She sank to the floor.

Chapter Fifty-Four

Mirry laid Marcus' carry basket slowly on the hall floor. His mewing had stopped by the time she had got him up to the flat. He seemed exhausted, and Mirry felt the same. She bent down and unhooked the latch, opening the door for him to come out. He stayed put, just staring suspiciously out at her from the back of the basket. She put her hand in to stroke him, but Marcus responded by hissing at her.

Mirry stood up, the blood rushing from her head making her feel dizzy. She shrugged off her raincoat and absentmindedly hung it on the coat hook. Even this simple gesture brought immediate images of Debs back, frightening images of Debs, like a blow to the back of her eyes. She was so very tired after the questioning down at St. Leonard's. John had managed everything, explaining Mirry's reasons for finding Debs, but she had still needed to make a statement which Fee had taken gently from her.

She had so many questions, but for now, she needed to lie down, just lie down and close her eyes. She went through to her bedroom, flopped on the bed, and was asleep within seconds as the weak early morning winter sun started to show through the curtains.

Mirry awoke to a soft purring in her ear. She opened her eyes to see Marcus curled on the pillow beside her.

'So you came out, brave boy?' She reached over and gently scratched him behind his ear. He opened one eye and stared at her. His purring increased.

'Oh, Marcus, looks like you're with us for a while, mate.'

When John came in after two in the afternoon, Mirry had got herself up, showered, and dressed, the normality of performing these simple tasks reassuring her.

Debs' family had been informed of her death and were on their way up from London. Her mother and father brutally shocked, her younger brother coming back from his job in Amsterdam. They couldn't stay at Debs' as it had been cordoned off. Mirry had booked them into the Ettrick Hotel just down the road from the flat. They were due to arrive in the early evening. John had organised for them to be picked up from the station and brought straight to the hotel. They wanted to see Debs, but sadly that wasn't going to be possible until after her post-mortem. Fee was going to be left to break that news. An added insult after injury.

On the day of Debs' funeral, the greyness of the sky reflected down onto the many mourners who had gathered outside the crematorium chapel at Mortonhall. There were various groups of people standing around talking in hushed tones, greeting friends and colleagues as people arrived. Mirry had a hold of John's arm tightly, the solidness of him giving her some comfort. They saw Cath and Liz standing apart from the crowd and went over to join them. Helen, Pen, and Colin arrived together, their faces grim. Pen had no makeup on for once, in anticipation of the tears that would very quickly fall. They all embraced wordlessly before standing back to look over the rest of the people gathered. Mirry could feel eyes on her from a small group of women standing in the door of the waiting room. She recognised them as the nursing staff from the Infirmary's ICU. They all quickly looked away when she glanced in their direction. It was too late though; Mirry knew how their conversation would have gone, with them identifying Mirry as the one who found Debs. Something that would follow her now for a long time, irrespective of staff changes.

'I don't fucking believe it.' This came from Pen, staring incredulously across the heads of the other mourners.

'Pen,' hissed Helen warningly, as a few people turned to see who was swearing.

'You have to be fucking joking with me, right, what the honest fuck is he doing here?'

Mirry turned and followed Pen's gaze to see Simon excusing himself past a couple of groups. Her heart leapt in her throat and began hammering almost deafeningly in her head.

'Oh no, no, no! He can't be here!'

It was too late, Simon had now joined their small group, oblivious, or so it seemed, to the blank stares.

'Not sure you should really be here, mate,' said John, the only one able to speak.

'I came to pay my respects to Debs,' Simon said. 'She was a colleague of mine too, you know.'

Mirry could feel the tears welling up in her eyes as she remembered conversations she'd had with Debs not even a month ago. They had talked more about what had happened at Christmas and how her and Simon had continued to see each other. Mirry had known something was up at the time. No new relationship should cause such angst in a person. Debs had not gone into details with Mirry other than to say that they weren't really suited at all. Mirry knew that Debs' confidence had been shot. Her usual bright and sunny manner had seemed tarnished. Mirry had put it down to a broken heart at the time but was now suspicious that there was so much more to it. And he had the gall to turn up to her funeral and expect everyone to just accept that he was here.

'We're going in.' Helen indicated the queue moving forward. Nothing more was said as they got into line. Simon coupled up with Colin who looked uncomfortable having the tall blonde man beside him. He reached up his hand to brush the hair away from his face, and it was at this gesture that Mirry saw the scratches just above his hand. Neat and brown - healing, but in a pattern Mirry recognised from when Debs first got Marcus. He would not let her near him, he would lash out, his claws sharp, rending, marking straight red lines that would take days to heal properly. Mirry couldn't believe what she was seeing, like slow motion. It brought memories of another time that Simon had an injury to his hand when he first started, blaming it on a slipped Stanley knife when he was opening his packing crates. Mirry had noticed afterwards that his story of a knife cut didn't match the rough scabs that were there when he took the dressing off. She hadn't thought anything about it at the time, but now? There was something at the back of her mind, a small warning light going off in her memory, but she couldn't pin it down.

Debs' service passed in a blur. Mirry could not stop the tears from falling as she sobbed, leaning against John. His face set expressionless. His arm around her, preventing her from literally dissolving into a puddle of grief on the cold concrete of the crematorium floor. It was over very quickly, too quickly. Her family left slowly as 'These Foolish Things' played softly, one of Debs' favourite songs that she could play so beautifully on the piano. Her mum was barely able to put one foot in front of the other, sobbing into the side of Debs' father's jacket. Her dad held his wife as they walked, his face stony and expressionless, but his eyes burning with grief.

Helen led their small group outside and they gathered together, murmuring about the eulogy so beautifully delivered by Debs' brother.

'Are we going to the wake?' said Helen eventually. 'It might be too much.'

They all looked at one another until John said, 'Yeah, come on, we need to pay our respects to Debs' family and toast her life. She dedicated so much, we have to show our solidarity and grief too.'

With the decision made, the small group of grieving friends made their way to the car park and joined the queue of leaving mourners.

Chapter Fifty-Five

The office was quiet when Mirry went in the day after Debs' funeral. The plants on her desk had been removed by Helen and taken home. They didn't want any more dying in their workplace.

Mirry turned her laptop on and went straight to her emails. She had only been off for a few days but, already, there was so much to attend to. She was so lost in thought that she didn't hear the office door swing open and wasn't aware of anyone around her until a shadow fell over her screen. She jumped and looked up. Simon was looking down at her. He looked like he hadn't shaved, there were shadows under his eyes, and his hair looked like it needed cut.

'Hi Mirry.' He spoke first, rubbing his hand through his hair, moving it back from his forehead. Mirry saw the scratches on his wrist again as his sleeve moved. Simon saw her looking at them and pulled his sleeve down.

'They look sore,' she said, staring straight up at him.

'Hmm, yeah, they were from Marcus. You know what he's like, doesn't like strangers.'

'No, he doesn't, usually hides from anyone he doesn't know… When did you see Debs last, Simon, by the way?'

'The day before she died.'

'How do you know what day she died?'

'Well, you know, after what was recorded as her date of death.'

'That doesn't make sense, Simon, when did you see her last?' Mirry pushed.

'Couple of days before the weekend you found her, we were not getting on that great… you know Debs, she could be pretty full on sometimes, and I really wasn't into having a serious relationship with her, you know how it is, Mirry?'

'Yeah, I do, so Debs was more into you then?'

'Did she say something to you then, Mirry? I know how close you two were.'

Mirry felt her eyes fill up, remembering all of Debs' kindness, care, and beauty.

'What did you do to her, Simon?' Mirry asked outright. 'She completely withdrew after you two got together.'

'Ah, nothing, we had a bit of fun but don't think we were really suited in the end.'

'Really? Not kinky enough for you and your exotic tastes, eh?'

'What's that supposed to mean, Mirry?' said Simon, backing away from her desk and straightening up.

'Debs was a kind soul, and I suspect you were taking her for a ride, Simon.'

'Really, Mirry? Is that what you think? You don't think there was a wee, green monster going on there when me and Debs hooked up. I know you were into me for a while, remember the wine bar?'

'You arrogant git, get the fuck out of my office.'

Simon laughed as he turned to leave. 'Don't like the truth much, do you, Mirry? And as for Debs, she was just too trusting in the end, a bit of fun, but I bore easily.' He walked past the whiteboard and tapped her name as he was leaving. 'See you're still top of the leaderboard, so you're successful at some things in your life, just relationships and getting pregnant not your strong point.'

Mirry jumped to her feet, aghast at those words. 'Get the fuck out of here,' she raged.

Mirry watched his retreating back in hurt astonishment. Her mouth was dry, her heart racing, all thought of work now completely disintegrated. She picked her bag up from beside her desk and grabbed her coat off the back of her chair. Her breath was starting to come in sobs as Simon's words hit home. How did he know she'd been trying to get pregnant? She quickly realised that Debs must have told him. The tears were falling even before she got to the glass door, her mind reeling with what had just happened.

'The utter bastard,' she thought to herself. 'The cold utter bastard.'

Mirry yanked open the office door and made her way quickly down the corridor, taking the back stairs so as not to run into anyone. She ran across the car park and jumped into her car, fumbling in the glove compartment for the hidden packet of Marlboro Lights. 'Only for emergencies,' she remembered laughing with Debs when she had found them. Well, this was an emergency. She flicked the window down a little and lit up, inhaling deeply, waiting for the hit of nicotine to calm her. The first drag tasted foul, tasted stale, tasted like old tights. She looked at the lit end and grimaced, taking another drag. The taste got worse.

'Ah, fuck,' Mirry said, throwing the burning cigarette out the window and banging the steering wheel with both hands, 'fuck, fuck, fuck, fuck, fuck!' And just at that, her pager went off loudly in her bag.

When Mirry got home that night, she was exhausted. The referral had been from ICU, and although the case had been relatively straightforward, Mirry had found it hard to concentrate. The donor had made his wishes very clear to his family when he was alive. There was no doubt in their minds that donation would be what he would have wanted. Even so, it was painful to watch a family go through the heartache of being confronted with the harsh reality of donation. It had only been a harmless discussion around the kitchen table a few years before. That unlikely event that nobody really thinks will arrive when they sign up had happened.

His retrieval was going ahead later that night. Helen had taken over from Mirry, having picked up the slack in the on-call due to Debs' death. Handing over had been hard for them both. Although Helen had been an excellent coordinator in her time, she had been away from the clinical area for so long, Mirry could tell that she was nervous. It also didn't help that Cameron was the retrieval surgeon and rumour had it that things had cooled between the two of them, Cameron apparently not wanting to risk his reputation with an extramarital relationship being made public. Life can be so complicated at times, Mirry thought as she climbed the stairs to the flat, her steps slow, an overwhelming tiredness enveloping her like nothing she had experienced before.

The flat was warm when she removed her coat and hung it up in the hall. There was a smell of something delicious cooking, and she realised she hadn't eaten anything since the morning; just hadn't felt like anything, especially after her run-in with Simon. The smell was now making her ravenous as she pushed the kitchen door open.

Sitting at the table was Fee and John, the remnants of a meal before them.

'Hi babe, I didn't think you would be back until later, thought you had a donor?' John looked up from the table, a half drunk glass of red wine in his hand as he pushed his empty plate away from him.

'Helen's doing the retrieval tonight. I'm bloody exhausted, don't know what's wrong with me. Hi Fee,' she said, turning to smile at Fee. 'What's for tea? Smells great, and I'm bloody starving!'

John looked immediately sheepish as he started to push his chair back. 'Oh, sorry, love, I didn't make anything for you, thought you would get something at work.'

'Oh, cheers.' said Mirry, taking in the empty pots and realising John had made curry.

'There's loads of naan and some dahl left if you fancy?'

Mirry bit back the retort that had nearly surfaced. 'That would be great, love.' She pulled a chair out beside Fee and flopped down as John got up to warm some leftovers and toast the naan.

'We were just talking about Debs,' said Fee, pushing a full glass of red wine across the table to Mirry.

'Yeah, that git was in my office today.'

Fee raised her eyebrows. 'You mean Simon?'

'Yeah, something bad went on between those two, I'm sure of it. Debs had completely withdrawn after they got together.'

'Is that why she did what she did, do you think then, Mirry?'

'Debs wasn't into all that weird shit. I know that for a fact, and as for that get-up I found her in… Jesus Christ, she never liked that kind of thing. I lived with her for long enough - she used to go red when John and I would joke about shagging outdoors. "Unsavoury" was what she called it.' Mirry smiled ruefully and her eyes filled once more as memories of laughing at Debs' prudishness came flooding back.

'So what do you think happened then?'

'I think that bastard had something to do with it. I think he got her into that shit and I think it all went wrong, that's what I think. I don't like him, I don't trust him, and I think he knows way more about what happened to Debs than he's admitting to.'

'Woah, Mirry, that's a pretty bold statement,' said John as he placed a steaming aromatic bowl of dahl in front of her and a huge slice of naan.

'You don't know the half of it. Things haven't been the same at work since he joined the team. He's always around, listening in. Helen's idea of the leaderboard turned out to be his. He acts like he's in charge of all things donor-related with suggestions for this and that. A total pain in the arse. Last week I saw him scanning through the donor register for Lothian, and when I asked him about it, he said he was checking data for a stats meeting he had with management.

Just weird shit like that, what does he need that for? But what he did to Debs is beyond the pale. I met one of his ex-colleagues from Dundee at the Christmas party and she warned me about him. I wish I had said something to Debs.'

At that, Mirry burst into tears. She cradled her head in her hands and sobbed. Fee reached round and held her wrist. 'Oh, come on now, Mirry, Debs dying wasn't your fault. You can't go blaming yourself.'

'Shit, I'm sorry,' Mirry said, rubbing her face roughly and wiping her nose with the back of her arm as Fee passed her a bit of kitchen roll, 'don't know what's wrong with me, I'm all over the place.'

'It's okay, Mirry, have something to eat and get that wine down you.'

Mirry scooped some dahl onto a piece of naan and barely chewed it before swallowing. As the taste of coriander and cumin reached her brain, she took a large gulp of wine and exhaled loudly.

'God, that's good, John,' she said, 'you know you make the best dahl in town.'

'Are you saying you think Simon had something to do with Debs' death, Mirry?' John asked as he placed a bowl of onion salad and some raita in front of her, his face serious as he glanced over at Fee.

'Yeah, I am. He was the last person to see her alive, and nobody seems to be bothered.'

'Well, it was put down as an accidental death, Mirry, you know that, it looked like Debs had done that to herself.'

'Oh for fuck's sake, John, you knew Debs, how bloody likely is that?'

'Who knows what goes on behind closed doors, Mirry,' Fee said. 'I think we've all seen it ourselves at work. People never cease to amaze me with the stuff they get up to.'

'Debs wasn't just people, Fee,' Mirry said, pushing her empty plate away from her, 'Debs was one of my best friends, and I wasn't there for her. Too caught up in my own shit.'

Mirry looked over at John who caught her eye and quickly looked away. They both knew the tension between them had been building again, the hiatus of the joy at Christmas fading fast.

'Sorry for putting a downer on your evening,' Mirry sighed, standing up, 'I'll head for a shower and then bed. Bloody tired and emotional all the time, it seems. Good to see you, Fee.'

Mirry gave Fee a quick hug and kissed the top of John's head before heading out the door.

'Night, Mirry, sleep tight,' Fee said, watching her leave. They heard the door of the bathroom close and the shower start.

'Do you think there's anything in that?' Fee asked.

'Och, I don't know anymore, Fee. Like you say, you don't know what goes on behind closed doors. Not sure I want to go dragging anything up now, maybe just let Debs rest in peace.' John rubbed his face hard. 'Anyway, who's for a cleansing ale?'

'Ah, go on then,' Fee said, smiling, 'just the one before I head home.'

Chapter Fifty-Six

A couple of weeks later, Mirry pulled her earphones out as she came through the door of the flat. Her breath easing from her run, cheeks cold and pink, fingers numb, the post-exercise glow beginning to warm her. It had helped to clear her head but made her all the more determined. John had gone back to work but had become morose and short-tempered. She had to have this out with him, enough already. His mood was doing her head in. Mirry hated this tension in her stomach, like acid and steel, rusting and corrosive. She hated it. Well, no more, it wasn't her way, and John knew that.

She could smell the morning coffee brewing. Just what she needed, a cup of strong coffee with hot milk, fantastic.

'Hey you,' she said, coming into the kitchen, pulling her running fleece over her head, her body heat rising with the cessation of exercise.

John had his back to her. He was looking out the window at the cold February morning, staring at the now-barren lilac tree, pouring coffee into a mug.

'Not sure there'll be enough for you,' he said without turning round, the coffee pot being put to the side, empty.

'Oh, cheers, John, you knew I wouldn't be long, could've made enough for two.'

'You never said where you were going.'

'Really? Eight o'clock on a Sunday morning, and I'm out in my joggers, and you can't think where I was going?'

'Thought we were going for a run together today, that was what you said last night.'

'Oh, I know, just couldn't face your boot camp tactics this morning, I'm way too tired.'

'You're always bloody tired these days… Here, have mine, I'll make a fresh pot.'

John pushed his mug over to her as he took the top off the pot and emptied the dregs down the sink.

'Could you not…' Mirry stopped herself from saying any more. What was the point? He never bloody listened, didn't care about her recycling obsession. He hated the stinky bucket under the sink.

She picked up the proffered coffee and took a gulp, the taste of it weird in her mouth, like burnt wood and nicotine.

'Did you get some new coffee?' Mirry said, trying to sound non-judgemental, but he knew her too well.

'What you talking about? It's what we always have.' He smelt the bag in his hand. 'Nothing wrong with it.'

'Maybe the milk has turned,' Mirry said, searching for excuses. 'Taste it yourself if you don't believe me.' She pushed the steaming mug of coffee towards him. John picked it up and took a drink.

'Like I said, nothing wrong with it.' He looked over at her, his mouth set in a firm line.

'Ach, you would say that, even if it tasted like shite, you stubborn git.' Opportunity for reconciliation now lost.

She stomped out of the kitchen, deaf to John's retort, her stomach churning. Too fucking early in the day for fighting.

She jumped in the shower, letting the hot water fall on her as she stood still, breathing slowly, trying to calm her irritation. It worked. After a few minutes she lathered, rinsed, then dried. Wrapping herself in her dressing gown, she padded through to the bedroom. There on the dressing table was a plate of marmite on toast, a cup of tea, and a glass of orange juice. A hastily badly drawn flower on a post-it stuck to the mirror.

Mirry looked at John's reflection where he was lying on the bed.

'Aw, cheers, love,' she said, smiling broadly at his reflection, 'you know me so well.'

She took an enormous bite from the toast and sipped at the tea, testing the temperature. 'Just bliss,' she thought.

'So what we doing today then?' she asked. 'Got the whole day off together. Fancy a walk? Lunch and pub crawl?' The day was beginning to brighten.

'Sounds a plan. I did say I'd drop Fee's wallpaper stripper off to her today.' John said, looking at his phone.

'John, Fee's is out past Haddington, that'll take ages.' Disappointment was starting to replace the warm glow.

'We can't leave it any longer, Mirry, we've had it since we changed the sitting room. Fee and Chloe want to get on with their stuff.'

'Okay, okay.' Mirry finished the last bite of toast and washed it down with the tea. She definitely didn't want to revisit that time again, knew that the memory of that wall was still with John. 'Better get our skates on then.'

'Time for a quickie?' John said, his eyebrows raised, moving his dressing gown to the side to show his very obvious erection.

Mirry burst out laughing, the atmosphere between them moving like mercury.

'Not this morning, sunshine, just had a shower. Anyway, how many times do I have to say, never a quickie, always a longy!'

'There was a time, Mirry.' John jumped up, closing the robe around him, catching his pants that Mirry threw at him.

'Let's get on with the day, the sooner we're in Haddington, the better. I'll drive,' Mirry said, leaving the room before John could protest. She knew her driving infuriated him. He watched her like a hawk, commenting all the time, his feet moving imaginary pedals beside her. She hated when he drove, all testosterone and cavalier, the stop-start braking like sitting beside someone driving on speed.

The air was crisp as they headed out, their breath steaming in clouds in front of them.

'When I was wee…' Mirry started.

'You used to pretend you were smoking,' John said. 'Every cold winter's day we're out, you say that.'

'Oh, sorry for being so predictable,' Mirry retorted. The knot in her stomach had returned, coiling and growing, coiling and growing.

They walked to Mirry's car, which as always was jammed in tight by a van and the street bin.

'I'll guide you out,' John said, stepping into the road, looking up and down, checking for traffic, gesturing with his hand.

'Fuck, he is annoying at times,' thought Mirry, her temper starting to fray.

'Left hand down… down, Mirry, down,' he shouted, gesticulating.

'And up yours,' she said under her breath.

She manoeuvred carefully out then waited for him to jump in.

'Well done,' he said as he climbed in beside her, rubbing his hands together and blowing on them. 'Shall we go via Porty?'

'No, I just want to get to Haddington first, and then we can chill.'

She drove slowly over the speed bumps, jealously watching the late morning Sunday brunchers making their way up to Bruntsfield. She couldn't be bothered going out to Haddington, what a waste of a morning but needs must. Mirry drove through the town, loving the morning brightness. The weak winter sun was forming a faint haze over the rooftops of the city.

John, checking his mobile the whole time, started giving directions.

'Roadworks at top of Morningside,' he said, 'might be best to avoid there.'

'Ah for fuck's sake, John, can you not just appreciate the scenery and stop looking at your bloody phone? I know which way I want to go, so sit back and enjoy the journey.'

John sat back in the seat, annoyance bristling from him.

'Right oh,' he said, chucking his mobile in the glove compartment, kicking it shut with his knee.

'Oi,' she said, 'gently.'

'Just fucking drive, Mirry,' John said under his breath, 'just fucking drive.'

Their journey continued in silence out on to the city bypass where it was slow until after the Sheriffhall roundabout. Mirry accelerated through the last set of traffic lights as they came to the open road. Her stomach was in knots, but the beginnings of the wide skies of East Lothian started to act like the balm that they always did. Maybe they could go to Tyninghame for their walk, it'd be lovely in the winter sunshine.

'Which way you going?' John asked, as she turned off the bypass, heading for Dalkeith.

'Wanted to go a different route today, take in the countryside.' Mirry gripped the steering wheel, waiting for the retort, and here it came.

'Thought we were in a rush, thought you were going to take the quickest route?' John tutted and pulled his hands through his hair, sighing loudly.

Mirry drove on in silence, taking in the beauty of the frosted bare fields, the bright pale blue sky, breathing slowly, calming her frustration.

The first signs for Haddington came up when John swore and smacked himself in the forehead.

'Wa fuck!' he shouted. 'I don't believe it.'

'What is it now? Get a bloody grip, will you, we're nearly there.'

'I've forgotten the stripper,' he said blankly, not looking at Mirry, addressing the windscreen.

'You're having a laugh,' Mirry said, glancing over at him.

'Wish I was, babe, we'll need to go back for it.'

'Oh, John, we're nearly there for fuck's sake. Why don't we just stop off in Haddington and buy Fee a new fucking stripper? They're not that dear, we've had the bloody thing long enough.'

'Since when were we made of money, Mirry? You'll need to turn back, it was Fee's dad's, and you know what she's like about his stuff.' Mirry remembered when Fee's dad had died. The only time she had seen her cry, inconsolable at the funeral, her grief open and raw.

Mirry braked hard in the middle of the road, glared at John, and before his protestation was out his mouth, yanked the wheel round as she accelerated into a U turn.

'Right, fuck it, let's go back.' She accelerated away, her speed matching her climbing anger. She reached forward and hit the CD button, the bassline of Lust for Life matching the thumping of her heart and the banging in her head.

'More please, Iggy!' Mirry shouted as she increased the volume, nodding her head in time to the beat.

'Mirry, turn that old shit down,' John shouted, hating this music, hating the noise. He reached forward to turn the volume down only to have his hand slapped away by Mirry.

'Leave it,' she shouted, turning the volume up further.

'Mirry, for fuck's sake.' John leaned forward again but, before he could do anything Mirry shoved his arm hard. At the same time the car swerved, swerved and hit the verge, swerved and hit the verge and lifted, lifted and spun, spun over, over then crashed, crashed then stopped.

Everything stopped.

Chapter Fifty-Seven

It was the pain in John's shoulder that woke him. He groaned as he opened his eyes.

'Hey, you're awake.'

John heard Fee's voice, but everything was swimming, swirling. He couldn't focus, just pain, not just in his shoulder now but everywhere, aching everywhere. He scrunched his eyes tight and groaned again.

'Fee?' he croaked, his voice cracked and broken.

'Here, have a sip.' A straw was pushed into his mouth. He sucked up warm water and swallowed. His head stopped swimming enough for him to make out Fee sitting at his bedside, holding the glass and straw.

'What's going on?'

'You guys had an accident outside Haddington, do you remember?'

John closed his eyes again, trying to orientate himself.

'Accident?' he mumbled, breathing slowly out of his open mouth. 'Accident?' he mumbled again as images started to flash before him. Green and grey, fast and loud, turning his head to look as Mirry screamed and disappeared into a cushion of white.

'John, John?' from Fee, her hand shaking his arm. Her touch crystallised him, brought everything into sharp focus.

'Oh my God, Fee, we crashed, the car spun over… Mirry, where's Mirry?'

'She's in ICU, John, she's poorly,' Fee's voice quietened. 'Pen is with her.'

'I need to see her,' he said, pushing himself up in the bed, grimacing with pain, a moisture sheen appearing on his forehead.

'You're in no fit state, babe, wait 'til the morning.' Fee placed her hand back on his arm firmly, almost restraining. 'Mirry got out of theatre a couple of hours ago, needed her arm pinned and plated.'

A flash of clear memory came to John, of Mirry slapping him as he reached for the volume in the car.

'But she doesn't need to be in ICU for that, surely?' John shook his head as if this would stop the faintness.

'She's got chest injuries, John, broken ribs and a collapsed lung. They need to ventilate her for now. She's in good hands, you know that. They know Mirry really well; the staff have been amazing, you know what they're like. They take good care of their own.'

'Oh, Fee, it was my fault, I was stressing her out.'

At that, a nurse came in.

'Hey John, you're awake, good… managed a drink then? How's your pain doing?'

'He's sore,' Fee said as she moved out of the way to let the nurse in to take his blood pressure.

'I bet you are.' The nurse smiled warmly at him, placing a cool hand on his forehead. 'I'll go and get you something.'

'I need to see Mirry,' John said, clearly this time, 'I need to see her.'

'Not tonight, I'm afraid, John, you're way too wobbly to be getting out of bed. Tomorrow, I promise. I'll take you there myself.'

There was a tentative knock at the door. It was pushed open and another nurse popped her round.

'Pen is here to see John, is it okay?'

John's nurse looked at him with raised eyebrows; he nodded.

The door was pushed open and Pen came in hesitantly. John could see she had been crying, her usually perfect makeup non-existent, her hair tousled on one side, flat on the other as if she had been lying sideways for a long time.

'Oh John,' she exhaled in a long breath, quickly moving to the side of his bed and taking his hand. 'Oh John, look at you.'

'How's Mirry, Pen?' John looked up at her, his eyes searching her face, worry and trepidation gnawing like a sharp whirlpool in his chest.

'She's stable now, John. They've fixed her arm, and her chest is okay. They're keeping her sedated overnight as a precaution, what with the baby and everything.'

'The baby, what baby?'

Pen looked down at him, her brow furrowed. 'Did you not know, John?'

'Know what, Pen? Stop this, what are you talking about?'

'Mirry is about two months pregnant; they've scanned her and there is still a heartbeat.'

John could not take this in. How could it be? And yet, they had not stopped trying despite all the arguing. The late nights with this damn case and Mirry's grief after Debs' death. They had still come together when they could, like an agreed unwritten rule that they would continue to try… and now this?

An unbidden sob came from deep within him. 'No, I didn't know, I don't even think Mirry knows either, she would have said.'

'What happened, John, do you remember?'

'Not really, I think we were arguing…' John had a couple of flashbacks then, shaking his head, 'I think we hit black ice.'

'The car's a write-off but it could've been so much worse, work have organised a car for you in the meantime.' Fee squeezed John's arm. 'Don't think Mirry will be driving for a while.'

Pen stifled a sob and wiped tears that had sprung from her eyes away in a gesture that was so unlike her, John felt his heart lurch.

'I'll hopefully get to see her tomorrow, the nurse said. I just need to set eyes on her.'

'I know, John, in the meantime I'll get you and Mirry some stuff from the flat and bring it in tomorrow. Rest up, I'll leave you in peace.' With that, Pen bent down and kissed John on the top of his head, stroking his face as she turned to leave.

'Thanks, Pen, thanks for everything.'

After the nurse had given him an injection for the pain, it wasn't long before he fell into a deep dreamless sleep.

Unfortunately, the dreamlessness only lasted for what seemed like moments, as John woke several times during the night, the pain in his shoulder deep and throbbing. He refused any more strong painkillers but accepted a couple of tablets after persuasion from the night nurse.

In the morning, the ward round was quick and efficient. He was to be discharged home with an appointment to be seen in six weeks. After he washed and dressed, the nurse took him along to the ICU to see Mirry.

John couldn't believe his eyes when he walked in. Mirry looked so tiny and defenceless, the ventilation tube pulling her perfect mouth into a grimace. A nurse placed a chair behind him so he could sit down. John mumbled his thanks as he carefully lowered himself down.

'I'm Wendy and I'm looking after Mirry today,' the nurse said, gently placing her hand on John's shoulder.

'Is it okay for me to touch her?' John asked, desperate to connect but scared to, as Mirry was surrounded by so much machinery with various lines and tubes attached to her.

'Oh, of course, John, just let me help you,' Wendy said, gently pulling back the sheet covering Mirry's arm and carefully tucking it beside her. 'You can speak to her too, you know, she may be able to hear you.'

With that, Wendy spoke to Mirry quietly. 'That's John in to see you, Mirry, looks like he's been in the wars too!' She smiled at John, encouraging him. 'Don't be scared.'

John took Mirry's hand, which was lifeless and floppy, and held it with both hands.

'Oh Mirry, Mirry, my love, I'm so sorry.' He laid his head on her hand and held it close to his lips. 'I love you so, so very much.'

'We're hoping to wake her up tomorrow, John, looks like her lung has reinflated and all her recordings have been stable.' Wendy paused before continuing. 'And baby is doing well.'

'I didn't know,' mumbled John, 'I don't think Mirry knows either, she would have said, we've been trying for a while, and it just wasn't happening, and now this…' John stopped himself, aware he was beginning to ramble.

'Would you like to see a picture of your baby? They did an ultrasound again this morning and printed one off for Mirry when she wakes up.'

John nodded his head, not quite taking in what Wendy was saying to him until she handed him a small black, white, and gray image inside a folded plastic pouch.

'There it is,' Wendy leant over, pointing at a small curled object. 'Isn't it beautiful?'

John caught his breath and felt tears well in his eyes as he looked down at the picture of his baby.

'Oh my God, is that the baby there?' John said.

'It is indeed,' smiled Wendy, 'think you should be here tomorrow when she wakes up, do you not?'

'Wild horses couldn't keep me away.' He leant down and kissed Mirry's hand again. 'You amazing woman, you,' he whispered. 'Love you so much.'

John stayed for a little while longer until Wendy gently persuaded him that he should really go home and rest. He would need all his strength for tomorrow when Mirry woke up.

Fee was in the relatives' waiting room when he came out. He was so very glad to see her. She put her arm around him and gave him a gentle squeeze. Before leaving the unit, she helped him on with his jacket that Pen had brought in. They made their way slowly along the corridor, down a flight of stairs, and out into the main concourse. John's head was spinning and the frenetic activity of the main thoroughfare of the hospital was in sharp contrast to the calm of the ICU. He needed to get out, to breathe fresh air and see the sky. He had never felt like this before, so vulnerable and out of his depth.

When they got back to the flat, Fee led the way up the stairs, checking with him at every landing. She unlocked the door and held it open for him as he walked in. The air was stale but smelt of home. Marcus ran to greet them, his tail erect and proud.

'Hallo old boy,' said John, leaning stiffly down to rub him behind his ears as Marcus weaved himself in and out of his legs.

'Somebody's pleased to see you,' said Fee, smiling down at the cat.

'Yeah, he seems to like me for some reason,' said John, continuing to rub Marcus' head. 'Thanks for looking after him, Fee, you're such a great mate, I really appreciate it.'

'No worries, you'd do the same for me. Anyway, let's get you in and settled. I've done a wee shop for you: couple of M&S meals, milk, bread, and some Hobnobs. I know how much you like them!'

'Yeah, Mirry, won't have them in the house, thinks they're the food of the devil.' At the mention of Mirry's name, John's heart took a lurch and the joy of coming home disintegrated. 'Oh Fee.' John caught his breath, stifling a sob.

'Come on, mate,' Fee said, walking ahead of him, 'get yourself sat down, and I'll stick the kettle on.'

John made his way through to the sitting room and gingerly lay down on the sofa. Marcus jumped up beside him, purring loudly and pushing his head against John's chest. Fee came in with a couple of steaming mugs, balancing a plate of biscuits on top of one of them. He reached forward to take them from her, but the sudden searing pain in his shoulder reared up as a reminder of his injury. He caught his breath and leaned back against the cushions.

'Drink this, John, take some more painkillers, go and have a sleep, then I'll run you back up to the Royal later tonight. I'll leave the keys for the work car in your bowl so you've wheels for tomorrow. It's parked just outside, you'll recognise it.'

'Cheers, Fee,' John said as he cradled the steaming mug in front of him, shaking his head when Fee offered him the plate of biscuits.

'All the more for me,' she laughed.

Once Fee had left, he made his way into the bedroom. Nothing had been disturbed since the morning of the accident. His yellow Post-it note of a badly drawn flower was still stuck to the mirror. There was evidence of where Marcus had been sleeping on Mirry's side of the bed, a collection of small ginger hairs and his faint imprint still visible. John lay down and instantly fell asleep.

He woke a couple of hours later, his mouth dry with a metallic taste that he put down to the painkillers. He looked over at the clock on Mirry's bedside table and saw that it was half past five. He checked his phone for messages, scared that he might have missed something, but it was just Mirry's smiling face on the screen. 'What a woman she is,' John thought to himself, 'so, so beautiful.' He was as surprised as Pen that Mirry hadn't told him she was pregnant; she knew how important it was to him. Maybe she didn't want to scare him after the problems Cath had had. Did she not think he could deal with it? Or was it perhaps something else?

The more he thought about it the more sure he was that Mirry must have known she was pregnant. He couldn't get the thought out of his mind. Why hadn't she told him? Did she not want their baby? Had she changed her mind? He knew their relationship had been rocky at times, but he thought that, after Christmas, things were getting back on an even keel. Perhaps he was wrong. Debs' death had shaken Mirry to the core.

He rolled over on his side and saw Mirry's journal next to the clock. Picking it up, he manoeuvred onto his back slowly, protecting any sudden movement of his shoulder. He flicked to the middle, reassuring himself that what he was doing was okay, that this unspoken infringement of Mirry's privacy was justified. The page had opened at the end of May and the first words that John read were 'I wonder what his story is.' Mirry went on to write about Simon joining the team. John vaguely remembered Mirry mentioning Simon at the time. He couldn't believe what he was reading. Mirry seemed obsessed with the man; she'd written about some publicity work she had done with him in Glasgow and about the frisson between them both… and he'd kissed her. The fucking cheek of the bloke! And then it was obvious something had happened when he was in Newcastle. There wasn't much documented but enough for John to suspect that they had slept together. The sudden realisation that Mirry's pregnancy might not be his hit him like a bolt out of the blue. 'Surely not,' he thought to himself, 'Mirry wouldn't do that.' Yet once the thought was present, it would not leave. It wormed and grew, all rational thought leaving John. They had been trying for months with no success and finally she was pregnant, but was it even his? He slammed the journal shut and threw it across the room, his anger now fizzing and whirring like a Catherine wheel in full explosive circles. This needed to be dealt with and now. He looked at Mirry's on-call rota in the kitchen which had the whole team's names and addresses printed on the bottom. He found Simon's name last, his address was in Corstorphine. John pulled his jacket on and headed out.

Chapter Fifty-Eight

By the time John had made his way out west of the city, his anger was beginning to dissipate. He was starting to regret coming this far out, away from Mirry at the Royal. He drove into the parking area at the back of the block of flats where Simon lived and reversed slowly into the only space available. He looked out at the car park, lit by the pale orange glow of the street lights, casting strange shadows on the ground and buildings. Looking up at the flats, he could see some windows illuminated, with curtains drawn as the occupants got on with their evenings.

He released his safety belt, grimacing at the pain in his shoulder, before picking up his mobile to check there were no new messages. The screen was blank other than the picture of Mirry. Her head thrown back in laughter, sitting on the pier at Brodick, the grey December sky of Arran in the background and memories of their Christmas hideaway came flooding back. That holiday now seemed so long ago, so much had happened since then. How could Mirry have let him down in this way? His resolve returned and he pocketed his mobile and got out of the car.

As he made his way to Simon's block, he wondered if Mirry had been here too. He could feel jealousy starting to gnaw at him as he stopped in front of the entry-phone at the entrance door. He quickly found Grey and pressed the buzzer firmly. He was here now; he had to go through with this. Just as he was about to push the buzzer again, he jumped when the intercom responded with a crackle.

'Yes?' John heard Simon's voice coming out of the speaker.

'Simon, it's John here, I'd like a word.' The intercom went quiet and then the buzzer went as the lock was released, and John pushed through the door. The entrance hall gave an odd welcome in the soulless way of new buildings. It was clean and sparse, a range of bicycles padlocked to the frames under the stairs. John made his way to the lift and pushed the button for the first floor. When the lift doors opened, he could see an open door at the end of the corridor, and he knew this must be Simon's flat.

He knocked as he pushed the door open.

'Hi? Simon?' For some reason, John began to feel uneasy; this all felt very weird, and the hairs on his neck began to rise.

'In here,' came a voice from the end of the hall. There was a soft yellow glow coming from a lamp sitting on a small table. John made his way to where Simon's voice had come from. Walking into the sitting room, John was immediately struck by the starkness of the room. There was a grey sofa and a matching chair. The walls were bare except for a large flat screen TV, and the drawn curtains were nondescript, plain, functional, giving the room an even more desolate air. Simon was sitting at a desk in the corner of the room, the glow from his PC illuminating the room and his face. He stood up when John entered the room and outstretched his hand in a welcoming gesture, as if John turning up on his doorstep was an everyday occurrence.

'John, how are you? I heard about your accident. How's Mirry?'

John was taken aback for a couple of seconds and then he remembered his reasons for being here.

'Oh, cut the crap with the bonhomie, Simon, will you? I think you can probably guess why I'm here.'

'No, not really, John, mind reading was never my best feature.' Simon smiled slowly as he took in John's discomfort. 'Why don't you sit down and tell me what's up?' Simon gestured at the sofa with a sweep of his arm.

'What was your relationship with Mirry?' John blurted out. 'Or rather when were you fucking my girlfriend?'

Simon threw his head back in laughter. 'Relationship with Mirry? Are you off your head? I wouldn't have dallied too long around Mirry, not really my cup of tea. I tend to go for someone a little more up-market, she was fun for a while…' Simon didn't get any more words out as John swung at him, his fist connecting squarely with Simon's nose. John heard the satisfying crunch of cartilage under his fist.

'Fuck,' they both said simultaneously. Simon bent over, clutching his face with two hands, the blood already visible between his fingers. John was breathing deeply, holding his injured shoulder as the room spun before him. He sat down heavily on the sofa before he passed out. Simon sank to his knees and continued to swear.

'You mad fucking bastard, what the hell?'

John's head began to clear and the room stopped spinning. He looked around for something to give to Simon to stem the bleeding, but there was nothing. John got up and made his way through to the kitchen and found a dish towel hanging on the radiator. He went back to Simon and handed it to him.

'Here,' he said gruffly, 'do you want me to have a look?'

'Are you fucking kidding me?' Simon said, pushing the dish towel to his face as he got to his feet. 'Get the fuck out of my house.' He started towards John, the anger evident in Simon's blue eyes.

'And just for the record, I didn't touch that mad bitch, the two of you make a good couple!' Simon threw the dish towel at John who caught it as he turned on his heel and made his way out of the flat, his heart racing, his shoulder screaming in agony as the reality of what he had just done hit home.

By the time he made it back to the car, the adrenaline had kicked in. John reversed quickly out, spinning the wheel with one hand as he threw the bloodied tea towel into the back seat. He drove out onto the main road. His phone rang and he quickly drove to the side of the road and answered. It was Fee looking for him. She was furious and demanded he get home now. He didn't need to be told twice.

Chapter Fifty-Nine

Mirry could hear a voice calling her name in the darkness. She was tired and just wanted to sleep, but the voice was insistent. There were other voices and noises she couldn't understand. Then she felt she was choking, and there was a burning, a burning in her throat and more choking, she couldn't breathe, she couldn't… her eyes opened, and she was blinded by bright lights and people leaning over her. The voice again saying something, and she was coughing and gurgling again. Then suddenly she gasped a full lungful of air and her vision cleared. She knew immediately where she was, the voice started to sound familiar as he encouraged her to breathe. A mask was put on her face, and the smell of plastic was strong, and the airflow was high, like breathing in a wind. She heard the voice say: 'Good extubation, 40% for next couple of hours, then we'll see,' before she fell back to a dreamless place.

When Mirry woke, she lay still and opened her eyes. She looked down to the bottom of the bed and saw a woman leaning over a table writing something.

'Hallo,' Mirry said, but what came out was just a whisper. She tried again. 'Hallo.' But it was nothing more than a feeble croak. Mirry moved her hand up to take the mask off her face and immediately there was the sound of beeping from beside her and the woman looked up. On seeing Mirry awake, a broad smile came across her face and Mirry recognised her. It was Sandie, her trusted colleague. A feeling of relief passed through her.

'Well then, Mirry, you've come back to us,' Sandie said, coming round to the side of the bed and placing her hand on Mirry's. 'You had us worried there for a while.'

'Jesus, Sandie, what the fuck?' Mirry croaked as the reality of where she was started to dawn on her. She tried to sit up, but there was a sudden intense pain in her chest which drew her up short. She collapsed back on the covers.

'Slowly, Mirry, you've been in the wars, babe, let's get you sorted.'

Sandie helped Mirry to sit up, taking her time, all the while encouraging her. She explained what had happened, about the accident, about Mirry's injuries, how she had ended up in ICU.

'What about John?' Mirry immediately asked.

'John was discharged yesterday, Mirry, we've virtually had to shoo him out of here to get him to go home to rest. I'll call him now and let him know you're awake… Do you want to speak to him?'

'God, yes, please.'

'And I'll let your mum know too. First things first though, I want the midwife to come and see you now you're awake just to make sure everything is okay with the baby.'

Mirry shook her head. 'The baby?' she asked Sandie, her eyes wide and barely focusing. 'What baby?'

'Your baby, Mirry,' Sandie said and went to the table where she picked up the scan picture in a plastic folder and handed it to her. 'Your baby.'

Mirry looked down at the grainy image and knew immediately what she was looking at. Her breath caught in her throat as she stroked the small dark shape. 'My baby?'

'Well, it ain't anyone else's, that scan's got your name on it, and I've heard the wee one's heartbeat when they came to check on you both.' Sandie grinned at Mirry, stroking her hair. 'Did you not know, Mirry? You're about 8 weeks gone.'

'No, no, no… I mean I've felt lousy for a couple of months but just thought I had a bug or too much on-call or…' Mirry stopped in mid-sentence. 'I need to speak to John.'

'I'll get the mobile and, whilst you're speaking to him, I'll call the midwife.'

Sandie left the bedside and said something to the nurse who was in the next cubicle. She returned with a mobile and helped Mirry rearrange her intravenous lines and monitoring leads so she could make the call. He answered after three rings. 'John, love, it's me.'

Chapter Sixty

Mirry was discharged from hospital ten days later and, although very sore, was delighted to be going home. She was even more delighted knowing that her baby was safe and had come to no harm in the accident. The news of her pregnancy was out now, and she had had numerous congratulation texts on her mobile and excited calls with her family. John was so very solicitous, wheeling her out to the car, helping her up the stairs, gazing across at her as she rested on the sofa.

'What are you looking at?' Mirry asked.

'You,' John answered. 'Just you. Do you know how much I love you?'

'I know,' Mirry said, 'nothing like a brush with death to concentrate the mind, or heart for that matter.'

'I thought I'd lost you, Mirry, I can't believe how lucky I am to have you and our baby.'

'Took us long enough,' Mirry chortled, rubbing her lower belly. 'Still trying to get my head round it.'

'We're good, Mirry, aren't we?' John asked. 'You're happy about the baby?'

'Absolutely, John, what's brought this on?'

John felt he had a confession to make but wasn't sure what to say.

'John, what is it?'

And then it came out, he couldn't help himself. He told Mirry how he had felt when he found out she was pregnant after all the time they had been trying. He didn't think it was ever going to happen and had given up hoping. The hardest part for him was admitting to reading her journal. He had wanted to know if she'd known she was pregnant and didn't want the baby. What he hadn't expected to find was what she had written about Simon. There was a silence then as Mirry took in the full extent of what John was telling her. His words were rushed; he looked so distressed that she wasn't sure how to react. Finally, he came to the part about when he went round to Simon's flat to have it out with him.

'You did what?' Mirry couldn't believe what she was hearing. 'You hit him? Jesus Christ, John, are you off your head? What on earth got into you?'

It was difficult for him to explain in the cold light of day, when Mirry was sitting safely on their sofa at home.

'I don't know, babe, he was just such a supercilious arse about you that it made me mad. Like he was so cool and you were beneath him in some way.'

'Yeah, well, that sounds about right, given what's happened,' Mirry said. 'Pen always said not to trust him and look what happened to Debs. For sure he knew what happened to her. But, John, what the fuck, I've got to work with the guy!'

'Well, not for another month yet,' John reminded her, 'deal with that when it happens.'

Mirry looked at him sitting across from her, trying to make sense of what he was saying.

'Okay, if we're being open, yes, I fancied Simon for a while, had a bit of a crush on him, but I never took it any further. You do believe that, John, don't you?'

'Yes.'

'And you know that I really want our baby and for us to be a family?'

'Yes.'

'So can we just put all of this behind us and look to the future?'

'There is nothing more that I want, Mirry.' John's eyes filled with tears as he went down on his knees and made his way over to her, pulling her into his arms. They held each other for a few seconds until Mirry shifted slightly.

'Fuck's sake, I'm so bloody sore!'

'Me too,' said John, leaning back and holding his shoulder, 'right couple of crocks, aren't we?'

They both laughed and gently brought their foreheads together and kissed.

'I love you, Mirry Colville.'

'I love you, John Sneddon.'

'Cup of tea?'

'And some marmite on toast? Eating for two now!'

'Ah, careful, Mirr, you're pushing it,' John laughed, kissing the top of her head and standing up. 'Won't be long.'

Mirry stretched and carefully rearranged herself on the sofa. She took out her mobile and found the ultrasound picture of their baby.

'Hallo little one,' she said, 'we're going to take such good care of you.' Mirry closed her eyes and waited for her tea and toast.

Chapter Sixty-One

It was the beginning of March before John was fit enough to get back to work. Mirry was still off but improving every day. Walking up the stairs to the office, he could feel the pull of work. He'd really missed the team and, although he had kept up to speed with Fee about what was happening, he was looking forward to getting back in the driving seat. He'd had a call with Charlie the day before and she had happily handed the reins back over to him. Other fish to fry apparently, and perhaps less troublesome than this case, John had thought to himself.

It was still early when John came into the main office, no one else had arrived. All was in darkness until he switched the lights on and the room burst into life. He saw that there had been another whiteboard added to the back wall and there was a confusing melee of coloured lines between the victims' photographs. Their images were ingrained in his memory and seeing them up close again was disconcerting.

Going into his room, there was a faint, bizarrely recognisable aroma. Looking around for the source, he noticed a small bowl filled with dried purple flowers sitting on his desk. Lavender, a leftover from Charlie. He pulled his chair out and sat down in front of his PC, wincing slightly at the ache in his shoulder. The chair had been adjusted for someone much smaller so, with some irritation, he fiddled with the lever until his eye line was level with the screen. Taking a deep breath, he switched his PC on and exhaled as the screen illuminated and he was asked to sign in. He went straight to his emails and began working through what had come in overnight. He zoned in on the email Charlie had said she would send, outlining what progress had been made with the case and where the team were. He knew that two of the team had been moved on as other cases had come in that needed attention. Serious crime didn't stop just because there was a serial killer on the loose.

His office door opened and, looking up, he was delighted to see Fee coming in backwards with a tray of coffees and what looked like something edible in a brown paper bag.

'Morning Boss,' Fee said with very obvious delight, 'great to have you back. How's Mirry doing?'

'Oh, morning Fee, can't tell you how good it feels to be sitting in this chair!' John said, taking the coffees from her. 'Mirry is getting better everyday; she's got a couple of more weeks off, but she's doing really well.'

'I never got a chance to say congratulations properly, when's the baby due?'

'Thanks, Fee. Not for ages yet - end of August is her due date.'

'You want to have a quick catch-up before the team briefing at eleven?'

'Sounds a plan,' John said, opening the brown paper parcel and finding, to his delight, a warm bacon roll. 'Grab a chair and we'll crack on. I just need to get rid of this before we start.' He picked up the bowl of lavender, went out of his office, and threw the contents into the main bin.

'Can't stand the smell of lavender,' he said, screwing his nose up. 'Reminds me of that air freshener they use down at the City Mortuary.'

'Oh yeah,' Fee laughed, 'I wondered why I hated it so much!'

'Anyway, what you got for me?'

Fee went over everything that had happened in the six weeks he had been away. There had been more interviews done with the victims' friends, family, and colleagues as well as the massive response from the public after the last reconstruction.

'How did you get on down in Newcastle?' John asked, flicking through some of the files on his PC.

'Yeah good, Jason's team went back and interviewed Susie's work colleagues like you asked. Their results came through just at the end of last week. Don't think there was anything significant, otherwise they would have said.'

'Why don't I have a look through that this morning, fresh eyes and all that.'

'Great, I'll leave you to it and get on with organising the team. Catch you at eleven, meet in here?' Fee asked as she crumpled up the brown wrapping from her bacon roll and threw it in the bin on her way out the door.

'Eleven it is,' John said, aiming his own wrapper at the bin and lobbing it successfully straight in.

'Result!' He laughed with satisfaction.

John turned his attention to his PC and opened the Newcastle interview file. He could see that there had been a number of new interviews added, so he made himself comfortable and began reading. There was nothing of any real interest to be gleaned further from the family interviews.

Kay had reiterated that she thought Susie had been seeing someone but she had no definite proof. By half past ten, John was beginning to think he should take a break and collect his thoughts before the team meeting when a name on the page in front of him caught his eye. That name was Simon Grey. It brought him up short. Reading on, it seemed that Simon Grey had been the team lead for Susie in the months before she had died. He had left a few weeks before, so nobody had thought to mention him until the second round of interviews. A statement had been taken on this occasion from the cleaner who came in after office hours. He had said that there were a few times when it was just Susie and Simon who were still in the office, even after he had finished his rounds. He had commented that either they were really dedicated or something had been going on between them. John slowly continued to scroll through the file until he came to a photograph that had been taken at what looked like a work Christmas night out. Everyone was smiling, some with paper hats on, glasses raised in a cheers. There in the middle of the group was Susie, smiling up at the man sitting beside her, who was none other than Simon Grey, their Simon Grey.

A wave of nausea came over John as he took in what he was looking at. Simon knew Susie. Susie knew Simon. The perpetrator was known to Susie. They were thought to be intimate. His hair had been found in her earring. It was just after Simon had moved to Edinburgh that Jenny had been strangled.

John's thoughts were scrambled, pinball flicking from one image to another. Simon Grey rode a top of the range bike and his blond hair was receding. Simon's interest in the case. Debs had died from asphyxiation. She had been in a relationship with Simon. Mirry's uncharacteristic outburst about him. No, this couldn't be, there must be a rational explanation. But there was no quieting his thoughts. John recognised this feeling, could feel it in his gut. This was it. There had been nothing before this. He looked out at the main office and saw his team coming together for the eleven o'clock meeting. Without thinking, he grabbed his phone off his desk and his coat from the back of his chair and headed out. Fee looked up with surprise.

'Boss?' she said with a puzzled look.

'Take the meeting, Fee, there's something I need to do,' John said as he strode past her, awkwardly putting on his coat. 'I'll catch up later.'

John left the office to a stunned and confused silence. He took the stairs two at a time before heading out to the car park. Before he reached his car, he activated the key and heard the sound of the doors being released. He went straight to the back door, his thoughts racing in one direction now. And there it was, and had been for weeks now, the bloodied dish towel from Simon's flat the night John had assaulted him. There was only one thing to do with it - he had to get it to Mark as quickly as possible.

Chapter Sixty-Two

Despite it being mid-morning, the traffic on the way to Mark's office was still slow. It gave John time to think about what he would say when he got there. He had called before leaving the car park, saying it was a matter of urgency that he see him. Mark knew by the tone of John's voice that there was something serious in the offing. He'd cancel his lunchtime meeting, he said.

Pulling into the visitors parking space, John's thoughts were now more ordered. Opening up the boot, he found the forensic kit that he always carried with him. His heart was in his mouth as he took out one of the larger plastic bags. Putting on a pair of disposable blue gloves, he went into the back of his car and picked up the stained dish towel, gingerly, as if it would explode. He dropped it in the bag and sealed the top. Shutting the boot with a firm push, he tucked the bag inside his coat, locked the car, and headed into the building.

The receptionist gave him a visitor's pass after he had signed in. John found it hard trying to make the usual small talk with her and was anxious to be let through. He took the stairs two at a time and arrived slightly out of breath. Mark was waiting for him at the door to his office, a look of concern on his face.

'John,' he said gravely, 'good to see you. What's going on?' He stepped aside to let John through, then followed and quietly closed the door. The pair looked at each other.

John couldn't keep quiet any longer. He took the bag from under his jacket and placed it on Mark's desk.

'I would like you to run some DNA tests on this please, Mark.'

'I'm not sure what you're asking me here,' Mark said, with a hint of warning in his voice, staring at the obviously blood-stained material in the bag.

'I think it may belong to the killer, but I don't have any proof. It's all just supposition at this point.'

'And this sample,' Mark said, 'was it taken with consent?'

'Not exactly,' John said, 'it was flung at me after an altercation.'

'John, I think you need to sit down and tell me exactly what's going on,' Mark said, going behind his desk, 'and then we'll see if there is anything we can help with.'

John exhaled loudly and sat down. 'Where do I start?'

'I always find the beginning is often the best place,' Mark said, gently.

Mark's face didn't flinch as John related what had happened in the last few months with the case, Debs' death, and Mirry's accident. When he got to the part where he had hit Simon and grabbed the tea towel in the bag in front of them, Mark frowned.

'So let me be clear,' he said, 'you want me to run a DNA test on this to see if it matches the other samples we have?'

'I do,' John said, 'today.'

'And at this moment, this is purely speculation on your part, and you haven't brought this Simon in for questioning.'

'Correct, up until now we have had no suspects,' John said, looking Mark straight in the eye.

'But you are suspicious enough to think this warrants going way outside normal policy?'

'I am,' John answered unflinchingly.

'Okay,' Mark said, 'we've known each other a long time, John, if you think this is right, then it's good enough for me. Leave it with me - should have some results back by close of play today. I'll run it myself. Now, get out there and get some corroborating evidence before the shit hits the fan.'

John stood up and held out his hand. 'Cheers, Mark, you don't know what this means.'

'I think I do,' Mark smiled, 'could be curtains for both of us if we don't handle this well.'

'Right, you've got my number.'

The two men shook hands.

'Speak later,' Mark said and showed John to the door. 'Let's hope for everyone's sake that you're right.'

John headed out the door, checking his watch. It was nearly one o'clock, he could be back in the office before two. He needed to speak to Fee. He knew she would be absolutely furious with him going off-piste like this, but what choice did he have? It had started raining heavily when he got back out to the car park, the sky grey and oppressive. The east coast wind was starting up, sending the raindrops horizontal. The weather matched his mood. He felt no elation that Mark had agreed to the test, just an overwhelming feeling that this was the right thing to do.

Fee was sitting at her desk eating her lunch and studying her phone when he came back into the office. She looked up at him with raised eyebrows. He nodded to his office and she gathered her sandwich, drink, and crisps and followed him in, shutting the door behind her.

'Sit down, Fee,' John said.

She didn't need to be asked twice, pulling up a chair opposite him.

'There's something I need to tell you, and you're not going to be happy with me. I might have fucked things up completely and, if I have, I'll take full responsibility for it.' He rubbed his hands through his hair as he exhaled loudly.

'Boss?'

For the second time that day he ran systematically through everything that had happened, including the assault on Simon. Fee couldn't believe what she was hearing.

'You hit him?'

'Och, Fee, it was a total heat of the moment thing. Mirry was lying in intensive care and he was just being a total dick, making out that she wasn't good enough for him. My Mirry! How dare he!' A flash of that feeling that Simon had provoked in John boiled to the surface. Fee had never seen him so angry before.

'And now you've asked Mark to run DNA tests on the dish towel he flung at you?'

'Yes,' John said sheepishly, realising when admitting it to Fee the enormity of what he had asked Mark to do.

Fee looked at John, taking in his obvious distress, anger, and frustration. She had known him a long time and never doubted his integrity. If he was willing to put his neck out like this, there must be something in it.

'Better get back to finding something relevant then to match your theory. Why don't we both go over CCTV again and see what you think. You know what this Simon looks like, don't you? See if we can spot him.'

John couldn't believe what he was hearing, Fee was going to stand by him. Relief coursed through his veins.

'Brilliant,' John said, 'grab that chair and we'll do that now.'

'Time to finish my sandwich first, Boss?' Fee asked with a glint in her eye.

'S'pose so. Any left for me?'

Fee gave him the other sandwich in the packet as she pulled her chair nearer his desk, and the two of them got down to work.

It was the CCTV images that really brought John up short. He felt like he was seeing them again for the first time. How could he have been so blind? Even though the images were dark and grainy, the resemblance to Simon's build and movements was uncanny.

'It's him, Fee,' John said, shaking his head, 'it's definitely him.'

'Okay,' Fee said, 'now we just need to work out how we're going to proceed. I have to say, you hitting him doesn't make this easy.'

'Fuck, I know, Fee.' John put his head in his hands. 'I just need to give Mirry a call to make sure she's okay and let her know I'm going to be late. We're not going to be going home anytime soon.'

But before he had the chance to pick up his mobile, his desk phone rang, the suddenness giving both of them a start. They looked at one another, knowing fine well what this call would be about. John inhaled fully before picking up.

'Sneddon,' he said. Fee watched him intently as he released his breath slowly, listening to the voice of the caller. He looked over at Fee, but his expression was unreadable. He made some agreeing noises and grunts before saying thanks and goodbye.

'Well?' Fee asked, the tension killing her.

'It's him, Fee, we've fucking got him.'

Chapter Sixty-Three

Mirry now realised why coffee had been tasting so bad and she could only tolerate tea. She smiled as she squeezed the tea bag and took it out of her mug. Pouring in the milk and giving it a stir, she took the first few sips, looking out onto the lilac tree in the garden as she waited for her toast. Pregnancy had been playing tricks with her body and she just needed to listen a bit better, now that she knew. The little ultrasound picture had pride of place on the fridge, and every time she looked at it, her heart lifted. There it was, their baby, curled safe within her. She stroked her belly. Her dwalm was broken by the pop of the toaster, and she quickly spread the butter so it melted before adding the Marmite. There was a squeak from the kitchen door as Marcus weaved his way in. On seeing her, his tail straightened, the squeak turned into his full throated greeting that Mirry was getting used to as he padded over to her.

'Morning lovely boy,' she said, finding a pouch of food for him and emptying it into his bowl. Watching him eat, Mirry's eyes filled with tears as she remembered the laugh she had had with Debs about his odd habits. Mirry wanted to tell Debs that Marcus was all right now, he didn't mind eating in front of them. She pulled off a bit of kitchen roll and wiped her eyes. There was a vibration from her mobile in her dressing gown pocket. It was a text from Pen.

'Morning hun, how's you? Up for a visit after work today?'

Mirry replied straight away, 'Absolutely, going stir-crazy here!'

'See you after five,' Pen replied.

The rest of the day Mirry spent tidying up the flat and sorting out the pile of clean washing that had built up in the bedroom. After lunch, an overwhelming tiredness enveloped her and she went back to bed for an hour, listening half-heartedly to the radio and dozing. She still needed some painkillers to ease the ache in her chest from her injury, but she felt it was a small price to pay for what might have happened.

At four, she got up and baked some scones for Pen. The intercom buzzed just as she was taking them out of the oven.

'Great timing,' she said to Marcus who was curled on top of his special bed on the radiator.

She went to open the front door and shouted down the stairwell.

'Scones are ready, I'm the hostess with the mostest!' Going back into the flat, she left the door open and went into the kitchen to finish off laying out the scones, butter, and jam. The kettle was just boiled and she filled the teapot. She heard the front door close.

'In the kitchen!' she yelled. 'I was just away to…' Mirry said as she turned round to face the door, but her words faltered when she saw who was standing in the doorway.

'Hi Mirry,' Simon said, 'I thought I'd pop round to see how you were doing. I brought you these.' He held out a large bouquet of white roses.

'Simon, what a surprise… em, thank you.' The hairs on Mirry's neck stood fully upright, shouting, warning, yelling.

'Sorry are you expecting someone?' Simon said, nodding his head at the domestic scene on the table.

'Yeah, Pen's coming round about now.'

'Oh,' Simon said, 'what a disappointment, I thought I would have you all to myself for a little while. No matter, I'll just leave the flowers.' He placed the flowers down next to the scones. 'I thought I would let you know I'm leaving and I wanted to see you before I go.'

'Leaving, what do you mean?' Mirry asked, moving behind the safety of the kitchen table, the coldness in her stomach like ice.

'Work has been impossible since Debs died. The atmosphere in the office is toxic and that's even before you come back. I know you'll just make it worse, and as for that arse of a boyfriend of yours, he's lucky I didn't get him lifted.'

Mirry stared at him, for once lost for words.

'Anyway, you take good care of yourself, maybe we'll meet up again one of these days.'

'I very much doubt that, Simon.' Mirry said with determination.

'Before I go, I think you should know that what happened to Debs was her own fault, you know. She was just too trusting.'

'Too trusting?' Mirry said, memories of Debs' hanging body came flooding back, making her head start to spin.

'Yeah, it was for my entertainment. I watched for a while, but I got bored and left.' Simon leaned over the table, holding Mirry in his ice blue stare. 'Doubt I would have felt like that if it had been you though, Mirry. For you, I would have stayed all night.'

'I think you should go,' Mirry said, but didn't move, her voice wavering slightly, the ice in her stomach spreading as fear started to take hold.

'Okay,' Simon said, straightening up, 'I'll see myself out.'

She followed him out into the hall and, just before he got to the front door, he turned and looked at her intently.

'Glad you're feeling better, Mirry, you take good care. Consider yourself lucky.' He smiled, nodded, then turned and left as quietly as he had come in.

Mirry's heart was racing as she inhaled deeply and ran quickly to the door, putting on the double bolt. Leaning her back against it, she tried to get her panic under control.

'What the fuck was all that about?' she said out loud, her head spinning, her heart hammering.

She ran through to the sitting room and looked down onto the road below. It was still raining and the pavements were wet, black, and shining. There was a car moving out from the other parked cars, its lights bright, the indicator flashing. Mirry gasped as she watched Simon open the passenger door and jump in. No sooner had the door closed than the car left, the red tail lights heading off down the street at speed.

Going back into the kitchen, she looked at the huge bouquet of flowers sitting on the table in disgust. She didn't want them in the house. Didn't want anything from that man. How dare he. Taking out a large pair of scissors from the drawer, she started hacking at the stems and beautiful white heads until there was nothing left other than a huge mound of florist paper, destroyed flowers, and broken stems. Her fury spent, she pulled the bin over and swept the remains in, sobbing loudly as she did, tears falling in amongst the debris. A sharp pain in her chest at this exertion took her breath away for a moment. She hung on to the table with two hands until the red mist dissipated and she was able to draw air in again. The loud buzz of the intercom made her jump. She picked up the receiver. 'Yes?' she said tentatively.

'It's me, you daft mare, let me in!' came Pen's dulcet, distorted tones. Mirry hit the buzzer for the second time that afternoon. She went to the front door and didn't open it until she could see Pen's face clearly though the peep hole.

'Hi Mirr,' Pen said, sweeping into the hall, bringing the smell of fresh air and cold with her. She grabbed Mirry in a huge hug, causing her to let out a spontaneous yelp. 'Oh shit, sorry, forgot about your ribs!'

'Oh Pen, it's so good to see you.'

'Wow,' said Pen looking at the scones, teapot, and jam on the table, 'I should come round more often. You okay Mirry?' Pen asked, taking a closer look at her. 'Shit, I haven't hurt you, have I? Your colour's not so great.'

'No, no, I'm fine,' Mirry said, sitting down at the table and gesturing for Pen to join her, 'I just had a visitor that's totally freaked me out.'

'Who?' Asked Pen, sitting down and accepting the side plate Mirry was offering her.

'Simon.'

'Simon?'

'Simon.'

'What the fuck did he want?' Pen said, her full attention now focussed on Mirry.

'He brought me flowers.'

'Where are they?' Pen asked, looking round the kitchen.

'In the bin,' Mirry said, 'didn't want them in the house.'

'Best place for them,' Pen said, 'what a total creep.'

'I know, weird.'

'You know he's handed his notice in, don't you?' Pen said, taking a scone, splitting it in two, and loading jam on precariously.

'Yeah, he said. When was this?' Mirry asked, pouring tea into two mugs.

'Hmm, last week sometime. Helen came to tell us, something about a toxic atmosphere after Debs. I should coco. He cleared his office out at the weekend, working his notice from home with annual leave. He'll not be back in. Can't say I'm disappointed, good riddance. Just wished he'd gone before, you know, then maybe Debs would…' Pen couldn't finish her sentence, her eyes filled with tears as she shook her head. 'Cold bastard.'

'Oh Pen, definitely for the best, I was dreading coming back in. Did I tell you what happened with John?'

'No!' Pen said, her eyes wide.

'Well,' Mirry said and she went on to relate everything that had taken place after the accident. From John reading her journal and thinking she had been having an affair with Simon to the part where John had gone round and clocked Simon. Pen's eyes were the size of saucers before she burst out laughing.

'Good on you, John,' she said, 'couldn't have happened to a better person. He's not going to get into bother for it though, is he?'

'Doesn't look like it. If Simon was going to press charges, you would have thought he would have done it by now, but now he's leaving, well…'

'Bloody hell, Mirry, you don't half get in some scrapes! Enough already, you've got my god-niece to think about!'

Mirry laughed and came round the table to engulf Pen in a hug.

'God, I've missed you!' she said. 'Now eat that fucking scone, will you, I made them specially for you.'

'You know me, don't need to be asked twice,' Pen said and bit down hard, jam squishing out around her mouth. 'MMMMM, amazing!'

Chapter Sixty-Four

J ohn couldn't believe it - after all this time, it was somebody under their very noses. Previous conversations he had had with Simon came flying back, the drinks and food they had shared, he'd even been in his house!

'So what now?' Fee asked. 'This is going to be impossible to navigate without the shit hitting the fan.'

'I know,' John said, his mind racing. 'I'll need to let Charlie know about him having worked with Susie and what happened with Debs. Then we'll bring him in for questioning. Maybe then we can get a DNA sample from him.'

'You can't question him, John, you know that, don't you?'

'I know, you'll need to do it with Charlie.'

'When?' Fee asked. 'Surely the sooner, the better, you never know what he might be up to.'

'I'll call Charlie, see what she says.'

Whilst John called Charlie, Fee made them a couple of cups of coffee to take out. It was going to be a long night by the looks of things. When she came back into the office, John was still on the phone, making arrangements. Charlie couldn't understand why John didn't want to do the interview with Simon but accepted his reason that he was too close to what had happened with Debs and Mirry. She agreed that Simon could be brought in for questioning and gave them the order to go and pick him up.

'Right, grab your coat, we're heading,' John said to Fee. 'Charlie will meet us down the road once we've picked him up.'

Fee headed out to the office and let the rest of the team know what they were about to do. John heard a faint cheer, and he smiled; on any other occasion he would have been elated, but this was just too close to home.

It was still raining when they ran out to the car park. The wind had died down but it was dark, with just the streetlights, shops, and car headlights illuminating Edinburgh. John put on the blue lights and siren whilst Fee radioed for back up to meet them in Corstorphine. Her calm tones as she gave a description of Simon helped John focus on driving at speed through the rush hour traffic. Cars pulled to the side and buses slowed to let them through. Pedestrians stared as they flew by in a blur. Just before arriving at the car park behind Simon's apartment, John turned off the siren and lights. He wanted there to be an element of surprise and didn't want Simon having prior warning. A couple of squad cars came in behind them.

John released his safety belt and jumped out. Fee joined him as he jogged over to the other officers to bring them up to speed. He didn't think there would be any issues, but just in case, he ordered them to stand at the fire exit behind the building and not let anyone leave.

'Right, Fee, this is it.' John said, looking up at the outside of the building. There was a faint glow in the sitting room window of Simon's flat but the curtains were closed. 'It's first floor, second door down.'

'Let's do it then,' Fee said, checking that her handcuffs were firmly attached to her belt as she pulled her jumper down.

They sprinted to the communal glass entry door. Fee pressed the service button and the door buzzed open. The entrance was surprisingly warm after the cold and damp of outside. Looking around, John indicated that they should go up the stairs rather than the lift. There was the smell of cooking in the stairwell, someone was frying onions, oblivious to what was about to unfold in their building.

Coming out onto Simon's corridor, John was amazed at just how calm he felt. All his previous anger had dissipated and he realised that what he wanted above all was resolution and justice. Standing outside Simon's door, he nodded to Fee as he knocked firmly on the door.

'Simon Grey?' he said loudly. 'It's the police, open up.'

There was no noise or movement from inside. John knocked again and rang the bell.

'Simon, open the door otherwise we'll have to break it down.' Silence. It was so quiet that there was a little flicker of anxiety starting in John's stomach. He knocked again. Absolutely nothing.

The other door in the corridor opened slightly and a small voice said, 'Hallo?'

Fee walked down to investigate. There was an elderly woman's face peeking from behind the crack in the door.

'Sorry for the disturbance, ma'am,' Fee said, 'please go back inside.'

'He's not there, you know,' she said, 'he moved out a couple of days ago.'

John couldn't believe what he was hearing. He came quickly over, pulling out his warrant card.

'We're the police, madam,' he said, showing her his card, 'do you know where he's gone?'

'No, he kept very much to himself, good neighbour mind, would take my bins out for me. His mum came to give him a hand. Has he done something wrong, like?'

'You could say that,' John said. 'You don't happen to have a key, do you?'

'Funny you should ask that,' she said, opening her door wide, 'the landlord always leaves me a copy for emergencies - he happens to be my son.' She chortled. 'I'll just get it for you, don't want you breaking the door down.'

She disappeared into her flat, leaving John and Fee standing perplexed in a cloud of furniture polish. Fee radioed to the officers outside to remain vigilant. Returning with a large multicoloured bunch of keys, she handed them over to John.

'It's the one with the red fob on it,' the woman said. 'Can you hand them back in once you're finished? Don't know if you'll find anything - as I say, he left a few days ago. Okay if I get back to my programme?' They could hear the opening music to a soap emanating from behind her.

'Of course,' Fee said, taking them from her, 'we'll knock when we're done.'

John took the keys from Fee and went back to Simon's door. He knocked again before unlocking the door and walking in.

'Police, anyone here make yourself known.'

Going through to the sitting room, there was a small lamp sitting on a cardboard box in the corner of the room, its yellow glow illuminating the emptiness. The curtains were drawn and there was a stale smell of neglect.

'Shit,' John said, looking around, 'fucking shit, Fee, he's not here! Check the other rooms.'

They went from the sitting room to the kitchen, the cupboards open and empty, the hum of the fridge the only noise. The bedroom too was bare, the double bed's mattress exposed without sheets, no lights on the bedside tables and coat hangers rattling in the wardrobe when the sliding door was pulled open.

'Christ, Fee, where the hell is he?' John said. 'We need to find him. He knows, doesn't he? He knows we're on to him.'

He called Charlie's number to deliver the bad news as they locked the door and returned the keys. There was nothing for it but to return to the station.

Chapter Sixty-Five

Pen stayed for a couple of hours, drinking tea and catching up. Although Simon leaving featured heavily, it was Debs that they wanted to talk about. Talk about and grieve. They shared some of their memories, and there was a lot of laughter in amongst the tears. It felt like a part of them had been lost, and they both knew that the Spice Girls would be no more.

Mirry was open with Pen about whether she wanted to come back as a co-ordinator after her maternity leave. The on-call and John's work were not going to be compatible with family life. Childcare was definitely going to be an issue as no family lived nearby. Pen said she also had a confession of her own. She had applied for a tutor's job at Queen Margaret University and had been invited for an interview at the beginning of April.

'So looks like it will be all change then,' Mirry said, absentmindedly rubbing her lower belly.

'Yeah, might be a good thing though, Mirr, sometimes a clean out of staff can revitalise a service,' Pen said. 'Anyway, it's time I was away, you're starting to look a bit tired.'

Mirry stretched and tentatively got up off the sofa.

'Yeah, I think I might just get my jammies on and head for bed. Thanks for coming round.'

'What time will John be back?' Pen asked, shrugging on her coat and pulling her long ponytail out over her collar.

'God knows,' Mirry said, 'I've told him to stop calling me every five minutes, that I'm fine.'

'He's just worried about you and the baby, Mirr. Can't help it, even though it's a bit nauseating if you ask me.' Pen laughed as she made her way out into the hall. 'Maybe catch up at the weekend? I'm not on call.'

'Sure, that would be great,' Mirry said, opening the front door and letting the cold night air in, 'now feck off and leave me in peace.'

Pen gave Mirry a final hug and a peck on her cheek.

'Love you, babe.'

'Love you too, take care.'

Mirry closed the door and sighed. Her thoughts strayed to Debs once more and all the changes that her death had caused. What Simon had said made her feel sick. She couldn't quite come to terms with what he had meant, didn't want to. Going through to the sitting room, she picked up the empty mugs and plates and carried them to the kitchen. Looking out the long sash window, she could see the lights from the flats opposite and a reflection of herself. She washed the dishes and put them on the draining board to dry. Fatigue was beginning to take its toll and the ache in her side had worsened. Mirry poured herself a glass of water and walked slowly through to the bedroom to take a couple of painkillers that were beside her bed. After brushing her teeth, she changed into her pyjamas and curled up under the covers to read. She was asleep within minutes.

It was the sound of the book falling to the floor with a soft thud that woke her up. She looked at the clock: 22.23, it blinked at her. The bedroom was in darkness apart from the orange glow from the streetlights, casting blurred shadows around the room. Mirry listened to see if John had come home but there was no noise. She got out of bed and went over to the window to close the curtains. Looking down into the street below, it was still raining, still black, still wet.

Her mouth was dry and her stomach rumbled. She went through to the kitchen to make herself something to eat. Going past the front door, she suddenly felt uncomfortable, the hairs on the back of her neck starting to rise. She stopped and put her ear to the door. The feeling that someone was just outside was unbelievably strong. Then she heard shouting from the street coming in through the closed door; it was the noisy student neighbours. She could hear laughter and babble as they made their way up. There was a muffled conversation just outside her door and then footsteps running down the stairs. Mirry peered through her peephole and saw her neighbours looking puzzled. She opened the door, putting the chain on.

'Was there someone there?' she asked.

'Oh hi Mirry, yeah, tall bloke with blond hair. Seemed in a bit of a rush.'

'Fuck!' Mirry swore. 'Has he gone?'

'Yeah, looks like it. You okay? You look a bit shaken.'

'I'm fine, I just need to make a call.' Mirry closed the door and immediately dialled John's number. When he answered, she burst into tears, and it took him a couple of seconds before he could make out what she was saying.

'John, Simon has been here, I'm scared, you need to come home now!'

It took John a long time to calm Mirry down once he got home. He and Fee had driven at full speed across town with siren blaring and lights flashing. They were now sitting in the kitchen with a teapot between them, listening to Fee in the hall relating the recent developments to Charlie. Mirry was in shock, still reeling from learning that Simon was responsible for the deaths of four people.

'I knew there was something about him,' Mirry said for the third time, shaking her head, 'but I didn't think it would be something like this. God, John, this is just horrific.'

'He knows we're onto him, Mirry,' John said, cradling the top of her head, 'he would be insane to come back here.'

'Is that meant to reassure me, John?' Mirry whispered. 'Not sure sanity is Simon's greatest trait, do you?'

Fee came back into the kitchen and sat down.

'Everything's in place, Boss, he'll not get far,' Fee said, the concern etched across her face.

'Well, there isn't anything more we can do tonight, Fee, think we should turn in, try and get some kip, and pick this up in the morning.'

'Agreed,' Fee said, 'Charlie knows that this has turned into a bit of a shitshow. I'll grab a taxi back to the station to pick up my car. Leave you here with Mirry.'

'Cheers, Fee, catch you tomorrow.' John saw Fee out and Mirry could hear their muffled conversation at the front door. She was finding it difficult to make sense of everything. So much had happened in the last few weeks. Debs' death, their accident, finding out she was pregnant at last. But this with Simon - he had been here, in their flat. A shiver went up her spine as the realisation of why he had come round to see her had begun to sink in. What he had said when he had left, that she was lucky. Had that been what she thought it meant? Had he wanted to harm her? Questions that she didn't want answered.

John came back into the kitchen and put his arms around her.

'I think you should go to bed, my love, I'll tidy up in here.' He pulled her gently to her feet. 'Go on, there's nothing else to be done tonight.'

'John, I'm so scared,' Mirry whispered.

'I know, Mirr, but I'm here, and everyone else is out looking for him. He won't get far.'

They slowly walked through to the bedroom together, arms around each other, John supporting Mirry whose legs felt like jelly.

'I still can't believe what's happened,' Mirry said as she climbed into bed and lay down, 'how could he have done what he's done? And why for fuck's sake?'

'Nothing is making much sense, everything seems so random. He obviously has an obsession with you though, Mirry.'

'I don't want to think about it, it's just too weird.' Mirry curled into herself, thinking of the little heart beating within her. 'Don't be long coming to bed.'

'I won't be,' John said, stroking Mirry's hair. 'Try and get some sleep, Mirr.'

By the time he joined Mirry in bed later, John was exhausted. It had been one hell of a day. He curled up next to her and was asleep within seconds.

Seconds was all it felt like when he was woken by the sound of his mobile going off at the side of the bed a few hours later.

'Simon has been found, John,' Charlie said, 'he's presented himself down at Fettes. Apparently his neighbour let him know you had been looking for him. I'll see you there at nine.'

'Okay, ma'am,' John said, looking over at Mirry whose eyes were wide open, looking up at him from her pillow. 'We've got him,' John said to her, closing down his phone and pulling her into his arms, 'we've got the bastard.'

He showered and dressed, paying careful attention for once about what he would wear. His actions were measured as he mentally planned how the interview and questioning with Simon would proceed. He didn't want to make any mistakes, this was too important. A lot of the evidence was circumstantial, it was the DNA that was the clincher. If the questioning went well, maybe Simon would slip up, but John doubted that very much. Finding a motive was a big part of this case - why had Simon done what he had done?

Going out to the car, John called Fee. She was heading to Fettes too, and he shared his thoughts about how the interview should be tailored.

Arriving at Fettes, he was buzzed through by the duty sergeant on the desk.

'Morning sir,' she said, 'I think the chief is waiting for you upstairs.'

'Thanks,' John said.

Arriving at Charlie's office, he was surprised to see her through the glass wall in deep conversation with a well-dressed man. She shook her head when she saw him, so he took a seat on the leather sofa outside her office. Fee joined him soon after and the two sat in anxious but companionable silence.

'What's going on?' Fee whispered out of the side of her mouth.

'I've no bloody idea,' John said, 'but this isn't looking good.'

John could feel a tightening in his stomach. Whoever Charlie was talking to it must be important as time was ticking and John was impatient to get on with interviewing Simon. Surely Charlie must realise this?

'Maybe it's the guy from the press office, maybe they're deciding how to release that we've finally got a suspect,' Fee said.

'I don't know, Fee, I don't like it.'

John could see Charlie had now picked up the phone on her desk as the man stood up. He watched as she spoke to someone, then put the phone down and stood up herself. The man offered Charlie his hand, which John could see Charlie was reluctant to take. They shook and then he picked up his leather case from beside him and headed for the door. Coming into the hall, he nodded at John and Fee who, by this time, had stood up in anticipation of finally getting to speak with Charlie.

Going into the office, John was surprised to see Charlie with her head in her hands. Hearing him come in, she looked up and John instantly knew that something was terribly wrong.

'Boss?' he said questioningly, and then his world came crashing down around him.

The man was Simon's lawyer who had come in to speak with him overnight. He was adamant that the police had nothing concrete against his client, it was all supposition. As far as the DNA profile found on some random dish towel was concerned, it would not be admissible as evidence. Was Charlie aware that her senior detective had assaulted his client after accusing him of having an affair with his pregnant partner? Charlie had been completely blindsided by that information and could give no response. He had insisted that they could not question his client until they had something definitive. They would be leaving now. His client was more than happy to come back in for questioning if anything changed.

John and Fee couldn't believe what they were hearing. Charlie understandably was furious with them both. Not only had she felt like a complete fool but John had completely compromised the case with his actions. He was to be suspended with immediate effect.

John could barely see as he walked out to his car. He passed Simon's lawyer in the car park and couldn't help himself when he spat out, 'How do you sleep at night?'

'As the saying goes, officer, on very expensive pillows,' came the sardonic reply as the man flicked his keys at his car and strode away without a backward glance.

John stood stunned in the car park, the cold morning air chilling him to the core. He looked around, trying to reorientate himself to the world around him. There was the familiar imposing edifice of Fettes College with its ornamental spires, the supermarket with its impossible brae leading to the car park on the second floor, and the never ending traffic on Crewe Road as people made their way to the Western General for treatment and care. All familiar to him but at just this moment it all felt so very alien, so very wrong. The sound of a car horn to his left broke his reverie and he turned round to see Simon in the passenger seat of a dark red car and, beside him, Karen driving. They both smiled as they drove past, Simon winking as he raised his hand in farewell, his smile almost sympathetic. Dumbfounded, John watched as the tail lights disappeared out of the car park. It was then that reality hit him. Simon had won; he had always been one step ahead, playing with them all like some elaborate chess game. The master manipulator with the coldest core. John knew then that they had lost him, there would be no going back now. Everything seemed to be moving in slow motion after the frenetic events of the last few days. With a heavy heart and a measured slow movement he took out his phone and dialled Mirry, the only constant in his life. When she answered there was only one thing that he could say,

'I'm sorry, Mirry, I've lost him. I'm so terribly, terribly sorry.'

Epilogue

I t was the last day of August when Mirry and baby Iona were discharged from hospital, three days after her birth. John came to pick them up, his new-father-nervousness very evident to the midwife on duty as she helped Mirry pack her belongings together in the small hold-all John had brought. He looked away as a huge pile of sanitary towels was placed on top of Mirry's pyjamas. The two women joked about how quickly she would go through them. Iona lay gurgling in the cot and John found it almost impossible to take his eyes off her. When they were finally ready to go, Mirry handed John Iona's outside suit for him to put her into. Picking Iona up out of her cot, she startled and snuffled before he placed her gently on the bed.

'Hallo beautiful little one,' he said, 'let's get you all cosy. You're coming home today, and I can't wait for you to see your new bedroom.' He wrestled awkwardly with her little limbs, trying to fit them into the suit which was way too big for her. Mirry winked and shook her head at the midwife who looked eager to help. Eventually, he managed to zip her in so it was just her little dark head that was peeking out. He picked her up and tucked her into the car seat he had brought, making sure three or four times that the clasps were firmly closed.

'Hometime,' Mirry said brightly. 'Thanks for all your help, Carol, everyone's been amazing!'

'Take good care, Mirry,' Carol said. 'Remember the district midwife will be in tomorrow morning and just keep some cabbage leaves in the fridge for soothing. Your milk is coming in good and fast.'

She opened the door for the three of them to go through. They headed out of the ward slowly, John carrying Iona in one hand and the hold-all over his shoulder. Mirry gingerly walked behind them. It wasn't long before they made it out to the car. John triple checked that Iona's car seat was fully secure.

He jumped in beside Mirry, a broad grin on his face as he reached across and kissed her.

'You are amazing,' he said, 'I love you so, so much. Let's get you home and cosy.'

Mirry stroked his cheek and kissed him on the mouth. 'I love you, John Sneddon. Going to be a bit of a roller coaster, but I can't think of a better person to be doing it with. Take us home.'

John drove slowly for once, not getting irritated at the traffic. There was a parking space right outside the flat, and he reversed into the tight space.

'That was lucky, eh?' John said, freeing up his safety belt. 'Stay there and I'll get the door.'

They walked up the front entrance to the flat, and John shoogled the key in the lock until it caught and he pushed the door open.

The first thing that hit Mirry was just how grubby their stairwell was after the cleanliness of the hospital. The afternoon sun was streaming down through the cupola, lighting up the fine dust motes. She climbed up the first two flights slowly.

'Christ, I'm uncomfortable,' she laughed, 'feel like my fanny's been turned inside out!'

'Well, pretty much had from where I was standing,' joked John, 'bloody amazing you can walk at all if you ask me!'

Mirry snorted as she bent over, breathing deeply in and out. 'It's even sore to laugh!'

'One more flight to go, Mirry, you've got this,' John said, leading the way. 'I've got cake and...' His voice tailed off as he went round the last flight of stairs.

'Cake and what?' said Mirry slowly coming up behind him. 'Don't be teasing me.'

She stopped then, a few steps behind John who was standing stock still in the middle of the stairwell looking up.

'What is it, John?' Mirry asked, sensing that the atmosphere had become suddenly charged.

'Fuck,' John swore out loud. 'Fuck!' he said.

'What is it, John? You're freaking me out.'

John moved aside so Mirry could see the top of the stairwell. There sitting on the newel post, lit from the light from the cupola was a Chinese Cat, sitting on a pink envelope, its arm rhythmically see-sawing back and forwards.

Mirry felt bile rise in her throat as she instinctively reached for Iona in her car seat resting on the landing.

'John, for fuck's sake, he's been here.' The enormity of what she was saying caused the blood to drain from her head. Stars spattered across her vision.

'Let's get in the flat, Mirry,' John grunted, quickly picking up Iona and striding up the last few stairs before opening the door to their home.

Mirry followed, taking a wide berth around the swaying ornament as if it were on fire.

She could hear John on the phone speaking to Fee, his words rushed and panicked.

'Yeah, get down here now and bring anyone who's free, that bastard has been in our stairwell.'

He shut the phone down and helped Mirry through to the sitting room and quickly brought Iona to her. Mirry cradled her sleeping baby in her arms, her heart hammering in her chest.

'What does it mean, John?' she whispered. 'Can't believe he's been here.'

'We'll find him, Mirry,' John said, stroking Iona's head, 'we'll find him, the arrogant bastard, if it's the last thing I do.'

Mirry could hear a siren coming down the road as she leant into John's arms and cried.

About the Author

Chris was born in Edinburgh but has lived in various villages, towns and cities around Scotland as well as a stint abroad. She has finally settled down, at least for now, in the beautiful coastal town of North Berwick.

Reading voraciously throughout her life Chris embraces the joy of storytelling and the impact it can have on us mere mortals! There is nothing more pleasurable than losing yourself in a good book.

A successful career as a nurse spanning over forty years has given her a rich experience of humanity which is reflected in her writing. Having retired from the clinical environment a few years ago Chris now has the time and focus for her creative writing.

Her first book The Beckoning Cat is a psychological crime drama set in Edinburgh.It draws from her life experiences and also her vivid imagination. When not immersed in a book you will probably find Chris immersed in the sea instead or looking after her bees.

Chris Lerpinière

Chris Lerpinière